RUN

It is just after Christmas, and the New England weather has worsened. Doyle has dragged his reluctant sons to a speech by Jesse Jackson, despairing at their indifference to politics. The two boys, both adopted, are close in age, but in character they couldn't be more different: Teddy, warm and affectionate, believes his calling is in the Catholic Church. The older by a year, more serious by nature, Tip is happiest alone in his lab, labelling and categorising fish specimens. When they are involved in a violent accident on the icy road, the family is forced to confront certain truths: about how the death of Bernadette, Doyle's wife, has affected the family, and about the anonymous figure, never discussed, who is the boys' real mother.

ANN PATCHETT

RUN

Complete and Unabridged

CHARNWOOD
Leicester

First published in Great Britain in 2007 by
Bloomsbury Publishing Plc
London

First Charnwood Edition
published 2008
by arrangement with Bloomsbury Publishing Plc
London

British Library CIP Data

Patchett, Ann
 Run.—Large print ed.—
 Charnwood library series
 1. Adoption—Fiction 2. Bereavement—Fiction
 3. Large type books
 I. Title
 813.5'4 [F]

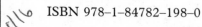 ISBN 978–1–84782–198–0

Published by
F. A. Thorpe (Publishing)
Anstey, Leicestershire

Set by Words & Graphics Ltd.
Anstey, Leicestershire
Printed and bound in Great Britain by
T. J. International Ltd., Padstow, Cornwall

The author wishes to thank Jack Baughman for his invaluable help with the fishes.

To my sister, Heather Patchett
and my stepmother, Jerri Patchett

1

Bernadette had been dead two weeks when her sisters showed up in Doyle's living room asking for the statue back. They had no legal claim to it, of course, she never would have thought of leaving it to them, but the statue had been in their family for four generations, passing down a maternal line from mother to daughter, and it was their intention to hold with tradition. Bernadette had no daughters. In every generation there had been an uncomfortable moment when the mother had to choose between her children as there was only one statue and these Irish Catholic families were large. The rule in the past had always been to give it to the girl who most resembled the statue, and among Bernadette and her siblings, not that the boys ever had a chance, Bernadette was the clear winner: iron rust hair, dark blue eyes, a long, narrow nose. It was frankly unnerving at times how much the carving looked like Bernadette, as if she had at some point modeled in a blue robe with a halo stuck to the back of her head.

'I can't give it to you,' Doyle said. 'It's in the little boys' room, on the dresser. Tip and Teddy say a prayer to it at night.' He kept his eyes on them steadily. He waited for an apology, some indication of backing down, but instead they just kept staring right at him. He tried again. 'They believe it's actually a statue *of her*.'

'But since we have daughters,' Serena said, she was the older of the two, 'and the statue always passes on to a daughter — ' She didn't finish her thought because she felt the point had been made. She meant to handle things gracefully.

Doyle was tired. His grief was so fresh he hadn't begun to see the worst of it yet. He was still expecting his wife to come down the stairs and ask him if he felt like splitting an orange. 'It has in the past but it isn't a law. It can go to a son for one generation and everyone will survive.'

They looked at each other. These two women, these aunts, had supported their now dead sister in her limitless quest for children but they knew that Doyle didn't mean for the family's one heirloom to pass to Sullivan, his oldest son. He meant for the statue to go to the other ones, the 'little boys' as everyone called them. And why should two adopted sons, two *black* adopted sons, own the statue that was meant to be passed down from redheaded mother to redheaded daughter?

'Because,' Doyle said, 'I own it now and so I'm the one who gets to decide. Bernadette's children are as entitled to their family legacy as any other Sullivan cousin.' Bernadette had always predicted that without a daughter there was going to be trouble. Two of the boys would have to be hurt someday when it was given to the third. Still, Bernadette had never imagined this.

The aunts did their best to exercise decorum. They loved their sister, they grieved for her, but

2

they weren't about to walk away from that to which they were entitled. Their next stop was to seek the intervention of their uncle. As both a priest and a Sullivan they thought he would see the need to keep the statue in their line, but much to their surprise, Father John Sullivan came down firmly on Doyle's side, chastising his nieces for even suggesting that Teddy and Tip should be forced to give up this likeness of their mother, having just given up Bernadette herself. If he hadn't closed the argument down then, chances are that none of the Sullivans would have ever spoken to any of the Doyles again.

It was a very pretty statue as those things go, maybe a foot and a half high, carved from rosewood and painted with such a delicate hand that many generations later her cheeks still bore the high, translucent flush of a girl startled by a compliment. Likenesses of the Mother of God abounded in the world and in Boston they were doubled, but everyone who saw this statue agreed that it possessed a certain inestimable loveliness that set it far apart. It was more than just the attention to detail — the tiny stars carved around the base that earth sat on, the gentle drape of her sapphire cloak — it was Mary's youth, how she hovered on the line between mother and child. It was the fact that this particular Mother of God was herself an Irish girl who wore nothing on her head but a thin wooden disc the size of a silver dollar and leafed in gold.

Bernadette's mother had given her the statue for a wedding present, and it wasn't until they were home from their wedding trip to Maine and were putting things away in their overlarge house on Union Park that Doyle really stopped to look at what was now theirs. He got very close to it then and peered at the face for a long time. He reached a conclusion that he thought was original to him. 'This thing really looks like you,' he said.

'I know,' Bernadette said. 'That's why I got it.'

Doyle had certainly seen the statue in her parents' house, but he had never gone right up to it before. His did not have the kind of faith that believed religious statuary was appropriate for living rooms, and now here it was in his own living room, staring down at them from the mantel. He mentioned this to Bernadette. In that bright empty room there was no place else to rest your eyes. The Virgin looked so much larger, holier, than she had in the clutter of her parents' house.

'You don't think it's a bit overtly Catholic?' her young husband asked.

Bernadette cocked her head and tried to divorce herself from her history. She tried to see it as something new. 'It's art,' she said. 'It's me. Pretend that she's naked.'

He looped his arms around this beautiful girl who was his wife. They very word, *naked*, made him kiss her ear. 'So where did it come from?'

Bernadette looked at him now. 'My mother never told you this story?'

Doyle shook his head.

Bernadette rolled her dark red hair around one hand and then stuck a pencil from her back

4

pocket through the knot to secure it to her head. 'That's because my mother's afraid of you. She's afraid of boring you. She tells this story to everyone.'

'I don't know if I should be flattered or offended.'

Back then there was only one sofa, one dinged up chair, one round leather ottoman that looked like a button. They left the boxes and sat together on the couch, her legs draped over his. 'It's a sad story,' she said.

'I'll remember it,' he said. 'That way you'll only have to tell me once.'

The story she knew began in Ireland, where her great-grandfather was a boy full of stories and high expectations. When he was still young he settled those expectations on the lovely shoulders of Doreen Clark, a redheaded girl whose beauty was outmatched only by her piety. Doreen Clark had made it clear that she had no interest in any of the boys who took such a keen interest in her. She was leaning towards the convent as if a strong wind were blowing her there. No boy who tried had been able to distract her from her prayers and good deeds, so despite all his best efforts, the great-grandfather's courting met with no success. Despondent, the boy left his hometown of Easkey and was gone for more than half a year. If Doreen Clark ever noticed his absence she did not mention it once, even to her sisters.

'When he came home again he was seventeen,' Bernadette said. 'He looked leaner, handsomer than anyone had remembered, and he had a lumpy bundle tied to his back. He said he had traveled all over the world trying to put Doreen out of his mind but the cause was hopeless. No one could forget Doreen. When he was in Rome — '

'He went to Rome?' Doyle said. 'At sixteen? What year is this?'

'Listen to the story,' she said.

The great-grandfather was quick to point out he had traveled all the way to Rome and sometimes implied he had gone even farther. He met a sculptor there whose job it was to carve saints out of exotic woods for the pleasure of the Pope. On one especially golden Roman afternoon the great-grandfather, sick of his own loneliness, sat down beside the sculptor who was turning a block of rosewood into Saint Francis of Assisi. He told this man, a stranger, the story of Doreen's beauty. There was pleasure in hearing himself say the words. No mention was made of there being any sort of language barrier between them. It was only said that the sculptor was so moved by the descriptions he heard of her slender neck, her delicate ears, the red wings of her eyebrows, that he set Saint Francis aside in order to carve a likeness of Doreen Clark, but the statue, because he didn't want anyone to think he wasn't doing his job, was also a statue of the Virgin. In the end it was this merger of the two women, one an Irish teenager and the other the Mother of God, that made the finished product seem to speak of both heaven and earth. The great-grandfather had no money to pay for the statue ('The suitors are always poor,'

Bernadette said, and she smiled at Doyle — a promising lawyer, who had not been poor at all) but the sculptor insisted he take it on the one condition that it be carried home and presented to the young woman as a gift. It was clearly implied that the sculptor himself had fallen more than a little bit in love with the face he had made.

To win the heart of a beautiful girl, have her represented in art as someone of even greater beauty. To win the heart of a pious girl, have her be the model for Mary Queen of Angels. Not a chip of paint was knocked from her long blue cloak, not a single fingertip on her graceful hands was missing. The statue possessed a kind of ethereal beauty that poor children in Ireland had never been acquainted with, not even in the church, and so this girl who was scarcely sixteen herself was moved beyond words. She had been good her whole life without any thought of reward and yet a reward had come to her. She could reach out her finger and touch it. Standing at the front door of the bakery in the center of town where the great-grandfather had begged her to meet him for just three minutes, Doreen Clark fell in love with the statue. While he told her his story he batted away a bumblebee with his open palm as it tried to menace Doreen Clark, drawn as they all were to the vague lemon scent of her hair.

Soon thereafter they married. The three of them, boy, girl, and Virgin, set themselves up on the top floor of her parents' humble house and promptly had five children. Every morning the girl, who was now a mother and a wife, knelt to say a prayer to her own likeness and was happy. The boy, who was quite grown by now into a man, had won the only thing he had ever wanted in life and so was happy as well. People came by their little apartment on the pretense of visiting or borrowing some tea or admiring a new baby, but really it was just that they never got tired of seeing Mother Mary as Doreen. The women crossed themselves and said its beauty was exactly like hers, though the ones who were jealous added on the phrase 'had been.' Exactly like her beauty had been.

Bernadette smiled. 'That's what you'll say when I'm old,' she said to her husband. 'Look at that statue over there. That's what Bernadette used to look like.'

Doyle leaned over and kissed the part of his wife's hair. 'You'll never be old.'

No one implied that Doreen and her husband lived a perfect life. They owed the butcher. Their eldest daughter came into the world with one leg that was shorter than the other and her thump thump thump coming up the stairwell was the sound that broke her mother's heart every day. He drank too much, the great-grandfather, but then so did half the island. These were still lean years a scant generation after the Great Famine, and they would have had no more or less than anyone else they knew but for the statue, which was not only a glorious object but the proof of their love. Love between hardscrabble young married people with five children was a thing in short supply, and so in that sense they were better off than the other hardworking men and their once beautiful wives.

'Then one day something turned inside the Bay of Easkey. Suddenly the sea could not do enough for my great-grandfather. Every fish within twenty miles swam into his net. The more fish he pulled out, the more people lined up to buy them. He made three times as much as he had ever made in a day, and that led to three times as much drinking and the generous buying of drinks, and soon the men were talking about the statue of the Virgin.' Bernadette raised her hand and made a slight gesture towards the woman on her mantelpiece to underscore the fact that they were one and the same. 'The men were making some mildly scandalous toasts to her beauty and his wife's beauty and my great-grandfather's adventuresome youth. A man called Kilkelly, who was as drunk as the rest of them, leaned himself across the bar and with the drink his friend had paid for in his hand, said, 'Tell the truth for once now. You stole it, didn't you? You walked into a church and took it straight off the altar.''

Kilkelly would later say he had never in his life had this thought before and that he didn't actually believe it was true. The comment was born in the spirit of a joking sort of cruelty that one has towards a fortunate man. But he did say it, and in all of the merriment and the slamming down of glasses on the bar and the drinking to a sea full of fish, the great-grandfather heard him and the words went through his heart like a spear through the side of Christ.

9

It happened on a night when he was seventeen years old and far away from Easkey. He was as drunk that night as he had ever been and still been standing, in some town he never bothered to ask the name of, swaying through the streets in a cold fog. He was looking for a dry place to sleep it off and, praise God, the side door to the church was open. A lucky oversight, because those priests kept their property locked up tight from drunks like him. He felt his way along and found a cushion in a pew to put his head on. He went to sleep right there in the first row. When he woke up the light was pouring in through the blue and gold windows, spreading out across the polished floors and the pews and the worn cloth of his own muddy trousers and who did he see in that light but Doreen Clark, the singular dream of his youth right there on the altar smiling down at him. Those were her eyes, those were her little hands, that was her incandescent hair that he had longed to touch every Sunday he had sat behind her in mass since he was a child. This could only mean that God had called on him to go home and win her back. He had to go to Easkey, collect Doreen Clark, and bring her here to see the statue that pointed him to her so directly. But then he closed his eyes and tried to think again. She would never travel to another town in his company if she hadn't even been willing to go down to the harbor with him to watch the fishing boats come in. Logic instructed him to borrow the statue for the week it took to walk it home and back. Surely God made allowances for borrowing in certain severe

10

situations. He took off his jacket and wrapped it gently around the Virgin Mother, whom he was already coming to think of as his little Doreen, then left the church by the same door through which he'd entered. It was an unnervingly simple departure. No one saw him. No one cried out, *Thief!* Mile after mile he looked over his shoulder waiting to see the hoards of angry Catholics chasing him down for kidnapping, but none of them came. The farther away he got with this pleasant weight in his arms, the more he knew the statue was never going back. He had the entire long walk home to imagine different scenarios for what might have happened. Once, he came upon an abandoned church in a town where every last person had died of a fever and so he picked the Virgin up and carried her away. Once, the church had burned to the ground and he found the statue standing unsinged in the embers, her arms raised to him. He thought of winning it in a game of dice with a priest, or receiving it as a gift for performing some act of heroism as yet unimagined, but then he worried that a better man would show benevolence and decline to take what was offered. On the third day of his trip home he decided it would be better if the statue had come from someplace very far away, someplace holy that would sit above all suspicions, like Rome. He had had the statue made for her. It was not a coincidental likeness but a tribute of his own design. It was then he began to see himself as a great man coming back in glory. As ridiculous as his story was, no one had ever doubted it. His proof was

11

in the irrefutable likeness of Doreen Clark's face, in her iron rust hair. His proof was in the fact that when he finally found his way home and told her the story she'd agreed to marry him.

Every man in the bar saw the truth now, the terrible crumple and blanch of a lie come undone, and the great-grandfather, who was then only twenty-five, turned his back on the crowd and fell on his drink in silence. By the time he had finished, settled the bill and walked home, the news of his crime had swept across the valley like a soaking rain. All the riches the fish had supplied had been consumed by himself and his kind and he had been exposed as a fraud. By the time he walked through the door of his own home, there wasn't a detail of the evening that his wife had not been told.

It was at this point that Bernadette fell quiet. She leaned her head against her husband's shoulder and for awhile they simply waited in the low, gold light of early evening, as if someone else might walk through the front door and finish the story for her. 'Well?' Doyle said. He was interested now. He wanted to know.

'Things go downhill from here,' Bernadette said. 'There's no redemption.'

'You only have to tell it once,' he said.

Doreen Clark, now Mrs. Billy Lovell, had come to see in one night that her happiness, her marriage, and her children had all been based on thievery and willful deception. The Catholic Church had been robbed and so had she, but there could be no extrication for her now, no returning to her youthful dreams. She lifted the statue of her own likeness into her arms, touching the cheek that had once been her cheek. There was no imagining how empty the apartment would be now. She bagged it gently in one of the wedding pillow-cases her mother had tatted with lace, a case she had wrapped in tissue paper and stored in a chest at the foot of her bed without ever once laying her head on it. Then she sent the great-grandfather out of the house and into the horrible darkness. 'Take it back,' was all she said.

Of course he couldn't take it back, any more than he could take back a leaf in a cluttered autumn forest to the rightful tree from which it fell. Ireland was crowded with pubs and crowded with churches and all he was sure of was that eight years before he had stumbled out of one of them and into the other. He did not know which saint the church was named for. How could he walk to every one of them in the country asking the question door to door, 'Have I stolen this from you?' So he walked to no place in particular. He thought about his sins and his intentions, one of which was quite bad and the other of which was pure. He carried the Virgin in his arms like a child and from time to time he would pull the pillow-case back from her beautiful face and weep for the love of his wife. Then he would go home. That was more or less the way it went for the rest of their lives, she turned him out and he came back again. Every time he walked down his own street his children would rush to meet him, their dirty little hands stretching up towards his neck. 'Da, did you bring her home?' they'd cry. His wife would let him stay two days or two months or sometimes even two years until she couldn't stand it anymore, living with the burden of their sins. But she was like the children, too, and her heart always stuttered with joy and relief to see the bulky shape inside the pillowcase as her husband started back up the stairs. She would lift the statue from his arms and carry Mary Mother of God back to the dresser, studying the face that had been her face, the serene and tender face that she had outgrown. Had that ever been the color of her hair? Then she would cross herself and say a prayer.

'And she didn't give it back to the church?' Doyle said. 'I mean her own church.'

'Well,' Bernadette said. 'It didn't belong to them, not them specifically. And the Lovells were all pretty attached to it. In the end she gave it to my grandmother Loretta, the one with the short leg, and all of her siblings were so furious that Loretta had to pack up the statue and her family and take the boat to Boston.'

'It might have been a bit of an overreaction.'

She shook her head. 'People in my family take this very seriously. When Loretta moved to Florida she gave the statue to my mother, and from there, well . . . ' She pointed again.

Doyle kissed her hair. He kissed the narrow path of skin beside her eye. 'That isn't such a bad story. There are certainly worse ones out there.'

But Bernadette was true to her word and Doyle never heard her tell the statue's full history again. Later on there was a shorter, cheerier version she used for the boys as a bedtime story that did not involve theft, and when a guest would comment on a peculiar likeness between Bernadette and the Virgin in the years that the statue stayed in the living room she never gave out anything more than a slight, flattered smile.

From the moment of their childhood in which Bernadette's sisters figured out who looked like the statue they had sung a never-ending chorus of petulance behind her: *Bernadette's the lucky one*, so she couldn't help but feel it was true. She had the statue after all, the image of herself and her mother and her mother's mother before her all the way back to Ireland. How many hours had she lain on her stomach staring at those blue robes as a child, touching her finger ever so lightly to the sharp edge of the halo as she prayed for better grades, prayed for better boys, prayed to find money on the sidewalk?

Once she was married, Bernadette managed to give up praying to the statue for years. She sometimes prayed to a vague idea of God, more out of respect to her Uncle Sullivan than anything else. If he thought there was something to faith then there must be something to faith. After their son Sullivan was born and was baptized, the religion of her childhood started to creep back into her daily life, maybe because there was more to pray for, that her boy would stay healthy, that he would be safe. She did not pray for Doyle to be elected to the City Council, though sometimes she prayed unconsciously for

15

the speeches and the fund-raising dinners to come to an end. She did not understand her husband's love of politics but she prayed for him to have what he wanted because she loved him. She prayed for what she wanted as well — the day she would have her own redheaded daughter to pass the statue on to — and then she simply prayed for another child. She prayed for her pregnancy to hold to term and then she prayed for another chance at pregnancy, and then another and another, but the praying didn't get her anywhere. She prayed for the strength and the wisdom to be satisfied by all that she had, a beautiful son, a loving husband. She prayed to accept God's will. She prayed to stop praying, a pastime that never failed to make her feel selfish and childish, but she could not stop. By then Sullivan was twelve years old, independent and wild, and Doyle was starting to talk about running for mayor. They had spent two years on the adoption wait-list, standing in line with everybody else. She did not ask for anything as ridiculous as a redhead or a girl, just a baby. Any baby would be fine. Bernadette's religion was the large, boisterous families she had come from and she believed in them deeply. She had meant to put two beds in every room in the house. She believed that Sullivan needed siblings as badly as she needed more children to love. She waited and looked to her statue, and she prayed.

Happiness compresses time, makes it dense and bright, pocket-sized. Of those four good years between Teddy's arrival and Bernadette's death, Doyle can somehow assemble only about two weeks' worth of memories: Teddy coming to them when he was five days old, and then the agency calling back only a few days later to say that the mother had changed her mind, not that she wanted her baby back but that she had decided her sons should stay together. Would they consider taking his brother in addition, a good boy who was fourteen months? It was exactly the windfall Bernadette had dreamed of, something too good, too rich to even pray for.

Did Doyle want another child? Another two? By the time they arrived he could no longer remember. Early in their marriage he had wanted to fill up the house as much as Bernadette, but in the years those children failed to materialize he ceased to want them for their own sake. In those years all he wanted was for his wife to be happy. So when the little boys arrived he did not think, *Finally I have all the children I want*, he thought, *Now Bernadette can be happy*. Seeing Bernadette happy after so many disappointments was Doyle's truest desire, and that was how he came to love the boys themselves. He loved them for the joy they brought Bernadette. For four short years the house was full. The Virgin moved into the little boys' room and watched them from the dresser while they slept. It was in January after the extravagant rush of Christmas that Teddy got a cold. There was nothing unusual about that. Teddy always caught things first. Then Tip's cold leapt into strep throat and Sullivan started to cough. Sullivan got strep throat and then it went to Doyle, and they passed it around like that, one

17

to the other, back and forth, with Bernadette doling out antibiotics and taking temperatures and running herself down, further and further down as she climbed the stairs with Popsicles and bright, shivering bowls of Jell-O. In taking the children to the doctor she never went to see a doctor herself. It was the pediatrician who touched her neck. He reached up from Tip, who was sitting patiently on the table, turning the pages of a picture book, and put his hand on Bernadette's neck without asking her first.

'Do you feel this?' he said, touching the lump that was there.

2

In the basement of the museum of comparative zoology, Tip stood alone with the fishes. Threats of bad weather that had not yet materialized sent everyone else home early, and while he was quietly fond of the people he worked with there was always something thrilling about having the place to himself. He walked through the catacombs of dead fishes, filing back the jars that had been taken out for study that day. Over the dull thrum of fluorescent lights overhead, Tip kept listening for the sound of his brother coming down the hallway. All he heard were his own feet on the cement floor, the squeal of tennis shoes and the musical clink of the glass jars touching in his basket. Teddy was late, a fact so basic and essential to his nature that Tip could hardly believe he had ever expected it could be otherwise. His brother was late. The sun would come up in the East. One would think he could remember that.

'Just meet me and Da at the lecture,' he had said on the phone that morning, thinking then at least one of them would be on time.

'But I'll be at the museum by five and the lecture doesn't start until seven.' Teddy had sounded perfectly logical. 'I'll just sit at your desk and study while you work.'

A two hour margin of error, even Teddy could manage that. But now it was six forty-five. If Tip left this very minute he'd barely be on time himself, and he couldn't do that anyway because then Teddy would have walked all the way to the museum just to find a note taped to the door saying he'd left. Teddy had lost his last four cell phones and had not pursued a fifth, so there was no way to head him off. It wasn't that Tip minded being late exactly. He didn't have the slightest interest in hearing what Jesse Jackson had to say. It was only the knowledge that their father would already be in the auditorium by now looking at his watch that made Tip feel uncomfortable about the time. How much better the night would have been if the sky had thrown down the bank of snow that was predicted and locked him in with the fishes.

He took a jar containing eight small warmouths from his basket and put them back on the shelf where they belonged. There were six rooms in the Department of Ichthyology, which was located beneath the museum, six brick-walled cells in the subterranean hive, each one a maze of metal shelving, fishes stacked floor to ceiling like bins of nails in a hardware store, 1.3 million dead fishes suspended in alcohol. A dozen or more tiny fish clustered together in small jars, single fish folded over in larger jars, huge fish alone in metal boxes. There were fish that had been recently discovered in the Amazon and a fish dating back as far as the 1700s. Put a jar in the wrong spot and you can pretty much say goodbye to it altogether. Tip followed the numbers with a librarian's precision, setting his basket on the floor so that he could handle the jar more carefully when he returned it to its proper location. Tip Doyle had a position of importance in the lab, even if his father didn't see it that way. Historically, the recataloguing of fishes was work for graduate students. That this job had come to Tip, a senior, was a sign of his seriousness and demonstrated his sense of responsibility.

'Does the country need another ichthyologist?' his father would have said had he been following Tip through his rounds. Tip was looking for the empty spot to which the next jar, eleven small blue-gills, should be returned. 'Would the country lay down its foreign wars, its need for health care and education, in order to turn its collective gaze to the splendors of the cod?' Tip stopped for a moment, using the buzz of the lights to work the voice out of his head. His father liked to say he paid more than forty thousand dollars a year to one of the finest universities in the world to give his son the right to peer into glass jars at dead fish. While Jesse Jackson's son went to Congress, his own son had wandered into the stacks of the Mayr Library, never to be heard from again.

Every jar Tip replaced introduced him to a group of specimens he had never seen before. Whenever he put a fish back he stopped to pick up three or four of its neighbors and contemplate their connections, and inevitably those connections led him to other fish, which might lead him to someday making a real scientific discovery of his own. The warmouth, for example, was in a bin next to some nearly translucent banded pygmy sunfish. Normally, had there been more time, that would have been enough to make him put the blue-gill down on the floor and lift up all the sunfish. Once he got going, Tip could often manage to shoot through half a night, finally turning the lights out behind him and locking up with his own key.

Tip's father resented his son's love of fishes. He thought that the fishes and possibly even science were a waste of Tip's serious consideration if he wasn't even willing to go to medical school, but Tip knew the exact point of origin of this interest and his father was completely to blame. It was Doyle who had driven them over the Sagamore Bridge and down the straight and narrow shot of Route 6 when he and Teddy were little, Sullivan, the oldest of the three boys, was twelve years older than Tip and much too grown-up for trips to the beach, and so they left him in his bedroom with the headphones on. On the drive, the two little boys asked their father questions about the ocean: What made the waves and why was it salty and where did the seagulls sleep at night? They did not ask to stop at the ice cream stands and taffy shacks that dotted the Cape with bright distractions. All they wanted was to get to the water. Everything about those perfect afternoons stayed with Tip, the parking lot blown over with sand, the tall sea grass bunched by the wooden steps that led down to the water, the matching red swim trunks he and his brother wore, and Doyle holding their hands. It was Doyle who settled them at the edge of the tide pools and there, for their benefit, identified every living thing in that shallow slice of ocean. Those were the earliest summers in Tip's memory, long before he had ever heard of Carl Linnaeus. On those sunny days with the wild roses blooming red against the dunes to their right and the ocean sliding back and forth over the sand to their left, his father was the inventor of taxonomy, the namer of living things. He instilled in Tip the sincere belief that there was nothing more fascinating than a tommycod and a string of kelp. Every day at the beach was gorgeous: in rain and sun, with noisy crowds carrying bright towels and in utter desertion, they found the same clear, cold water over the small pulsing universe, a fully comprehensible world.

Had Doyle been asked to tell this story he would have included the fishes but assigned them a much smaller role in history. He would admit that his youth had been marked by a great interest in marine life, but that it came along with an interest in the Red Sox and Latin, twentieth-century American novels, Schubert, the Democratic Party and the Catholic Church. His plan had been to pass all of those interests and dozens more along to the boys in equal measure in hopes of making them well-rounded, well-educated citizens. He did not mean for any of his sons to become ichthyologists. He had meant for them, at least one of them, to be the president of the United States.

From far away Tip heard a banging on the door and then the sound of his own name called out again and again. Teddy made a lot of noise in the lab ever since the time he startled Tip, coming up behind him unexpectedly and causing him to drop a jar. It had been neither forgiven nor forgotten. Tip took his basket down the hallway towards the sound of his brother's voice, turning off lights behind him as he went.

'Tip,' Teddy called.

'Late,' the brother answered back.

At six feet three inches, Teddy, a year younger, was the taller of the two, though Tip was more inclined to stand up straight and so made up for the difference. 'I'm sorry,' Teddy said, the expression on his face genuinely sorry and surprised, as if he had never been late before. 'I forgot to check the clock.'

'You always forget.'

'I had to go see Uncle Sullivan.'

Tip sighed and pointed to the door. 'Go.' He regretted leaving behind seven jars unshelved, not to mention the fact that it was reading period and exams were one week away. Tip did well on his tests because he studied for them. Everyone seemed to think his grades came in with no effort on his part. He grabbed his red jacket from the coat tree and threaded one arm through a sleeve while stuffing his books into his backpack.

'Is that the coat you wore?' Teddy said, his own parka was zippered from his knees to his chin. 'It's freezing.'

'That's the coat I wore.' Tip should not have let his tone be short. Teddy was the better of the two of them, making them late so that he could visit their ancient uncle in the home downtown

24

where old priests were stashed away, but still the whole thing grated on him. It grated on him even more when Teddy told him their uncle had sent his love.

'You told me that after you saw him yesterday.' He wiped his hand across the last row of light switches, casting the kingdom of fishes abruptly into darkness. Teddy stepped behind his brother through the open door and followed him down the hall.

'It's crazy down there,' Teddy said, shaking his head. 'It's completely out of control. There were so many people lined up to see him when I got there today I could barely get to his room. Sick people, people in wheelchairs, women with screaming babies.'

'A regular miracle at Lourdes.'

Teddy was talking faster now and he raised his volume slightly as if it needed to keep pace with his words. 'Sister Claire told me a news crew came today to do a human-interest story. It was bad enough when they put it in the paper. Once it's on television no one is ever going to leave him alone. It's like he's being crushed by a stampede of sick people. If I'm not there to make them go he never gets any rest.'

'So you cut class.' Just because his brother went to Northeastern didn't mean he didn't have to show up. In Tip's food chain, academics sat on the top and everything else was there to be eaten. In Teddy's food chain, nothing even came close to their uncle. 'Why doesn't he just tell these lunatics he can't actually cure the sick?'

'He tells them every day. He tells everyone

who walks in the door.'

'Well, he ought to be more convincing. And you ought to go to class.' Tip could not abide the Regina Cleri home. There was some vague antiseptic odor in the hallways that all but brought him to his knees. Tip, who spent half his life elbow deep in dead fishes, could not endure the smell of old people.

'Didn't you hear the weather report?' Teddy said. 'We were supposed to get covered up. I didn't think I'd be able to get there tomorrow, maybe not even the next day.'

Tip locked the final door behind him and together they walked out of the museum and into the clear winter night. 'So where's the snow?'

Teddy looked up at the sky. Both boys had wanted the same thing: to be stranded in the place that they loved, to have the situation taken out of their control by nature. 'The storm missed us.'

'Well, tell it to Da, he's the one who's going to be pissed off.'

'Take my hat,' Teddy said, reaching up for his stocking cap. The air was hurtful, too cold to breathe.

'I'm not taking your hat,' Tip said. He had found a pair of mittens in his pockets. At least that was something.

Doyle would be irritated that the boys were late, but it was Tip who was angry, not really at his brother but angry because he hadn't paid attention to the weather and it was at least twenty degrees colder now than it had been

26

when he'd left for class that morning. Without his winter coat the wind fell down the back of his collar like handfuls of snow. He was angry to have to leave his work unfinished, and with every step they took towards the Kennedy School he thought of something else in the lab that needed his attention, another set of notes that deserved review. How much longer could he afford to waste all this time on his father's naïve obsession with politics? It was one thing when they were little boys, a captive audience happy to be dragged along in tow, but now Tip had other things to do. He started to grouse about it all to Teddy, but when he looked back he saw his brother was lagging, nothing more than an outline behind him. He squinted. It was already dark as midnight.

'Hurry up!' Tip waited until Teddy trotted up beside him. 'Do you think we need to be later than we are?'

Teddy was almost too preoccupied with his own thoughts to walk a straight line, but he kept quiet about it now.

The farther they went, through the cluster of chem labs, the music practice hall with four bars of music slipping out a half-open window (it was Schubert, a piano sonata, but Tip could not think which one), the applied science center, and the economics building, the more they passed, the more certain he was that tonight was the night he would tell his father, Enough, this had to stop. He could barely manage the work he had. He couldn't keep dropping everything to hear some politician who hadn't been viable for twenty years just because it was what his father felt like doing on a Tuesday night. If he had gone to Stanford, every minute of his day would have been his own. Even at Princeton he would have stayed mostly out of reach. But no, he had let his father propagandize the superiority of Harvard as a means of keeping him close. Tip and his brother had been dragged to lectures since a time before memory, lectures and City Council meetings and rallies and funerals. Oh, did his father love funerals! The countless city fathers, sons of Boston, and daughters of Massachusetts whom they had laid to rest. How Doyle loved to explain the importance of the deceased on the drive to various churches, what the dead had done and why they merited respect. Well, Tip was sick of it. And yet when the next streetlight swept over him, he held up his wrist reflexively and checked the time. He felt sick to see the hands tilted past the place they should have been. 'We're already eight minutes late.'

'So run,' Teddy said. 'I'm freezing anyway.'

They ran. Both of the brothers were fast, long legged and graceful. They had both been on track teams at different times. Tip had quit after his freshman year of college. Even when there were drills and meets and hours of practice, running always felt like playing around. Teddy was thrown off the team while he was still in high school. Fast as he was, he had no talent for showing up. All through childhood they had run together, as far back as those first days on the beaches of Cape Cod. Sometimes in the summer they would drive all the way to Provincetown to

28

spend the day at Race Point, a famous beach, Doyle told them, where boys came to race. And so they raced each other back and forth from towel to towel, first Tip winning and then Teddy, though Tip always suspected his brother of throwing a few of the wins to him. Doyle stood in the bright sun, pale as a fish and clapping, cheering his sons on. They thought of that now, both of them separately, wordlessly, as they cut through the yard, passing the freshman dorms, avoiding the hard white lumps of old snow frozen solid to the tough winter grass. They thought of their father clapping his hands and shouting their names as they pumped their legs up higher and finished with a long kick back. As they ran down JFK and turned onto Eliot Street they remembered being children and the feeling of running barefoot in soft, hot sand. They remembered their father's cheering voice, his pride in them, and so for the moment Tip didn't feel as bad about leaving his work and Teddy didn't feel as bad about leaving his uncle. They saw the crowds of people still pouring into the building and were pleased to think they weren't going to be so late after all. Teddy and Tip went through the double doors at the Kennedy School like they were breaking tape at a finish line. They stood panting in the bright crush of students: quilted parkas and Polarfleece pullovers, magenta stocking caps with floppy yellow pom-poms that did not call serious intellectual pursuits to mind. Everyone was talking, waving, all of them push-ing forward like a tide. There were too many winterized bodies smashed together, the sharp

29

intersection of the too-cold night and the too-warm room. The crowd spilled out in every direction. For Jackson? Tip pushed his way forward, kept his head down like a swimmer. There were more black students in the lobby than a person usually saw around this place. Most of the time they were diffuse, scattered, always in the landscape, never all together. But tonight they held a slight majority. Tip would have said it made no difference to him, when in fact that alertness he always carried in his neck, the alertness that stayed with him so consistently he never even noticed it anymore, temporarily released its grip and disappeared.

If they were late then everyone was late. The entire evening was late. There were so many people milling around looking for seats that they had a hard time even finding Doyle, but he was there, two-thirds of the way down, saving the seat on either side of him with a coat on one chair and the blue scarf Bernadette had knitted him for a Christmas twenty years before across the other. Half a dozen young people, hopeful that he was merely being thoughtless and spreading out his winter baggage, had asked him if the seats were taken. One young man went ahead and sat on the scarf without a word and Doyle had to tell him to move. Standing in the aisle not ten feet in front of Teddy and Tip was a girl with a head full of long braids and a piece of fabric wrapped around her neck that was covered in tiny round mirrors. She was asking Doyle about the availability of the seat while throwing little circles of light around the room.

'My sons are late,' Doyle said.

'Your sons are here,' Teddy said, and he smiled at the girl. She eyed them skeptically. She started to say something but sighed and turned away instead, taking her little rings of light with her.

'Not very friendly,' Tip said, watching her go.

'Of course she isn't friendly,' Doyle said. 'She doesn't have a place to sit. She doesn't have a father who gets there early to save her a seat.'

Teddy leaned in from the aisle to kiss his father on the head. 'I'm sorry we're late.'

'You're always late.' Doyle reached over and pulled his coat into his lap.

'But so is everyone else,' Tip said. He let Teddy scoot past their father's knees and took the aisle seat for himself on the off chance an opportunity for an exit might be presented.

'The program starts at seven-thirty,' Doyle said.

'You said seven,' Tip said and dropped into the chair with all the heaviness his thin frame would allow.

'I know.'

Tip looked at his watch. Seven twenty-three. His father had finally found a way to beat the system. Bernard Doyle was sixty-three years old. He was five foot nine inches tall. He tried very hard to think of ways to keep ahead of his sons.

Doyle touched the back of his hand to Tip's cheek. 'You're frozen. Why aren't you wearing a coat?'

Tip inhaled slowly, deeply, trying to bring his pulse down. He still felt like he was running. 'It wasn't all that cold this morning.'

'Didn't you know the weather was going to be bad?' One of the countless outcomes of Bernadette dying when the boys were small was that it had had the effect of turning Doyle into something of a hen.

'If the weather was going to be so bad then what are we doing here?'

Doyle sighed. 'You'd think I was dragging you to Providence for a boat show.'

'I need to finish my work,' Tip said.

'Work never gets finished. I walked out on a stack of incorporation papers. My secretary chased me down to the elevator with letters to sign. I imagine it will all still be there tomorrow. Jesse Jackson will not be.'

'He was great the first time. I'm sure he'll be great again.' Teddy nodded to the stage, the empty podium, a glass of water reflecting light balanced on top.

Doyle shook his head. 'You saw Jackson at the '88 convention. You don't remember seeing him in '88.'

'Everybody remembers Jackson.' Teddy didn't want to be there any more than his brother did but there he was and he was going to make the best of it.

'You were five,' Doyle said. 'You remember him from television, not San Francisco.'

'COMMON GROUND! . . . ' Teddy said, his voice too loud even in the crowded hall. 'Easier said than done. Where do you find common ground? At the point of challenge.' His eyes fixed on Doyle's. Tip turned away in his seat, twisted his torso to face the aisle as Teddy filled his voice with a preacher's articulation. 'This campaign has shown that politics need not be marketed by politicians, packaged by pollsters and pundits. Politics can be a moral arena where people come together to find a common ground.' He had the intonation in his pocket, the heartfelt power rising to the end of every sentence. People turned around and looked at the young black man reciting Jackson's convention speech to the older white man. Jackson himself in the front row turned back and looked over the top of his narrow glasses to see who was using his voice. He nodded at Teddy, who smiled and gave a small but enthusiastic wave in return. The people in the auditorium wondered if the younger man was mocking Jackson or if he was crazy. There was always at least one crazy person at these talks. They wondered if he was making the older man uncomfortable. No one coming in late, searching for a seat that was not there, wondered if they were father and son.

'Why do we need to stay for Jackson when Teddy can do the whole show over dinner?' Tip said.

'You can recite it on the way home,' Doyle told him in a low voice. He had come in the car and as far as Doyle was concerned Teddy could say anything he felt like saying in the car. Teddy often worked on his memorization while riding back and forth on the T. He thought it was a good use of time, but Doyle worried that people would take his son for a schizophrenic.

Teddy shook his head. 'I don't know the whole thing.' But when he thought about it, he had

33

almost all of it. Only the part about Michael Dukakis was a little fuzzy.

'This is insane,' Tip said to no one. 'It's reading period.' But no sooner had he spoken than the lights dimmed briefly and came back up again, signaling the audience for their attention. The ones who were still milling around created a fire hazard by sitting down in the aisles where they stood. Teddy was going over the rest of the speech in his head. There were so many different versions. He knew it was time to stop talking and so he mouthed the words silently: *My right and my privilege to stand here before you has been won, won in my lifetime, by the blood and the sweat of the innocent.* Doyle didn't hear his other son, the one who was longing for fishes, because his attention was now on the front of the room and what was to come.

The man in the herringbone jacket who approached the podium was Lawrence Simons, called Lawrence and never Larry, a friend of Doyle's. He stood motionless, staring out into the crowd, until the audience noticed him, finished the last half of the sentence they were speaking, and quieted down. Lawrence Simons was the one who had told Doyle about Jackson's lecture, knowing that he was always looking for things like this for Teddy and Tip. Doyle had a fondness for politicians when they weren't running for anything, when they were out of the game altogether. That was when they were willing to take the kinds of impossible moral stands that would get a man thrown out of Iowa in the first week. Lawrence Simons, a professor at the Kennedy School, was making his introduction in a voice that could not affect enthusiasm even though he admired the speaker and had taken a hefty chunk out of the lecture budget to bring him there. Like Doyle, he was white, past sixty, and dependent on a pair of heavy glasses that corrected an astigmatism. He catalogued Jackson's life into the microphone, checking off the major points on the list: poor childhood, Dr. King, run for president, peace negotiator. All the while Jackson sat in the front row, listening to the litany for what must have been the thousandth time. How many times had he been introduced? Doyle remembered the feeling, the stages he had waited on, the head tables where he turned his gaze down the long row of glistening water glasses to the speakers who were speaking of him. It was like reading your own obituary over and over again.

Not that Doyle was ever introduced anymore. Not only was he never the speaker, he was not spoken of. He was no longer a source of reverence or scandal or pity. It was very rare that someone who passed him would turn around to look again or lean in to whisper some version of his story to the person beside them when he walked into a restaurant. After so many years people had forgotten about the adoptions and the death of his wife and the scandal surrounding his oldest son. They had long forgotten anything he had ever accomplished for their city. In fact, Bernard Doyle had slipped so completely from the public consciousness that on the rare occasion some stranger said, 'Hello,

Mr. Mayor,' he found himself brightening inordinately. It was that last vestige of his own vanity that struck him as the most humiliating thing of all.

'We are Democrats,' Jackson said urgently from the stage. 'We have a responsibility.'

Doyle gave one small, reflexive nod of agreement. It was that sense of responsibility that made him continue to drag Tip and Teddy towards the cause of leadership. They didn't want to go, but then they never liked having their teeth cleaned either. It wasn't entirely up to the child to be free to decide what was best. Doyle knew these were the last moments of his ability to exert any sort of parental authority. Most parents had lost theirs years before, some as far back as junior high school. It was the essential closeness he had always shared with his boys that had allowed this to go on for as long as it had, the closeness that was born out of their own bad luck. Both of the boys allowed themselves to be pulled around by Doyle now only because they had clung to him for so long. Their loyalty had become their habit. As children they had been so eager to please him that they had spoiled him into thinking that they would grow up to be exactly the men he wanted them to be. Even now, when it was abundantly clear that Doyle had failed, he could not entirely abandon his drive to shape them. They should be leaders, smart boys like these, boys with lives of such advantage. The call to service should be coded in their bones. But Tip could not seem to extend himself past the lower vertebrates. He reserved

36

what little passion life afforded him for the jaw structure of teleosts. Doyle felt the cold prick of a headache just thinking of it. What profits a man if he saves a fish and yet loses his soul? That of course led him to Teddy, the sweetheart, the darling, who was poised to give his most valuable of souls away to the Catholics. Had Doyle known what would be enticing to boys, he would never have shown them the Cathedral of the Holy Cross or the Atlantic Ocean, for that matter. Doyle blamed his late wife's uncle John Sullivan for Teddy's dreamy infatuation with the Roman Church, though Father Sullivan always replied to the charge with a big song and dance about having a calling and how he wasn't in the business of minting priests. These days, according to what one reads in the paper, he was in the trickier business of raising the dead, and Teddy could not get enough of it. Lose Teddy and you'll find him sticking around for the second mass of Sunday morning, or visiting the sick in the home for decrepit clergy. He had to be pulled out of there the way boys of Doyle's generation were collected from pool halls. If Teddy was given to leading, couldn't he think to lead something more ambitious than a Boston flock?

Doyle sighed and shifted in his seat. And then of course there was Sullivan, but where Sullivan was concerned even Doyle was a realist. Teddy and Tip would each hold a second term in office before his oldest child ever managed to become a notary public.

'Suffering breeds character,' Jackson said from the stage, 'character breeds faith. In the end, faith will not disappoint.'

Teddy leaned over and whispered in his father's ear. 'He said that in '88.'

Doyle nodded, not wanting to encourage whispering. With the noticeable exception of his own sons, whose eyes glazed over the moment the lights dimmed, the audience was rapt. None of the other children were rustling in their seats. Jackson didn't lecture so much as hypnotize. Once you gave over to the swinging cadence of his oratory you found yourself agreeing with ideas you could never completely remember. Bit by bit Jackson took over Doyle, washed him down in the waves of mellifluous repetition until the speaker and the listener were one.

But Jackson never got to Tip. Tip was still in the MCZ, reviewing the notes he had taken that afternoon on the jaw structure of regional fishes. That's what it meant to concentrate. Jackson's voice was nothing but a metronome in the background, the steady ticking that regulated the artistry of science in his head. Politicians would always be talking. They had been talking forever. If Tip had chosen to listen to them every time they chose to tell him something he would have gone out of his mind by the seventh grade.

That was the way it was in any room where one person took the center stage; some of the people would listen with concentration while others couldn't tell you a single thing that was said. It didn't really matter who the speaker was, or if they were boring or passionate. You never got everyone's attention, not if you were the Pope saying mass in St. Peter's Square or Renée

38

Fleming in recital at Carnegie Hall or Czeslaw
Milosz reading his poetry in Polish for the very
last time. The only way to make everyone listen
was to start a fire in the middle of the room and
then identify the location of all emergency exits.
And even then, if you took the time to notice,
there would always be someone running
frantically in the opposite direction. Doyle knew
this. Jesse Jackson knew this. But Teddy and Tip,
at the ages of twenty and twenty-one respec-
tively, each believed that he was the only person
there who had drifted off to other things. Teddy
was thinking about his great-uncle lying in bed
and how he was no wider than a pillow, no
higher, and just as pale. He believed that Father
Sullivan had cured those two women even if the
old priest swore on Teddy's head that he had
nothing to do with their sudden onset of
miraculous health. The weather report had
promised that the snow would be blinding by
three and so Teddy decided if he waited he could
get caught at the Regina Cleri home. He had
been sure he would be forced to stay the night
rather than be sent into the howling drifts alone.
He waited and waited. The sick were dispersed
and his uncle fell asleep, but the snow never
came. Finally one of the nursing sisters said the
weatherman had changed his story altogether
and already his snowstorm was pushing up the
coast to bury Maine.

Once Jackson finished his lecture and opened
the floor to questions, Tip had a harder time
blocking out his environment. It seemed to him
that every hand in the place was raised except for

the hands belonging to his family. It could be four o'clock in the morning before they got this circus wrapped up. Tip felt that he had reached the end of his evening's allotment of obedience. 'I need to go,' he whispered.

Doyle shook his head almost imperceptibly and Tip released a long, audible sigh. As children, both Teddy and Tip had been so good. They were practically legends of patience in certain circles, sitting quietly in their white shirts at dinner tables full of adults, occasionally offering up a single insightful and utterly charming question. But now they twisted in their seats and scratched their ankles. At the very point they should have been able to make a full connection with the material they were instead so often restless, itchy.

A nervous white girl stepped up to the microphone in the over-crowded aisle and asked whether Jackson would ever consider another run. 'We need you,' she said. The crowd exploded in cheers and then the rhythmic repetition of the name, 'Jes-*SEE*, Jes-*SEE*.'

Tip pushed one of his fingers, which was only now starting to warm up, under his sleeve and pulled the sleeve back to look at his watch. He leaned across his father and tapped Teddy on the thigh. Once he had his attention he held up his wrist.

'It won't be that much longer,' Teddy said quietly. 'He'll shut it down.' He motioned towards Jackson, who was nodding his head slowly and then holding up his palms to signal to the audience that their point had been taken.

40

Doyle, without so much as glancing in Tip's direction, put his hand over his son's wrist.

Tip started to review the material that would certainly be included in his advanced marine biology exam. How many times had jaw protrusion occurred in the evolution of fishes? Simple enough. Everyone knew it had in sharks, in some chondrostians, in the *Ostariophysii*, and in the higher teleosts. Maybe it would seem too obvious to favor the higher teleosts the way he did, but fascination didn't always have its origins in obscurity. While Jackson answered questions about the inherent cruelty of the Republican domestic budget, Tip considered the fully movable maxilla and premaxilla and tried to draw conclusions about the teleosts' homocercal tails. In this way he managed to pass the time. Teddy was right. At nine-fifteen Jackson called for one final question and at twenty minutes past the audience produced a thundering ovation and struggled into their coats.

'Didn't I tell you that would be worth it?' Doyle said, his face as bright as Christmas morning. 'He's still got the fire in him. Even when you've heard it all before, you never have the feeling he's just putting it through the paces.'

'He was putting it through the paces,' Tip said flatly.

Doyle shook his head. 'He has a message. He's still trying to get people to listen.'

Teddy picked up his own long scarf and looped it twice around his brother's neck. When Tip started to object, Teddy pulled the scarf tight across his mouth. 'He's good all right,' Teddy said. 'It's the minister in him.'

'What the party needs to find is another Jackson,' Doyle said.

'What's wrong with the Jackson it's got?' Teddy followed his brother down the aisle and into the crowd of slow moving, winter-wrapped bodies.

Tip turned around and spoke over his shoulder as he walked. 'He means we need a Jackson who's white and centrist, which means we don't need Jackson at all. We need Clinton, and we've already had Clinton.'

'Is that what I said?' Doyle asked.

'It's what you meant.' It wasn't what Doyle said or what he meant, but Tip felt entitled to a mean-spirited remark. It wasn't just the fish that needed to be put away. Even Tip knew that was nothing. But there was still so much to read, and the weight of all the work there was to be done on his thesis balanced like a piano on his head. The swirl of people in the front hall of the building overwhelmed him. Everyone seemed so energized, so motivated by the event. Was he the only student there who had work to do?

'Try to straighten out your disposition on the way to the reception,' Doyle said.

'A reception?' Teddy said.

His brother held up both hands, his red woolen mittens making two sharp exclamations. 'Not a chance.'

'It's at Lawrence Simons' house. Thirty minutes tops. He was good to invite us.'

'And we would be good to go, but we're not going, or I'm not going with you.'

'Tip!' a boy called.

Tip turned around. 'Hey,' he said and raised his hand. It was Jacob Goldberg, his lab partner from inorganic chemistry last year, the only other kid in the class who was interested in science and wasn't just another insanely cutthroat premed. Before they had a chance to speak, the crowd pushed them apart and moved them forward. The crowd made the decision about which of the doors they would use to exit. They were all just a school of fish bumping around in a wave. The whole time they shuffled ahead, Tip and Doyle bickered lightly about Jackson. Teddy tried to keep his place between them, putting his hand on one coat sleeve and then the other. When they were finally pushed out of the warm foyer of the Kennedy School and into the great cold world of the night, it was snowing. Not the heavy, wet flakes that come down like silver dollars and melt a minute later, and not the very dry tiny snow that blows around and never really settles on anything. This was a hard, steady fall of a medium-sized flake that meant business. To tilt your head back and look straight up into a streetlight was to have some comprehension of infinity. They came and came and came. The huge crowd dispersed almost instantly, everyone looking for shelter while Tip and Teddy and Doyle continued to stand on the street corner, trying to agree on their destination, their heads and shoulders quickly glittering with snow.

'They said the storm missed us,' Teddy said, looking at the soft fall as if it had lied to him personally. He should have waited longer with Uncle Sullivan. He should have been more patient.

'I told the Simonses we were coming. This isn't going to take all night.' Doyle felt the cold deep inside his ears. He wanted to step back inside, preferably into the Simonses' warm living room where he could have one drink and talk for a little while to friends, to his sons.

'Sometimes it takes all night.' Teddy was trying to be light-hearted but the intention got lost in all the weather. Cars slid past. Already there was the sound of tires crunching and spinning.

'You should go home now anyway,' Tip said. 'You're never going to be able to drive in this.' All he would have to do is walk back to the museum. The heater was always running on overtime there. Tip wore a T-shirt under his shirt and sweater all the time because the colder it was outside the more likely it was to get too hot down in the basement near the boiler.

Doyle took off his glasses and wiped them on the end of his scarf. 'How many people do you think were in that room tonight who would be able to make the time to go and shake Jesse Jackson's hand?'

'Let them go,' Tip said.

'We'll be out in ten minutes,' Teddy said. 'We won't even take our coats off.'

For a minute Tip closed his eyes against the snow's luster. He thought about the teleosts, about jaw structure, about what mattered in his life. 'I'm not going to do this anymore.'

'Why is your schedule — '

44

'Not tonight, not anymore.' Then Tip opened his eyes and looked at his father. There, he had said it, and it wasn't even that difficult. Other people from the lecture trudged around them, past them, muttering about the weather. No one stopped and stared. 'You don't care about the things I care about. I don't care about the things you care about. I'm not dragging you over to look at bluegills.'

'I'm trying to teach you about something that matters,' Doyle said.

Tip nodded his snow-covered head, and the snow-covered branches of the snow-covered trees leaned over and bent down close to him. He was walking backwards, away from his father and brother. Snow like this took away all the familiar markings. It erased the environment, the place where Tip and Teddy and Doyle had all grown up. They were on Eliot Street, but it snowed so hard they could have been in a forest outside of Copenhagen. They could have been on a city street in St. Petersburg. They could have been anywhere in the world where snow fell in endless repetition, the three of them together having this very conversation. Tip was wishing his brother would walk away with him because he knew Teddy was tired of politics, too. This wasn't what he wanted for himself any more than Tip wanted it. *I'm going with Tip*, he would say to their father, and they would walk together back across campus to the MCZ, maybe stop in one of those cappuccino places on the way to warm up from the snow. And even as Tip was wishing his brother would come with him, he was also wishing he could stay. He wished he were more like Teddy, able to just let things roll off of him, be pleasant, think of the good. If they were alone, Teddy would have brought up Sullivan. Remember all that Da has been through with Sullivan, he would say, and the thought of their brother would shame Tip into keeping quiet. Tip was right in between those two thoughts as he was backing away, as he was hit by someone he thought for a second had just slipped into him in the snow. But the hit was much harder than that, hard enough to push all of the air out of his lungs. His fall to the ground was soft with all the snow and still it stunned him. Immediately he heard the sound of another hit and then another. He was far from where he'd been standing, down on the ground and all he could see was the endless field of white gliding towards him. He felt a pain in his leg but the pain, like everything else, was very far away. There was a girl somewhere screaming and his father's voice calling out to him, 'Tip! Tip!' But when Tip opened his mouth he found he didn't have the breath to answer. He closed his eyes and felt the snow melting on his tongue.

3

There were three separate hits. They were so close together that someone who was not directly involved might not have been able to see them distinctly, but for Kenya time slowed down and gave her the chance to think of each one as its own act of a play. In the first, her mother left her on the sidewalk and ran to the older boy, Tip. She blind-sided him with the full force of her body, the momentum of the blow knocking him very nearly clear of the car. The second one was the car hitting her mother, and this hit was made up of many smaller hits: her hip against the high front fender — BANG — her chest against the hood — BANG — and then she rolled up until her head struck the windshield with a single clear crack, just at the moment when the car slid to a stop. The third act was the worst to see because it was the whole scene played back in reverse. Her mother's head leaves the windshield, her body rolls backwards across the hood, and then she falls to the ground with a wet, heavy thump and lies there, facedown in the snow in front of the tires of a light-colored SUV. One of her mother's arms was still in its coat sleeve but the rest of the coat was turned inside out and fanned the ground next to her, the slick green lining facing up. Kenya, who was capable of moving like lightning, of leaping, of vaulting, of being her mother's little gazelle, was there beside her

47

before the coat had settled out across the snow. Not only was Kenya fast, she had trained her young reflexes to snap like springs. Crack the starting gun and she was off the blocks. She ran. She was down on her hands and knees, calling, 'Mama, Mama,' but it didn't come out anything like the word. It was just a long, high sound that started with the letter M. She put her hand beneath her mother's cheek to turn her head. She needed to see her face. When did her mother's head get to be so heavy?

'Don't move her,' a voice above her said. It was an adult voice but she did not regard it. One of the first rules of safety in scouting was not to move a person after an accident, but that knowledge came second to the fact that no one can breathe facedown in the snow. When she had turned her mother just enough, she brushed the snow out of her nose and eyes. There was blood beneath her head, a bright and shocking soak of red against the white, but the sight of her mother's face, the weight of her head in her hands, calmed her and she was able to stop making that noise. She could hear a car door open and then there was a man's voice that everyone quieted to hear. Over and over again he said, 'I didn't see her. I didn't see her.' Doyle and Teddy ran to Tip, who was still on the ground. The other white man, the one who Did Not See Her, just stood there repeating the only sentence he knew. And then Teddy, whom she had always especially liked, left his brother and came and crouched down right beside her. He put his arm around her like she was someone he knew and

48

for a second he held her tight so that her shoulder pushed against his ribs. Then he let go and took off his own coat in the snow and put it over her mother. He put his own hand beneath her mother's head to keep it from being too cold.

'Will you get somebody to help?' Kenya said.

'Somebody will be here in just a minute.' Again he spread his arm like a wide wing over Kenya's back and they crouched together, their knees touching very close. He was a big man, tall and big-shouldered, and though she was tall for her age she felt like a little girl beside him. Both of the boys were handsome and tall and even though she liked Tip and knew he was very smart, Teddy had always been her favorite of the two brothers. He had a softer face. Several times in her life he had smiled at her when their eyes met in a crowd, not because he knew her but because he was the sort of person who didn't mind smiling at people he didn't know. He was only wearing a blue pullover sweater now and he did not shiver even though it was freezing. Sitting like this beside him, touching him, would have been the most remarkable thing that had ever happened to her except that now she could not think of him at all. Her mother hadn't opened her eyes and Kenya had to keep brushing the snow off her face. Teddy took off one of his mittens and pressed it tightly to the long cut across her forehead. Cars had stopped all around them and people stood in the snow and waited for something to happen. It seemed that there were almost as many people clustered on the side-walk as had been to hear Jesse Jackson.

'I didn't see her,' the man from the car told someone. 'What was she doing in the middle of the street?'

'She's your mother,' Teddy said.

The way he said it, not as a question but as a statement of fact, made Kenya wonder for a second if he knew this was her mother, but then she realized that wasn't the way he had meant it. She told him yes, and even though she couldn't put any volume behind the word, she saw her mother's chest very clearly rise and fall at the sound of her voice.

'What's her name?'

'Tennessee,' Kenya said, and she added, 'like the state.' Because that was the way her mother always said it. If she didn't introduce herself as 'Tennessee-like-the-state' then someone was always bound to ask.

'That's not one you hear every day,' Teddy said.

'No, sir,' Kenya said.

Doyle came over to them then, crouching down in the snow. He wasn't wearing a coat either. He had spread it over the other brother, who for some crazy reason was only wearing a jacket. 'Tip's okay,' he said to Teddy. 'I think he's broken his ankle but he's okay. The damn car went over his ankle.'

'She pushed him out of the way.' Kenya's voice was soft. The headlights from the SUV cut her into a silhouette. 'He was going to be hit by the car.'

Doyle nodded solemnly and Kenya could tell that he was thinking, yes, I saw it too. He looked down at her mother and very gently touched her forehead next to the place where Teddy was pressing down the mitten, and at that moment Tennessee blinked open her eyes. She looked at Kenya for a minute and the sides of her mouth bent up the smallest bit.

Kenya took hold of her mother's hand. It was cold and bare. Her glove had fallen off. 'Sleep,' Kenya said. 'They're going to be here to get you in one minute.'

And the mother, who had no energy to do anything but listen to an eleven-year-old, closed her eyes again. If she had seen just who it was that Kenya was huddled up against, she gave no sign of it.

Teddy sat and watched the whole thing. He had no idea if the woman whose head he now held in his hands would live or how badly she was hurt and he was sorry to think this little girl had to sit there and watch it all. Even if it had to happen, she shouldn't have to see it. 'Your loved ones were daring and brave,' Teddy said quietly, 'and they had that special grace, that special spirit that says, 'Give me a challenge and I'll meet it with joy.''

Kenya looked up at him. She had no idea what he was talking about but the words were beautiful.

''They had a hunger to explore the universe and discover its truths,'' Teddy said. ''They wished to serve, and they did. They served all of us.''

'Oh, for God's sake, Teddy,' Doyle said, pushing himself up from the ground. 'Not Reagan. Not now.'

51

★ ★ ★

When the ambulance came it seemed like only a minute had passed and it seemed like a day. One man came straight to the mother and one man went to Tip. Tip sat up and pulled his father's coat around him. He shook his head. 'I'm fine,' he said, and pointed to the woman lying a few feet away. He didn't look entirely fine but the man didn't ask him again. He also went to see about the woman. Now there were three policemen on the scene and they scattered the crowd and spoke to the man who had struck Kenya's mother with his car. He was back sitting in the driver's seat in order to stay out of the weather. Teddy rested the woman's head into the snow and pulled the girl back so that there was room enough for the two men from the ambulance to work. The first thing they did was slide her onto a board, a flat sled that kept her off the ground. The lights on their truck stayed on, cutting wide red circles around them.

'Are you her family?' the ambulance driver said to Teddy.

'His family,' he said and pointed to Tip.

'And she's yours?' The driver now pointed to Kenya.

Teddy looked down at the girl who was tucked under his arm like a permanent resident and she looked back at him. He had forgotten to ask her name. 'She belongs to her,' Teddy said, and motioned his head slightly to the black woman on the ground. This was how their connections were established. No one asked Doyle if he belonged

52

anywhere in this group. In fact there was a moment when a policeman tried to shoo him away.

'My son stepped in front of the car,' Doyle told the policeman. 'It was snowing so hard, I don't think he even saw the curb. None of us saw the car. This woman saw the car and she pushed him away.'

'The car hit her when she pushed him?' the policeman said.

Doyle said yes, that was the way that it happened. None of the things that had seemed so important ten minutes ago, Jesse Jackson and Lawrence Simons and the fish in their jars, none of those had any bearing on the story now.

Kenya watched the workers like the foreman of a construction site. She kept an eye on every move they made. The ambulance driver was a black man with some island accent. Of the two men who worked on her mother, one was white and one was black. All three of the policemen were white men. The white ambulance attendant snapped a white plastic collar around her mother's neck while the black ambulance attendant belted her legs. They worked like ants, their movements small and precise. One took his hands away and the other one's hands were there. One put a bandage on her head, the other sliced open the sleeve of her coat and wrapped a cuff around her arm. Kenya gasped to see him cut the coat when it would have been so easy to simply slip it off of her. Her mother would go straight to the little wicker basket on the top shelf of the closet where needles and thread were kept. Kenya herself did not know how to sew but surely it could be mended. One man opened up her mother's eyelid with a thumb and shone in a light. The other taped her head to the board with wide paper tape. They called out numbers and nodded to themselves. Every minute Kenya's mother became stiffer and straighter, locked into the equipment until every piece of her was bundled tight.

'What's her name?' the black attendant said to Teddy. He had forgotten already that Teddy did not know the woman and that he had no reason to know the answer to the question.

'Tennessee,' he said.

'Like the state,' Kenya said.

'Huh,' the white attendant said, and the black one said, 'Tennessee? Tennessee, can you hear me?' His voice was so loud that even the policemen turned around.

When Tennessee opened her eyes again Kenya rushed to put her face just above her mother's face. Her mother tried to smile but the men told Kenya to step back and Teddy took her arm lightly and pulled her away. They were very busy. It was as if they had rehearsed this accident before, as if they had practiced and practiced in anticipation of exactly this night. 'Tennessee,' the black man said. 'Can you tell me where you're hurting?'

But she couldn't tell them anything, and then her eyes were closed again. They reached beneath the board she was strapped to, counted to three, and picked her up like she was nothing more than snow. Then they slid her into the back of the truck.

When Kenya put one foot onto the step to climb inside the men all shook their heads. 'Not tonight,' the white ambulance attendant said, as if perhaps tomorrow it would be fine for her to ride along.

'I want to go!' Kenya could hear the panic in her own voice.

'You stay with your family, they'll drive you over,' the ambulance driver said. 'We can't have little girls in the back of the truck.'

Snap, snap, they locked the metal board down into place and each man leaned out and grabbed a door and pulled it shut. It was all so fast, as fast as the accident itself. There was no way to see her mother now. Once the doors were shut Kenya started to cry, though not in the keening way she had done before. She cried like a girl who was standing in a snowstorm without her mother. Her mother didn't let her ride the T alone and so she wasn't certain she would be able to get back home by herself. She didn't have any money for a token. For some reason she didn't have her keys tonight. She usually wore them on a cord around her neck. She had forgotten to ask which hospital they were taking her mother to and even if they had told her she wouldn't have known how to get there. The men in the truck hadn't gotten the story straight, even though Teddy had told them. They had left the black girl with the two young black men who didn't know her. After all, they looked like they belonged together. She wasn't hurt, she wasn't alone. They didn't think another thing about her.

'I'll call an ambulance for the boy,' a

policeman said. 'They should have sent two.'

'I don't need an ambulance,' Tip said from the ground. He had pushed a wall of snow against either side of his ankle in an attempt to freeze the swelling and the pain. He did not untie his sneaker or roll up the leg of his jeans. He didn't want to know.

Teddy had left her to go and see about his brother. It was much worse for Kenya now that her mother was gone. Not only did she have no idea how she was going to find her again, she could now see the size of the red mark left behind in the snow even as it was quickly being covered up. It was impossible not to try and calculate the extent of the damage. Without Kenya there to watch over things, to keep her mother safe, anything was possible. How could her mother keep herself safe when she couldn't even stay awake? The crowd had all gone away. Now that the ambulance had left, the remaining group of them were of no interest to anyone.

The few people who stayed behind had turned their attention to Tip. Kenya was sitting in the snow alone next to the spot where her mother had been. That's when she happened to notice something small and dark beneath the SUV. The shape of it made her wonder because it clearly was not a leaf or a piece of paper, and because she very much wanted to be thinking of anything other than her present circumstances, she crawled under the car to see what it was. The SUV was so high up that she could get beneath it quite easily by keeping low and dragging her legs behind her. Three feet back she found one thin, stretchy glove that was absolutely her mother's, and after brushing it off she shoved it in her pocket. Then she saw her mother's boot lying on its side. She had forgotten to look at her mother's feet. She took the boot by the laces and pulled herself backwards from beneath the car. If there was one boot off there could be two.

'Couldn't you just take us all over to the hospital?' Doyle said.

'We've got to call an ambulance,' the officer said.

Kenya looked behind the trees near a high brick wall. She looked beneath two bushes and when she stood up straight she found her mother's hat sitting neatly on top of one of them. Her mother's favorite dark green hat, purchased two years ago at the very end of the Filene's after-Christmas sale for three dollars! How her mother would have hated to lose that hat. Kenya brushed it off carefully and put it on top of her head. Her mother had been upset with her after they left the apartment that night because Kenya said she had put her own hat in her pocket when she hadn't. Kenya had lied about the hat because hats looked ridiculous on her when her hair was up in ponytails. They made her head look lumpy. Her mother put a strong hand on Kenya's shoulder while they waited for the T and she spoke to her sharply about keeping her head dry and not catching cold. How was she going to take off work if Kenya caught cold? There was for an instant the thought of her mother never scolding her again, of being alone in a night as dark as this one forever, but just as quickly she banished it. After all, her mother had opened her eyes. That was what she had seen herself, so that was what there was to trust. She would wear her mother's hat. She would find whatever else was missing. Everything had been flung around. That's how hard she was hit. She saw her mother's scarf right next to where she had been sitting, but now she couldn't see the blood anymore and she couldn't see the scarf either, just the shape of the scarf like a long flattened snake beneath the snow. She shook it out fast and wrapped it twice around her neck even though the wool was wet and cold and only made her colder. The snow was unstoppable, covering everything up, sifting into the smallest open spaces: the pockets of her coat, the tiny splits in the grill of a car. That was what made Kenya stop and think about looking for things in a different way and looking for them quickly. That's how she found her mother's purse pressed up tight against a brick wall, just a lump in the snow. It would have been so easy to miss it altogether, and then the purse would have stayed there until spring.

'We can't just go loading people in the cars,' another officer said. 'Nobody likes that.'

'Look,' Doyle said, running a hand across his head. 'I need to get my son out of this weather.' They were all soaked through by now, all bitter and wet. 'I'm Bernard Doyle. If you could help us out here.'

'Mr. Doyle?' said the oldest of the three, a man not so much younger than Doyle himself. He smiled hugely and then remembered himself and stuck out his thick, snowy glove. 'Mr. Mayor? Of course you are. Man, I've been looking at you all night trying to figure out . . . '

And then it was done. For one shining moment in history, Cambridge extended its hand to help Boston. Teddy got on one side of Tip and one of the younger officers got on the other and they lifted him up and put him in the backseat of the black and white. Suddenly it seemed hard to believe that they'd left him on the ground all that time. Tip Doyle. Teddy and Tip. They remembered them now. The black and white had been running all this time, the heater cranked up to high so that the car was tropically warm. Doyle got in beside Tip and called to Teddy. 'Get the girl and let's go,' he said.

But when Teddy looked up she was nowhere. He had her with him not two minutes ago. In every direction it was nothing more than an empty block filling up with snow. All of the people were gone, the SUV was gone. The footprints were all filled in. The street was shimmering, mirror-like. Even now the place where Tip had lain for so long was smoothing over.

'Come on,' Doyle said. He was shivering in the warm car. His hands ached.

'Just a second.'

The two younger officers got back out of the second car. It was late but the streetlights poured generously across the snow and lit up the night in resplendence. She was a skinny girl and tall, ten or eleven or twelve, with her hair in four high braids or six high braids and her coat was a dark color. Not that it mattered. There was only one little girl on this street on this night. They couldn't leave her out there in the cold. They couldn't lose her, whoever she was. For an awful moment Teddy tried to remember if he had seen her since the ambulance left. Had she followed it? Even though he saw nothing in any direction, he put his hands up to his mouth and called out as loud as he could, 'Hey! Tennessee's daughter!'

And out shot a head from beneath a snow covered Buick parked on the side of the street fifteen feet away. The child was underneath the car.

'What are you doing, girl?' Teddy said to her.

Kenya raised up her hand to show him. 'I found her other boot!' She was trying to shinny out but the snow was making a fast wall and she struggled. He went and took her hands and pulled her up into the night air. She seemed to be an empty coat, utterly weightless, and for a moment he held her aloft in his arms. 'It was all the way up here,' she said breathlessly.

★　★　★

'Kenya like the country?' said the officer driving the car.

'Like the country,' she said.

Kenya and Teddy sat up front with two boots, one purse, one hat, a scarf, one glove, and her mother's cut coat. 'You were smart to go looking for that stuff,' the officer said to her. 'Especially the purse. That's sharp thinking. Most people don't think so sharp when there's an accident.'

'It was everywhere,' she said.

'Things get thrown around, I'll tell you. The things I've seen.' He whistled. 'You wouldn't want to hear it.'

Everyone in the car stayed quiet because none of them wanted to hear it.

'I only found one glove,' Kenya said.

'She may still have the other one on,' Teddy told her.

'Maybe not,' Tip said. 'So then I'll know what to bring her in the hospital when I come to visit.' Tip was sitting with his back against the door and his leg up in his father's lap. The car had the wet, woolly smell of soaking overcoats. It didn't make any sense. A Chevy Tahoe had run over his ankle and someone else had been hit straight on trying to push him out of the way, they were all headed to the hospital in a police car and yet he was in a much better mood than he had been earlier in the evening. He thought about saying this but it would have been disrespectful to the girl.

Kenya turned around to look at Tip over the backseat. He was shivering. It made her feel shy all of a sudden to see him hurt.

'I think she wants to know how you are,' Doyle said.

Tip smiled at her. Poor kid, she had it worse than he did any day. 'I think my ankle's broken but it can't be too bad. I can still move my toes.' Or he could move his toes just after it happened. He couldn't move them now, though that was very likely because he was too damn cold to feel them.

Kenya winced in part at the thought of the pain and in part at the thought of her own ankle. A break would mean a whole season out of track. All of the events that she was bound to win this year would go to someone else. Maybe, if it was very bad, it would mean no more running for years, maybe until high school even. If that were the case she didn't know who she would be at all. The policeman's windshield wipers made a high squeak as they slapped the wet snow back and forth. All along the front of the dashboard were radios and thick, curling cords. It wasn't like the dashboard of any car she'd ever seen before. Every minute or so voices would come through, women's and men's, saying things that she didn't understand punctuated by loud, squelching bursts of static. The officer who was driving just ignored them and went on making conversation with Doyle about past elections and city planning commissions and the chief of police. 'I'm a guy who lives in the past,' the officer said. 'That's what my wife always tells me. I'm not saying there's anything wrong with this guy but it's not like it used to be, you know?' There were no other cars on Storrow Drive, and it was usually packed at any hour of the day. They crept along carefully. And all of that seemed right to Kenya. After all, she had gone down the rabbit hole just like Alice in the book. Her mother had been hit by a giant car and taken away from her, she was in the front seat of a police car riding with the Doyle family to the hospital in a snowstorm. If there had been other cars, if the weather had been fine, if anything in the world had seemed the same, she might have just shrunk down to the size of nothing and disappeared.

People treat you nicely when you come to the emergency room in a police car. The officer got out first and said to everybody there, 'This is Bernard Doyle. This man used to be the mayor of Boston.' There were a couple of other police officers standing around in the cold, talking with the guys who unload the ambulances. Two nurses were smoking cigarettes under the awning and they turned around from looking up at the snow to look at Doyle. They all seemed impressed, and a couple of them came over to shake his hand. It was late and they weren't very busy because of the weather. People who were sick decided maybe they weren't so sick that they had to go to the hospital, and people who would have been out getting into trouble that could lead them to a hospital chose to stay home as well. They put Tip in a wheelchair and he made a sorrowful sound when they touched his leg. Tip was feeling worse now than he had in the car or out on the street in the snow.

'I'm going back with Tip,' Doyle said to Teddy, but he was looking at Kenya. Doyle had never looked at Kenya before, all the countless times she had seen him he had never so much as glanced in her direction. Her mother said that was nothing to take offense at. 'He shouldn't see you,' she said. 'If he sees you then you're doing something wrong.'

'We'll wait for you,' Teddy said.

'I'll check on your mother first,' he said to her.

'As soon as I find out how she's doing I'll come and tell you.'

Kenya thanked him but once he was walking through the swinging electric doors she remembered something. 'Wait,' she said.

Doyle stopped and turned around to look at her again. It was almost too much, the way he saw her now, the way he looked at her like she was someone he knew.

'You'll need this.' She dropped to the ground and fished through her mother's purse for her wallet. It was big and brown and it looked like a dog had been chewing on it though they didn't have a dog. The zipper on the change purse and the snap on the billfold had both broken last year and her mother kept it together by putting two big rubber bands around the wallet at either end. As soon as Kenya had taken it out she was sorry because she knew that her mother wouldn't want anybody to see the rubber bands. But it was too late. She had asked him to come back and now she had to give it to him. She held it out in her hand.

'What's this for?'

'Her cards,' Kenya said. 'They're going to ask for her cards.'

Doyle hesitated. 'I think we can wait for that.'

'They won't see you without the cards.' She stretched her hand out to him. 'Don't worry. They just copy everything and give it all right back to you.' Kenya wasn't sure which cards they had to copy but she was certain they would be in there somewhere.

The attendant had already wheeled Tip

64

through the door and so Doyle nodded his head and took the wallet. Then he went inside.

'I think we should go in too, get warm,' Teddy said. 'There's bound to be some hot chocolate in there somewhere.' Teddy liked children. He liked this Kenya, who surely was having the worst night of her life but still managed to think so clearly, gathering up boots, handing out insurance cards. How old was Teddy before he understood anything at all about insurance cards? To be honest he wasn't sure he entirely understood them now. 'How old are you anyway?'

'Eleven,' she said.

'I'm twenty,' he said.

'I know that.' They were under the cover of the awning and she was looking at her toes. She used the heel of her boot to punch down a hard pile of dark gray snow that had fallen off the underside of a car.

'How do you know that?'

She looked up at him and blinked. She had said something stupid. She was stupid. She reached up beneath her hat and gave an uncomfortably hard pull on one of her braids. 'I'm a good guesser.'

'How old do you guess my brother is?'

She thought about lying, saying sixteen or thirty, but her mother always said that a lie never got you anyplace in the end, that it would always double back to bite you. 'Twenty-one?' she asked.

The girl looked nervous. Teddy was worried that she didn't want to be alone with him. Who knew the best way to comfort an eleven-year-old whose mother had just been hit by a car? He reached out and took the boots she was holding. 'You're a good guesser. Most people think Tip's older than that.'

'Because he's serious.'

'That's right.' He smiled at her like he was a teacher and she had just worked the math problem correctly on the board. 'You know lots of things.'

Kenya shrugged. 'Not really. I just thought he seemed serious.'

Teddy looked out at the snow for a minute. It was still streaming down every bit as hard. He wondered how they would manage to get home when the time finally came to go. 'I don't know about you but I'm freezing.' Teddy had picked his coat up off the ground after the ambulance left but it was wet all the way through now and he didn't want to put it on.

'I really hate hospitals,' Kenya said.

'Everybody hates hospitals but that doesn't mean they just stand outside all night.' The truth was that Teddy had no issue with this hospital at all. This was not the place where his mother died. This was not the place they took Uncle Sullivan when he needed Lasix. No one he had ever loved had been sick at Mount Auburn. He thought the place was fine.

Doyle wasn't in the waiting room and so they went to the main lobby where there was a coffee shop with a wide bar trimmed in chrome. They ordered hot chocolate in big Styrofoam cups and brought it back downstairs to sit and wait. Kenya

66

was wearing thick white tights and running shoes with her winter coat. She stretched out her long thin legs as far as she could and then slumped back in her chair taking small, quiet sips of her chocolate. Then she took off her mother's green hat and held it in her lap.

'Isn't there somebody you ought to call?' Teddy said. 'Somebody who could come and get you?'

'I'm going to stay here,' she said. Her eyes went around the room. She was looking at the sick people, the ones who were waiting to be seen and the miserable people who were waiting to hear the news about somebody else. Emergency-room waiting rooms were never nice like the ones they had in other parts of the hospital. Those were for the people whose families were already checked in and had a room. This place made its message clear: Don't get too comfortable. You're only passing through.

'Shouldn't you call your dad?'

'Nope,' she said.

Teddy took a sip of his chocolate and then tried again. 'Then who are we going to call?'

Kenya shook her head. 'Nobody. I'm going to stay with my mom.'

'I don't think they'll let you,' he said tentatively. 'You can't sleep out here.'

'I'll sleep in the bed with her. I sleep with her at home.'

It wasn't Teddy's place to tell the child what she could and couldn't do, but he didn't want her to be disappointed either. Any system that wouldn't let her ride in the back of the ambulance surely wasn't about to let her sleep in the hospital bed alongside her mother. 'You really may not be able to.' He was looking right at her. Another ambulance had just come in and there was a great flurry of activity around the electric doors, so many people coming in and out that for awhile they just stayed open, letting in all the cold air. They brought a very old woman into the hallway on a gurney. She was hardly any bigger than Kenya but she was white, dead white, her hands and blanket and thin white braid. Her blue eyes swept past them and did not see them there.

'Do you have a friend from school you can call?'

'It's too late,' she said, pointing up to the clock on the wall. Half past ten. 'Everybody's already in bed.'

'You can wake somebody up. Nobody's going to mind.'

'They aren't going to make me leave.'

'But what if they do?'

Kenya looked at him for a minute, weighing out the situation, weighing out him. 'If they make me leave I'll go home with you.'

Now there was a thought, a little girl climbing heavily up the staircase to Sullivan's empty room. Did you brush your teeth? Say your prayers? 'You don't know us,' Teddy said. 'I don't think your mother would let you.'

Kenya was never allowed to speak to the Doyles, or speak about the Doyles, but if it was a real emergency, then where else would she go? And if this wasn't a real emergency then what

68

was? 'I know she'd say it was fine.'

Teddy had planned to try again but his father came through a swinging door beside the nurses' station that said NO ENTRANCE in big red letters. He was talking to a doctor who was wearing a lab coat over his blue scrubs, and when they looked up and saw Teddy and Kenya sitting there they both let their sentences end in the middle of a word. Doyle introduced them to Dr. Ball. Teddy started to stand up, but then he thought better of it and sat back down again. If he stood up then everyone would be too tall. Doyle and the doctor both had such serious looks on their faces that for one awful minute Teddy wondered if they were coming out to tell this child who had no place to go for the night that her mother was dead.

Kenya asked the doctor if her mother was fine.

'I don't imagine she's feeling well at all right now,' he said. He was what some people would call a dark-skinned man, but he wasn't black. Kenya wasn't sure where he was from, India or Pakistan, maybe Lebanon. He pronounced each of his words very, very clearly and made every one of them beautiful regardless of what he was saying. 'It is a terrible thing to be hit by a car.'

'Yes,' Kenya said. 'I saw it.'

'And so you know,' he said.

'But she'll be okay,' Teddy said, because to him this was the piece of information that needed to be set out right away.

Dr. Ball looked down at the file in his hand as if to search for that particular piece of information. 'She has broken her hip — '

69

'The car hit her on her side first,' Kenya said, though she ought not to have interrupted.

'Yes, exactly. For that she will require surgery. It will be performed in the morning. Dr. Zhang is an excellent surgeon. You may have great confidence in him. Also she has a broken rib, a fractured left wrist, and a concussion. She has been through a great ordeal, your mother.'

'But she will be okay.' This time Teddy spaced the words out ever so slightly, making his voice crisp and distinct like the doctor's.

The doctor gave Teddy a hard look, perhaps because he thought he was being mimicked. 'For someone who has been hit by a car I would say she is a promising case.'

Kenya smiled, showing her straight white teeth. None of them had seen her smile before and each was surprised by the charm she had, by what an exceptionally pretty little girl she was with all those teeth to light up her face. 'And Tip?' Kenya asked charitably.

'It is a very bad sprain with a slight fracture to the fibula.' The doctor shut his file now and smiled back at the girl. 'It seems the car went right over his ankle. Clearly the boy has iron bones.'

'It was a huge car,' Kenya said.

'Exactly,' the doctor said. When Teddy asked if his brother would have to spend the night, the doctor said they would find the proper boot for him to wear and let him go.

'And my mother?'

'Your mother we are planning to keep, but you may come and see her before you go home.'

'That's good,' Doyle said, and patted Kenya on the shoulder. 'You go back and see your mother and I'll check on Tip.'

'We have given her something for her pain after all the X-rays. I'm afraid she will be sleeping now.'

'I can see her sleeping,' Kenya said.

Dr. Ball nodded and Teddy and Doyle and Kenya followed behind. It was even colder in the back than it was by the door. The nurses in their brightly colored jackets did not look up from their stacks of paperwork when they passed by the desk. The emergency room had the feeling of a busy bus station, everyone was restless, waiting to be taken on to some other place or let go. There were people waiting in the halls on gurneys. They stared up at the ceiling or kept their eyes closed. The old woman with the blue eyes was there and she looked at Kenya. 'Where's Jeannie?' she said, or at least that's what Kenya thought she said. It was very hard to hear her.

'I don't know.' Kenya reached out to pet the old woman's hand. She was not afraid of very old people the way most children were. Her mother worked with very old people just like this and some days she took Kenya along. The woman's skin was cool and dry and she could feel all the little bones of her fingers so easily. Teddy put his hand against Kenya's back and steered her away.

'Here,' Dr. Ball said, and Teddy and Doyle turned into the first room to see Tip, while Kenya went farther down the hall with the doctor to find her mother.

'So does this mean you won't be going back to work tonight, or are we going to drop you off on the front steps of the museum and let you hobble in?' Teddy said.

'Can you believe I was run over by a car?' Tip was improbably giddy, glad about everything: glad to be warm again, glad not to be dead, not crushed, glad that his brother was there, and his father. If they moved one step closer in this tiny space he could have touched them.

Teddy shook his head. 'Not nearly as run over as some other people around here. Does it hurt?'

Tip looked down at his ankle. It was wrapped in a white bandage and lifted up on two foam blocks while he waited for his boot cast. His jeans had been cut back to the knee and he was sorry about this. He didn't like the waste. 'I have been so thoroughly medicated I could probably go dancing right now.'

'Which is saying something,' Teddy said.

Doyle dropped himself down in a plastic chair beside the narrow hospital bed. He didn't listen to the boys, who gave the evening a tone of adventure. A sudden, sickening bout of vertigo washed over him. The room tipped forward, then left, then to the back. Doyle let his head fall forward into his hands. There was an awful tightness in his throat and a tremor came up through his shoulders. Why was it now, more than an hour later, that all of this was on him? How was it possible that this woman, a stranger, could act so quickly when it took him more than an hour to cry over what he himself might have

72

lost? If Doyle had her instincts he would be the one flat on his back now, waiting for surgery.

'Oh, Da, stop,' Tip said. 'Look, I'm fine. I was barely run over at all.'

He still had the wallet in his lap. Doyle took off his glasses and wiped at his eyes, but now that he was crying he found it difficult to stop. It was embarrassing. He was grateful that it hadn't happened out in the waiting room in front of the girl. Teddy was standing right up beside him, leaning into him slightly the way a dog will lean, as reassurance. Doyle would have been glad to keep them there, the three of them just like this, no arguing, no danger unless it was a methicillin-resistant *Staphylococcus aureus*. Doyle had read too much about those.

'Tell me about the woman, the girl's mother,' Tip said, hoping to change the conversation. He didn't want to think of how this had started: his walking away, his raising his voice to his father for the right to get back to the basement of the MCZ, some poor woman getting hit by that behemoth because he couldn't be bothered to pay attention. 'Is she all right?'

'She has a broken hip,' Doyle said, clearing his throat. He found a handkerchief in his pocket. 'I think that's the worst of it. There was a broken rib, a slight concussion, something else, I can't remember. The doctor says she'll have surgery in the morning.'

'A fish wouldn't have done that for you,' Teddy said.

Tip shrugged, looking dreamy in his light coating of Demerol. 'The question is, would I have done it for a fish?'

'You would.'

'I don't know if I would have done it for anyone,' Tip said. 'I might have wished I had in retrospect, but I don't think I could have gone from thought to action so quickly. Or maybe she didn't have time to think. It all happened so fast.'

'I would have pushed you,' Teddy said. 'So would Da.'

Tip raised up awkwardly on one elbow and smiled at his brother. 'Ah,' he said, 'but you didn't.'

'I didn't see the car,' Doyle said. And yet he must have. Even in the snow he would have seen the headlights. He tried to remember the moment. He wanted Tip to come to the party at the Simonses' house. Tip was walking away. They were arguing. The snow was coming down so hard. Doyle squinted his eyes. He did not see the lights behind his son. All of a sudden he felt quite certain that there were no lights. The driver did not have his lights on. For the rest of his life he would tell himself this and it would help to ease his grief.

'The little girl was very brave, I thought,' Tip said.

Teddy slid his back down along the wall until he was sitting on his heels. There wasn't another chair in the room as it wasn't meant to hold three people anyway. 'I'm not sure she has anyplace to go. She said she didn't have anyone she wanted to call. If they won't let her sleep here she said she wants to come home with us.'

'I don't think they'd let us walk out of here

74

with a random little girl,' Doyle said.

'Not a random little white girl,' Tip said from his hospital bed. 'But a random little black girl? I don't think anyone's going to stop us at the door.'

Doyle stared at his second son. 'Why would you even say such a thing?'

Tip turned his empty palm up towards the ceiling. He meant no harm whatsoever. 'Because it's true. When will we get out of here, midnight? One? I'm just saying there probably isn't a child-welfare agent parked at the front door of the emergency room. The ambulance driver was happy to turn her over to us, as were the cops. If she wanted to come with us I don't think anyone would stop her.'

'I'd stop her,' Doyle said, lowering his voice. 'We can't bring home a child we don't even know.'

'You've done it before,' Tip said.

'If she really doesn't have anyplace else to go, we might just have to take her,' Teddy said.

Doyle shook his head. 'It wouldn't be right.'

Tip moved his toes slightly but it hurt him. 'More right than leaving her in the waiting room to work it out for herself, I suspect. We do owe her a favor.'

'Then it may be right but it wouldn't be legal. I don't mean it wouldn't be legal the way double parking isn't legal. Walking out with somebody else's child is kidnapping, even if there's no one at the door who wants to stop you.'

Neither Teddy nor Tip said anything to that, and so they conceded the point to their father.

Doyle slid the rubber bands off either end of the wallet and looked at the driver's license. 'Tennessee Alice Moser. Five feet seven inches tall, born September 16th, 1966. Lives in Roxbury.'

'Maybe there's somebody in there we could call,' Teddy said.

Doyle did not feel right about going through this woman's wallet. He did not feel right to notice how very little it contained, seven dollars in cash, a card for the T, several crumpled receipts, a few pictures of the girl, Kenya, taken at department stores, one Master-Card, two Visas, no one to notify in case of emergency. There was no insurance card either. The girl had been wrong about that. 'We'll make sure she has someplace to go,' Doyle said, and put the rubber bands back in place. 'We aren't going to just leave her here.' But none of them had any idea what they would do with her.

'Speaking of which' — Teddy stood up and stretched — 'I should go and check on her. I'll come back in a little bit.'

When he opened the curtain the same doctor was there leaning over a chart at the nurses' station. Teddy stood and waited until the doctor noticed his stillness and looked up. He pointed to the cubicle across the hall and down from Tip's. 'Good that you are here. It is time to take the child out now. She should not stay back there for too long. Mother needs her rest.'

Tennessee Moser was in a room with a door rather than a curtain, making her seem like someone who was in for a longer stay right from

76

the start. Teddy tapped lightly on the frame. 'Hello?' he said.

Kenya came and pulled the door open just a bit, peered out. She looked like a girl who was playing house. 'She's sleeping.' Then she pointed at the doctor. 'He's the one who should keep his voice down if he wants her to rest.' There was nothing especially loud about Dr. Ball's voice, but every sound came through. Call bells chimed while a scratchy voice called indecipherably for Dr. X or Y over a loudspeaker, but Kenya's mother slept deeply, unaware and undisturbed.

'We need to go back to the waiting room now,' Teddy said.

'Don't you want to see her? You could come in and say hello.'

'I'll say hello when she's awake.'

Kenya looked over her shoulder and then back at Teddy. 'Say hello just for a second. I think she'd like it.'

Teddy walked into the tiny room and saw that the woman was sleeping. She looked so different in the bright fluorescent overhead lights than she had in the snow. Teddy wasn't even sure he would have recognized her. She was older than he had thought at first. She looked tired, average, not at all heroic, or at least she didn't look like the sort of woman who would be pushing people away from cars, not that he knew what such a woman would look like. She was tall and she wore her hair straightened and pulled back. She had a white bandage on the right side of her forehead and it covered up half of her right eye. On her right arm there was a cloth splint held in place by Velcro fasteners and her other arm had an IV tube running into it that connected her to a plastic sack that hung above her bed. Her heart monitor beeped with comforting regularity. She was so still, so profoundly asleep, that Teddy had to watch to make sure her chest was moving slightly.

'They're going to take her to a room in just a little while. That's what they told me,' Kenya said.

'That would be good.'

'A nurse came in and asked me a lot of questions. There were all sorts of forms to fill out but I told her your dad had the cards.'

'He'll take care of it.'

'They wanted to know what she's allergic to. The nurse said that was really important but I don't know. I don't think she's allergic to anything. There are things she doesn't like. She doesn't like olives but I don't think she's allergic to them.' Kenya turned her eyebrows down in a way that made her look particularly concerned.

'They probably won't be giving her any olives tonight,' Teddy said.

Kenya gave him a quick look that made it clear she wasn't a fool and then she let it go. 'Did you know they put fifteen stitches in her forehead? I don't think it's going to make any difference though. It's so far up it's almost in her hair.'

Teddy didn't follow her line of reasoning but he didn't think it mattered. 'It won't make any difference.'

Kenya stroked her mother's foot beneath the white sheet. 'She's so pretty.'

Teddy thought of the picture of his own mother that he carried in his wallet, how he would take it out to show people when he was younger and how he would ask them, 'Don't you think she's pretty?'

'She is,' Teddy said.

Kenya leaned over and kissed her mother on the cheek. 'You keep on resting and we'll be back to see you in the morning. Don't worry about anything.' She walked over to the door and stood next to Teddy. She touched her fingers lightly to the sleeve of his sweater. 'At least tell her goodbye,' she said.

So Teddy told her goodbye.

In his mind, Teddy made a list of all the people he could call if he were in some kind of trouble late at night. He thought of the people he could call now, tonight, no matter how late it was, and then he thought of the people he would have called when he was eleven. If it was serious trouble he would always call Tip first, and then his father a very close second. He could call his older brother Sullivan, if Sullivan was in the country. Even though his father wouldn't agree, Teddy knew that Sullivan would always come through to the best of his ability. His uncle Sullivan was certainly long past the point of being able to come and get him if that was what the situation required, but he would be the person Teddy would most want to talk to if there was ever real trouble. Even now he longed to excuse himself from the girl for a moment and find a pay phone so that he could tell his uncle what had happened tonight. Uncle Father

Sullivan often had a difficult time sleeping, so chances were he would be awake anyway, staring out at the same snow that Teddy was staring at now. He would know exactly what to do about the girl, where they should take her for the night, and he would tell Teddy what he should say to comfort her. Father Sullivan didn't have a phone in his room anymore since that story about him had run in the *Herald*, and the office at Regina Cleri had been overrun with calls. Still, Teddy knew that for him the nuns would take the phone up to his uncle's room.

Even in the very unlikely event that Teddy couldn't find the members of what he considered to be his immediate family, he could always call any member of his mother's family, four uncles and two aunts, their husbands and wives, their children, his cousins, who were scattered all across the country now. He could call his father's brother in Chicago or any of his uncle's daughters, who were Teddy's favorite cousins. He could call his friends, or Tip's friends for that matter, and they would come to him and take him home with them for as long as he needed to stay.

So how was it possible that Teddy could conjure up an entire phone book of people waiting to accept his collect calls and Kenya could think of no one? Every time Teddy asked her, all she said was no. He decided that she must have people, plenty of people, but for whatever reason she was holding out as a way of giving them no alternatives. She wanted to stay where she was, a short hallway away from the steady beeping of her mother's heart monitor. As they stood together by a large window, Teddy could think of no way at all to push her towards confession.

'Aren't you sleepy?' he asked.

She shook her head. 'I should be but I'm not.'

They stood and watched the snow coming down in the light and when the silence between them felt awkward Teddy started up, ''Yes, the newspaper was right: snow was falling general all over Ireland,'' he said. ''It was falling on every part of the dark central plain, on the trees, on the treeless hills, falling softly upon the Bog of Allen and, further westward, softly falling into the dark mutinous Shannon waves.''

'What are you talking about?' Kenya said. She didn't look at him like he was crazy. She just wanted to know.

Teddy shook his head. 'It's a story I like. The snow made me think of it.'

'You do that a lot, don't you?'

'What?'

'I don't know, repeat things. You did it tonight before the lecture.'

'You saw me at the lecture?'

'Everybody did. You were talking just like you were Jesse Jackson.'

He had been, he remembered now, although it seemed like that was years ago. It had never occurred to him that they were at the lecture too. Were Kenya and her mother sitting close by? 'Why did you want to go hear Jesse Jackson?'

Kenya shrugged. 'It was my mother. I didn't want to go. My mother likes politics. We go to

81

those sorts of things.'

Of course it made sense. Everyone there was coming out of the lecture. Why else would they have been on Eliot Street in the snow late at night, so far away from Roxbury? 'We must have come out at the same time then. I didn't see you.'

Kenya looked at her fingernails and then stuffed her hands in her pockets. She was still wearing her coat. She was still carrying her mother's purse, though she'd left the boots by her hospital bed. 'Maybe we did. I don't know. Tell me the rest of that story now, the one about Ireland.'

And Teddy was going to tell her, all about the snow falling on Michael Furey's grave, but Doyle came through the door pushing Tip in a wheelchair. Tip's foot was straight out ahead of him in a pale blue boot, a pair of crutches rested across his lap. Tip and Doyle looked tired in a deep and permanent way.

'They're letting me go,' Tip said.

'And I'm going to talk to someone about where Kenya should stay tonight,' Doyle said. 'We'll get you set up, don't worry about that.'

'I'm going to stay with my mother.'

'They won't let you.' Teddy put his hand on her shoulder. 'You know that.'

'You're going to have to go to a family member or a guardian,' Doyle said. 'We'd take you home with us but they don't let children walk out with just anybody at this hospital.'

But they all knew that wasn't true. There were very few people left in the waiting room now, and where they were standing, so near to the door, there was no one else at all. No one would see them or stop them. No one would care who she left with except for the Doyles themselves. Kenya sat down in a chair beside an artificial rubber tree. She was thinking things over. Maybe she was trying to come up with the name of someone she could call. Maybe she hadn't given up hope of staying there with her mother. When she finally spoke it was to answer the question that no one had asked her. 'It's the one thing I'm never supposed to tell,' she said.

'Then we won't tell either,' Teddy said. It was late. It was impossibly late, and if they were only now going to get involved with child services it could be hours still before they were home and asleep.

'Just take me with you,' Kenya said.

'We can't.' Doyle kept his eyes steady on hers. 'You have to understand, that would be against the law.'

Kenya sighed. She looked at Teddy and at Tip, but in the end it was Tip she decided to put the question to. It was all so complicated and Tip was the smartest one so he had the best chance at understanding. Look at your face, she wanted to say to him. Look at your eyes. But that wasn't the right way to say it. Tip in his red jacket sat in his wheelchair, his bare toes poking out of his blue boot. Doyle stood on one side of him and Teddy on the other, all three of them looking right at her, seeing her and no one else. They were all respectful of who she was, the daughter of the woman who had been hit by the car. They were waiting to hear whatever she had to say. No one was rushing her but the words *tired* and *late* hung over all of them like a blinking sign. She wanted more than anything to pull on her hair but she willed herself to keep her hands in her lap. She wanted them to see her as serious.

'Don't you ever wonder about your mother?' she said.

4

Tip was smarter and Teddy was sweeter. They had heard it since a time before memory. Sweet and Smart or Smart and Sweet. Either way it should have been a name of a magazine for teenaged girls or a brand of hard candy or a sauce for crispy duck. The teachers in their elementary school said it when the boys were a grade apart. They said it after Tip skipped the fourth grade and went ahead to fifth. They dressed up his English compositions in tin foil stars and red letter A's and pinned them to the cork board in the language arts center. They were slow to erase the math problems he had worked out in chalk. But they never longed to scoop Tip up in their arms. They didn't save his class picture or the cards that he made because, unlike his brother, Tip never made any teacher a card. 'Tip is one of the smartest little boys this school has ever seen,' the teachers would confide when Doyle came in for conferences. 'But Teddy is just so sweet.' Teddy did not get to skip the fourth grade. In fact, it was suggested that he repeat it. The principal was careful to avoid the word 'failed.' She made it sound like they enjoyed having Teddy in fourth grade so much that they were hoping he could stay and do it again. Doyle refused. It was bad enough that his sons, who should have been one year apart, were now two years apart. He would not see them go to three.

Besides, just because Tip was smart didn't mean that Teddy was stupid. Teddy wasn't stupid, he just wandered. Even as a little boy Tip could be pinned into place by an idea. Set him on the floor with a picture book and he would stay until the book was finished. Set him on the floor with a can of Lincoln Logs and he would stay until he'd built himself a woody Taj Mahal. Teddy, on the other hand, was more like a cloud. The slightest breath of wind could send him to the hall closet to hunt up a tennis racquet he hadn't seen in years, or out to the mailbox on the corner to see if the time for the pickup had changed even though he had nothing to mail. It wasn't that he refused to do his homework or even that he couldn't manage it, it was just that other things caught his attention, and anything that had Teddy's attention had all of him. Doyle got his youngest son through fourth grade the same way he would get him through fifth and sixth and all the grades to come: he sat there. He put his body in the room, at the table, beside the book. He brought Teddy to his office after school and had him sit beside him at the desk so they could work together. When Teddy's mind wandered from the project at hand, Doyle knew it before he did. He could smell the distraction as if it was something burning and he tapped the page with his finger. 'Right here,' Doyle would say. If Doyle had a meeting, a dinner out, he would pay Tip a dollar to take his place. He did not ask the baby-sitter to do it. She had a susceptibility to Teddy's charms that made her unsuitable for discipline.

The thing that was most likely to walk off with Teddy's concentration was the memory of his mother, the splendid redhead in the photographs, his own perpetual flame that he stoked with every available scrap of information. He *did* remember her. He was positive of that. He remembered her kneeling in front of him, buttoning his winter coat. He remembered sitting on the floor of the kitchen while she chopped carrots and talked to one of his aunts. He remembered lying beside her in a bed, his back to her chest, her long, pale arm draped over him so that he was looking at his pillow and her hand. He could still feel the even rhythm of her breathing. He had put his hand on top of her hand, stretched out his fingers and tried to cover hers and in her sleep she wrapped that hand beneath him and pulled him close to her.

There were many, many times that Teddy tried to mine his father for information because surely Doyle had enough stored away to keep his memory burning forever, but Doyle would always just tap the open math book with his finger. 'Right here.'

It was in fact a misunderstanding between them. Teddy wanted to talk about Bernadette. Doyle wanted to keep Teddy from spending his life in the seventh grade. He tried to ask Tip but all Tip would ever say was, 'I don't remember.' He said it curtly, like Teddy was nagging and he didn't want to be bothered. That must have been the case since it was impossible that Tip, who was a year older and certainly smarter, would actually remember less. Sullivan would have told him about their mother but Sullivan was never around and when he was around he tended to stay in his room with the door locked. Other people in the family, aunts, uncles, various older cousins, would cry when he asked them what they remembered. They would pull the boy to their chest and weep in his hair until Doyle had to tell him not to ask anymore.

That was how he came to be so close to his great-uncle, Father Sullivan. It turned out the priest had stories stacked up like dinner napkins. Father Sullivan said that they belonged to Teddy, hundreds of stories waiting to be unfolded. They all started simply, beautifully, 'When your mother was nine she got a yellow dress for her birthday. I was at the party. Everything she asked for that year was yellow. She wanted a canary and a lemon cake . . . '

Somewhere along the line Teddy's love for his mother had become his love for Father Sullivan, and his love for Father Sullivan became his love for God. The three of them were bound into an inextricable knot: the living and the dead and the life everlasting. Each one led him to the other, and any member of the trinity he loved simply increased his love for all three.

The question wasn't did he ever think of his mother. The question was did he ever think of anything else.

★   ★   ★

Doyle called for a taxi to take them home. When he asked how long it was going to be, the

88

dispatcher told him to go look out the window. Everyone who was out in the city tonight was stranded. Now it was clear that he should have made the call an hour ago. None of them even considered going back for Doyle's car, which by now was surely buried. Driving home was the smallest of the plans that had been laid aside. With everything that had happened, the only thing that stayed consistent was the falling snow. The streets had been swept into a single luminous valley. It was Teddy who announced that Kenya would spend the night with them, and neither Tip nor Doyle countered with the subject of kidnapping, though Doyle wondered if the child herself would bring charges against them later. Tip had signed all of his release papers and now he sat in the wheelchair and quietly ground his teeth. His left shoe, a puffy white Puma sneaker, rested uselessly on his lap beneath the two crutches that balanced across the wheelchair's arms. The wheelchair would only go as far as the front door. The crutches had been written out as a prescription and filled from a storeroom at the hospital. The boot, a complicated blue fiberglass construction trimmed out with Velcro straps, had been purchased and charged to the insurance company. It was Tip's to keep. They sat in the waiting room and looked out the window. The sets of headlights that slid slowly past the hospital were few and far between and the Doyles pinned their hopes to every one of them. Kenya yawned and then yawned again until her eyes were damp with exhaustion. She did the finger work for *Für Elise* against her knees. It helped to keep her awake.

'How long have you known?' Teddy finally asked, because of the million questions flying through his head at once this was the only one he could shape into words.

'About you?' Kenya shrugged. 'I don't know. A long time.'

But what was a long time when you're eleven — two months? three years? Teddy couldn't bring himself to ask her and so he said nothing. Tip wrapped and unwrapped the shoelace of his empty sneaker around his finger while Doyle kept watch for the cab. It came sooner than any of them expected, the first piece of good luck all day. Together they set through the electric door that sprang open to return them to the weather. Teddy helped his brother into the backseat and Doyle rolled the chair through the door of the hospital and said good night again to the nurse. Kenya sat by one window with her mother's purse in her lap, looking out, and Tip sat by the other window with Teddy in the middle. Doyle got into the front seat.

'We'll come back tomorrow,' Kenya said, looking at the sprawling building over her shoulder when they finally drove away.

'First thing,' Teddy said.

'What if she wakes up in the middle of the night? How's she going to know where I am?'

'The nurse will tell her you're with us,' Teddy said, though they had forgotten to tell the nurse anything.

'We'll have to call someone at your school and tell them you won't be coming in,' Doyle said. In the morning he would return her to the place he had taken her from. He would let her sleep and then it was right back to the waiting room. Now that they were in it that was the only thing to do.

'I don't think they'll have school tomorrow,' Kenya said. The taxi was only going about ten miles an hour. It pushed through the snow like a sleigh.

'No,' the taxi driver said. 'No school tomorrow.'

'Good.' Kenya put her head against the frosted window and watched the snow.

Doyle kept his eyes straight ahead until they ached from trying to focus on so much whiteness. He had felt a leap of viciousness inside his chest, the very viciousness that had made him a good prosecutor when he was a young man, when the girl first made her claim. He managed to catch himself before he laughed at her. He was able to remember the circumstances of this night and that she was only a child. He did not blame the child, but that didn't mean they weren't sitting in the middle of some elaborate ruse. Even if he was no longer the mayor, theirs had been a public life. An old white mayor with two black sons, they were almost impossible to miss. People had delusions. Women had called the office all the time when the boys were young and proclaimed their maternity. Everybody sees themselves at the center of the story. Still, the defense could find holes in his argument big enough to drive a herd of cattle through. The woman had put herself in front of the car to save Tip, that was true, but who knows what she was thinking at that moment? The girl, Kenya, was more troubling as she seemed to be the very body of evidence: long legs, long neck, the warm color of her skin. He had noticed her hands, her tapering fingers, the elegant beds of her fingernails. Those hands could be compared. Hands? Doyle felt himself more closely related to Clarence Darrow than the high-tech legal investigations that ruled TV. It was only a matter of DNA these days. The mother was or she wasn't, and as far as Doyle was concerned, even if she was, she wasn't. His boys had a mother, and their mother was in the Old Calvary Cemetery in Roslindale.

What Doyle wondered at even more than this sudden reappearance was his own lack of vigilance. Why had he never thought of a mother returning? Why was it that once the adoptions were finalized he never wondered about her again, never speculated about her to Bernadette? Even the claims of crazy women never drove him to consider the possibility of a mother waiting out there somewhere. How had he let himself be so emptied of any past, as if the boys had been pulled from out of the air? And why was it the boys had never asked about her either, never said, as children in similar circumstances surely must, what about our real mother? Maybe because it was natural to wonder about the one who was missing, the one who left you, and for their family that would always be Bernadette. It was enough to hold one absent mother in your mind, to love completely and completely believe in the love of this woman you never see. No one could be expected to hold up two empty places. The weight of it would surely crush the life out of a child.

'It's late for a little girl to be up,' the cabdriver said, looking back at Kenya in his rearview mirror. He was Jamaican. It was not a country that afforded any practice in driving through snow.

'I get to stay up late if there's no school,' she said, though not late like this. Even on a Saturday night she was asleep by eleven, and if her mother was working a late shift she called Kenya and told her it was lights-out and Kenya would do what she was told. She would go to sleep but still keep one ear cocked. What she would have given to hear her mother's keys right now, the jingle that preceded the deep click of the lock. Heaven would be home, to walk into their own apartment together right now. She would barely get out of her shoes. She would sleep in her coat and her dress if her mother would let her. She would collapse into their shared bed, melt into familiar sheets. Home, bed, sleep, mother — who knew more beautiful words than these? 'Anyway, I'm not even tired.'

'That would make one of us, girl,' the cabdriver said.

Just saying the word *tired* made her eyelids flutter down. How glad she would have been to sleep in this cab. But then she remembered her vigilance. That was the word her mother taught her. Don't stop looking around. Don't stop watching. Every moment you've got to know where you are, what's coming up behind you, who's staring you down. That's what her mother would tell her now. Kenya yawned once and then shook it off, made herself sit up straighter.

When they pulled up to the house all the lights were on, the only house lit bright on the dark street, and none of them gave it a thought. Doyle handed the driver twenty over the meter in simple gratitude for bringing them back. The street was a snow globe, a Christmas card. Doyle took a last deep breath of the cab's sour warmth before opening the door and stepping back into the cold. He went to get the crutches out of the trunk. Someone on the street was playing Schubert's C-sharp minor quartet. He could barely hear it but he knew, and for a second Doyle smiled. Then he stopped smiling. To reach the front door of the house they would have to climb fourteen steps, and while they had once been distinct they now blurred into a single slope of snow, a perfect bunny run. Back in the taxi Teddy put his hand on the girl's shoulder.

'We're here,' he said.

Kenya blinked, looked at Teddy and then looked down the street, suddenly, utterly awake, though she would swear that she hadn't been sleeping. 'We're here,' she said.

There was nothing Kenya did not know about Union Park Street. She knew the bus that came up Columbus Ave. through Roxbury, past Malcolm X to where the split makes it Tremont. She and her mother rode that bus to Union Park when she was a little girl. She knew the straight shot down to Cathedral. She knew when the neighbors moved away and who kept up their

94

tiny patches of lawn. She made note of the padlock on the iron spiked fence that surrounded the little park in the center of the street, the faded 'No Dogs Allowed' sign on the gate that might as well have read 'No People Allowed.' She watched as the snow was whisked away in the winter and how the street sweeper came and scrubbed down the street in the summer with water sprays and giant round brushes. Where she lived, what fell on the street stayed on the street, if it was precipitation or a Coke can.

Doyle and Teddy got Tip out of the car and stood on either side of him. Tip dug in his crutches and tried to hold his foot up but his bare toes touched down behind him and dipped into snow. 'Who thought it was a good idea to put the door so far away from the street?' he said. While they looked at the stairs and tried to figure out the logistics of transport, Kenya shot up ahead. She bounded and leapt. Never had she climbed these stairs or been allowed to sit down on them to catch her breath on a hot day, though people everywhere sat on steps that did not belong to them, people sat on *these* steps that did not belong to them, a fact that she pointed out to her mother often and to no avail. She wasn't even allowed to walk on the same side of the street as this house. She turned her eyes away from it every time but there was not one thing she didn't know about the window casements, the knocker or doorknob, the woman's face carved out of stone above the front door or the two urns on either side that were filled first with violets then hydrangeas then zinnias then chrysanthemums just this summer alone. If anyone had asked her yesterday how it might have felt to be right there at the top of the stairs like she owned the place, she would have said petrifying, paralyzing, and she would have been wrong. It was electric. It was King of the World, first place in the 500 meter. She could have roared, 'Look at me here!' her hot breath making a geyser of white steam. But she remembered herself. She looked down at the Doyles there on the sidewalk looking up at her and saw that they were stranded, waiting helpless for her lead, and so she started dragging her foot back and forth like a broom.

'I have a snow shovel,' Doyle said.

'I've got big feet,' Kenya said. Back and forth she traveled down each step until there was a wide swath cut from the center.

'You're going to get snow in your shoes,' Teddy said, but he admired her resourcefulness, the meticulous nature of her work.

'I already have snow in my shoes.'

'Sacajawea.' Tip put his crutches on the first stair while Teddy and Doyle stood close by to catch him in case he fell over backwards. Once, when Teddy was thirteen he had a cyst in the back of his knee that had to be removed and that cyst put him on crutches for six weeks. It was during that time that maybe twice, when the crutches were very new and still seemed glamorous, Tip took them for a spin around the kitchen. That was the full extent of his crutch experience. When they got to the landing at the top, Kenya said to none of them in particular, 'I get to go inside.'

'We weren't going to make you sleep on the stoop,' Tip said.

Doyle was still searching his pockets for his keys when the door swung open wide and Schubert poured out behind the sound of Sullivan calling their names.

'Doesn't anyone leave a note?' he said. He was wearing Doyle's red plaid bathrobe and a pair of bedroom slippers cut from an old oriental carpet that none of them had seen before. He put down his drink on the front table to put his arms around Teddy. Teddy, for embracing, was always the logical choice.

'Who knew you were coming home?' Doyle said.

'You knew it,' Sullivan said. 'I told you I was coming home.'

They hobbled into the front hall, wet and covered in snow. Doyle took off his hat and scarf and handed them to his oldest son, then he went to help Tip out of his jacket. Sullivan tonight? Think of all the nights they waited up, waiting and wanting Sullivan to come and then tonight there he was. They should have slept at the hospital.

'When did you get a boot?' Sullivan asked. He had put a fire in the fireplace but the flue wasn't open far enough. Everything in the living room was dim and slightly blurred with smoke. Teddy coughed.

'Tonight. That's where we've been. You said you were coming home for Christmas.' Tip had

had all the mysterious reappearance of family he could stomach for one day. *Surprise!* It's your mother! *Surprise!* Your brother shows up too! He felt like hobbling down the street after the Jamaican and hiring the taxi to take him back to the lab. Sullivan patted Tip on the back, a little too heartily given the circumstances of Tip's balance.

'It's practically Christmas.'

'On my calendar it was three weeks ago,' Doyle said. 'Could you turn the stereo down?' One child understood Schubert, only one of them, and he managed to make Schubert a point of irritation.

'And now you've adopted another child,' Sullivan said to his father. 'I think that's marvelous.'

Doyle looked at him, a look that Teddy or Tip would have understood instantly, but Sullivan simply turned away to shut off the stereo.

'This is Kenya,' Teddy said, his voice sounding abrupt in the new silence.

'Kenya, Kenya,' he said. 'What a beautiful name. I've been to Kenya. I was living not too far from there in Kampala.'

'You've been to Kenya yourself?' It was her own name, she heard it every day, and still it was thrilling to attach it to the place.

'This is Sullivan, by the way.' Teddy was always glad to see Sullivan. He loved his brother, and besides, Sullivan had the brilliant ability to turn all of the focus and anxiety in any room onto himself.

'Do you have a last name?'

'Moser,' she said and shook the hand that he held out to her. Kenya had only seen Sullivan a few times in her life. He had dark red hair and dark blue eyes and his skin was tan with a red undertone like a deeply polished wood, though she remembered it as being very pale before. They stared at each other without embarrassment, Kenya and Sullivan, while they held each other's hand.

Sullivan spoke to his father but he kept his eyes on the girl. 'If you were going to adopt another child it seems remarkable that you found one who looks so much like the two you've already got.'

'We didn't adopt her,' Doyle said.

'You think I look like them?' Kenya was awfully flattered. It was something she liked to think sometimes but when she asked her mother all her mother would say was you look like yourself.

'Not him, of course,' he pointed to his father. 'But those other two.'

'Sullivan.' Doyle lowered his tone.

'A first cousin at least.'

Tip crutched his way into the living room and fell into the sofa, pulling his leg up to the coffee table as he stretched against the cushions and closed his eyes.

'What happened to you, anyway?' Sullivan asked, following behind him. 'Did one of the fish bite you?'

'He was hit by a car,' Kenya said.

Sullivan raised his eyebrows, and it served to make him look halfway impressed. 'If you were hit by a car then I'd say you came through pretty nicely.'

'It was her mother who was hit by a car,' Tip said in a flat tone, though he looked like he was already asleep. Her mother. Let's be abundantly clear on this point: *her* mother.

Sullivan, who wasn't as tall as either of his brothers, crouched down to his knees in front of the girl. He pushed his hair, which had gotten too long, back from his eyes. 'Your mother was hit?'

'She broke her hip,' she said, 'her wrist, a rib, and she cut her forehead here.' She ran her finger along her hairline in the place that her mother was cut. 'But she's going to be fine. The doctor said she was going to be fine. She pushed Tip out of the way. He didn't see the car.'

Doyle clapped his hands. 'All right, enough stories. It's very late and there will be time for all of this tomorrow.' He stood behind Kenya and lightly touched her shoulder. He saw then that her coat pulled across her shoulders and was short in the sleeves, last year's coat. 'We should let our guest get some sleep now.'

But Sullivan did not stand up. 'Your mother must be very brave. I would never step in front of a car for someone else.'

Kenya started to say something but every single word she knew was inadequate for the necessary response. Her mouth simply opened and then closed, empty. Sullivan looked at Kenya and then he picked up her hand and held it again. 'Do I know you?' he said.

She blinked. Teddy turned around to face

100

them and for a moment Tip opened his eyes. 'I don't think so,' she said carefully. Where had Sullivan gone to all those years he stayed away? That was the thing Kenya and her mother couldn't figure out. One day he was there and then they never saw him anymore.

'Sullivan, let her go to bed now,' Tip said. 'You can grill her for details tomorrow.'

'Your mother won't appreciate our keeping you awake all night, school or no school.' Doyle gestured one hand towards the staircase.

At that moment Kenya remembered where she was. There was so much happening and it was all going by her so quickly. 'I haven't seen anything yet,' she said to Doyle. Here was the living room, two identical sofas with carved legs facing each other, bright throw pillows, big and soft, one that was needlepointed with a picture of fish, a real piano in the corner, a big one, photographs in silver frames. The draperies, whose lining she had seen so many times before, were striped on this side — red and blue and green on a heavy cream cloth. They were held back by tasseled ropes. She had to remember every last piece of it, the carpet, the candy dish, the basket of magazines on the floor. She had to go back and tell her mother.

Tip yawned hugely from the sofa. 'She might be hungry, you know. We could offer to feed her.'

'I'm not,' Kenya said, and then immediately regretted it because it would have meant seeing the kitchen.

'Let her sleep in our room,' Teddy said. 'Tip's never going to make it up all those stairs.'

'I'm going to sleep right here,' Tip said, and he meant it. He pulled off his red jacket and tossed it onto the farthest cushion. Then he swung his boot off the table and onto his jacket, stretching out long. Tip had a history of sleeping on couches, of studying too late and falling asleep wherever he was. Teddy went off to get him some blankets. Tip wanted them all out of the room. He wanted everything out of his head: fish and snow, car and politics, mother and sister. The ache in his ankle was like an angry conversation coming from another room, something persistent, irritating, abstracted, something you should get up and take care of but for whatever reason you don't.

'Good night,' the girl's voice said from someplace nearby. He raised up the fingers of his hand to her but kept his eyes closed.

Doyle found a toothbrush in its package and a tube of paste and laid them on top of a fresh towel and facecloth in the bathroom. He gave her an undershirt to sleep in because there was nothing in the house, not a single thing, that came anywhere close to being right for little girls. He took her up the long staircase with its steep angled turns and then worried that she might be afraid to sleep so far away from everyone else. Then he remembered that Sullivan would be across the hall and he wondered if that might frighten her more. He watched her narrow shoulders, her slender waist. He counted her six high ponytails and reminded himself again that whatever else was happening here tonight, this was a child whose mother had been hit by a car.

She would have to be scared to death and he would make a point to remember that.

When they got to the room, Doyle, who had very few occasions to venture so high up in his own house anymore, was struck by how perfectly preserved it was. It was a museum of a past life, and now Teddy lived up there by himself. Hardly anything had changed since the boys were in grade school except the addition of the crimson felt pennant that said HARVARD. Teddy had put it up over Tip's bed when Tip was accepted, and while Tip said it was idiotic and embarrassing, he never took it down. There was a map of the states and a huge map of the world that Doyle himself had put up on the walls with thumbtacks, a chart of the solar system, a guide to learning Morse code, pictures of Bobby Kennedy and Martin Luther King, Jr., the two pictures of Bernadette on the dresser in a double frame. On one side she was a bride of twenty-four, her hair twisted up and crowned in netting, on the other side she was a mother of three, the day they brought Tip home. Bernadette holds Teddy and Doyle holds Tip and Sullivan stands between them, twelve years old. Beside the pictures was the statue of the Virgin Mary, her arms open and ready to receive.

'This is where they slept?' Kenya said.

'Teddy still sleeps here. Tip sleeps at school.'

'Why doesn't Teddy get to sleep at school?'

Doyle glanced at Teddy's unmade bed and pulled the covers up. 'Because he doesn't go to classes when he sleeps at school.'

Kenya slowly turned her head, not so much

looking at the room as absorbing it. 'I used to make up stories about this house.'

How strange it was to think that a child he had never met could make up stories about the place he lived and that he would never have known it. 'What kind of stories?' It was his legacy, this house. Doyle had bought it when people said the neighborhood was too close to Roxbury, too close to Cathedral. He hung on to it when his neighbors chopped theirs up into condos and sold off their homes room by room.

'I said there was a dance club here, and a bowling alley, and a movie theater.'

'No movie theater.'

'I said that each of you had your own floor, you and then Sullivan, then Tip and then Teddy on the top, and that there was an elevator so you could go up and down and visit each other.'

'I'm certain the boys would have liked that.'

'Sometimes I said it was my house.' Kenya had tried to be on her best manners when she was downstairs. Don't ever stare at things, her mother always told her. If you stare at something people will think you mean to take it. But now she could not help herself. She walked from chair to bed to desk in the room, staring and touching and every now and then closing her eyes to inhale. She pulled *Moby-Dick* down from the bookcase, studied the cover carefully and then returned it to its proper place. She took down *Call of the Wild* and *The Voyage of the Beagle*. She opened them up and smelled the pages.

The winter that Tip was eleven and Teddy was

ten, Doyle read them *The Voyage of the Beagle* over twenty-eight nights. He billed it as their first completely grown-up book, so defined because it lacked any of the elements that had made the previous books he had read them so appropriate for little boys. There were no dogs, no beggar orphans, no Lilliputians, and no illustrations. Doyle had dragged an armchair up the stairs from his study a long time ago and left it permanently in the boys' room so that he could be comfortable regardless of chapter length. There the chair sat, now awkwardly pushed into the corner and covered in clothes that the housekeeper would pick up on Thursday. In the evenings, thousands of evenings ago, he had pulled that chair in between the boys' twin beds so that he faced them, Tip on his left hand, Teddy on his right, both of them pajama clad, both of them so wide awake with excitement for the story that it seemed impossible that in half an hour they would both be sound asleep. Doyle knew the adventure of it all wore them down to a thread in the end. He read the story of the young Charles Darwin in a strong and animated voice, and sometimes the boys would become so excited by the discovery of a toad or the painful wanting of water or the threat of various natives that they crawled out from under their covers so they could sit closer to him. If there was a terrible storm that pitched the *Beagle* violently in strange waters, Teddy would wind up coming over into the chair to sit on the side of Doyle's lap and then finally, a page or two later, Tip would follow, even though he thought of himself as too old for such things. What they loved so passionately about the book was that it was real. Darwin was a real man, the *Beagle* was a real ship, and this was the real world he wrote of, even though it was difficult to believe that the world contained such things as phosphorescent seas and natives who ran naked through the jungles and slept in the rain and the mud.

''All that at present can be said with certainty is that, as with the individual, so with the species, the hour of life has run its course, and is spent,'' Doyle read, and closed the book. 'And so ends chapter nine.'

The boys made small sounds of disappointment but they did not ask for more. Beg all you want, Doyle never read more than a chapter a night.

'When I'm bigger, I'm going to go and explore Brazil,' Tip said.

'I'm not sure what's left to be explored,' Doyle said. He stood up and swung Tip over into his bed, dropping him from a height great enough to cause a good bounce.

'I'll find something.' Tip scrambled to pull his covers up against the New England chill that no furnace could chase from the fourth floor. 'There are jungles there that no one has ever been to.'

'Very possible.' Doyle leaned over and kissed his son good night. 'Then you'll come home and be president.'

'After I've been a famous explorer,' Tip said.

'Not me,' Teddy said. 'I'm going to stay home with Da.'

'Good man,' Doyle said, and kissed him, too. 'You can be president first then, while Tip is in the Amazon hunting piranha. Now off with the light.'

Tip leaned up and pulled the chain on the table lamp but the room was never very dark. The curtains stayed open at night to let the streetlight in and a plug-in night-light that read *Brush Your Teeth* glowed brightly from the baseboard. Neither boy liked the dark. They liked to lie in bed awake and look at the maps pinned to the wall, including the map of Darwin's voyage on which they charted his progress.

'Say a prayer for your mother, boys,' Doyle said at the door, and then he said the words with them. 'Grant eternal rest unto her soul, O Lord, and may perpetual light shine upon her — '

Kenya touched the lamp, the bedside table. She went to the wall and touched the frame of Kennedy's picture. She put her hands flat against the windowsill and looked out. 'I know which window this is,' she said excitedly.

'You do?' Doyle stood beside the doorframe and watched her watch the world.

'I never knew which room they slept in. I thought it was the next window under this one but I was just guessing.'

They had asked for one child and then came home with two. So often they had said to each other how lucky they were. They hadn't thought of it before but it was so much better, infinitely better having them both. Each brother would keep the other from feeling alien or isolated in

107

this white jungle. But if there had been another call, the agency saying there was one more sibling in the set and this one was a girl, a daughter for Bernadette, oh, he would have given anything if she could have had a daughter. Even if she had come at the very end, even for a week. Doyle sat down on the edge of the bed and closed his eyes.

'This is your wife?'

Doyle looked at the pictures of his wife. 'That's her.'

'She's so pretty.'

'She was,' Doyle said.

'And this is her, too?' Kenya touched her fingertip ever so lightly to the fingertip of the Virgin. 'This is her after she died?'

'Yes,' Doyle said. 'That's her, too.'

5

In Teddy and Tip's room, Kenya slept openmouthed and dreamless, one hand falling over either side of the twin mattress. She did not snoop in drawers or say her prayers, the two things she had planned on doing once she was safely alone. This sleep had caught her off guard, swept up like a wave and pulled her in. Wearing a T-shirt that seemed to be the size of a ship's sail, she slept in Tip's bed. Doyle told her to because the sheets were clean.

Tip had made his bed where he said he would, in front of the smokey fireplace on the couch where he had first collapsed upon coming home. Teddy got an oven mitt and stuck his hand up the chimney to wrench the flue open wider, scorching his sweater slightly for his troubles, then he stretched out on the couch across from Tip in case his brother should wake and need something in the night. Besides, his room was occupied. Neither boy had taken off any of their clothes and the hems of their pants were still wet from snow. Their socks were damp and cold.

'Awake?' Teddy said. They had been saying it to each other all their lives, sleeping in their opposite beds or, in this case, opposite couches. It meant, *Are you there, are you listening to me, will you talk to me now?*

'I can't imagine why, but I am,' Tip said.

'So what do you think?'

'About what?'

Teddy pushed himself up on one elbow. 'Come on, there's nothing to talk about? The car, the girl, your ankle, your mother. Take your pick.'

Tip kept his eyes closed. He would have liked to have been asleep. He was tired enough. But his brother, once he got on a scent, would be relentless with his questions. There was really nothing to do but give in to him. 'The car: didn't see it. The girl: I have no idea about the girl, I'm skipping that one. The ankle: hurts more than you might think. The mother, whomever's mother she might be: absolutely no concern of mine.'

'Even if she saved your life.'

'No one said I was dying.'

'Tip, seriously, our mother showing up like that out of nowhere, you can't just write that off, not if she really is our mother.'

Then Tip did open his eyes. He rolled over to face his brother whose face he could make out quite clearly in the light coming in from the street. Teddy serene, hopeful, open-minded. Every word of it was written out on his face. If Tip had had the energy he would have pulled himself off the couch to slap him, but since he didn't have the energy he would have to try and explain. 'There are two choices as to what you can think. You can think this is a sad person or a dangerous person who has been following us around for God only knows how long because of something she read in the paper twenty years ago. She watches us go to school, she watches us pick up bagels, she tails us through the bookstore. I don't love this thought. In fact, I find it singularly disturbing. Next thought — this is our biological mother, the woman who didn't take you home from the hospital and set me out on the curb at fourteen months, and now she's following us around for whatever reason, jealousy, regret, who knows. What part of that am I supposed to embrace?'

Teddy sat with this a long time. Tip's logic was always going to be stronger than his own. Tip knew how to put words to things while Teddy knew how to follow what was in his heart. 'But she pushed you away.'

'I appreciate that. Maybe we can call it even now.'

'You have to at least give her a chance.'

'If she's some crazy woman, then no, I don't have to give her a chance. If she has a biological connection to us, then I already did. I gave her a chance for fourteen months.' Tip leaned into the void between the couches, the side of his face barely illuminated by the final licks of orange light from the fireplace. 'You want to think she's our mother? Then who is our father? Did you ask yourself that one? That's where babies come from, Teddy, a mother and a father. Open the door to one and you're going to have to start looking for the other.' He let his head fall back to the pillow. It was deep and sweet. 'I'm not interested.'

'Nobody's talking about fathers here,' Teddy said, feeling a rush of loyalty to Doyle.

There had been moments in his life when Tip

had considered another father, more so than he ever considered a mother. Whenever he got angry at Doyle he would try to imagine that other man, the one who was coded in his genes, but it was never very satisfying. He could not picture him as a scientist, a brilliant herpetologist or entomologist who had given his son away. He could only see a boy no older than he was now, walking through the streets, his hands shoved deep into the pockets of his sweatshirt. 'Go to sleep,' Tip said, and dismissed the image from his mind. 'It will be every bit as confusing in the morning.'

Teddy would have pressed the point but then they heard their father coming down the stairs and they fell into silence. There was nothing they meant to keep from him, but it was their habit from the days when they used to hear his footsteps coming back up the stairs to tell them it was late and time to stop talking. Doyle trained them this way, until the sound alone of his footsteps would quiet them.

Doyle came into the living room with extra comforters in his arms and draped one over each of the boys. Looking at them there, he thought of when he used to carry them, both of them together, when they fell asleep in the car coming back from the beach, how he balanced one on each hip and felt their shins tapping together. They were always so slight, so long-legged and weightless. He did not know how they could have grown into such enormous men. He unlaced the one shoe Tip was wearing and rested it on the floor. By the time he was finished, both boys had fallen for their own trick. Both of them were asleep.

Doyle knew for certain he would be awake all night. He had planned to worry about Tip's ankle and the little girl sleeping in Tip's bed. He had also meant to analyze the best way to extricate his family from the girl's mother, while at the same time being fearful that she had come to take from him the very thing he could not bear to lose. He told the story quietly to Sullivan in the kitchen after covering up the boys, about Tennessee and Kenya and how they had always known where Tip and Teddy had been. 'To hear this girl you'd think that she and her mother have been standing on a street corner every night of their lives making sure the boys got across.'

Sullivan took it all in, nodding slowly while Doyle talked, and when Doyle was finished Sullivan yawned. 'I guess that's why she looked familiar.' He poured himself a glass of grapefruit juice from the refrigerator. 'I must have seen them lurking around.'

Doyle watched while his son drained his glass in one long gulp. 'That's all?'

Sullivan's blue eyes were bloodshot and damp and he pressed them down with his fingers. 'No, I'm sure there are other things to say — 'how shocking,' or 'what a surprise.'' He scratched hard at his head with both hands. 'It's just the jet lag. I'm standing here but I'm sound asleep.'

Doyle tried to focus his attention on his first son for a moment but it was an effort. Bernadette was always telling him to think about Sullivan. 'You can't make everything about the little boys,' she would say. But right from the beginning Doyle saw the little boys as a fresh start, a chance to do a better job. It was remarkable in retrospect, seeing as how Sullivan was at that point still more than a decade away from complete ruin. Once Bernadette was gone and Sullivan did his best to destroy everything that wasn't already lost, it was all Doyle could do not to write him off completely. But he hadn't done that. He had stood by Sullivan, even if Sullivan would never acknowledge it. He had been an imperfect father to an imperfect son and as far as he was concerned they were even. Now that Sullivan was back, Doyle would do his best to walk the line between extending himself and playing the fool. He tried to make his voice sound kind. 'You know, we expected you home three weeks ago, and I can't remember the last time you picked up your phone when I called. Are there problems in Africa?' Sullivan's failure to materialize at Christmas had barely been commented on in their house. Sullivan not showing up when promised was the rule rather than the exception.

'I would say that the entire continent is nothing but one mammoth problem. Thus is the nature of Africa.' He yawned again, this time like a lion, his head went back, his mouth opened wide. When it was finished he shuddered. 'I'm going to sleep.'

Doyle said good night and let him go, feeling certain that whatever had gone wrong this time, it was serious. You could tell by the crispness of his manner. Even when Sullivan was a teenager

114

he had a certain formality when things were very bad, as if he was preparing to serve as the counsel for his own defense. Doyle wondered if he needed to spend some time worrying about Sullivan on top of everything else, even though he had sworn that off as a pastime years ago.

Once he was in his room with the door closed, Doyle realized he wasn't going to get to anyone on his list. He took off his shoes and socks and draped his suit over a chair, but when he sat down on the bed to pull off his tie he knew he had reached the end of the evening. There would be no brushing of teeth, no getting up again. He barely had enough time to pull a blanket up over his shoulders before he had fallen into a sleep so peculiarly untroubled it would last until nine the next morning.

As the hours passed in the tall house on Union Park, only Sullivan stayed awake. The clock in his chest that was still set to African time had left him in a relentless state of wakefulness. After spending half the night thinking that exhaustion would surely win, and looking hopefully in his dopp kit for the sleeping pills he had run out of months ago, he finally gave up. He blinked into the darkness of his childhood room, made out the shape of his oak dresser and the narrow door of his closet, and realized that coming home had been a mistake. He'd only gotten half the equation right: he absolutely had to leave Africa, but he hadn't spent enough time thinking about which plane to get on and where that plane should land. This was not a late Christmas visit. He had forgotten that he had ever volunteered for Christmas at all. This was another reshuffling of life, a complete reinvention that called for some time and a little peace, neither of which had ever been afforded to him in his father's house. Sullivan kicked off his covers, closed his eyes, and for a brief moment tried again. But sleep was a mirage, a wavy blue line in the desert that you never actually got to. He pulled himself out of bed and went to the window. The snow had stopped, and even though it was dark outside the world below the house was oddly bright. No one had driven down the street yet. All the disruption, the shoveling and tire tracks and footprints and dog shit that would be there in a few hours to ruin the landscape hadn't happened yet, so Sullivan decided to go out.

Because his exit from the African continent had been hurried, there wasn't much luggage involved, just his computer and some papers, a handful of books, a few sentimental pieces of clothing that worked well in Uganda but offered up no defense against a Massachusetts winter. Sullivan looked in his closet and in the dresser drawers and found sweaters and jeans and boots that had been left behind more than a dozen years before. He felt at once irritated because the clothing implied his eventual return and relieved because he needed something to wear. He found the mossy green sweater he had loved in high school and buried his face in the wool to see if he could find any residual traces of pot smoke. It smelled like cedar. He got dressed in the darkness and stepped out into the hall. Through the door that was left half open he could see the girl asleep in Tip's bed, her head and arm dropped over the mattress's edge, the fingertips of one dark hand curling just above the floor. It was so damn cold up there. They had always referred to the fourth floor of the house as the meat locker, and not without cause. He went back and took the comforter off his bed, spreading it over the girl who did not so much as change her breathing beneath this new weight that settled on top of her. Sullivan thought of all the strays he saw in Africa, the endless streams of parentless children who cycled through the various AIDS clinics he supplied, freshly minted orphans who had given up looking for extended family and were now trying to find a place to spend the night. They bore no resemblance to this Kenya who appeared to be utterly at peace in her sleeping. She did not twist herself in a ball or stuff herself beneath a cabinet. She did not sleep with open eyes the way the most unnerving children had learned to do. He had forgotten how American children slept. They stretched out long and wide, dreaming of sugarplums while they waited for handouts from tooth fairies. Even he had to admit that a clean bed on the top floor of the Doyle home on Union Park wouldn't be such a bad shore for someone to wash up on, no matter how cold it was, as long as that someone hadn't grown up there.

Sullivan went down the stairs in the dark. He thought he was moving quietly but when he passed the living room Tip raised a hand and waved. 'Leaving so soon?' he whispered.

'Can't settle down. I'm in the wrong time zone

117

again. I'm going to go look at the snow.'

'Well, in case you don't come back, it was good to see you.' Tip had not seen Sullivan in over two years.

'You should learn to be sweeter,' Sullivan said, drawing on an old joke. 'More like your brother.'

They both turned and looked at Teddy, who was still sound asleep. Sullivan thought of the girl in the bed upstairs, her cheek pressed against the pillow in such a similar way.

'Do me a favor,' Tip said. 'Bring me a glass of water.'

'Sure.'

'I don't want to get up. This thing is killing me.'

Sullivan came back from the kitchen with the glass. He watched Tip sit up enough to pull a bottle from his pants pocket and tap out a pill the size of a small bullet into the palm of his hand.

'I'll trade you,' Sullivan said. 'One for the glass of water.'

'Are you in some sort of pain?'

'Enough.'

'You don't even know what it is.'

Sullivan shrugged. 'I'll assume they aren't passing out Bufferin.'

Tip looked at his brother, held him still for a minute with his eyes, then they made that most basic exchange: narcotics for water.

'At least you're making me work for it, that's good.' Sullivan put the pill in his pocket and then patted his hip. 'This is for later, when it's time to go to sleep.'

Tip looked up at the clock on the mantel. There was barely enough light in the room to tell the time. 'It's five in the morning. You better take it soon.'

'How's the ankle?'

'Hurts.' Tip swallowed his Percocet.

'It's a hell of a story,' Sullivan said. 'Your own mother coming out of nowhere to snatch you from death.'

Tip smiled. 'Why does everyone insist I was dying?'

'It was an SUV. Anything's possible.'

'Somehow you showing up here feels like the bigger coincidence. What happened to the humanitarian efforts in Africa?'

'Let's just say everything comes to an end.'

'Is there a reason you're having this conversation now?' Teddy said, his eyes still closed. He pulled the comforter over his shoulders and then brought his hand back inside.

'Just to annoy you,' Sullivan said kindly. Teddy, no matter how tall he'd gotten, would always be the baby, the baby Sullivan liked to take out of his crib when he was sleeping, driving his mother crazy when he wasn't in the place she had put him down. Sullivan took him to the street to show the other kids. These were Irish kids like Sullivan himself, kids who under any other circumstances would have said nasty things about who is your mother fucking to get a baby like that? Instead they stayed quiet and watched while Sullivan bounced Teddy in the air above his head. They knew he was baiting them, they

119

knew that Sullivan was just waiting for the chance to prop this baby up against a light pole and kill one of them for saying what was on their minds. Every now and then he got lucky. Somebody's visiting cousin or a stranger who'd wandered foolishly in from another neighborhood would give him an invitation. Then he just handed the baby off to any kid who was standing around to watch that crazy Irish boy, the son of Bernard Doyle, unleash himself like a hurricane upon another child. Teddy was easy even then, round and smiling. He'd go to anybody.

'Go back to sleep,' Tip whispered.

'Did you take a pill?' Teddy said, still refusing to open his eyes.

'We did.' Tip gave the bottle a shake. 'Do you want one?'

'You're a riot,' Teddy said.

Sullivan pulled on his hat and fastened the toggles on the coat he'd worn at sixteen, feeling pleased to see how easily it fit over the heavy sweater. No one got fat in Africa. 'Both of you go to sleep. I'll be back in a little while.'

Teddy sat up then. There was a heavy scar running down the side of his cheek made by a crease in the pillow. 'You're going out?'

'Here I go,' said Sullivan.

Then Teddy was up, pulling on his boots. The comforter slid off the couch and puddled onto the floor with a smooth shush. 'Give me two minutes. I'm almost ready. We can go to the hospital and see how she's doing.'

'I was thinking more about a walk around the block.'

'Teddy, seriously,' Tip said. 'Wait until someone's called the hospital. Wait until Da and Kenya are up. It's too early.'

'Not if they're taking her into surgery this morning.' He jumped off the couch and was gone down the hall.

Sullivan watched him go. The sudden, miraculous ability to wake up astounded him. 'This'll teach me to go out the back door.'

'I did appreciate the glass of water though.' Tip believed that he was just starting to feel the warm ease of the Percocet seeping into his bloodstream. The pain in his ankle was becoming softer. He was starting to think it had never really bothered him at all.

'I don't suppose you're coming with us?'

'Not unless you're planning on carrying me.'

'You'd have to bend your knees up.' Sullivan looked at his wounded brother all booted up and wondered if he could carry him still. 'I hate you for being taller than I am, you know that.' If Teddy was a cupcake among babies then that left Tip to be the difficult one, stiff and intractable — a wailer, terrified of both the day and the night. You could always find him looking out the door, out the window, in the closet, under the bed. Nobody knew if he was looking to see if there wasn't somebody else coming to take him away or if he was trying to find the person who'd left him behind. Sullivan wondered if he would remember any of that now. Probably not. Tip wasn't easy like Teddy. He was suspicious, didn't want to be touched. And who could blame him? This kid had a memory. He was fourteen months old when he showed up on their doorstep like a basket of fruit. For two months and a year he had been somewhere else, had been used to someone else. Then he came to live with strangers who called him by another name. 'What's his real name?' Sullivan asked his mother.

'Tip?' she said. 'Thomas.'

Sullivan shook his head. 'I mean before that. What was his name where he used to live?'

She was bathing Teddy in the kitchen sink. Her hair was in one long braid over her shoulder and the baby kept reaching for it. She said she didn't know.

'You have to know. It has to be written down somewhere.'

'Maybe his name was Tip,' she said.

But Sullivan knew this wasn't the case. He had called out the name when Tip was sleeping and he never opened his eyes.

Sullivan invented a game for Tip that he called The Cape. 'Where's my cape!' Sullivan would roar and then get down on his knees and here would come Tip if Tip was in the right kind of mood. He would latch himself around Sullivan's neck and hang down his back, his head turned to the side and pointing down. Sullivan would hold on to his feet and they would careen through the living room, screaming. For awhile, a year or two, that worked for both of them, but it didn't make them any closer really. Tip was the kind of kid who could hang from your neck and still maintain a critical distance.

When Teddy rushed back into the room he

was wide awake, pulling on his coat and moving through the front door. 'I'll call you if anything happens,' he said to Tip. There was a great rush of cold air that blew through the entry hall and into the living room. The temperature would start dropping now that the snow had made its final contribution. Sullivan leaned over and picked Teddy's comforter off the floor and threw it on top of Tip, though he wondered if he wouldn't be better off taking it along for himself.

'We won't be long,' Sullivan said.

Tip smiled at him. 'You will be if you're going with Teddy.'

The snow was soft and deep and dry and it came very nearly to Sullivan's knees. January nights were epically long in Massachusetts. The sun was still two hours from coming up. It could as easily have been midnight as five a.m. as the brothers shuffled ahead in the dark. 'You don't really want to go to the hospital,' Sullivan said.

'Of course I do.'

'And what are you going to say to her? 'I know you're going into surgery, but why'd you give me away?' It might not be the best moment.'

Teddy stopped. The words stopped him. He stood so close to Sullivan that Sullivan had to lift his chin to meet Teddy's eyes. 'I want to see how she is. She was hit by a car. I want to tell her that we're taking care of her daughter. She did something pretty heroic, you know. Maybe you can't see that, not having been there.'

'So you have nothing to ask, just things to tell. You have no curiosity.'

Teddy pulled up the collar of his parka and

leaned in. 'Things come up by themselves over time.'

'Well, I'm thinking of myself then,' Sullivan said. 'If my mother had given me away and then turned up again twenty years later at the scene of an accident, I think I'd have some questions.'

'Your mother *is* my mother,' Teddy said. 'And if our mother had shown up at a Jesse Jackson lecture and pushed Tip out of the way of a car, well, then yes, I'd have some pretty serious questions myself about where she'd been.'

'A Jesse Jackson lecture?' Sullivan shook his head. 'Jesus, the old man just never lets up, does he?'

Sullivan and Teddy let it drop after that and walked the blocks towards the Back Bay Station in silence. It had always been about politics. If anything, it had been less about politics when Doyle had been mayor, when the wild aspirations he had to shoot the moon were only for himself. But after that was gone, and yes, Sullivan understood that this was in part his responsibility, Doyle simply turned the full weight of his expectations onto the boys. It had been made abundantly clear that Sullivan had proven himself unfit years before he was in the car accident, and every action of his adult life did nothing but provide more irrefutable evidence that he was not the son to provide his father's wish fulfillment. He was glad for it, glad to be off the hook no matter what disasters of conduct had been required, but why couldn't Doyle see that Tip and Teddy were no more likely candidates than he? Tip was never going to pull his head out of the aquarium long enough to vote, much less run, and Teddy, Teddy had all the political acumen of a koala. Still, Doyle continued to persist with their political education, their sentimental education. Once he admitted that Teddy and Tip were hopeless causes he would have to face the fact that there was no one else coming up behind them, no one else who was willing to be crushed by the heavy mantle of his expectations.

'What are you going to do?' Sullivan asked his brother.

'I'm just going to talk to her.' Teddy pulled off a mitten and fished around in his pocket for a Kleenex.

'No,' Sullivan said, thinking of the conversation in his head. 'I mean with your life, assuming that you don't have any plans to be the next Jesse Jackson.'

It was so absurd a thought that it caused Teddy to laugh. Then he shook his head. 'I don't know.'

'You do too know.'

'I'm twenty.'

'And I'm Jack Kennedy.'

They walked along for awhile, their feet shushing in the snow. They were alone in the city with the moon sitting high above their left shoulders. 'I think, sometimes,' Teddy said, and then he stopped. 'Sometimes I talk to Uncle Sullivan — '

'About the love and fellowship of our Lord, Jesus Christ.'

'Forget it.'

'Just say it. You can talk to me.'

'There's nothing to talk about.'

Sullivan clapped his hands and let out a howl to wake the street. 'I *knew* it. Dear God, you're going to sign on with the child molesters!'

'Sullivan, stop it.'

He laughed. 'I think it's fine. You might as well make one father in the family happy.'

'I didn't say I was going to be a priest.'

The older brother bowed. 'So you're not. I apologize. I am completely wrong.'

Teddy took the bait. He always took the bait. That's why there was so little pleasure in baiting him in the first place. 'I want to help people. Is there anything so wrong with that? Isn't that what Da taught us to do? Isn't that why you were in Africa?'

'Not exactly.'

Teddy stopped walking and then Sullivan stopped walking too. They faced each other in the snow until Sullivan started to shiver. 'Keep moving,' he said.

'"Your honor,"' Teddy said, '"years ago I recognized my kinship with all living beings, and I made up my mind that I was not one bit better than the meanest on earth."'

'Eugene V. Debs,' Sullivan said, and raised one gloved hand towards the starry night. '"I said then and I say now, that while there is a lower class, I am in it, while there is a criminal element, I am of it, and while there is a soul in prison, I am blah, blah, blah."'

Teddy nodded his head, grateful for once to be understood. 'That's what I mean.'

'No,' Sullivan said. 'That's what Debs means. He was on his way to prison. You want to be a priest. If you can't explain the connection between those two things, I'd be happy to do it for you.'

Teddy trudged forward in the snow, showing Sullivan his back. He was too good a Catholic to tell his brother to go fuck himself. 'I said I don't want to talk about it.'

'You like girls, Teddy. Remember that? And they don't let the girls come with you. You have to check them at the door. You're going to give up Ramona for a bunch of guys who can't get laid?'

Teddy reached up and pulled his hat down farther over his ears.

'Wasn't her name Ramona?'

'We broke up last year.'

Sullivan could imagine it. To the best of his memory, that Ramona wasn't the sort to wait around on a guy who was trying to decide between his girl and his savior. 'But it's not as if you've been spending your Saturday nights doing projects for the altar society. You're still seeing girls.'

'It doesn't matter who I'm seeing.' Teddy's voice was tight. 'I'm not a priest.'

'Yet,' Sullivan said. He could only imagine all the pleasure there was in the girls who tried to dissuade Teddy from his calling, just like the girls who tried to distract Tip from his fish. It was one of the few things Sullivan and his brothers had in common: whether it was serious or remorselessly casual, there was never a shortage of female companionship. It was the payoff for all they had suffered. All girls were suckers for motherless boys.

Sullivan wondered if his mother would be happy to think that the only sweet child she had was growing up to be a priest. He wondered if she would be horrified. He was genuinely sorry that he had no idea what she would think. He remembered his mother in the snow when he was still her only son, pulling him behind her on a bright blue plastic disc. He remembered the snow in her hair and later how when they were back in the warm kitchen she would rub his hair dry with a towel. He remembered how she sang to him, 'To know, know, know you, is to love, love, love you.' She was pregnant then. He could see her belly pushing out against her sweater. One more thing that never came to pass. *If Bernadette had shown up*, Teddy had said, but that couldn't happen, even though at some point Doyle was bound to throw that possibility out to him: *What would your mother say if she knew what you've done?* But his mother wasn't there, and as long as the universe continued to operate in the same way it always had there was no chance she was coming. If she had shown up even once, just to him, he believed that things wouldn't have turned out like this at all, and if she had lived, there was a chance that even Sullivan might have gone so far as to make someone proud. He might have been a politician or a scientist, even a priest. He wouldn't have made the same mistakes because he would not have been in those places at those moments. If his mother had lived, the chain of events would never have begun. There never would have been an accident. He would not have been sent off in the world by himself. Surely he would still have made mistakes, but they would have been smaller ones. He shook the thought out of his head. It got him nowhere.

When they arrived at Back Bay, Sullivan dug his hands in his pockets, but all he found there was a Percocet. It was a very small thing but still something to look forward to later on. He looked at Teddy.

'I've got it,' Teddy said and pulled out his wallet. His face was soft again and he smiled at Sullivan. Teddy, unlike the other members of his family, never held a grudge about anything.

*   *   *

Like Sullivan, Kenya's mother had been awake off and on for most of the night. Every time she fell asleep for a second there was someone there to wake her up. It seemed to be the responsibility of every person in the hospital to wake her up, and they took their job seriously. They shook her shoulder and called her name and shined a light in her eyes. 'Miss Moser, how you feeling? Can you tell me how you feeling?'

But Tennessee couldn't say how she was feeling. The only word that came to mind was suspended. She was hanging off a thousand tiny wires. She didn't tell them that. It wasn't worth the effort to make the words. She couldn't take in a proper breath. How was she feeling?

She looked at the woman standing over her bed. She was tall and bony with jet black skin and three gold chains around her elegant neck. African, you could hear it in the voice. That wasn't a Boston voice. That wasn't Roxbury. She closed her eyes and wondered where in Africa she was from, but when she started to ask, there was an Asian man holding her wrist. He wasn't as tall as the African woman but he was even thinner, no bigger around than a six-year-old. Didn't anyone eat in this hospital? Did they hire starving refugees to come in and wake you up at night? 'Miss Moser, can you open your eyes for me now?' It was an Irish girl, fat and sickly pale, who was checking the line going into her hand.

Tennessee thought of Ebenezer Scrooge and wondered if this last girl was her ghost of Christmas future. She had a vague memory of Christmas, Kenya sitting cross-legged on the floor with a present in her lap. She could see her tearing the paper but she couldn't be sure if the Christmas she was seeing in her mind was the most recent or a year ago. She had a terrible feeling she had left Kenya someplace she wasn't supposed to, that she had forgotten her, though how could that be possible? She would never forget her daughter. Had Christmas come and gone? It was winter. For all of her uncertainty, that was the one thing she was sure of, she had been so cold in the snow. She blinked her eyes and everything shifted like magic. People were there at a distance, and then touching her, and then she was alone. She was awake in one room and then later on she was awake in another, or at

130

least she thought it was another room. It seemed larger and not nearly as bright. She didn't think there had been any window before. She had no memory of being moved, but that didn't tell her anything either. She had no memory of coming to the hospital in the first place. The room was mostly dark except for a long, thin light that was mounted on the wall above her headboard, and that light fell directly into her eyes. She would have liked to turn it off so that she could better see out the window, but turning off a light seemed like the single most impossible task she had ever considered and so she left it alone. She could never seem to remember to ask anyone about the light when they were there.

What she thought about, what consumed her past the point of speaking, was the pain. There was a web of pain that extended from the top of her head down to her knees. First she tried to stay very still so as not to disturb it, but then it would get disturbed anyway and so she would experiment: she moved a hand, she flexed her toes. She was at all times very careful to keep her pelvis straight and pointed up, as she knew it was her pelvis, or more precisely her stomach, that was the center of what was wrong.

'Miss Moser, I'm taking your blood pressure now. You're going to feel a pressure.'

When there weren't people talking directly to her, there were still people talking. Their voices came out of the ceiling. People called for doctors. People called Code Blue. Bells rang out a little symphony. Again and again they woke her up.

And then Tennessee woke up alone in a room and everything was different. As soon as she opened her eyes she remembered. The great fog that was dripping down the little plastic tubing into her arm burned off in the bright light above her head and she remembered Jesse Jackson was speaking at the Kennedy School. She had barely made it in time, rushing home from work to pick up Kenya. She made them both peanut butter sandwiches, standing in the kitchen with her coat on, and put the sandwiches together in the bottom of a paper sack with an apple.

'I don't know why we can't stay home,' Kenya had complained. 'It's freezing cold and I've got homework.'

'You should have done your homework already,' Tennessee said. 'You can do it on the train.'

'I can't do it on the train because then my handwriting gets all sloppy and it's points off.' Kenya bent over and put her hands on the floor then straightened out her legs. Bend and straight, bend and straight, until her torso rested flat against her thighs and the backs of her hands were pressed beside her shoes. 'There was an extra-short recess today because it was so cold outside, so I went and ran circles in the gym until Miss LaPiana came and said I wasn't allowed to be in there by myself and that I had to go back to the cafeteria with everybody else.' She was like a dog that had spent the day penned up. Tennessee had to figure out a way to get her into a better school. Cathedral Grammar had offered her a scholarship of four thousand dollars last year, but that wasn't any more helpful than offering four. She had to figure out a way to make them pay for all of it. She had to get someone from the school to come see Kenya run. Kenya could be their fleet-footed child star. She could run and earn her keep.

'I could run all the way to Cambridge if you'd let me,' Kenya said, turning a deft finger inside the peanut butter jar. 'I could run beside the bus and then beside the train and you could watch. I'd stay right next to your window.'

'Quit horsing around and put your coat on. Wash your hands first. Did you get your hat?'

Kenya said it was in her pocket, but once they were halfway to the stop and Tennessee told her to put it on, Kenya admitted to leaving it at home, saying that it made her head look lumpy. The child went out into the freezing cold night with no hat on and Tennessee scolded her while they stood on the corner and waited for the bus that would take them to the Park Street Station.

She saw the lights of the bus coming from a long way off. She saw the lights of the car.

Kenya had been on the sidewalk. She was sure of that. She could not say where her daughter was now, asleep in the waiting room probably, not too far from here, but she was positive that when the car came, Kenya was nowhere near the car.

She was less sure about Tip. She had been half surprised to see them at the lecture. More and more often now she saw Mr. Doyle alone. The boys were growing up. They were busy with school. Tennessee had not been able to find a seat and she watched the boys from high up in the auditorium where she stood behind the back row against the wall. There was nothing she did not know about the backs of their heads. She listened to Jesse Jackson, but her eyes stayed fixed to her sons' heads. Why was Tip only wearing a jacket? She wanted to ask Jackson a question but she never raised her hand when the Doyles were there, and anyway, Jackson only seemed to call on the dreamy-eyed students. *I do appreciate your inspiration and leadership,* she wanted to say, *but I need some more specific advice. I need to know how to keep my child safe in public schools, safe from guns and chipped lead paint and pushers and bullies who have been bullied too much themselves. I need to know how I can walk her straight to the door of her classroom in the morning and still get to work on time and how she can learn enough to get to college when there are thirty-five other children in the room and half of them did not get breakfast. Can we talk, sir, about those things?* All these speeches were so inspiring, yet every time she left the building with no more information than she had come in with. Politicians never mentioned the details of life because of course the details that appealed to one person could repel another, so what you wound up with in the end were a long string of generalities, stirring platitudes that could not buy you supper. For years Tennessee had wondered how Mr. Doyle and the boys could stand it, so much talk that added up to nothing. She thought that Mr. Doyle must have been obligated to go because he had been a politician himself.

Mr. Doyle had led her to politics, but when she actually started to understand it all she was with her neighbor, a girl who didn't go to hear speeches. It was years ago, and Kenya was just a baby, and she was cooking dinner with her neighbor, who was also her best friend, in the apartment three floors up from hers. It was January and freezing cold and they were making soup the two of them with the baby held in place on the sofa with a nest of pillows. The two women were talking with the radio on, and then they heard Dr. King's voice. Her friend leaned over and raised the volume until that giant baritone covered them whole. 'It's his birthday today,' she said, and Tennessee said she knew that because there wasn't any mail.

For another minute they tried to continue their chopping and then they simply stopped and stood, eyes closed. Tennessee had read the speech in school when she was a girl but it meant nothing to her then. They had even played it from a record album once in the school gymnasium and made the children listen, but she had managed not to listen by looking at a magazine instead. So, truly, when it came over the radio in her girlfriend's kitchen the year she was twenty-nine it was nothing she had heard before.

'Now is the time to make real the promises of Democracy,' Dr. King said.

'Now is the time to rise from the dark and desolate valley of segregation to the sunlit path of racial justice.

'Now is the time to open the doors of opportunity to all God's children.'

That was the first time Tennessee saw just how politics, once you dug through everything that was worthless, could leave you stunned. There were some people who had the ability to tell other people what was worth wanting, could tell them in a way that was so powerful that the people who heard them suddenly had their eyes opened to what had been withheld from them all along.

When it was over, Tennessee turned off the radio and her friend wiped her hands on a towel. 'Now that would be worth getting shot for,' her friend said thoughtfully.

'What a thing to say.'

The friend shook her head. 'Think about it, to have the chance to say all that, to have it played every year on your birthday so people remember you. I would die if I could do as much as that.'

At the time, Tennessee had not understood the logic, but five months later her friend was dead from a sepsis that had seemed at first to be nothing more than a fever. She had decided she didn't need to go to the emergency room until it was very late. She kept saying that she could tough it out. Later, when Tennessee was alone with the baby, she thought often about that January night in the kitchen and Dr. King's speech and how her friend had been right: it was better to have done something, to have stood for something great and gotten shot for it than it was to never stand up for anything and die like everybody else. Tennessee had meant to do

136

something with her life. She had thought that one day she would make a speech that addressed the simple details of daily existence that the politicians all neglected. She had always thought that one day she would find a way to stand up for the things that people were afraid to say, and let them know it was fine to ask for what you needed. She had thought there would be plenty of time, that she would go back and finish college and how people would respect her for that. But now she was in a hospital bed and she wondered if she might in fact die just like her friend, which was to say, die like everybody else.

While Jesse Jackson gave his speech, Kenya sat on the floor of the auditorium finishing her math homework in a spiral notebook. Afterwards she lost a glove and it had taken them awhile to find it under the bank of seats in front of them. The glove was the reason they were among the last people to leave. So Tennessee was surprised when she saw the boys and their father standing out in the snow. Most of the crowd had gone already. It was a lousy night. She saw the three of them talking and she turned away, wanting to get Kenya, who had no hat, out of the weather as soon as possible. But then Tip was walking towards her, wearing a slight red jacket that would not have been enough to keep a cricket warm. When he stopped he wasn't more than three feet away from her. She could see that he was talking to Mr. Doyle but she could not understand what he was saying for the relentless thud of her own heart beating in her ears. He had passed her countless times in his life and it never failed to cause a flush of adrenaline: a singular desire for flight. Would this be the one time he would notice her? *Are you following me?* She pushed her hand down on Kenya's shoulder harder than was necessary, as if forgetting that Kenya knew better than to say anything. But there was nothing to worry about, Tip never saw them. He passed by them, still talking, into the night thick with snow. Then walking halfway backwards he stepped off the curb and into the street, into the lights that she only at the moment realized were coming towards them. He could have been anybody. He was a boy stepping out in front of a car he clearly did not see. Tip kept his head in his books, in the clouds, with the fishes. He didn't pay attention. She pushed him, but not because he was hers. She pushed him because he was there and the car was there. She pushed him so hard she was certain she had sent him sailing up through the falling snow and into the night like a punch from a cartoon character. *POW!* He spun off towards the stars. Had she knocked him clear to safety? She had never hit anyone as hard as she hit Tip, and then, as if in reply, she was hit by the car. She held up her hand and felt it crack against the front fender. For a single second she had touched him, and even if it happened through gloves and coats, it was miraculous. She had not touched him in over nineteen years.

The car had not hit him. She had pushed him away. She had saved him.

The Asian nurse in the bright blue scrubs was back and slid a thermometer beneath her gown and under her arm. He wanted to know how she was feeling.

There was a night two years ago she could have touched him easily. She was coming home from work, changing trains at Park Street, when she saw Tip leaning back against a wall, a backpack hanging from one shoulder. He was reading and he was alone, no Teddy, no Mr. Doyle. Tennessee had never thought of it before but in all the years she had been looking for the boys she had never seen either one of them by themselves, though of course they were older at this point and surely went places without each other all the time. The station was crowded and she didn't have to stand too far from him. She liked the way he seemed so comfortable. He wasn't looking around or shifting his weight from side to side. He was handsome, but handsome wasn't the thing you'd think of first because his head was tipped forward and he didn't smile. What you'd think if you saw him was that he looked smart. He looked like someone who had a purpose in this world. He wasn't some kid who was hanging out riding the trains. He looked exactly like what he was, a college boy. While he was waiting, a pretty Spanish looking girl walked by, black hair long down her back and big gold hoop earrings, high heels on her black boots, and for a second she glanced back over her shoulder at the boy who was reading, the boy who didn't notice her, and Tennessee smiled.

The B train to Boston College pulled up and Tip got on and without even giving it a thought

Tennessee followed him up the steps and into the car and sat down across from him. All the people and all the trains and all the cars on the trains and seats on the cars and yet there he was right in front of her. It was dark by then and she could see him and see his reflection in the glass behind his head. She kept her eyes out the window but it didn't even matter. She could have been looking anywhere, and he never once so much as straightened up his neck. After a concerted effort she could see that he was reading a book called *Inland Fishes of Massachusetts*. It was written by three people, Hartel, Halliwell, and Launer. She took a pen from her bag and she wrote their names on the palm of her hand. Normally when she saw him she didn't do more than sweep her eyes briefly past the places he was, but now they were together on the gently rocking train. For once in her life there was nothing but time. When the train finally made its last stop, Tennessee felt a prickly sweat of dizziness come over her. Everybody stood up and gathered their packages and scarves. It was October and dark and she followed Tip nearly two blocks down the street before she remembered that Kenya was still at the after-school program and she was now very late picking her up. She stood where she was and watched him until he finally turned at a corner and the night swallowed him whole. She didn't know why he'd be going out to Boston College or who he was going to see, it wasn't her business to know, and she paid a second fare to get back on the train going home.

140

For the rest of the fall and that winter Tennessee made no effort to find Teddy and Tip. She didn't take Kenya to lectures or political rallies. She did not save her money to buy symphony tickets on the rare nights they played Schubert. Something had shaken her on the train. It was time for her to think of the boys as grown now, time to focus her attention on the daughter she had. She did, however, work hard to get a copy of *Inland Fishes of Massachusetts*. She tried for weeks to find it in a regular bookstore, but she didn't have any luck. She was starting to think that Tip must have bought the last copy for himself. Then, finally, on a Saturday it occurred to her to look for it at the Coop. There were three of them, but the book cost forty-five dollars. For an hour she stood in the aisle and read the first chapter while Kenya looked at a textbook on ornithology, beautiful photographs of birds with drawings of their feathers and bones. On the train home, Tennessee wrote down the things she could remember in her notebook while Kenya stared out the window at the sailboats cross-hatching the Charles. There was nothing she liked better than taking the Red Line over the river.

'What are you doing?' Kenya asked.

'Writing down what I read in the fish book.'

Kenya waited only for a second. She wanted to be patient, but there was such a short time before they lost the view. 'Mama, look at the boats,' she said.

Tennessee put down her pen and glanced up. 'Nice,' she said, and then went back to her work.

'Why do you care so much about fishes?' Why, when there were so many pretty boats.

'They're interesting,' her mother said.

The next nurse didn't ask her anything. She couldn't see him very clearly for the bright hall light behind him. He could have been reading a chart or checking the pills that he had, maybe he wasn't sure he was in the right room. Tennessee closed her eyes and fell back to sleep or didn't, but when she looked again there were two of them there and one of them said, 'See, she's awake.'

'She's awake,' Tennessee said quietly. Her tongue was heavy in her mouth and she had trouble making the words. The skin on her lips had cracked and bled and the blood had dried. This time there was something she wanted and she remembered to ask for it while they were there. 'Water?'

'I'll get you some,' one of them said.

'You can't get her water.'

'Why not?'

'She's probably having surgery in a couple of hours. She may not be allowed to have any water.' Then the voice turned to her. 'Has anyone else given you water?'

Tennessee thought about all the comings and goings. Water would have been nice, a little ice even. She felt like she had a fever now. 'I don't remember.'

'I'll go ask.'

'I'll ask,' the other one said, and he was gone.

Now the second one, the one who was left in the room with her, walked towards the bed. 'I think this is harder than he realizes,' was what he said.

Tennessee tried to fix her mind on all the nurses to think of which one had been shy. When the nurse was closer he sat down on his heels so that his face was just a foot away from hers and slightly lower. He wasn't wearing scrubs. He was wearing jeans and a heavy green coat. The strip light above her bed that had been such a source of irritation made it possible for her to see. Even in the wake of medication and pain and a sharp blow to her left temple she knew him. She had not seen him in years but she knew him like he was one of her own. How was it that he was the one who had come to her? Had he heard about her accident and come to see if she was okay? But that didn't make sense. Maybe she was still asleep. Maybe the sleeping and the waking and dreaming had finally become one thing. She looked at the light in his hair. It was still that same strange dark red color it had been when he was a child. Tennessee pressed her eyes closed tight.

'Are you in a lot of pain right now?' Sullivan said.

'Where have you been?'

'Excuse me?'

'All those years you haven't been home.' She felt like she had no experience talking. Her mouth was hot and dry.

'I've been a lot of places. I've been in Uganda for awhile now.'

When he was a child, when she was a little bit more than a child herself, she had been afraid of

Sullivan. Everything Sullivan could do to her boys could be done secretly, with no way for her to protect them. He could shove them up against the wall when passing in the hallways or smother them with pillows in their beds at night until they were too frightened to sleep. Did he pinch her boys when no one was looking? Whisper in their ears that his parents had reconsidered the adoption and now the orphanage was coming to take them away? Her children had stolen his sweet life as the baby, after all. He would never again be the only child, the only son. She watched him closer than his parents did. Sometimes she watched him closer than Teddy and Tip. But this boy dragged her boys around. They hung from his neck and propped on his hip. This boy seemed nothing but patient in the afternoons when she sat in the far corner of Blackstone Park and waited with a book that she pretended to read for hours at a time. Even when he thought no one was watching, he was good to them.

'No water,' Teddy said from the door, his voice so small and apologetic it was difficult to hear him over the hum of the light strip.

'What did I tell you?' Sullivan kept on looking at Tennessee.

'Who's that?' she whispered.

'Teddy,' Sullivan said, and took her hand.

There was so much churning inside her chest she wondered if her heart could stab itself on that one broken rib. She had not meant for this to happen. She had not. For a moment she allowed herself to believe they didn't know. They were only coming to see her as the woman who had acted to save their brother. But this was not the visit of grateful strangers. She thought of her own face now, cut and bandaged, ugly. To see her in bed like this. When Teddy walked up to stand beside her, Tennessee closed her eyes, even though everything in her said to open them.

'I wanted to check on you,' Teddy said in his church voice. 'See if you were okay.'

She pulled up the corner of the sheet in her other hand, the hand that Sullivan was not holding, and she wiped her nose and eyes.

'The doctor said you're going to have surgery this morning.'

She nodded.

Teddy started over, as if every sentence he spoke was his opening line. 'I wanted to tell you that Tip is okay. His ankle is hurt but he's fine. He would be here with us but he needs to stay off his leg for now.'

'It's sprained?' she asked. Her voice sounded so strange to her.

Teddy started to tell her but Sullivan looked up at him and said, 'It's sprained.'

'Did you see my daughter?'

'She was still asleep when we left the house,' Teddy said. 'We kept her up too late.'

And now Tennessee did open her eyes. She looked at Sullivan and then at Teddy, one of them on either side. Sullivan did not let go of her hand even though she couldn't imagine why he held it. Teddy was so close to her. She could hear him breathing. She could see the way his eyelashes curled up. He had the face of someone who had never been hurt before, never been disappointed. She felt certain that he didn't lie to anyone, and yet in her mind she could see Kenya sleeping on a sofa in a bright waiting room, her long legs tucked beneath her, her coat over her shoulders, fast asleep. The picture was perfect in her mind. 'She's here,' Tennessee said. She must be here. Why hadn't she asked one of the nurses where her daughter was?

'We brought her home with us last night,' Teddy said. 'We couldn't leave her at the hospital. Da's with her now, and Tip.'

The Ghost of Christmas Future came back into the room. She did not care who was having a conversation. She had her schedule to keep to, and anyway, there was nothing in the world she hadn't seen. 'Miss Moser, are you in any pain?'

Tennessee nodded her head, and the nodding served to increase the pain.

'We're going to have to say goodbye to your guests now and start thinking about getting you ready for surgery.'

'Give us one more minute,' Sullivan said.

The nurse shook her head but at the same time she turned away. 'One minute and then you go. Visiting hours don't even start until nine.'

'Nobody asked us to leave,' Sullivan said. There was something sweet in his voice, as if he meant to charm her.

'Stick around much longer and somebody *will* ask you to leave,' the girl said, but with a lilt that matched his.

'She shouldn't have gone off with you,' Tennessee said, hoping that by saying it enough

146

she could change the outcome. 'She was supposed to stay.'

'They wouldn't let her stay.' Maybe this wasn't exactly the truth but Teddy thought it was close enough. 'She argued with everybody. She wanted to sleep here.'

'I can't ask you to keep Kenya.'

Sullivan stood up and touched Tennessee's forehead as if he was checking for fever. 'Given the circumstances, you could ask us to do anything.'

'She's a nice girl,' Teddy said. He did not know the woman in the bed. He knew his mother, Bernadette, who smiled at him from a thousand photographs. He was glad they were being sent away. His hands were starting to shake and he stuffed them in his pockets.

Tennessee's head was aching. She wanted whatever medication the nurse was going to bring her. Before they left she would remember to ask them to turn out the lights. 'She's a nice girl,' Tennessee said as a way of saying goodbye to them, as a way of saying thank you and I'm sorry, as a way of saying, I wish I had never let you go, and I wish we had never met. 'Just be sure you take her out and let her run.'

6

Father Sullivan had lost his talent for sleeping. It was his problem long before anyone ever said he had the ability to take cancer from a thyroid with prayer, though certainly this persistent rumor didn't help. It was the condition of his heart that kept him from sustainable rest. He still fell asleep, he fell asleep constantly, but the sleep was like a bean he managed to balance for a moment on his nose. He had no ability to hold it. There was a tide inside his chest now and whenever it crested and broke around his heart he tried to find a better position to lie in. Try sleeping in the ocean with the water rushing into your nose and mouth the second you cease to float. Late at night, Sister Claire pulled up the railing on the far side of the bed and lined it with pillows so that in those restless hours when she wasn't nearby he could shuffle them around on his own. He stacked and unstacked and restacked, looking for the perfect angle at which to prop himself up, then finally got out of bed and sat in the chair by the window so that he could look out at the snow, the gorgeous sea of sugar-ice that he was no longer responsible for shoveling. His heart woke him up to remind him that in life there was never a limitless number of nights.

The floor was cold on his bare feet, but getting out of bed had been effort enough. He didn't want to spend the little energy he had left walking over to the closet for his slippers. Let cold feet be the worst of it. Little Johnny Sullivan, the fastest Catholic boy the South End had ever seen, climber of trees and chain link fences, the ruler of ice hockey and hardball, now weighed out the benefits and perils of walking five feet across linoleum and wisely decided against it. When he was a pirate boy of ten and twelve the apostle Paul himself could not have convinced him that this was where it would all wind up one day, and if he had been convinced he no doubt would have thrown himself into the Charles to drown. So sure was Johnny Sullivan's belief in God's impassioned love for him that he had felt certain he alone would never age.

Not that the misconceptions he held dear to his heart as an adult were any more advanced than the ones he had had as a child. There was a time when Father Sullivan would have thought this confinement was God's retribution for the enormous restlessness that had driven his life, or for the cigarettes he managed on the sly. He believed in a carefully ordered universe: action and reaction. But now he could no longer picture a God who kept track of such minutiae or would think to punish anyone for it. Over the course of his lifetime, God and Father Sullivan had changed together. When he was a young priest teaching American and European history to Catholic boys and coaching basketball in the winter and baseball in the spring, God was made of sterner stuff. Those were the days of confession and penance, Lenten offerings and Friday fish. As a teacher he ran the boys after school in large loops around the playing field and then out into the neighborhoods, over the broken sidewalks, past the dismal row houses with missing shingles. He kept pace beside sixteen-year-olds in the rain and the snow and the last scorching days of August. They ran in the name of athletics and in the silent understanding that what was in each of them needed to be exhausted, wound down like a clock. When Father Sullivan was a young man he kept up a crushing pace in every waking moment so that sleep was like falling down a mine shaft — straight to the bottom of something nameless and dreamless and dark. It wasn't a specific desire within himself that he tried so hard to break. It was his thoughts of God, a God and a Church with which he might not be in peaceful accord.

Now, at the very moment when there should have been no distractions, when he should have had nothing but time to examine the very things that had kept him from a total communion with his faith, he had somehow become the star attraction in his own circus. His undoing had started out simply enough, as undoings so often will. Three months ago, a woman from his old parish had come to visit at Regina Cleri. Nena DeMatteo brought him some banana bread and a book of crossword puzzles and sat by his bed to talk. It was church gossip mostly, the battle over how to manage the capital campaign for the new addition. In the course of their conversation she told him other things as well. She talked about her children (disappointments every one) and how she had developed a painful bursitis in her hip. She had given up her tennis game and then could no longer manage the stairs in her home. Cortisone shots and anti-inflammatories had done nothing to help her and the doctor had run out of suggestions. Nena asked Father Sullivan to pray for her and he said of course he would. When she was leaving she stood for a moment beside the priest's bed and he reached up and touched her hip, her left hip exactly where it had been hurting and the hurting stopped. The way she told it to the newspapers later on, it had startled her the way a sudden silencing of unendurable noise is startling. She shifted her weight from side to side, gently experimenting with the absence of pain, and then she thanked the priest and said goodbye. Nena passed the elevator in the hall. Sixty-eight years old and her legs carried her down the stairs and out to her car with the even clip of a girl. After a week spent without the slightest trace of discomfort she came back with her friend, Helen Cain, who had been diagnosed with thyroid cancer. They said nothing to him of Nena's recovery. They brought another loaf of banana bread and a crossword-puzzle book by way of superstition.

'If you could touch her neck,' Nena said in what she hoped would be an offhanded manner, 'and say a prayer for her health, it would mean a lot.'

Father Sullivan thought nothing of the request. He had been putting his hands on sick people since he was twenty-three years old. He believed in the comfort of human touch. He was sitting up in his chair by the window that day, and Helen Cain, who was barely forty with three small girls at home, leaned forward and he touched her neck and closed his eyes and prayed that she would have peace. That was all he asked for. That was all he had ever asked for. Later Helen would say that she felt something at that moment, a small shock in her throat, and three days later when she went to the doctor the cancer was gone.

'How should I know where it went?' Father Sullivan said to the bishop when the bishop came to Regina Cleri. 'It's not as if I hid it in my chair.'

Awash in their health and good fortune the two women had talked: to each other, to their families, to the press. Soon the hallway outside his room was clogged with the suffering and the sick. Women with colicky babies crying in their arms, a man with leukemia in a wheelchair, his young wife standing behind him looking sicker and more exhausted than he did. There was a ten-year-old boy who had been blind from birth. Blind! What did they expect?

Sister Claire would let them in one at a time. Father Sullivan would explain over and over that there was nothing he could do, but of course the person would insist that he try. He was a priest after all. He could at least offer up a prayer. So Father Sullivan spent his days praying, trying and failing in a seamless continuum until finally Teddy would come and shoo everyone away. He had come by just this afternoon and driven them out, enduring all of their bitterness in stride. The sick were a ferocious lot. They'd walk right through you if they thought that health was on the other side. 'He's sick himself,' Father Sullivan heard Teddy say out in the hallway. 'You have to understand. It's not going to do anyone any good if he dies trying to make you well.'

That's telling them, Father Sullivan thought.

When every last one of them was gone the boy came in and sat down beside his bed. 'Give me your hands,' the priest said.

'I can't. They're freezing. It's freezing outside.'

'If I can give sight to the blind I should be able to at least warm up your hands. Anyway, mine are cold, too.' And so they sat there, the two of them alone, holding each other's frozen hands.

'You should try and get some sleep,' Teddy said.

'Not when you've just gotten here.'

'I'll stay and study. If I sit right here no one will bother you. When they look in your door I'll shake my head at them and they'll go away.'

'Shake your head gravely.'

'I will shake my head so gravely they won't even think of coming again for a week.'

'Oh,' Father Sullivan said, the very thought of rest sweeping over him in a warm wave. 'That would be good. You would wake me if it's something very important.'

'If it's life and death.'

He thanked him and then closed his eyes. 'Now give me a speech. Something nice to send me off.'

Teddy asked him what he had in mind and Father Sullivan thought about it. 'Something with a little conscience, shall we? But nothing too stirring. I mean to rest.' There were so many good choices. He considered something perfectly classic, maybe the Gettysburg Address, but then he thought of all the pleasure that came in being surprised. Teddy said he knew just the thing, simple and true, full of humility. All the qualities his uncle admired.

Teddy leaned forward and began, ''Your honor, years ago I recognized my kinship with all living beings, and I made up my mind that I was not one bit better than the meanest on earth.''

'Dorothy Day?' He liked to guess, though he never got them right.

'Eugene V. Debs.'

'Debs, of course. Day was hardly one for speeches.' Father Sullivan yawned. 'What I wouldn't give for a good American Socialist now.'

Teddy continued the speech meant for the judge about to hand down Debs' prison sentence in his best bedtime story voice. ''I said then, and I say now, that while there is a lower class, I am in it, while there is a criminal element, I am of it, and while there is a soul in prison, I am not free . . . ''

Night after day Father Sullivan was awake with his thoughts. The visit of the two women and all of the subsequent visitors that followed had shaken him. It made him realize how helpless he was to do anything of substance for anyone. He tried to see what was ahead for each of them and he could see nothing at all. It would be incorrect in every sense to say that so near the

154

end of his life he had lost his faith, when in fact God seemed more abundant to him in the Regina Cleri home than any place he had been before. God was in the folds of his bathrobe, the ache of his knees. God saturated the hallways in the form of a pale electrical light. But now that his heart had become so shiftless and unreliable, now that he should be sensing the afterlife like a sweet scent drifting in from the garden, he had started to wonder if there was in fact no afterlife at all. Look at all these true believers who wanted only to live, look at himself, clinging onto this life like a squirrel scrambling up the icy pitch of a roof. In suggesting that there may be nothing ahead of them, he in no way meant to diminish the future; instead, Father Sullivan hoped to elevate the present to a state of the divine. It seemed from this moment of repose that God may well have been life itself. God may have been the baseball games, the beautiful cigarette he smoked alone after checking to see that all the bats had been put back behind the closet door. God could have been the masses in which he told people how best to prepare for the glorious life everlasting, the one they couldn't see as opposed to the one they were living at that exact moment in the pews of the church hall, washed over in the stained glass light. How wrongheaded it seemed now to think that the thrill of heartbeat and breath were just a stepping stone to something greater. What could be greater than the armchair, the window, the snow? Life itself had been holy. We had been brought forth from nothing to see the face of

God and in his life Father Sullivan had seen it miraculously for eighty-eight years. Why wouldn't it stand to reason that this had been the whole of existence and now he would retreat back to the nothingness he had come from in order to let someone else have their turn at the view? This was not the workings of disbelief. It was instead a final, joyful realization of all he had been given. It would be possible to overlook just about anything if you were trained to constantly strain forward to see the power and the glory that was waiting up ahead. What a shame it would have been to miss God while waiting for Him.

The old priest shifted in his chair and pulled the blanket up high on his shoulders. All around him Boston was waking up now. He could see the lights outside his window switching on one by one. He thought of all of those people in their beds burrowing down for a last minute of sleep and his damaged heart went out to them. Small wonder people longed to stay alive, that they would line up in his hallway on the misinformation that he could save them. Father Sullivan did not believe he had been a part of any sort of miracle, but wouldn't that be a glorious transition to make so late in the day, to go from the business of saving people's souls to the business of saving their lives? If he was right and God showed His face to the living then it was the surgeons to whom we should offer our novenas. Let us pray to the ones who keep our tired hearts pumping.

More than anything, Father Sullivan wished he could say all this to Teddy, but he worried that suggesting an absence of afterlife would be like killing off poor Bernadette all over again. After so much time he could hardly suggest that he no longer believed his mother was waiting for him. If he could have wished a second life for anyone it would be for his favorite niece. She would have made such good use of eternity. At her funeral Father Sullivan had promised the congregation that they would all be together again, as if Bernadette had simply run ahead to secure good seats for her family. Now when he should have had thoughts of joining her, he found his own words to be foolish and hollow. *We always said that Bernadette was the lucky one*, he had told the weeping crowd, *and now we know it is her greatest luck to be sheltered in the arms of Christ*. But was that even true? Bernadette's luck had been her life, her love for her husband and her sons, the joy in her home. Her existence did not add up to a handful of tests meant to win her place in heaven.

Father Sullivan had come to these conclusions too late to put them to any good use. His health would never be such that he would once again clip a lavalier microphone onto the front of his vestments and expound on his theories of the day. But Teddy wasn't even at the start of his vocation yet. If he did become a priest he would have his entire life to direct people away from some incalculable unknown in favor of valuing the lives they led. Father Sullivan smiled to think of how much he sounded like Bernard Doyle, looking to a son for the fulfillment of his dreams. Maybe that was the definition of life everlasting:

the belief that the next generation would carry your work forward.

Had he wasted his life, or, far worse, wasted the lives of the people who had entrusted him with their faith? Father Sullivan shifted in his chair, trying to find a better angle to breathe. No good would come of exhausting himself, not when the sick would be at his door early. If he couldn't heal them he could at least show them the courtesy of his full attention. He tried hard to clear his mind and watch the snow in peace until finally he closed his eyes against the city of Boston and fell asleep in his chair. It was just before six in the morning, and when Sister Claire came in with his coffee, she put down the cup and went to the closet for his slippers. With his feet suddenly, inexplicably warm, he managed to rest more deeply than he had in weeks.

It was because he was soundly asleep that he could not say exactly when Teddy came into the room or what part of the story he had heard and what part he had been dreaming. He tried to make sense of the details in his mind but they were coming so quickly he was certain he had missed the beginning: another mother, someone other than Bernadette, a little girl, an accident, Tip and Doyle, even Sullivan was there. No one had seen Sullivan in years. Father Sullivan nodded, hoping to jar the sleep from his brain, while Teddy stood nervously by the door and told everything he knew: an ambulance, a hospital, some talk of kidnapping. He couldn't find a place to grab hold of the thread and so nothing in the story made sense to him. He could only think that he must have opened his eyes when Teddy came in and that Teddy must have understandably mistaken that gesture for his being awake. Now the boy paced in front of the door, now he stopped to close it as if someone might be listening. He left a slushy gray trail of ice behind him on the floor, the fallout from the tread of his boots. Teddy could not get the words out fast enough. Had he done something or had something been done to him?

When finally there seemed to be a break, a breathing spot in the narrative, Father Sullivan picked a random question from the hundreds he could have asked. 'This woman was just standing in the snow with her child?'

Teddy nodded and he sank down onto the unmade bed. 'None of us saw them. We've never seen them.'

'And she pushed Tip into a car.'

'No, no. Away. She pushed him away to save him and she got hit herself.'

Father Sullivan shifted his position in his chair. As was so often the case he was having a hard time finding his breath upon waking. The tide in his chest seemed to fill up his rib cage. He knew it would be easier once he changed positions but the story distracted him. 'Was Sullivan with you?'

'Sullivan was at home. He was there when we got back from the hospital.' Teddy was taking short, shallow breaths like his uncle. He pulled off his coat and his gloves. He crossed his arms over his chest and stuffed his hands into his armpits.

159

'No, was Sullivan with you this morning at the hospital?'

Teddy nodded. 'I tried to get him to come here with me. I wanted him to see you but he said he was tired. He's just come back from Africa. He said he needed to go home and get some rest.'

'You might think about doing the same thing.'

'It's all straight in my mind and then it flies to pieces.'

'It would be too much for anyone.' He took the pillow that was under his left arm and forced it behind his back. He closed his eyes and tried to inhale through his nose. For a moment he saw himself running, not as the priest but as one of the boys in the pack, pale and slight as a stalk of wheat.

Teddy looked out the window. 'What I don't understand is how I never saw them.'

'It was snowing very hard.'

'How I *never* saw them. I think she's been standing there since I was a baby. She was there when my mother was alive.'

'There must be people everywhere we never see.' Father Sullivan wanted to touch the boy, to put a hand on his wrist, but he was too far away.

'You would have seen her,' Teddy said dully, his eyes turned down to the snowplow that was digging out the front drive of the Regina Cleri home. He was quiet for a long time and Father Sullivan thought that he was going to help him up and into bed but then Teddy made his point. 'Maybe you could come to the hospital and meet her.'

160

'The mother?' There was so little air in the room that he had to work to keep from gasping.

'I need you to.' They both realized simultaneously that this was the reason he was there, though honestly it had not occurred to Teddy before. It was the purpose of the story. 'I think if you met her you could help me understand what's happened. And since she's in the hospital, since she was hurt so badly, I thought you might want to pray for her.'

Teddy looked at Father Sullivan and in that look was the hope of all the people who lined the hallway to his room every day, the people who could be lining up right now for all he knew. 'Teddy, I didn't make those women better.'

'You don't know that.'

'Of course I know that. Do you think that from time to time I just become some sort of unwitting conduit for God?'

Teddy never answered quickly when the answer was important. That's why his father thought he wasn't as smart as his brother, that's why the teachers discounted him. But Father Sullivan always told him there wasn't any fault in thinking something through. 'There are things that go on that none of us can understand, that even you can't understand. I want you to come and see her. Maybe you can't make her better but you could come and see. You know I wouldn't ask you if I didn't have to.'

'It would be very difficult for me to go to the hospital.' It would be difficult to get out of the chair and into the bed, and that was the only thing he wanted.

'But you do go to the hospital. It's the one place you go. You'd come if I was the one who'd been hit by a car.'

And then Teddy had him because it was true: he would come. He would walk there in the snow for Teddy even if it was all just a gesture in which his sacrifice would be to die trying. His students had cycled through his life every year, his parishioners came and went, all of the nieces and nephews he loved, his own brothers and sisters, they meant nothing to him compared to this boy. Everyone changed, the Church changed and the city changed, God changed, but Teddy was constant. Sometimes Father Sullivan would think, I could have adopted this boy. Had I found him first he could have been my son. 'Help me back to bed,' he said to Teddy.

Teddy leaned forward and Father Sullivan put his hands around Teddy's neck and Teddy put his hands beneath his arms. He lifted him up so that his feet barely brushed the floor. As soon as he was standing straight Father Sullivan felt the air pouring back into his lungs and he yawned, trying to pull it in faster. 'Let me just stand here for a minute.'

Teddy did not take his hands away. His uncle had once been a great man, straight and tall. He had swung Teddy up on his shoulders when he was a little boy. He walked out of mass with Teddy on his shoulders, stood at the front door of the church shaking hands with the people coming out, and there was Teddy, high enough to touch the arch of the door which was higher than any man was ever tall. Father Sullivan was not a young man then but the light of Teddy's youth poured down on him and everyone who saw them felt it. It was not so different now, only less metaphorical: the young man held him up.

'I'm asking for too much,' Teddy said.

'I'm fine. I'm just catching my breath.'

'If anybody else told you you had to go out in this weather I'd tell them they'd have to get through me first.'

'Well that makes it easier then. You won't have to get through yourself.' Father Sullivan breathed again. He moved his hands to Teddy's shoulders and took his weight onto his feet. 'I'm better now. I can lie down.'

He felt stronger when he was in bed, even though the head of his bed sat nearly upright. As his strength came back to him he thought that maybe a small trip out would be fine. He shouldn't be so quick to embrace his limitations. He certainly managed to go to the hospital for himself from time to time. He didn't see how it could be so different to go for someone else.

'Tell me she's in Mass. General.' Mass. General he could practically see from his window.

'Mount Auburn.'

'Ah,' the priest said.

'I shouldn't have asked.'

Father Sullivan smiled and took Teddy's hand. 'As long as you don't expect that I can mend her bones and make her walk, we should be fine. You won't do that, will you?'

'I won't,' he said, and he tried to make it true in his heart.

'I would certainly want to meet the person who brought you into the world. I'd like to see those brothers of yours, too. Maybe if I could get out of this place they would meet me.'

'I will promise you that.' Teddy felt better having something that he could offer up in return. It was not unlike the sensation his uncle had, a sudden subsiding of pressure in his chest. He felt he would be able to make sense of things once Uncle Sullivan was there with him.

There was a light tapping on the door and before anyone spoke Sister Claire put her head in the room. 'Father, are you up now? There are people waiting to see you.'

★   ★   ★

On the other side of the city, Father Sullivan's namesake realized that he had made a critical error. Teddy had asked him to come to the old priests' home and he had managed to sidestep that easily enough by claiming exhaustion. But once Teddy had left the hospital, Sullivan remembered he had nothing of value on him save a single Percocet. In the course of one transatlantic flight he had gone from being a moderately well-to-do man in a poor country to being indigent in the land of plenty. His wallet, which was sitting on the bedside table of his boyhood room, had been exhausted by the wildly overpriced taxi ride from Logan. He sat down heavily in a chair near the front door, not too far away from where his father and brothers had sat the night before, and thought about the long haul back to Union Park. Boston was a walk-in freezer turned to its lowest setting and the men with shovels and blowers were only now starting to venture out to cut a path where the sidewalks had been. In the same way Sullivan believed that his clock was still set to African time, he believed his blood was still suited for an African climate. He had finally learned how to remain temperate in the tropical heat, but now he was physiologically unprepared for this kind of cold. It could not be good for him. It was possible that he could go back to ask Tennessee Moser for assistance. She was family in some sense, the mother of his brothers, and he felt for her genuinely. He would be glad to help her, and so it was reasonable to think she would want to help him in return. He wouldn't even need cab fare, he would take a dollar twenty-five for the T. Still, the thought of tapping a woman who had probably already started preoperative sedation, even for such a small amount of money, made him uncomfortable. Why hadn't Teddy remembered that he didn't have any cash? Why didn't any of them seem to remember that there was another brother? Teddy wouldn't have walked out of there if it had been Tip who had forgotten his wallet, but that was hardly a reasonable example, seeing as how Tip had never forgotten anything in his life. Tip probably had a stash of backup tokens sewn into the linings of his pockets. Now Sullivan would have to call the house and Doyle would have to come and pick him up while he stood on the corner, shivering in his high school clothes. No, that he would not do.

Sullivan took the elevator back up to the third floor, thinking at the very least he could get a cup of coffee before setting out. The day shift would be coming on soon and he might as well go up while there were still people working who had seen him before. None of the nurses and doctors understood what they had in this hospital, certainly the patients didn't, the clean floors, the working elevators whose doors opened and closed without complaint, the drugs and the beds, the water and light, such abundance that the situation practically demanded waste. Had he taken something from a hospital like this one it would never have been missed, but then again there would be virtually no market to sell what was stolen. Everything was too readily available in America, nothing was contraband. 'Is there some coffee around here?' he said to the young Asian man in bright blue scrubs behind the desk.

'Coffee shop, first floor.' He was sifting through an enormous stack of charts as if the one he really wanted was the one he couldn't find.

'That's good to know,' Sullivan said. 'But I don't want to go down to the first floor. I don't want to leave this floor.'

The young man put his thumb in the pile and glanced up.

'She's on her way to *surgery*,' Sullivan said.

The man nodded and separated the stack into two piles. 'Sorry. Black?'

'Milk actually.'

The nurse brought back the coffee and a glazed doughnut resting on a napkin. Sullivan thanked him for the kindness.

And then there was the Irish girl coming down the hall towards him like an old friend. 'I shouldn't have run you off. Turns out they're not taking her down for another hour at least.' She didn't have a bad face. It wasn't the kind of face that Sullivan liked, and she was fat, but he gave her credit where credit was due. People must have said it to her all her life, such a pretty face.

'Really?' He took a bite out of the doughnut.

'It's the snow. Everybody's running late. Dr. Zhang isn't even here yet. It's one big parking lot out there.'

'So you're not leaving?' He gave up half a smile. There was no reason not to. For an instant she reddened and then faded back to chalk.

'Just as soon as someone comes to take my place.'

'Well, I'll be here too. My brother walked off with my wallet.'

'That kid was your brother?'

'Long story.'

'He stole it?'

Sullivan shook his head. 'Nothing like that. There was just a little mix-up in the coat closet. My fault, really.'

'So she's your — '

'Aunt,' he said. 'By marriage.'

'Sally,' said the Asian nurse, bearer of doughnuts, and pointed to the phone. 'Anesthesia.'

Sally waved Sullivan on like a doorman at a club. She seemed to take enormous pleasure in her own largesse. 'Go back and sit with her. She

167

seems pretty out of it, your aunt.'

Sullivan nodded and took a long sip of coffee. 'She was hit by a car,' he said by way of explanation, and he headed down the hall.

The electrical light that had burned over the bed was off now but the sun was pulling up over Boston and the walls and the floors were washed over in strips of gold that fell through the tilted Venetian blinds. It was a hospital room, and nothing could soften the seafoam walls or the gray tile floors. A hospital room could only be made beautiful by light, but the opportunities for light to come into 315 were rare and fleeting. Tennessee Moser was folded into stiff white sheets, her arms down straight by her sides. Her eyes were closed. The bed next to hers was empty and it looked like an oasis of rest and peace the likes of which Sullivan had never known. He could fall into that bed and sleep until June. He should have told the nurse that he was her husband, since husbands, unlike nephews, could probably lie down in the empty beds and not be made to move. But the Irish girl wouldn't have gone for that. It was one thing to have a black aunt or a black brother, those were matters beyond your control. A black wife was something else entirely.

Sullivan finished off the coffee and doughnut and washed his hands in the little sink.

He kept his eye on the woman sleeping in the bed. Her face was swollen, sliced and stitched, undone and reassembled. There were bits of gauze tape holding her together and flecks of blood clinging to the roots of her hair. It hurt

168

him to look at her but Sullivan did not turn his eyes away. He saw her as a box of clues. He tried to assemble the faces of his brothers and the face of the little girl they'd brought home from the features she provided. Doyle could deny it all day long but there they were: Tip's forehead, Teddy's mouth. Most of all he tried to remember her in the landscape, to scan the faces on every street he had walked down as a child to see if she was there, but there was really no remembering something like that. Besides, he imagined the woman he saw in this bed only bore a faint resemblance to the woman who was hit last night by a car. The question was, what did she look like smiling? What did this woman with blood in her hair look like when she was standing up? What if it was springtime and a breeze stirred the branches of flowering apple trees over her head? That was how he wanted to see her, in the brilliant light of late April, standing in a rain of apple blossoms, but it was too large of a gap to cross. In this bed she looked tired in a way that was greater even than last night's violence could account for. It was clear that she had been tired for years before she ever saw the lights of the car. Sullivan understood this because he was tired himself. He wanted to lie down in the bed beside her as much as he had ever wanted anything in his life. He wanted to sleep for both of them.

'Maybe you'd get me that water now,' she said, and he startled. He was leaning over her, his face too close to hers.

'I'll ask again. They're running late.'

'Where's Teddy?'

169

'He had to go home.'

Tennessee stopped talking. She had not opened her eyes. There was no way to be sure if she was actually awake, but Sullivan made his way down the hall to see about getting her something to drink. Everything was quiet there. The patients were still sleeping and the visitors had been kept away by snow. The nurses clustered together at their station, complaining idly about a certain doctor who never returned his pages. 'Just like the boys I used to date in high school,' one woman said, leaning a hip against the counter, and the tall Ethiopian woman replied, 'He wants you to beg.' Sullivan motioned for his friend Sally, and when she came to him, standing a half a step too close, he pressed her for the favor. She relented easily this time, coming back with a few chips of ice in the bottom of a cup. She was tired after working all night and what difference was it going to make, really? The surgery was looking later all the time. She handed it over with all the gravity of a first visit to a methadone program. 'Give it to her slowly. Don't let her have it all at once.'

He assured her that he understood.

'I looked at her chart,' Sally said. 'We don't have any insurance information. We need to get her cards.'

'If I don't have my own wallet I certainly don't have hers,' he said.

Sally gave him a stern look. 'Well, call someone, okay? I need to get this in the computer.'

Sullivan nodded and went back to the room.

He held a piece of ice against Tennessee's lips. 'Don't go crazy on this stuff because I don't think we're getting any more. It looks like you're not covered for ice.'

'You didn't go,' she said.

'I stayed with you.'

She kept her eyes straight up, fixed on the acoustical tiles of the ceiling. 'I don't understand.'

'Let's just say you're interesting to me.' Sullivan pulled up a chair beside the bed. 'You're like the spy who came in from the cold.'

Tennessee tried to open her mouth a little wider but her jaw was sore and her lips were swollen. She felt like somebody had beaten her with a fender and asphalt and a thick sheet of glass. She tried again and Sullivan took his finger and pushed the bit of ice inside. He knew about these things. He had sat with the sick before. To look at the expression on her face a person would think that nothing in her life had felt as kind or tasted as sweet as that silver of ice on her tongue. She took a moment to savor the melting before she answered him. 'I'm not a spy.'

'Of course you are,' Sullivan said. 'You've been following us around all our lives. What else do you call it?'

Tennessee thought for a minute. She tried to get the right words because words were so hard to come by. 'Wanting to make sure your boys are okay.'

He shook his head. 'You knew they were okay. If anything had happened to the sons of the former mayor of Boston it would have wound up in the paper. Our entire life winds up in the paper.'

She sighed then and closed her eyes. She said what every woman said. 'You don't understand.'

Sullivan considered the assessment and found it to be fair. 'I probably don't. I probably couldn't understand why you were spying, but at least I know that you were. And believe me, you have my complete admiration. You've been at this for a long time and none of us knew you were there. I don't think you ever would have slipped up if that car hadn't caught you.'

Tennessee stayed quiet and Sullivan shook his head. 'People like you never open up. You just get used to not telling anything. Spies always have a lot more information than they let on to. There are lots of spies in Africa, you know. You don't see them for a long time but they're always there: contractors, tour guides, kids with back-packs. They blend in like those moths whose wings look like dried out leaves. It was all a sort of game for me, learning how to spot them. The good ones were just like you, very low profile, very discreet. You won't find one getting drunk in a bar and going on about Dubai. You just get a sense about them. Spooks, they're called. As soon as you notice one they're gone.'

'What were they spying on?' It was better to talk about spying in general rather than the specific ways it might apply to her.

'That part was never completely clear, though in the end I guess some of them were spying on me.' There were two black men who were too often together, too often in the places Sullivan went. For a time he thought they were looking to buy, but then he noticed their clothes weren't right. They were shabby enough but they changed all the time. Two poor men and every day they had on different filthy shirts.

'What did you do?' It was an effort for her to make the words and so he patted his hand lightly against her wrist. Sullivan told her she should rest while she could, that he would leave so that she could get some sleep. 'I won't tell anyone about this. It will be our secret.'

'What did you do?'

Finally he held up an ice chip and when she looked at him he put it in his own mouth. 'I stole.'

Tennessee blinked as if this had managed to surprise her.

'I thought you knew everything about us already.'

'No.'

'Well, that isn't fair. You couldn't have known that. Nobody knows that. If you knew what I was doing in Africa I would spend the rest of my life trying to secure your position as the head of the NSA.'

'What did you steal?' she said.

He did not like the question, even though he had made the declaration himself. To announce a theft seemed cavalier, but to be asked about it felt like an accusation. Now he wanted to reword his statement. It wasn't stealing exactly. It was skimming. He simply took a little bit off the top of everything he had to make more for someone else. He could turn twenty vials into twenty-one.

Then he could turn ten into eleven. Then five into six. It was a kind of mathematical genius. In a country where the demand exceeded the supply by hundreds of thousands of vials he was saving lives and making money hand over fist, and then spending it fist over hand, pumping the fruits of his labor directly back into that fruitless economy. In that light it wasn't even wrong. It was an expansive redistribution. 'Retrovir,' he said, but there was no reason she would have heard of Retrovir unless she was HIV-positive herself. 'Anti-retrovirals.'

He waited for her shock and reproach but she just kept staring at the ceiling. One of her eyes was full of blood where a vessel had broken the night before. He wondered if she was unable turn her head and then he wondered if she knew what the word meant. Anti-retro-viral. He was ready to tell her. He had been ready to tell somebody since he saw those two men in the street outside his apartment two nights ago. All along he had been waiting for someone to ask him, at the airport, on the plane. The woman sitting next to him put on her headphones and an eye mask and turned her chin towards the window. The flight attendants made their soulless trek up and down the aisles like members of the living dead. Someone should have turned to him and asked what had happened. Why was he leaving so quickly, what had he done? Had the balance of the scales tipped over from the living to the dead? Had he, without ever knowing exactly when it happened, started taking too much medicine out and putting too much purified water in? He had made up so many stories, fashioned credible lies out of pieces of absolute truth, but in the end no one had questioned him about anything. He had bought a one-way ticket, after all, and thanks to his hurried departure he had only the small bag. At every checkpoint they let him pass. In Logan, the customs officer stamped his passport and said, 'Welcome home.' No one took a firm hold on his upper arm. No one asked him to step aside. He had steeled himself for the barrage of questions from his father, from his brothers who would certainly pull him off into the kitchen and whisper to him when they were alone, but then there was that scene that blew in through the front door with the snow, Tip in his boot, Teddy and Doyle so shaken. There was that doe of a girl who remained the focus of everyone's attention. No one was asking him anything. He wondered if this was the way it felt to the spies. They wanted to tell what they knew but they were doing too good a job and so nobody ever asked. Criminals lingered near their crimes like narcissistic teenage girls who longed to unburden their souls with talk. But he wasn't a criminal, nor was he like them. The drugs were his to begin with, or at least they were in his control. It wasn't hard. He delivered to the hospitals, to the doctors. Tip was not the only one who had a grasp of basic science in this family. It wasn't all fish. Measure out what you need and what you have and it becomes perfectly clear that they allow for a certain amount of waste in the dosage. All you have to do is take the waste off the top.

'Is there any more ice?'

Sullivan slid out a piece and gave it to her. It was small. 'You should take what's left. It's melting.'

'I don't feel well,' she confessed.

'Should I go get the nurse?'

'Have you been in Africa all this time?'

He wondered if she had heard anything he'd said to her. She must be at least as tired as he was. She had been hit by a car and was pumped full of what he imagined to be a complicated cocktail of painkillers and antibiotics. It was even possible that her hearing had been damaged in the fall. They probably hadn't understood a single word the other one had said. 'I'm going to let you get some sleep.'

'Why did you leave?'

'I told you.'

'Boston,' she said.

'Why did I leave Boston?'

'It's your home.'

It had been a long, long time since anyone had asked him that. Leaving Boston for Sullivan was just a given. What amazed people was that he ever came back at all. *It was the weather*, he wanted to say to her. *I couldn't stand the way they pile the snow up in walls between the sidewalks and the streets so that you spend half the winter wandering around like a goddamn rat in a maze. And the business of having to always move your car to the opposite side of the street when there never was a spot for it, I hated that. I hated all the colleges and their sweatshirts, the* self-righteous *liberalism* that made all the children feel so good about themselves while their parents coughed up $45,000 a year in fees to keep them safe. There was also the construction. *It would never be finished in my lifetime. I left because my father gave up on me as soon as there were those other boys for him to bank on, and I hated those other boys, your sons, because they took his attention and his love without any effort at all. Besides, everything reminds me of my mother. That was reason enough to go. Every day I am in Boston I think of how she died and I will tell you that the Christ to whom you pray knew nothing of suffering compared to what she endured at the end. Outside of Boston I do not see her face on a daily basis.* He could come up with a list that was longer than the phone book and every bit of it was true, but she was a spy and the only answer she'd settle for was the answer she already knew, and so he told her: he left because of the accident.

'Tell me.'

'What am I supposed to tell you? If you know where we eat dinner then you certainly know I was in a car accident. People who don't even know my name know I was in a car accident.' Sullivan stopped and rested his forearms against her bed. There was always that sound of the lights in a hospital. He could hear them from the hallways and for a second it made him think of Africa, that relentless buzzing just off in the distance and how in Africa it was another thing entirely.

'How long ago?'

He closed his eyes. Certain things exist outside of time. It was ten years ago, it was this morning. In that way the accident was like his mother's death. It did not recede so much as hover, waxing and waning at different intervals but always there. It happened in the past and it was always happening. It happened every single minute of the day. 'I was twenty-three. I'll be thirty-four in June.'

'You were hurt.'

'You know this.'

'I read some things.'

'Oh,' Sullivan said. 'But you want to know what happened because you never believed that story anyway? No one believed that story.'

She stayed quiet then and she waited. Sullivan admired her tactics. He thought of the snow outside. The sky was bright blue now and the wind coming straight down from Toronto would be bitterly cold, but he could have walked it. Sally the nurse could have given him the fare to get home. He didn't know why he hadn't thought to ask her in the first place. He could have promised her something, a phone call later on. The promise of a phone call was worth a dollar and a quarter to a fat girl. 'Natalie always wanted to spend the weekend in Boston, but I liked to come up to Amherst. I had talked her out of spending her junior year abroad. Her three best friends had all gone to Paris and I managed to talk her into staying even though I had graduated. I wasn't even there and I made her stay.' Sullivan tilted back the Styrofoam cup and took the little bit of water and the last shards of ice down the back of his throat. Tennessee Moser was right about that ice. It was brilliant. 'It's funny, but when I think about Natalie and everything that happened, the thing I feel worst about in some strange way is that I cheated her out of a year in France. I never came right out and said she had to stay, but everything I did made it clear: my mother left me and everybody leaves me and now you're leaving me, too. She was twenty years old and she was so bright, A's in everything, but she wasn't smart enough to see through such a simple bit of bullshit. The truth is I would have been fine if she'd gone. I would have sulked around and slept with other girls and she would have memorized every painting in the Musée D'Orsay and spoken French like Simone de Beauvoir and we both would have had a great time. But I missed being in college. I liked going back on the weekends and sleeping in her little twin bed in the dorm room. I liked the idea of a girl giving up something as big as a year in another country for me. That was the kind of proof I needed in those days. That was love.'

Natalie was a Jewish girl from Cleveland whose paternal grandfather had brought home the unfathomable surprise of a Japanese bride from his peacekeeping tour of the Pacific. And while no one would have been able to name it by looking at her, the one-quarter Asian blood swimming around amidst the three-quarters Eastern European, there was something quietly exotic in the planes of Natalie's face and in the heaviness of her hair that she wore in a braid down her back. There were a million boys like Sullivan, Irish all the way back to the dawn of time, but Natalie was a singular genetic concoction. The finest elements from every part of her heritage had managed to step forward. No matter how many grandchildren those four-quarters produced, there would never be another with Natalie's balance, the warm light of her skin, her intelligence and grace. She was not the girl you saw at first. She did not turn heads coming into a room. But once you saw her, really saw her, there was no looking anywhere else.

'Natalie died.'

'You know she did.'

'I'm sorry.'

'We should be talking about you, anyway,' Sullivan said, and suddenly he was irritated with her. This is what spies do, after all. They get you going on about yourself. She was flat on her back and barely able to open her mouth and still she had gotten him talking about things that should not be discussed. 'With all due respect to your impending surgery, any person looking at this exchange would say that you are the one who should be answering questions. We could start with the simplest one: Why did you give up your children? Teddy I can see. Maybe you're poor and you're young and you've already got one kid and so you have to give the second one away, but then to give away the first one, too? How did you give up Tip? How did you go back to your house and pick up this child who is more than a year old and give him away?'

'She was driving,' Tennessee said.

'You don't get to make all the decisions.' He kept his voice low, even as it was edged in fury. He managed to stay seated in his chair. She did not flinch at all and again he wondered if she could hear him.

'Finish this,' she said.

He only listens to you, his father had told his mother. She was already sick and moving in one inexorable direction and still his father was complaining to his mother about Sullivan. He could hear their voices from where he stood outside the bedroom door and from that moment on he thought yes, I will only listen to my mother, and if she is gone I will not listen to anyone ever again. So what he could not understand at all was his desire to listen to this woman. He wanted to finish this story. No one ever asked him about the things he needed to say. They were always so busy asking him about things that couldn't possibly matter. 'I drove up Friday night after work to pick up Natalie like I said I would, but by the time I got there I'd changed my mind. I wanted to sleep in her bed and go to a movie on campus. I let it get later and later but she said she wasn't falling for it. I had promised we were going back to Boston and we were going back. She was restless that year. I was gone. Her friends were gone. I was in a bad mood. I'd taken something, a couple of Darvocet Natalie had in the bathroom from when she'd had her wisdom teeth out over winter break. We were drinking Jack Daniels out of tea cups. She kept laughing even though I knew she was getting mad at me. She was saying, 'You're not doing it this time. We're going to go. We're going to go.' Until finally there was nothing I could do. I had to take her back. I had promised to take her back.'

The rest of it he really didn't remember. Whether that was the time or the drugs, the concussion or the loss or the willful release of knowledge he may once have held, he couldn't say. He walked into the winter night with Natalie, snow blowing in circles around them, a soft, enveloping sweep. She held his arm. He had her suitcase, a quilted bag containing a toothbrush and a nightgown, underwear and extra sweaters, a copy of *The Magic Mountain* that she was reading for a course called Twentieth-Century Classics in Translation. Sullivan had taken the class himself three years before and had done well in it. He could remember the contents of her suitcase but nothing about getting in the car, nothing about Natalie getting in beside him. Nothing at all until he saw his father sitting by his hospital bed in a room that was not unlike the one he was sitting in now.

'When I woke up my father was there and he told me that Natalie had died. My memory is that he was kind about it. He cared for Natalie, I think. He saw her as a good influence. I honestly didn't understand at that point that she had died with me or that my being in the hospital was connected to her death. The accident had shaken everything loose in my head and it was very difficult for me to figure out what part of what was happening was real.'

'I know,' Tennessee said.

He nodded. 'Yes. Exactly like that. So it was awhile, a few minutes or an hour, I don't know, before I put it together: Natalie, me, the car, and I asked my father what I had done.' At this Sullivan stopped for a minute because it was not a sentence he ever said, not to himself, not to anyone. He tipped back the cup for some water but it was already gone. 'In my memory, and I don't know if this is true or not because there were only two of us in the room and God knows we never talked about it again, in my memory my father took my hand and leaned over the bed.' And Sullivan, in a moment of genuine feeling, took Tennessee's hand and leaned towards her. 'He said, 'She was driving the car. If you don't remember, that's fine, but I'm telling you, Natalie was driving the car.''

'Maybe she was.'

Sullivan shook his head. He didn't think about her so much anymore, not like he thought about his mother. He thought about how he was adrift in the world, but for the most part he managed to block out the source of his launch into darkness. Sweet Natalie. Forever in her junior year, locked out of Paris, eternally twenty in winter, laughing. 'Never.'

'That night — '

'I always drove. She would have been sleeping. If it was dark and we were in the car, then Natalie was sleeping. There was a story that I was sick that night or I'd had too much to drink and she was taking me home. You read those stories.' He looked at Tennessee and smiled. 'You never believed them. I didn't believe them. The whole thing proved to be an enormous miscalculation on my father's part. He thought that by telling a lie we would all be spared the pain and embarrassment of my killing my girlfriend, but it never worked out that way, not from the very beginning. The press hounded him straight to hell. They rounded up Natalie's parents, Natalie's friends, and gave airtime to their opinions. They kept her picture on the front page longer than they would have if she'd been kidnapped. They waited outside his office, outside the hospital, outside the house. It was over for him after that, even though they were never able to prove what I'd done. Not a single cop ever changed his story, my God they were true to their mayor, but Boston proved to have less devotion. I really do believe if he had just kept his hands off of it and let me stand accountable no one would have cared. Saintly Bernard Doyle with the dead wife and the two black orphans, the people would have forgiven him one murderous fuck-up of a son. It might even have helped him in the next election. But people hate to be lied to. It belittles them. They could smell him saving the hide of his privileged boy, and for that, I'll tell you, they turned on him like feral dogs. My father had a plan, you know. He was already set to run for governor. He had it laid out like a chess match. My father had a plan for the people, not just the people in his family or the people in Massachusetts. He had a plan for All The People and he threw it away on the one person he didn't much care for to begin with. He ought not to have lied, Bernard Doyle. We might have gotten over Natalie, both of us, but no one ever recovered from him lying.'

'He meant to protect you.'

'Or he meant to protect himself. Either way he made the wrong choice.'

Tennessee breathed in the stale hospital air and felt a sharp pain in her ribs. 'You were his son.'

Sally knocked on the door as she opened it. 'They just called. They're coming up to get her now.'

'I'm ready,' Tennessee said, her voice so quiet that Sally didn't know she had spoken.

'No,' Sullivan said to the nurse. 'We need more time. She has things she has to tell me.'

'She can tell you everything when she wakes up.' Sally raised her voice. 'You have a very nice nephew, Mrs. Moser. He's been worried about you.'

Tennessee kept her eyes closed but she nodded her head.

Sullivan leaned closer to her ear. 'It isn't fair.'

'Later.'

He took her hand again and pressed it. He could not imagine letting it go. 'I never told that story before. Do you believe me? I promised my father I would never tell the truth and from that day on I never did, not about anything, not until now.'

'Thank you,' she said.

'But why?' His heart was enormously open to her now. She had taken his burden for a moment, lifted the thing he had carried with him for so long he hadn't even understood that he was still holding it. 'I'm not the son you're interested in.'

Tennessee opened her eyes again, but it seemed to take everything she had this time. He knew those eyes. They had been looking at him since he was twelve, asking him why he had done all the things he had done. 'I wanted to know why you stole,' she said.

7

When Kenya opened her eyes it was to a flood of astonishing sunlight. So bright was this room, so radiant, that for the first few moments she was awake she did not consider her mother or the Doyles at all. She did not think of where she was or what had happened. She could do nothing but take in the light. It had never occurred to her before that all the places she had slept in her life had been dark, that her own apartment had never seen a minute of this kind of sun. Even in the middle of the day, every corner hung tight to its shadows and spread a dimness over the ceiling and walls. Draw the curtains back as far as they could possibly go and still the light seemed to skim just in front of the window without ever falling inside. No matter what time of day it was she had to switch on the overhead bulb to do her homework, or her mother would shout at her, *Your eyes!* But in the light that soaked this room a girl could read the spines of the books on the very top shelf. '*The Double Helix*,' she said aloud. '*A Separate Peace*.' She stretched her arms down the comforter and admired them. She spread her fingers wide apart and took her fingernails under consideration. Every bit of her was straight and strong and beautiful in this light. She glowed. She felt it pouring into her and yet she could tell by her skin, which looked ashy most mornings where she lived, that it was pouring out of her as well. It was just like the leaves they had studied in science class. She was caught in an act of photosynthesis. The light was processed through her and she was improved by it. She wondered if there wasn't some way that light was divided and somehow, even though it didn't seem logical, more of it wound up in better neighborhoods. How had she slept so deeply in the presence of all this sun? She sat up and pulled the blankets up with her. The room was cold but not as cold as it got when the radiator shut down at home. It shut down more reliably than it came on. Besides, there were plenty of nice things to offset the chill. For example, it was a very comfortable bed, something she hadn't taken the time to notice when she had collapsed into it so late the night before. It was a very fine pillow. She knew she had been tired beyond any tired she had achieved through running in her life, but that didn't account for her good night's sleep. She swept her gaze around the room. She saw the pictures of Mrs. Doyle and Dr. King, the maps tacked into the wall, the enormously high windows through which light poured in to saturate every surface. She saw that lovely statue with her arms open wide and saw how the light painted the side of the woman's face and made the halo shining on the back of her head seem almost like a living thing. She would like to have a statue of her own mother to take with her through life and put on various dressers as she grew up. It was a comfort to sleep beneath that watchful eye. The woman on the dresser made

188

everything peaceful and quiet. And with that thought Kenya realized what was so strange about this room, stranger and more wondrous than the light or the pillow or the bed: it was the quiet. Not a single sound floated up from Union Park, not kids screaming, not the drivers of passing cars laying on their horns, not the shouts of men arguing with each other or crazy women arguing with themselves. The radiator did not hiss or clang or make that awful sound like there was someone standing right there beside you whaling into it with a metal bar. There was nobody banging around in the halls, saying things her mother told her not to listen to, banging on their door either by mistake or because the person wanted to come inside without knowing them at all. There were no car alarms or police sirens, no Fire Station Engine 3, no inconsolable babies wailing. All the sounds that woke her up in the morning and woke her up half a dozen times every night were gone. How had the Doyles managed to take all of the light and none of the noise? She got out of bed and pulled the comforter around her like a cape against the cold. She went to the window to see if it was a holiday of some sort and no one was allowed outside, the one day a year when everybody had to stay in and keep their thoughts to themselves. But what she saw from that fourth-story window was the snow, beautiful and silent, as deep as the second step on the house across the street. She had forgotten the snow, but the minute she remembered it she remembered everything. A sudden gasp came up in her throat and she made a small sound she could not hold back. She leaned her forehead against the frosted glass and closed her eyes, though her tender eyelids were ineffectual at blocking out so much light. What she wanted more than anything was to take time back one day to her own dark apartment where she would just now be waking up with her mother.

Kenya got dressed quickly. The doors in the hallway were open and she could see that the bed in the room across from hers was empty and unmade and she went back and made her own bed up. She knew that her mother would want her to show them that she had been raised to know better. She heard her own footsteps on every stair coming down, no matter how weightless she tried to make herself. Was she supposed to come downstairs at all, or should she have waited in her room until they called her? The entire house was luminous. It was clean down to the dowels that held up the banister and the corners of the baseboards, so clean that it was impossible to believe no woman lived there. The glass in the windows looked like something you could put your hand through in order to touch the cold air on the other side. She came down into the front hallway and then stretched her neck to look around the door into the living room. There was Tip sitting up on the couch with a textbook in his lap. As quiet as she was he looked right up like he had been expecting her.

'Where is everybody?' she whispered.

'Teddy and Sullivan went out for a walk a long time ago,' Tip said. 'And my father I don't know about. He may still be asleep.'

She stared at him, her eyes enormous and round.

'Did you sleep?'

'Like I was dead,' she said.

'You can come in here, you know.'

Kenya had lost some of the bravado she felt under the cover of last night's snow and darkness. She moved slowly into the room and sat on the couch where Teddy had slept, carving a modest place for herself in the jumble of pillows and blankets. She made a point of keeping her feet hanging just above the floor instead of sitting on them when sitting on them was her natural inclination. 'How's your ankle?'

'It's going to be fine. I just have to get used to it.'

'Any news about my mom yet?' She hadn't heard the phone ring but maybe the phones didn't ring on the fourth floor.

'Yours is the first voice I've heard since Teddy and Sullivan left at five. They might know something. They were talking about going to the hospital. We can ask them when they get back.'

They stared at each other, both of them thinking the same thing.

'Thank you for letting me use your room,' Kenya said, feeling that she was mining the depths of whatever manners she had.

Tip nodded. 'It's cold up there,' he said. 'I should probably sleep down here when I come home anyway. It's so much warmer.' He waited a minute, and when she didn't jump in he managed to add, 'I always liked this couch.'

'It's nice.' Kenya ran her hand over the fabric of the couch she was sitting on. All her life she had thought about this: sitting in the living room, talking to Tip, but she realized now for as many times as she had dreamed about it waking and sleeping, the movie in her head did not include sound. She felt like now she was straining to hear the interesting conversations they must have had, because as hard as she tried she could think of nothing to say to him. 'So you like fish,' she offered up finally. It was the best she could come up with. Tip didn't even seem to be trying.

'How do you know that?'

Kenya shrugged. 'My mom said you did. She said that's what you were studying in school.' She waited but her conversation starter had started exactly nothing. The silence sat back down on top of them, causing them to stare and look away in perfectly timed intervals. 'Did I say the wrong thing?'

Tip had a sort of pinched expression on his face and she was kicking herself. 'It's just that you know a lot more about me than I do about you.'

'I've known you longer.'

Tip closed the book in his lap and rested his hands flat on top. She could still see a picture of a pale blue fish beneath his thumb. 'So if that's the case, we should be talking about you and not me.'

Kenya waited. She knew he was trying to think of something important that he could ask her about. Tip was at an even greater disadvantage than she was, seeing as how he hadn't been thinking about her for years. 'What do you want to know?' She wanted to get the ball rolling.

'Something about you. Anything. What do you study in school?'

'Just the regular stuff. Math and science and social studies, English.'

'But what do you like?'

'Running,' Kenya said.

'I meant which subject.'

'PE is a subject, sort of. I always get A's. I run in the all-city track meets.'

There was a way that Tip had of holding his head perfectly still and straight and giving equal weight to each of his words that made him seem very much like his father. Kenya wondered if he realized he was doing it. 'Is that what you want to do when you grow up? You want to run?'

Kenya reached up and pulled sharply on one of her pigtails. It was what she did when she was uncomfortable. 'I'll run in the Olympics. You can do that a couple of times until you get too old and then I'll be a coach.'

'Teddy and I used to run,' he said, though he sounded unsure. 'But we both gave it up awhile ago.'

'Didn't you like it?'

'We liked it fine but neither one of us took it seriously enough. There are only so many things you can keep up with. I guess running just got dropped.'

Maybe that was true and maybe that was a reason not to finish your geography homework, but how did a person give up running? No more that beautiful moment of lacing up your shoes before a race, no bouncing on your toes, the loss of your own speed, the power to cut past everyone using nothing but strength, to stretch your legs out long in front of you, kick up high behind you, to say in your head again and again, *fleet, fleet, fleet*. He had given that up for fins and gills and buckets of slimy water? 'So what do you like?' she asked him. 'Other than fish.'

Tip did not answer. Kenya waited so long that she wondered if it would be impolite to repeat the question. He let his eyes stray over the room until an interest presented itself to him. 'I used to play the piano,' he said finally. He hadn't really been listening to her though. He was not thinking of other things he liked now, he was thinking of the things he'd liked at another time in his life and then had given up: soccer, the Catholic Church, politics.

Kenya did not correct him in the excitement of the moment. 'I can play a little!' She had had her eye on the piano in the corner, its polished wood and sweet, rounded curves. Though she could not devise a scenario in which anyone would ask her to play, she could imagine herself doing just that. She had only ever played on an upright before and it had always been true in her mind that real pianos had long, elegant bodies like this one. Real pianos lived in concert halls and the living rooms of the very rich, while uprights toughed it out in school gymnasiums and the small apartments of elderly piano teachers.

'Play something, then,' Tip said.

She was already on her feet, heading magnet to metal towards the Steinway before the invitation could be rescinded. 'I really only know a couple of songs. I practice in the gym when there's a teacher who'll stay after school. Someday I'm going to take lessons again.'

'I stopped my lessons, too,' Tip said in solidarity. 'I was older than you, though.'

Kenya nodded, so pleased to finally have this one thing that united them. 'Last year I got to take for four months, but it cost too much. Our math teacher, Mr. Morris, he shows me something every now and then. He had lessons the whole time he was growing up. He said when he was my age that music was just another subject and everybody took it like math.' Even the sea of framed pictures that covered the piano top could not distract her now, graduations and weddings and baby portraits, she overlooked them all. Kenya lifted the lid and set it smoothly back without so much as a tap. She could have cried to see such perfect keys, every single one of them even, none sitting higher or lower than the others, none of them yellowed or split. The white gleamed white and the black gleamed black. She wanted to press her cheek against them, to absorb their coolness. She wanted to sound E-flat with her forehead. 'It's beautiful.'

'It was my mother's.'

For a second Kenya started to say the wrong thing but she caught herself. 'Your mother played piano?'

Tip nodded. 'That's one thing I remember about her.'

She slipped down quietly onto the bench. It would have been enough just to sit there, to never even play. If she had had a piano like that she felt sure she could have done something great with it.

'Are you going to play?' Tip asked.

Whenever she played the upright in the gym at school she always imagined herself in a beautiful auditorium, but now she knew for the rest of her life whenever she played a piano she would imagine herself right here. She set her fingers lightly on the keys, pulled in all of her breath, and played as much of *Clair de lune* as she had in her head. She could not believe how beautiful it sounded, how good she was on that piano. When she got to the end of what she knew she doubled back and played it again, hoping that Tip wouldn't realize she was just repeating. She could not break away from the sway of the melody and force herself on to the other songs in her modest repertoire. She might have gone on all day if Teddy and Sullivan hadn't come in then, their noses wet, their faces stiff from cold. She pulled up her hands and let the last notes rise slowly and wait and then release.

'Christ in His heaven, but it is cold out there.' Sullivan slammed the door and stomped the snow from his boots onto a mat in the entry hall.

'You're missing the concert,' Tip said.

'We heard someone playing.' Teddy bent down to begin the business of unlacing. 'We thought it might have been you.'

Tip laughed at the thought. 'That was a ridiculously long walk you took, by the way.

Shackleton came back sooner than that.'

Sullivan shook his hair out from underneath his hat and pulled off his coat. 'You don't know the half of it. So how is our little Van Cliburn this morning?'

'Can we go to see my mother now?' Kenya asked Teddy.

'We might want to wait a little while,' Teddy said.

Kenya shivered, either from the dull tone of his voice or the wind that followed them in through the door, she didn't know. She left the piano bench with regret and went to them. 'Is there something wrong?'

'Nothing wrong except what you know about already. She was just going into surgery when I left her this morning.' Then Sullivan quite unexpectedly leaned over and folded Kenya in a tight embrace, as if he had just that moment seen her and realized that he loved her. His hair was cold and soft against her face and he smelled of limes and soap. When she looked up at him, surprised, he kissed her cheek. 'That is from your mother,' he said, planting one hand firmly down on each of her shoulders. 'She told me to give you a hug and a kiss and there you go.'

All of the light that Kenya had stored up from the bedroom flooded through her now. It was better even than getting to play the piano. She had most certainly felt her mother. She could only imagine her mother had held on to Sullivan and Sullivan had somehow managed to carry her home in his arms. 'Thank you,' she said, though thank you didn't begin to cover it.

He held up his hands. 'I'm only the messenger.'

'What else did she say?'

'Not very much, other than the usual things about loving you and being worried about you.' Sullivan said this as if her mother passed messages along through him all the time. 'Oh, and she was worried that you were causing us a great deal of trouble and eating all our food.'

'She didn't say that,' Teddy said. Teddy did not take kindly to the teasing of children, but Kenya only laughed.

'Maybe she said it and she didn't mean it,' Sullivan said. 'She was pretty sleepy still. We got there too early.'

'You should have taken me with you.'

'I went in your room to wake you up,' he said, 'but you were sound asleep. I gave you my blanket so you wouldn't freeze to death up there.'

It was true, because now Kenya remembered that there had been an extra comforter in the morning when she woke up.

'I don't think they would have let you in anyway,' Sullivan said. 'They're pretty strict about visitors on the surgical floor.'

Kenya studied him. 'Then how did you get in?'

'I told lots of lies. Teddy is completely incapable of telling lies, you know. If you ever want to circumvent the system you may as well leave him at home. He's useless.'

'Is any of this true?' Tip asked.

'We were at the hospital,' Teddy said, hanging

198

up the coat that his brother had dropped on a chair in the entry hall.

Sullivan took Kenya's hand and led her back to the sofa opposite Tip where they both sat down. 'I spoke to the doctor before I left and he said he would call us when the surgery was over.'

'I want to go now,' Kenya said. 'I want to wait for her.' And she did, in part because she loved her mother more than anyone in the world and wanted to be close to her, and in part because she was feeling very guilty all of a sudden for having such a good time.

'There's simply no point. We'd only be sitting over there staring at the carpet and it's not worth looking at. The very first minute you can see her we'll know it. We'll be there before she ever opens her eyes. In the meantime, there are plenty of things to think about.'

'Like what?' Kenya said.

'Breakfast, for one. I somehow doubt that this one offered you anything to eat.' He tilted his head towards Tip.

'I thought people would be bringing me breakfast this morning,' Tip said.

Kenya came to Tip's defense. 'I haven't been up very long, really, and we started talking about the piano. We would have gotten around to breakfast.'

'And after you've been fed I think one of us should take you back to your house to get your things. Your mother's going to be in the hospital for a few days at least and she thinks it's best that you stay here with us. Do you have your keys?'

'I have my mother's purse.'

'Then they'll be in there,' Sullivan said, as if he had an intimate knowledge of that purse. 'Now we have a plan: breakfast, packing, and then you'll go for a run. Your mother said you were essentially worthless if you didn't go running.'

Was it possible that she should think of Sullivan as another brother, perhaps even more of a brother than these other two who seemingly had no ability to speak to her, or was it the fact that he wasn't her brother that made him so easy in his conversation? Certainly Teddy had talked to her plenty last night in the hospital when he thought she was nothing but some poor little stranger with no place to go. But even then Teddy hadn't kissed her. It was Sullivan's ease she found so mesmerizing, the way he told the truth about everything, even if it meant showing himself in a poor light. The very few times she had seen Sullivan around when she was younger, she had always thought of him as her brothers' impediment. Worse than being black in a white family was the burden of being an imitation in the presence of something real. Kenya always thought that things must have been better for Teddy and Tip when Sullivan was gone because then there was no other child against whom they could be judged, there was no one there who by his very presence reduced them to outsiders. But the things that had been the clearest to her when she stood far away from the house on Union Park were now the very parts of the story she seemed to have wrong. Without Sullivan, this house would be unbearably serious. In fact it was hard for her to imagine how they managed for such long stretches when he was gone.

'Do you run?' she asked him.

'It depends on who's chasing me.'

'I'll take her out,' Tip said. He sat up straight and put his feet on the floor.

'You're not going running,' Teddy said. 'In the boot, in the snow? I can take her.'

'I didn't say *I* was going to run. I'll take her to the track over at school. She's not going to run in the snow.'

'I can,' Kenya said, but they weren't listening to her now.

Sullivan smiled benevolently. 'And how will you get to the track?'

'The same way I'll get anywhere. Did you think I was going to sit on the couch for six weeks and stare at my foot?' With that Tip was up decisively, taking his crutches off the floor and stepping forward. The throb in his ankle that came with lowering his foot was both a devastation and a surprise. The Percocet turned out to be nothing but a mask for a deeper truth. His ankle seemed to be breaking all over again. He leaned forward to pick up his blankets and Teddy did the same, folding everything up in neat piles. 'I've got to go to the lab today anyway.'

'You're going to *work?*' Sullivan said.

Tip laid his blankets back on the couch. 'Imagine that.'

' 'I think that we have no hope at all if we yield in our belief in the value of science,' ' Teddy said, clutching a pillow to his chest. ' 'In the good that

201

it can be to the world to know about reality, about nature . . .''

'And they're off,' Sullivan said.

'' . . . to attain a gradually greater and greater control of nature, to learn, to teach, to understand. I think that if we lose our faith in this we stop being scientists, we sell out our heritage, we lose what we have most of value for this time of crisis.''

'Oppenheimer,' Tip said, choosing to ignore his entire leg. 'No one had the sense to say those things but Oppenheimer.'

Kenya leaned in towards Sullivan and dropped her voice. 'Why does he do that?'

'It's a game,' Sullivan said. 'We were all supposed to memorize speeches when we were kids. Teddy just turned out to be so freakishly good at it he never stopped playing.'

'Do you know any speeches?' she asked.

Sullivan shook his head. 'I make a point of forgetting everything.'

'I'll start breakfast,' Teddy said. 'What do you eat?'

'Anything,' Kenya said.

'Peanut butter toast and cereal?' Tip said. 'That's what *I* eat.'

It was as if Tip was extending his hand to her as best he could and so she nodded. 'That's good,' she said. The truth was that she liked peanut butter toast quite a lot.

'I'm going to take mine to go, if that's all right.' Sullivan stood and stretched and yawned. 'I suddenly feel like I might be able to go back to sleep now. You'll wake me up when you hear anything from the hospital?'

'Sure we will,' Teddy said, but even he wasn't able to make himself sound very convincing.

Then, instead of turning for the kitchen, Sullivan headed up the stairs, as if he had forgotten about the food as soon as he had mentioned it. 'Good night, family,' he said. 'I'm going to put every blanket in the house on my bed and go to sleep and dream of Africa.' He waved to them and blew a kiss to Kenya. With every turn in the stairwell he was more convinced by his own exhaustion. He could barely even make it up to the top floor. Certainly he would go to sleep. He took his heavy comforter back and fell into his bed and this time the bed felt right, a deep feathered nest. It was perhaps even a bit warmer in the room now. He would stay asleep for the entire day and dream of the hot sun coming down on the dark red earth, of the children in the Catholic orphanage who wore those bright white shirts, of the pale green house geckos that clung to the walls of his room.

But for the first time in nearly a dozen years, Sullivan dreamed of Natalie instead.

★ ★ ★

'You were at the hospital all this time?' Tip asked his brother. He was sitting at the table in the center of the bright kitchen while Teddy filled up the four-slice toaster.

'What can I do?' Kenya asked. What she wanted to do was open up the cupboards and look at all the plates.

'Make the coffee,' he said.

'I can't make coffee.'

'Of course you can. I'll talk you through it. First step, the filters are in the drawer and the coffee canister is the second one over.'

'We went to the hospital for a little while and then we both left. I wanted to tell Uncle Sullivan what had happened and Sullivan didn't want to go.'

'No surprise on either count.'

Teddy closed up the plastic bag and returned the loaf to a smart wooden bread box whose front panel scrolled down like a garage door. 'I ran into him again when I was coming home. He said he had stayed in the hospital because I'd forgotten to leave him a token. He'd left his wallet at home.'

'So how did he get on the T?'

'One of the nurses gave him the money.'

'No surprise there as well. Okay, now put the coffee filter in the basket and put in five scoops of coffee.'

Kenya closed the drawer with some hesitancy. Everything in it was interesting: a tin of mints, a handful of old corks, long wooden matches.

'I can make the coffee,' Teddy said.

'So can she. Everybody has to learn how to make coffee,' Tip said. 'Heaping, not level. So Sullivan stayed with her all that time?'

Her. Kenya thought the pronoun was cold.

'He said they talked.'

'What did they talk about?' Kenya asked.

Both of the brothers turned and looked at her.

'Water. Fill up the whole pot with water and then pour it into that hole on the side.'

Teddy put boxes of Cheerios and Raisin Bran on the table and got the bowls and spoons. 'Sullivan said they talked about me. I don't believe him though. I think he was just giving me a hard time.'

'But you saw her. What did you talk about when you were there?'

Teddy stopped to think for a minute and then he looked at Kenya. 'We talked about you,' he said. 'She wanted to know if you were all right. She'd gotten confused from all the medication. She thought you were still at the hospital.'

The words came down on Kenya like a blow and she lowered her arms to her sides and rested her fingers on the edge of the countertop. 'I should have waited.'

'Nobody ever knows what time it is in a hospital. It was dark outside when we were there. She probably thought it was still night. I think she thought that everything had just happened.' Teddy looked over to Tip.

'Turn the power switch on now,' Tip said. 'The red button right on the front. There, perfect. Now you know how to make coffee. When your mother comes home from the hospital you can make her coffee in the morning.'

'We don't have a coffeemaker,' she said dully, when what she wanted to say was, *Shut the fuck up about the coffee.* There were tears sitting up high on the lower lids of her eyes and she tried her best to hold them there. She should have stayed at the hospital and never said a word to any of them. She should have brought her hat with her the way her mother told her to. She knew right from wrong. She knew what she was supposed to do and what was expected and she didn't do it.

'I'll buy you one,' Tip said.

The three of them sat at the table and ate their peanut butter toast in silence, one of them trying not to cry and the other two holding their breath for fear she might start. Would it have been like this if they had stayed together? The breakfast table, the talking and ignoring one another. Two brothers alone was nothing like two brothers and a sister. If they had had a sister all along they would have been better talkers. They would have known when to take things lightly. If she had had two brothers she would have been protected. All of the kids who gave her a hard time in school, in the apartments, they would have known to stay away from her with two brothers who were so much older and so much taller than everybody else. She would have gotten respect because Tip did well in school and all the priests knew Teddy. Being an only girl meant being resourceful and strong, but to have two brothers would have meant not always having to work so hard at being safe. They would have all protected one another, teased and softened and shaped one another. But if they had stayed together, then either the boys would have had to have stayed with their mother and never known Bernadette, or Kenya would have had to give up her mother and been adopted out to the Doyles.

206

For the three of them to stay together, one of the mothers would have had to lose completely. If that had been her mother then she would be alone in the hospital with no one to look after her. But who *was* looking after her now? At that thought a second wave of tears pushed up and knocked out the ones that were waiting, spilling those well-held tears down her cheeks and into her cereal bowl as fast as she could wipe them away with her hands.

Teddy put down his toast. 'What?'

Kenya shook her head. She held her hand up to shade her eyes as if the light was suddenly more than she could bear. 'My mother,' she said.

The two boys looked at her with genuine feeling, but neither of them was able to do the thing that for Sullivan would have come so naturally: put a hand on her wrist or touch her hair. 'She's going to be fine. She'll come through the surgery okay.' Tip handed her a paper napkin from a basket on the table so that she could blow her nose. 'They fix broken hips all day every day at that hospital.'

'But what if she had given me away, too? She'd be all alone now.'

The boys hadn't realized that she was crying for what her mother was enduring, or might have endured. They had thought that she was like any other child and so would be crying for herself. They had cried for themselves when their mother died. They were younger of course, they understood less, but they had never cried because their mother was suffering. They cried because they wanted her to take care of them the way she always had before. They cried for her reassurance.

'She didn't give you away,' Teddy said. 'She saved you. She loves you.'

They were all three sorry he had put it that way since it raised the question of people only keeping the children they loved. Similarly, they were all three relieved when Doyle arrived in the kitchen and threw them off their conversation. He was dressed in dark wool pants with a shirt and sweater, an outfit that said that the snow had defeated him and he had no intention of going into work today. The law office was closed due to weather. He looked rested and calm, like someone who had been up for hours, possibly sitting in a chair in his bedroom reading after a long night's sleep.

'Is this what happens when you come down so late?' he asked. 'Someone else makes the coffee? I would have started sleeping late years ago.'

'Kenya made it,' Tip said.

'I thought she looked like a clever girl.' Doyle had resolved to stand by his pledge of the night before. He would not put his hesitancy and doubt off on the child. When he smiled at her she pressed the wet napkin into a ball in her fist and tried to breathe through her nose. 'Are you feeling all right?' he asked her. 'You didn't catch a cold up there?'

She shook her head. 'I didn't wear a hat last night in the snow,' she said. 'My mother told me to.'

'Mothers always turn out to be right about these things. I'll make you some tea and honey.

You don't drink coffee, do you?'

She told him she did not.

'I hate to see children drinking coffee. I don't even like to see my boys drinking coffee now. So, good for your mother.' He liked that. He thought it sounded generous. 'And speaking of your mother, I need to call the hospital.'

'I went over there this morning,' Teddy said. 'She's in surgery now.'

'You've been all the way out there and back? I didn't even hear you.' Why had Teddy gone to the hospital? What could he have wanted there? Doyle did not ask. Instead he went over to fill up the kettle and for an instant the three of them looked at one another with conspiracy. They had not had to explain Kenya's crying.

'Sullivan couldn't sleep. We were going to take a walk together and then we decided to go to the hospital and see how she was doing.'

She, Kenya thought. *She has a name.*

Doyle raised his eyes to the ceiling for a moment and then looked down at the stove. 'Sullivan. I actually hadn't thought of him yet this morning.'

'You wouldn't have forgotten him for long,' Tip said.

Doyle sighed. 'No, I'm sure you're right, but for once Sullivan isn't on the top of the agenda. Tell me about your mother instead.'

'She's having surgery now,' Kenya reported. 'And when she wakes up I'll go and see her.'

Doyle nodded in approval as he poured himself a cup of coffee. 'I like a person who has a plan. When your mother wakes up I'll take you to the hospital myself.' And then it might be nice to take a trip, take Teddy and Tip to Paris for a week. Leave a note for Sullivan by the door.

'I'm going to take her over to the track to run first,' Tip said. 'Burn off a little energy instead of just waiting around.'

'Do you run?' Doyle asked her.

Everything about him seemed animated, interested. How was it she had always imagined him to be so stern? In her mind she could see him walking through lecture halls and museums, outside in the lobby just before the symphony was about to play. He was always wearing a suit and he never looked at anyone. Over and over she had smiled at him just to see if he would ever smile back. More than once her mother had to tell her to stop it. 'How could they be happy with him?' Kenya asked, even though the boys looked happy enough. Now she wondered if she had been right about anything at all. 'I run all the time.'

'These two are both excellent runners. If they'd stuck with it I think either one of them could have been real contenders.'

'They're not too old now,' Kenya said.

Tip nodded to her for the vote of confidence.

'I'll take you over to your apartment,' Teddy said. 'That way you can get some things to stay over. You can get your running clothes.'

She would not be staying over again but they would work that out once they got to the hospital. Doyle lifted up from the table. 'I'll call for a taxi. We might as well learn a lesson from last night and get a jump on it this time. The

210

wait's going to be even longer this morning.'

'I don't need a taxi,' Kenya said.

Doyle shook his head and picked up the phone. 'I'm not going to have you walking over to Roxbury, and you don't need to take the bus. We'll have the taxi wait for you. You can just run in and get your things.'

'But I don't live in Roxbury,' she said.

Doyle put his hand over the receiver. 'Taxis will go pretty much anywhere. Where do you live?'

Kenya pointed south towards the dining room. 'Cathedral.'

'The church?' Doyle cocked his head. When he thought about it for a minute he hung up the phone and moved backwards, drawing himself down to the table again.

The three of them were staring at her. When they did something all together at the same time it was very clear that they were family.

'No,' Tip said, keeping his voice measured and slow. 'The housing project, Cathedral. That's what you mean, don't you? You live at the end of the street.'

'It's not the end of the street,' Kenya said hesitantly. 'It's more than three blocks over from there.' She could have run it in five minutes, four and a half without the coat and the snow. She had done it before. Her address should not have been a betrayal and yet she could feel them each pulling away from her. It was too close. She had been too close to them all along. It wasn't just that she came to their neighborhood from time to time, she lived there, just on the other side of that narrow line that divided them. Sometimes she and her mother went to church at the Cathedral of the Holy Cross when her mother didn't have to work on Sunday morning and Kenya didn't have a track meet but they almost never saw the Doyles anymore and the Doyles had never seen them, so what difference did it make? That was Boston: on one block there were houses so beautiful the mayor himself could be living in one and three blocks away there was a housing project where it maybe wasn't always so nice but it was still a lot nicer than some other places. Her mother had waited for years for an opening at Cathedral to come up. They had been lucky to get in at all, they had waited in line with everybody else and they got their spot fair and square. It wasn't like they bothered anybody. They stayed down there like mice. They didn't take any of the air away from the Doyles, any of their sunlight.

Doyle took off his glasses and pressed the bridge of his nose between his forefinger and thumb. Then the kettle began to whistle and he got up and turned off the burner on the stove without making Kenya her tea.

'Her driver's license said Roxbury,' Tip said. They had gone through her wallet, after all, looked at its sad contents, counted her money.

'I don't know.' Kenya's voice was breaking apart. 'We used to live in Roxbury when I was little. What difference does it make where we live?'

Doyle, who should have had the presence of mind to lie, instead said, 'It's very close, that's all.'

Kenya looked at her hands. She wanted to ask

212

them how far away she and her mother were supposed to stay but she knew she wouldn't be able to make the words come out of her mouth without some kind of bleating sob and she would not do that.

Doyle would have preferred to not know any of this. If given the choice between yesterday and today he would have opted for yesterday when Tip stood on two solid ankles and complained about having to see Jesse Jackson speak about the responsibilities inherent to democracy. Yesterday Doyle only worried about Teddy cutting his American history survey in order to seek out the company of his uncle. Yesterday Sullivan was scarcely a thought that crossed his mind, seeing as how he never returned phone calls from Africa. Yesterday he did not know that this girl Kenya and her mother lived in unnerving proximity to his family. They could have brushed past him in the aisles of the grocery store or stood beside him on the train and it never would have mattered. After all, he had apparently spent the past twenty years in a state of complete oblivion to their presence, and if he could roll back the clock even slightly then he could slip back inside the comfort of all he didn't know. But no one was offering him yesterday over today. No one got to choose anything where time was concerned. If time could be rolled back then what would be the point in stopping someplace so close? He would go all the way to the year before Bernadette died and find another outcome for her illness by catching it sooner, and in doing so he would lay down a different set of cards for Sullivan as well. This child who presently sat at the wide-planked kitchen table that Bernadette had purchased in Vermont and lashed to the roof of her car would return to the crowd scenes, another face that blended in with so many others, were it not for a fact that too much of life unfolded beyond his control. But then he looked at his son picking at the edges of his peanut butter toast. Had all of their circumstances been different, he doubted very much that Tip would have been different. Tip's interest in ichthyology was a transcendent force. No matter what had happened in their life, Tip would have grown into a man who saw Jesse Jackson as a waste of his evening, and he would have stood in the snow to argue against attending a reception. If things had been shuffled ever so slightly so that Bernadette had lived and Tennessee had followed them less, who was to say that the car would not have hit Tip squarely in the back last night, snapping his beautiful and much beloved neck as it pushed him forward? Working against every natural inclination, Doyle had to make himself consider that what had happened might not have been the worst thing at all, not by a long shot. It was possible in fact that they had all gotten off easy, everyone except the woman in the hospital. He cleared his throat. He forced himself to try again. 'Lucky for Tip you stayed close,' he said to Kenya.

'Lucky for all of us,' Teddy said, as he had been thinking much the same thing.

Tip considered the point and then he nodded. 'True.'

214

Kenya put her hands flat under her thighs and sat on them. She wanted to compress herself, be smaller. 'We weren't even looking for you last night,' she said, her feelings stung. 'It's not like all we do is follow you around.'

'Then why were you at the Jackson lecture?' Doyle asked her.

'You're hardly *ever* at the lectures anymore. We go all the time. We go lots of places where we don't even think about you.' Kenya knew that her tone was rude but she meant every word of it. 'Sometimes one will be really good and my mother will say, 'I sure wish Tip and Teddy had come to hear that.' Or it will be boring and long and she's glad you stayed at home. I wish we got to stay at home more but my mother says we have to hear what they have to say.'

Teddy leaned towards her. Anyone could see how patient he was. He looked like he wanted nothing more in the world than to make sense of what she was talking about. 'You have to hear what who has to say?'

'You know, the guys who make the speeches.'

'Why in the world do you have to hear all that?' Tip asked her.

Kenya reached up and gave one of her braids a single sharp yank. 'She likes politics, I guess.'

'So you're saying that she goes to hear lectures not because she thinks we'll be there but because she enjoys it herself?' Doyle felt an unmistakable flutter in his chest. No matter how he felt about this woman, he had a desire to slap his hand flat against the table and shout to his sons, *Are you listening to this?*

'I don't know how much she enjoys it but she thinks it's something that a person has to do.'

'If that's the case, then it proves that certain interests can't be passed on genetically or environmentally,' Tip said.

'I think it's brilliant,' Doyle said. He patted Kenya's shoulder and then sent her up to the top floor to get her coat and her mother's purse. 'And get the hat,' he called after her. 'You can wear her hat.'

They remained very quiet, the three of them listening to her footfall on the stairs going up and up. 'We have an eleven-year-old stalker,' Tip whispered.

'I don't think we can blame the child. The child just follows her mother,' Doyle said. His coffee was cold and he pushed it away.

Tip stretched his leg up into the chair where Kenya had been sitting. 'I was making a joke.'

'Why do we have to blame either of them?' Teddy said.

'Because they follow you,' Doyle said. 'They lurk behind bushes without your knowledge. Even if they're doing it to save your life it is not a natural relationship.'

Teddy stood up and stretched his arms over his head while he yawned. He had gotten up too early. 'Forget it. They're nothing to us, okay? They're political groupies following a former mayor, but I'm still going to take her over to her apartment and help her pack. Now that I know where they live I don't suppose I'll be gone very long.'

Tip shook his head. 'I'll take her,' he said.

216

'Then we'll go straight on to the track. After that she can come with me to the lab for a minute. I still have some work to finish and then we're practically there at Mount Auburn. I'll take her to the hospital and drop her off.'

'You don't think the dead fish could manage one day without you?' his father said, though not unkindly.

'If there isn't time I'll do it later.'

'You can't expect yourself to crutch all over Cambridge in the snow,' Teddy said.

'So go dig the car out and meet me.' Tip swallowed another Percocet and pushed the bottle down in his pants pocket. Normally he would have just left them on the kitchen table and never given it a thought. Normally Sullivan lived in Africa.

'You're exhausted,' Doyle said to Teddy, then he turned to Tip. 'And you've got one functional foot. I'm taking her over to Cathedral.'

'I said I would take her running,' Tip said.

But Doyle wasn't going to budge. Suddenly, with some strong and nameless desire, he wanted the boys at home. 'You'll still take her running. I'll bring her back here and you can take her over to school in a cab. It will take you that much time to get cleaned up anyway. Then Teddy can get some sleep and we can all meet up at the hospital later on.'

At that moment Kenya was back in her coat and her mother's deep green hat whose brim swallowed up her forehead and shadowed her eyes. She held up the keys in her hand, two keys on a silver loop. 'I can go now,' she said.

Doyle stood up and put his cup in the sink. 'Good. I'm ready.'

'It's okay for me to go by myself,' she said. She hadn't thought it would be Doyle who would walk her over. She was sure it would have been one of the boys. 'My mother wouldn't mind.'

'But I would mind, and for the time being you're my responsibility. I don't want you getting caught in a snowdrift.'

Both Teddy and Tip had meant to come along but once Kenya was standing there in the kitchen they didn't want to argue with their father anymore. What they found was that neither one of them was sorry not to go. By telling them they had to stay home, Doyle had made them feel younger than they were, and that, oddly enough, made them think how nice it would be to be younger again. They had liked being the little boys. There was an ease in obedience, never thinking past their father's instruction. For a long time after their mother's death Doyle was able to protect them, and all there was in the world to worry about was what would happen that night on Darwin's *Beagle*. It made the brothers think for a moment that Kenya was the lucky one. At eleven, not only could her life be ordered, she still had all those books to look forward to. She could be foolish enough to go to bed at night believing that one day she might grow up to be president.

At the bottom of the steps Doyle and Kenya turned in the same direction, walking down Union Park Street away from Tremont. It was not yet ten o'clock in the morning but most of the sidewalks had been cleared and the snow was neatly banked on either side. 'What I always wanted to know was what happened to the people who lived in that house?' Kenya said, and pointed to a house that was exactly like Doyle's but four doors away. 'I don't think it ever was for sale but one day there were different people living there.'

Doyle nodded. 'The Baughmans. He was a lawyer. The house sold quickly. It might not have even gone on the market, I can't remember. I know they went to New York.'

'They had twin girls.'

'That's right, Scarlett and Lucy.'

'I always thought that would be a lot of fun, having a twin.'

'Did you know them?'

'The girls?' Kenya shook her head. 'Oh, no.'

The wind whipped across the narrow park and Doyle snapped up the collar of his coat so it stood straight. It was so much colder now than it had been the night before. The leafless trees looked brittle standing naked in this little park. The bowls of the two black fountains were filled with snow.

They followed the street past Shawmut, past St. John the Baptist Hellenic Orthodox Church with its enormous mosaics of a sad-eyed Christ on the front of the building. They passed the Cathedral of the Holy Cross where Bernadette's uncle had baptized the boys, where they made their first communions and first confessions with their grade school class, and where John Sullivan came back to say the mass for Bernadette when she died. It was not her uncle's parish but it was theirs and the bishop made special allowances for Doyle's family. Doyle saw the cathedral as a joyless structure, the granite Gothic Revival so massive and foreboding that it was impossible to imagine that anything as light as faith had ever existed within its walls. He wondered if it was all those years of going to mass at the cathedral that had ground religion out of him. Perhaps if he had attended a more modest church, maybe even the Hellenic Orthodox closer to the house, he might have done a better job of holding on to God, or perhaps religion had only ever been a campaign device for him, as Sullivan so often suggested. When he knew that he was finished in politics, he let himself be finished with his faith as well. As a law partner he was no longer required to be the good Catholic son of Boston.

'Are you and your mother Catholic?' Doyle asked.

Kenya nodded. 'Sure. We're all Catholic.'

Cathedral Grammar School sat between the church and the housing project, a tall chain link fence wrapping up its basketball court tight. It would have been full of children normally but this morning everything was empty with the snow. Doyle had a real affection for this building. He thought of the countless plays he had attended to watch his boys dressed up as shepherds or sheep, the parent-teacher conferences spent sitting beside the teacher's desk in undersized chairs to hear how well Tip was doing and how mightily Teddy struggled. He thought of the hallways lined with lockers, the construction paper butterflies stuck to classroom doors, the primordial spaghetti suppers that were the cornerstone of a Catholic education. Sullivan had gone to Cathedral Grammar as well. Teddy and Tip had followed him there. Later, Teddy went around the corner to Cathedral High and Tip took the bus to Boston Latin. It was one of the reasons Bernadette had wanted to buy their house in the first place. She had looked at the schools before they ever had children to enroll. She loved the idea of walking her imaginary children over in the morning and picking them up in the afternoon. Doyle had asked her if she loved the idea of the school being next door to a public housing project. 'I'll thank God if it saves them from only seeing other Irish kids all the time,' she said.

Of course in the end it was Doyle who wound up walking the boys to school in the morning and rushing home when he could to pick them up in the afternoons. He blessed Bernadette for having the good sense to keep them all so close together. 'Do you go to school here?' Doyle said, and pointed up at the building. She was a smart little girl after all, and he knew there were a certain number of scholarships. He had served on the scholarship committee.

Kenya shook her head. 'It's private.'

Past the school they walked into the first courtyard of the housing project, but now he let her lead him. 'We're towards the back,' she said. 'It looks pretty in the snow, sort of like everything's just been painted.'

He knew what it looked like without the snow. He had been the mayor after all and on the City Council before that. He was familiar with the housing projects, their budgets and statistics. He was especially familiar with Cathedral, sitting as it did in his own backyard. It was better than a lot of places. The sprawl of mustardy-yellow brick buildings turned into something of a maze and no good ever came of mazes, but there was a playground that kids actually used. Because it sat hip to hip against a better neighborhood, it was patrolled with greater regularity. The police pushed down hard on the nefarious elements and in doing so managed to hassle most of the decent citizens as well, so the crime rates stayed down and for the most part no one was happy. Boston Medical Center was only blocks away. There was a women's shelter, a food pantry, plenty of resources and yet every one of them was stretched thin enough to snap. If Doyle could have been the mayor again he liked to think there were some things he would do differently.

Once they were through the second archway they passed three Hispanic girls standing against a wall smoking cigarettes in the cold. They had on puffy nylon jackets but none of them wore hats. 'Hey,' Kenya said lightly because they had turned their eyes to her, to Doyle walking behind her.

'Fucking freezing,' one of the girls replied, as if she had been asked about the weather.

Kenya quickened their pace slightly and led him through an exterior door that was propped open with a brick. A fine wedge of snow had dusted into the hallway and was marked with foot-prints. She unlocked the door to her ground floor apartment, using the larger key for the top lock and the smaller one for the knob. She switched on a light inside the door and when they were both safely in she closed the door behind her and locked it again. *Just like you've been taught*, Doyle thought. The lightbulb was weak and the apartment stayed dark. 'My mother wouldn't be thrilled about you coming over,' she said. 'She'd get all worried about cleaning everything first.' She went to pull back the curtains and when she did she kept her gaze out the window for a minute, looking at a narrow walkway and then another covered over window like her own. 'We don't have that many people over.'

But the apartment, albeit small and dark, was perfectly clean. There was a long floral sofa and an easy chair on one side of the room, a table and two chairs beside the kitchenette. There was a round-faced clock on the wall with a pendulum that swung behind a small pane of glass. The place was stuffy and had the vague smell of something that had burned. Doyle wondered if that came from another apartment.

'I don't think I've ever been in one of these apartments before,' Doyle said.

'You can sit down if you want to,' she said. 'The couch is really comfortable.'

Doyle sat down obediently and the couch pulled him back. It would have been impossible to sit there for any length of time without falling into a coma-like sleep. 'Very nice.'

'People give my mom lots of stuff. The clock and the couch, both of the lamps. It all came from the people she works for.'

'Where does she work?' Doyle wondered how they had come this far without him knowing what Kenya's mother did for a living.

'She takes care of old people. It's called assisted living.' Kenya said the words carefully because it was what she considered to be a grown-up phrase. 'She used to work in a nursing home but the assisted living place is a lot nicer. Sometimes when the people die their families give you furniture. It's still hard work though. A couple of the old people are really mean but my mother says they can't help it. They're frustrated.'

'I suppose old people are like everybody else,' Doyle said. He had a sudden, uncomfortable vision of himself as an old person, the furniture of his little apartment winding up in the little apartment of the women who cared for him. 'I can call them if you'd like, let them know that your mother's been in an accident.'

Kenya nodded. 'That's a really good idea. I've been worried about them firing her for not coming to work.'

Doyle looked around the little room. There was a door on the other side, surely a single bedroom, a bathroom. 'Where do you stay when your mother's at work?'

'I'm at school, or I'm at after-school.' Kenya swept her hand over the kitchen counter and pulled some loose mail, bills, and fliers, into a neat stack. 'On Tuesday nights I go to the Girl Scouts. She tries not to work at night but if that's the schedule then I stay at home. I used to go with her to work but if anybody finds out she gets in a lot of trouble. I used to stay in a room that was empty but then the old people told on her. They all liked me fine and they still told.'

'You stay here by yourself?'

Kenya slipped out of her coat and laid it over the back of the chair. She took off her mother's hat. 'It's no big deal. I put both of the locks on the door and I leave the television on. Someday she'll get a job where she'll only have to work while I'm in school. That's going to be perfect.'

Doyle was glad he'd left the boys at home. He did not want to see them here. He did not want to picture them sitting on the too soft sofa, their too long legs pressing the edges of the coffee table. He used to find Bernadette sitting in their room sometimes after they had gone to sleep. She did it even more once she was sick, when she still had it in her to climb all those stairs. She would be sitting in the dark and he would come and sit on the arm of the chair beside her and for awhile they would listen to the boys breathe. 'They could have gone to someone else,' she'd always say to him. That was the part of it she never could get over: that these sons who were so unquestionably hers could just as easily have gone to another home, a different fate. But what they never said was that they had already belonged to someone else, and they could have just as easily stayed where they were.

'What do you want me to bring over?' Kenya said.

Doyle felt himself flush with emotion and he was ashamed. 'Whatever you'd bring over to stay at a friend's house.'

'I don't go overnight,' she said. 'My mom doesn't like me to go.'

He tried to find a handkerchief in his pocket. 'Do you have a Kleenex? All the cold is making my nose run.'

Kenya went through the door of the other room and came back with a handful of toilet paper. Doyle thanked her. She stood in front of him while he blotted his eyes. There seemed to be something she didn't know how to say. There was an old white man crying in her living room. What was she going to say about that? 'Don't worry about me,' Doyle told her. 'I'm fine.'

She twisted back and forth on one foot, just the slightest movement of nervousness. 'I don't know how to pack exactly,' she said.

He blew his nose and stuffed the paper in his pocket. The child stood in front of him nibbling her lower lip and he smiled at her. 'Kenya, I have no doubt that you could land a plane if the situation called for it. Packing for someone as smart as you wouldn't require any thought at all. Besides, if you get it wrong we can turn around and come right back.'

With those few words, so true and therefore easily given, she all but fell down next to him on the couch in a swoon of happiness. He took her hand and patted it with authority. 'Bring a nightgown, the warmest one you've got. Underwear, socks, an outfit for tomorrow, something to run in. Bring your schoolbooks.'

'Tomorrow's Saturday.'

'Bring them anyway. The boys are going to

226

want to see what you're studying. You know that Tip's going to want to help you with your homework so if you don't have any just invent something. It will make him feel good.'

She got up then and went into the other room on her mission. He could hear the sound of drawers opening and closing. He wanted to take her back to the house and play her some Schubert. Not the lieder. The lieder would be too overwhelming for a child. One of the quintets would be exactly right for her. He wondered if she had ever listened to Schubert before. She had only just now gone and he wanted her to come back to him. He found he could not bear to be in this room without her. 'Let me know if you need any help,' he said.

'What do I put it all in?' she called to him, and he was able to catch himself before he said the wrong thing.

'Put it in a pillowcase,' he said. 'Then we're going home.'

8

After all the pills it was hard to follow the story but it went something like this: two men came into her room, two different men, and they took the sheet she laid on at either end of the bed and they said, 'On the count of three,' and they lifted her. Sweet Mother of God. She never knew that pain could form a light, a bright and blinding pool of heat. It poured through her. It broke open in her hip and flooded through her gut — her fingertips and teeth and hair, the rounded pads of her feet — everything that she was belonged to the pain. The pain jarred loose the very deepest part of her heart, a place so secret that she never went there herself. The stone was rolled away from the mouth of the tomb and in that moment she forgot herself and called out the name of her friend, the one whose name she never called, the one she tried her best not to think of.

'That's right,' the man at her feet said, working to make his voice sound soothing and being no good at it. He had already forgotten her name. He forgot it the second he crossed her off his list. 'We're going to Tennessee.'

The hallway was paved in cobblestones and they banged forth over them with inhuman violence while rattling through every conversation two men could have about basketball. Full-court and half-court pickup. NBA or college ball. Eastern versus Western Division. It was impossible that a hospital could be so enormous. She didn't know where they were going but it would have taken less time just to wheel her back to Cathedral. It occurred to her they might be steering around aimlessly just to have more time to talk. Every corner they turned put a knife in her side and soon, she knew, that knife would cut her in half. 'Celtics? Man, tell me you're making this up. You could not be interested in the Celtics.'

The man at her feet scolded back. 'Loyalty,' he said. 'Loyalty. Do you even know the word?' They chattered on like women, a basketball of happy banter thrown back and forth from head to feet. They weren't even interesting to each other. It wasn't worth the effort it took to make sense of the words and after awhile Tennessee stopped trying. She let the voices float above her like an unbroken string of lights. The entire room was going down now, abruptly stopping, starting again. People came in and stood very close beside her, not speaking to her but laughing with the basketball men. Then somewhere a door slid open and just like that the first group left and new people came on. Everyone agreed that there hadn't been a snow like this since '78.

'Thomas, did you get caught here?'

'All night, Mister,' Thomas replied. 'All day and then all night.'

'That's too much,' the Mister said. 'You tell them I said they need to let you out of here soon.'

Thomas acknowledged that this was his last

delivery. 'I drop her off and I am gone.'

It went on this way until they reached some ground floor in hell. 'Last stop,' the man above her head said in a jolly voice. They pushed her out and bumped into another hallway, this one congested with people like herself laid out on rolling slabs. That was when the two men left her. No goodbye. No good luck. She could only tell they were going because their voices receded, dribbled off towards the edge of her vision and then disappeared. Later on a woman came and stood beside her table.

'Ms. Moser,' the woman's voice said. 'Did you have some ice?'

'My stomach hurts,' Tennessee said, surprised that she was able to find the words, but it *did* hurt, and the pain was both deep and wide.

'It's your hip.' The woman said it with such simple authority that Tennessee wondered if she had a way of knowing. Her hip hurt, yes, she knew that, but the stomach was something else altogether.

'Stomach,' she said again.

The woman snapped the chart shut, making a breeze that fanned Tennessee's forehead in a lovely way. 'Did you have some ice?'

Drop the curtain. After that there was nothing, maybe some sleep. It was very hard to say what was real sleep and what was a lapse in memory or a smooth slope of medication that strapped her into a luge and sent her straight over the icy edge of a cliff. She knew how to go with it. She did not try to grab hold of anything to slow herself down. When she woke up she was in a regular room again and the blinds were pulled high. She blinked her eyes a couple of times against the honeyed light.

'You can flat sleep,' a woman's voice said. It wasn't the one who was asking her about the ice. It was somebody else.

Tennessee ran her tongue around the inside of her mouth in order to loosen up the words. Her teeth felt small and unfamiliar. 'How long have I been out?'

The woman got up from the chair where she had been sitting and came and stood beside the bed. She was dark skinned and terribly pretty with her hair in a mop of short, tight braids. She was wearing a pumpkin orange shirt dress that buttoned up the front and a pair of scuff slippers.

It was the dress that was familiar first. Even when she could only see it as a field of color she remembered. Tennessee had loved that dress. The color put out a heat all its own. She would have asked to borrow it but she was at least three sizes bigger, six inches taller.

'I've been waiting for you to wake up all day,' the woman said.

It came to her one piece at a time, the dress, the voice. Her vision was blurry from all the sleep but Tennessee in her bed blinked and blinked again. She had no choice but to admit to what she saw. *Ne plus ultra*. It was a phrase a teacher had used in school. She hadn't thought of it in years but then she'd had no reason to. There by her bedside stood Tennessee Alice Moser, beloved, dearest and best. Tennessee

Alice Moser, who at the greenest age of twenty-five had died of urosepsis in the emergency room of Boston Medical Center before anyone had ordered the tests to figure out what was wrong with her. Her truest friend, Tennessee Alice Moser, the big-hearted, small-boned girl for whom she had named herself, was now almost ten years dead, but standing in this hospital room anyone would have to say she was as fresh as a blade of new spring grass. How perfect she was! The clock had stopped and left her twenty-five and twenty-five was young. Not one bit of her stooped forward. Her eyes were fire bright. Her shoulders were straight and back. She even smiled like a girl. 'My God,' Tennessee said. 'How sweet you are!'

Tennessee Alice Moser touched the back of Tennessee's cheek with her hand. 'You too, girl of mine.'

'Am I dreaming or dead?' Not that it mattered to her either way. It was fine if it meant getting to see her friend. She was always sorry she hadn't had those kind of dreams people say they have, the ones where the person you love the most comes back and sits by your bed and holds your hand after they're gone. She had not had a single vision of Tennessee Alice Moser since she had gone into the little cubical of the emergency room to say goodbye to the body that was there. In that last moment their roles were reversed from what they were now: Tennessee Alice Moser lay in her bed, eyes closed, chin tipped back, and Tennessee sat alongside, holding her cooling hand. Since that night she'd had only a few small photographs kept safe in a *Field Guide to North American Fishes* to rely on, and to tell the truth she hadn't looked at those in years. They broke her heart.

Tennessee Alice Moser looked down at herself, smoothed the sides of her dress with her hands. 'You are neither one exactly. Sort of in between the two. Or you can think of it as anesthesia.' She leaned over and pushed the automatic button to raise up her friend's head.

'Is it all right to do that?' Tennessee asked. 'I think I've just been operated on.'

'Don't worry. I'll put you out flat again before I go.'

'Thoughtful girl.'

'That surgery,' she shook her head. 'Be glad you weren't awake to see it.'

'Awful?'

Tennessee Alice Moser squinched up her eyes and then covered her face with her hands. 'It was so bloody.'

'You never were any good with bloody.'

She sighed and dropped down into a chair beside the bed. 'I was not.'

Tennessee was smiling now and couldn't stop, thinking of her friend having to watch not only the surgery but everything that happened in her life and in Kenya's life all these years gone by. 'Do you think I'll live through this?' She had meant to be teasing but Tennessee Alice Moser reached into her own hair and pulled on one of her little braids.

'I don't know yet. It's kinda up in the air.'

The vagueness of the answer should have

been, at the very least, a cause for more questions but at the present moment Tennessee was easily distracted. 'Kenya does that.'

'Does what?'

'Yanks her hair. I could tell her to stop it for the rest of my life and she couldn't. She doesn't know she's doing it.'

'You think she looks like me?'

'Carbon copy, but that's not even what I'm saying. She *is* like you. All the little things she does are you. Sometimes I just have to stare at her. It blows my mind.'

Tennessee Alice Moser looked down at her hands in her lap and she smiled.

Her friend in the bed went on, glad to have someone to say this to since she thought about it every day without anyone to tell. 'Sometimes I feel like my entire life has been some sort of study in genetics,' Tennessee said. 'There's Kenya doing things like you, and then I wonder if my boys are doing things like me.'

'I imagine they are. I imagine that's how it works.'

'You should see the way she runs, like it was born in her bones. The coaches always say to me, 'Were you a runner? Was her daddy a runner?' She's eleven years old and I couldn't keep up with her on a bike.'

'I think maybe Ebee ran. I'm not sure. You just tell them you were Wilma Rudolph in your last life.' She took her friend's hand in the hospital bed and turned it over. She lined them up palm to palm then entwined the fingers until they were locked up tight.

'In my last life I was somebody named Beverly who had two little boys and gave them up. In this life I'm you and I have a daughter.'

'You have my daughter, yes you do.' Her voice was distracted then, miles away.

Tennessee looked at her friend and worried. She had always worried if she'd done the right thing. 'I tried to find Ebee,' she said.

'What would you have done with him?'

'I thought he might have wanted Kenya,' she said, but she really didn't think he would have. He had hardly even wanted Tennessee Alice Moser. He had been less like a boyfriend and more like a couple of weekends, a couple of good nights out. Tennessee had only met him once in the stairwell. She did not exactly remember his face. What she could remember was Tennessee Alice Moser looking over her shoulder in that pumpkin colored dress that fit her so neatly, her smile wide enough to show even her back teeth. She would not think ill of any man who had made her friend so happy, but who's to say he would have been interested in a baby he hadn't known about to begin with? 'Here you go, total stranger,' she would say, handing Kenya over. 'Here is my beloved baby girl. You take her.' Not that it mattered. She didn't find him. She searched and did not find.

'No,' Tennessee Alice Moser said. 'I don't think Ebee would have been right.'

'I looked for your mother, too.'

'Well, you would have had to look for her where I am now.'

'Really?'

'She's dead, and one of my sisters, too. I guess we didn't turn out to be such a hardy bunch. The other sister I would have to say not a chance. I wouldn't have wanted her to get her hands on my girl.' Tennessee Alice Moser sighed and scratched off a dried clump of blood that was clinging to the bandage on her friend's forehead. 'No, you're the one I'd have picked if I'd ever given the whole thing five minutes of thought. Unless,' she said, and there she stopped.

'Unless?'

'Well, didn't you ever think of putting her up for adoption?'

Tennessee was frankly stunned. Kenya, who she had stood by every minute of her life as if she was her very flesh? 'Adoption?'

Her friend brushed the surprise aside without even considering it. 'It's not like it's a completely foreign concept. Your boys did pretty well in the system. They wound up in a big house, they went to good schools. Don't get me wrong, I think you've done a wonderful job and I'm grateful to you, I am. I know you love her and I know that counts for everything, but I have to tell you I've wondered. You were the one going back to college. You were the one talking about law school. Then you take my baby and all of that's gone?'

'I couldn't give her away. She wasn't mine *to* give away back then.' Tennessee worked to keep a steady voice. 'I kept thinking I'd find the right person, the person she belonged to. You can't just take a baby back once you've adopted them out.'

236

Tennessee Alice Moser lowered her eyebrows and looked at her friend hard, just looked at her and said nothing, giving her time to come to her own conclusion until finally Tennessee sighed and picked at the tape that held the IV line into the top of her hand. 'Okay, all right. So I didn't want to give her up. Is that what you want to hear me say? I was terrified that I was going to find one of those people I was looking for. But what you're forgetting is how sick I was over you after you died, and how Kenya and I made each other feel better. Don't you remember how good she was? I'd go and pick her up after work and she would just smile and grab for me. I'd pick her up in my arms and I thought I would die for loving her so much. I never wanted to put her down. I wasn't going to give her away to strangers. Things worked out for my boys, you're right, but I was stupid then and I was young. I didn't stop to think about all the really bad people there are out there who could wind up raising your child. I couldn't take that chance again, even if I had been lucky before. I'd already given up my own boys, you know. I'd given up my family. I'd given up you. At some point it's just enough.'

Tennessee Alice Moser nodded, looking like the wisest twenty-five-year-old that God had ever created. 'I never thought about leaving her. I remember when she was born I looked at her and I thought, I am going to be with you for the rest of your life.'

'Well, you meant to,' Tennessee said.

She brushed her hand against her friend's

forehead. She felt so wonderfully warm. 'What am I supposed to call you, anyway?'

In the hospital bed, Tennessee rolled over onto her side. She felt the stiff crunch of the bandages taped to her hip but no pain. There had been such a raging sea of pain and now there was nothing, not even a stitch or an ache. She flexed her foot back and forth to check again. 'Beverly? I don't know. There's nobody left who calls me Beverly now but I imagine I could answer to it.'

'I'll call you Tennessee.'

Tennessee shook her head, feeling guilty. 'You shouldn't do that. It's your name.'

'It's not like I'm using it for anything.'

Tennessee really didn't know what she needed to explain to her friend and what her friend already knew. It seemed possible that their lives, Kenya's and her own, were like a show that Tennessee Alice Moser watched, and all of their details and decisions were already understood. It seemed equally possible that from time to time she could have turned her face away, missing certain days or weeks that were important to the story. 'It was all I could figure out to do,' she said. 'I knew I couldn't adopt her myself. It would cost a fortune and take forever and they probably wouldn't have given her to me anyway.'

'No, you were smart. You were always the smartest person I knew. I really think you would have been a politician if you'd kept up with school.' Tennessee Alice Moser had dreamed big for her friend as was her inclination. 'That's what I think. You always had important things to say. You made a million times more sense than any of

238

those guys you used to go listen to.'

'I was never going to be a politician.'

'You were. You understood the system.'

Tennessee shook her head. 'There isn't any system. I found that out when I took Kenya. The law only goes to a certain point and then it stops. When all this was going on, when I wasn't finding Ebee or your mother and I knew I wanted to keep her for myself, that's when I realized there really wasn't anybody out there watching what we did. I mean, they still watched me in Filene's, they watched at the grocery store to make sure I didn't run off with a quart of milk, but take someone's child? Why, they all but held open the door for me. I left that apartment in Jamaica Plain with Kenya in my arms and moved to Roxbury and not one person had a thing to say about it. Even good old Mrs. Roberts next door who watched Kenya the night you died, she never asked me how I was managing to keep her.' Tennessee closed her eyes and thought about her daughter's face. It was too open, too bright, too beautiful like her mother's. 'That's why I keep her so close to me now. I make sure that no one's going to walk off with her.'

'Maybe you keep her too close.'

Tennessee shook her head. 'Forgive me, but you might not understand the way the world is today. It's a dangerous place. You've got to be careful now, especially with a daughter.'

'It's always been that way with daughters since way before either one of us was born, but that still doesn't mean you needed to keep her inside so much. You didn't have to turn her whole life into a big secret.'

'Her life's not a secret.'

'Sure it is. You drag her around everywhere after those boys. She's not allowed to talk to them, she's not allowed to tell anybody what she's doing. That's not fun for a little kid.'

Tennessee was hurt. She had only been trying to live her life in balance, to do her best for everyone concerned and that meant all of her children. 'You think I should have given up my boys?'

'I think you already *did* give up your boys. I think you should have paid more attention to the girl you had. If you were going to take on my name and my daughter then I wish you had taken on a little more of me. Instead you went to work some dead-end nursing home job like I had. Did you think that's what it meant to be like me? You know how much I hated that job. You were a secretary going back to school. You were the smart one. If you really wanted to be like me you could have at least had a little fun.'

Now Tennessee was crying. She kept her eyes closed and let the tears push out the sides. You should have stuck around, was what she was thinking, see if you could have managed it any better yourself.

Tennessee Alice Moser shook her head. She had waited such a long time to come back and now she was being nothing but critical. She had missed her friend terribly, this woman who had done everything she could to do right by her memory. 'You must be thirsty,' she said in a conciliatory voice, and her quietly weeping friend admitted that she was. Tennessee Alice Moser poured out a cup of water from the little Styrofoam pitcher on the night table, bending the straw down to reach her lips. 'What you realize after awhile,' she said, 'is that there are a lot of things you think you're going to do and it turns out you can't. I was going to keep Kenya with me but then I died. You were going to keep her with you and you got hit by that damn car. So part of it is intention and part of it is luck. We've got very fine intentions but our luck isn't so great.' She smiled then, suddenly remembering the way she was wrong. Tennessee opened her lips to take in the straw. 'Except we did find each other. That was luck.'

'That was the best luck I ever had.' Tennessee could see them in her mind, two girls in that rotten apartment building in Jamaica Plain, passing each other on the sidewalk in the summer heat, in the hallway in the winter bundled up in scarves, passing each other for such a long time before the constant recognition wore them down and they started to say hello. 'I couldn't get over your crazy name. When you first introduced yourself to me, I thought, who would name their daughter Tennessee?'

'My father used to tell me, just be glad your mama didn't want to go back to Mississippi.'

'I wouldn't have gone through with it if they'd named you Mississippi.' Both of them laughed like this was the craziest thing they'd ever heard when really they were just wanting something to laugh at to bring them together again.

'Now you're living out my curse. Everybody has to ask you the same stupid questions they always asked me.'

'Tennessee like the state. I say it every time.' She reached up and put one finger on her friend's chin. 'You didn't get old.'

'That's the way it works.'

'I miss you all the time. I miss you more than I miss my family, my boys.'

'Scoot over,' Tennessee Alice Moser said, and then she climbed into the hospital bed beside her friend. She was always the little one. There was always room for her on the sofa, in a chair. She tucked her head down on the shoulder that she had known best in the world when she was alive.

'How is it being dead?' Tennessee asked.

'It's good,' she said, but she didn't look up. 'It's not like streets of gold or anything, but it's nice. I hardly ever think about being alive.'

'But you must think of it a little bit,' Tennessee said. 'I mean, you're here now.' She put her hand on the back of her friend's head, touched the little ropes of hair. She was here. She could feel her.

'Well, yes and no. It's hard to explain. It really has more to do with you thinking about me.'

'But I used to think about you all the time and you never showed up before.'

'But now you're sick.'

Tennessee worked this over in her head and concluded that either she was just imagining things or she was about to die. Neither thought appealed to her, but neither thought particularly troubled her either. Maybe it had something to do with the medication they had given her for surgery. 'Did you know you were going to die that night?'

'Not one clue. Did you?'

'I did, but not until just before it happened. Even when we got to the hospital I thought you were just crazy sick. I'd been sitting in the waiting room half the night and all of a sudden I thought, She's going to die, just as clear as if someone had said it to me. About ten minutes later the doctor came out and told me.'

'I'm sorry about that,' Tennessee Alice Moser said, and she meant it. It must have been awful for her, leaving that hospital alone.

'It was nearly three in the morning by the time I got home and I woke Mrs. Roberts up. I took Kenya back to your apartment and we slept in your bed. She didn't even really wake up, just cried for a minute in her sleep and then settled down again. She was so good. She was right about eighteen months then, not too much older than Tip was when he went to live with the Doyles, but somehow when I looked at Kenya it all seemed so much sadder to me. It seemed like the cruelest thing in the world that this baby had to lose her mother. I couldn't stop thinking that if we had just left for the hospital a little sooner . . . '

'You tried to get me to go.'

'I should have made you.'

Tennessee Alice Moser propped up on one elbow and looked at her friend. She brought her face down close. 'You've been a mother too long. I said no. It was too expensive.' She smiled. She

243

had those pretty teeth just like Kenya. God had given her a short, hard life but a perfect set of straight white teeth to help her endure it.

'You were the one who wanted to be a nurse. You should have known something about medicine.'

'Yeah, I knew I couldn't afford it.'

In those better days when they were both alive and together, Tennessee had had the same apartment as her friend but she was three flights down. They both faced the street. They had the same little closet in the living room, the same bedroom that was not much bigger than a double bed. Tennessee had a better refrigerator because the guy who lived there before her was a junkie. He had torn the door off his refrigerator to put it in front of his window to block out the light, only it wasn't tall enough and never could do the job. When they finally got him out of there the whole thing was beyond repair and they had to buy a new one. It wasn't actually new but it was newer than Tennessee Alice Moser's. By the time they got to be best friends, better than the sisters either one of them was born with, they had each other's keys. They would run up and down the stairs in their nightgowns to borrow some money or lipstick or salt. Everybody called them The Girls, merged the two of them into one even though Tennessee was older, taller, lighter. She came from Rhode Island, though nobody knew that except Tennessee Alice Moser. Tennessee Alice Moser was as slim as a girl even after Kenya was born. She was darker, prettier, and launched into a state of perpetual movement. As close as they were, it was a long time before Tennessee told her friend about the baby she had at eighteen and how once he was born she found she could not take him home even though she had been planning to. She put down her story brick by brick, checking to see how Tennessee Alice Moser took what she heard before trying her out with the next chapter. There are some women to whom you could say, 'I gave away my son,' and they will finish up their glass of wine politely and ask you a couple of questions but when they rise to say good night they are gone permanently. She knew this because her mother was gone. Her sisters were gone. The friends she'd had back in Providence, gone.

'Do you know where he went to?' Tennessee Alice Moser asked.

Indeed she did, though finding out had been an accident. Five days after her baby was born she saw an article in the paper that said a Boston councilman and his wife had adopted a son. It was on the bottom half of the front page, human interest on a slow news day and only news at all because the councilman was white and the son was black. She had walked to the Quick Trip to get away from her family and buy a Dr Pepper and saw it there, a big stack of papers by the checkout and the top one turned over to a white man and white woman holding a baby, holding him up to show his shining face to the camera. They were that proud of him, she could see that. They were proud of his beauty. Tennessee put down the soda and took the paper instead. She went and sat on the curb outside the store and she read. The article said they were naming him Edward but planned to call him Teddy. He was five days old. Anonymous sources were quoted as saying the adoption of this child amounted to political maneuvering, but that wasn't true. She saw the picture. She saw the mother who was holding her baby. She saw the look on the woman's face. Nothing political there.

'How did you know it was your boy?' Tennessee Alice Moser asked.

They were sitting in the living room, drinking wine on Tennessee's mossy green sofa. All those years she had never told anyone and now she was telling because her friend was just that trusted, that dear. It felt like letting go of the breath she had sucked in on the day the nurse came and took him from her arms. It couldn't be a bad thing to tell one person, not when you've been lugging the secret behind you all by yourself year after year.

'I had seen him. I knew he was mine. I knew because the paper said he was five days old.'

'But there must be lots of babies.'

'He was mine,' she said. 'I knew my baby.'

'You would,' her friend said with deference, because at that time she did not have a baby herself.

'And when I got home I sat down and I looked hard at my older boy — '

'Your older boy?'

That was the complication, the thing that made the story into something unnatural. But once she decided to tell there was nothing to do but say every word of it. 'I had an older boy at home. I was keeping him. I could manage with one. But after I saw that picture in the paper I thought, One of you is going to go on and have a very sweet deal, get an education, live in a nice house, be safe all the time, and one of you is going to stay with me. I wasn't feeling so good then, and staying with me didn't sound like anything but a burden this child would have to endure. I started to tell myself that it should be all or nothing, that doing it halfway was a disservice to them both. I had an idea that Tip, he was my big boy, could look after the baby, little as he was himself. They could be together and look after each other. So I went back to the agency I'd given the baby to and I asked them to make the call. The woman I talked to said I was wrong, that it wasn't my baby with the councilman in Boston, but I said for them to take down my number anyway and to call me back. They called the next morning. I was right about it being my baby. I would have known him anywhere.'

Tennessee Alice Moser thought about all of this for a long time. She could see giving up a baby maybe. She could even see how that might be a good thing. But how did you give up the boy that you knew? The one you had fed from your body already, the one who had slept in your bed at night when he cried? 'What did you call Tip back then?'

But Tennessee just shook her head. 'He's Tip.'

Even though she had told all of her story, she waited months before asking her friend if she wanted to come along and sit on a park bench in the South End and eat a sandwich and pretend to talk while the boys walked by them on their way to the Montessori school. Teddy was four by then and Tip was five and they each intermittently held the hand of the redheaded woman and then swung their hands in the air. They were talking, talking, to Bernadette and then to each other, and she was talking back to them. As hard as the two girls on the bench tried they could not hear what was being said. Teddy laughed at something and then for half a dozen steps he hopped with his feet together. Tip kept his chin pointed up, looking at the formations of clouds.

'This is why you moved to Boston?'

'Yes.'

'Do you watch them all the time?'

The first time she had only come up for the day, thinking she would just hang around until she could get one look to see if they were okay, and then that would be enough. But it wasn't enough. She tore off half of the sandwich without looking down and passed it to her friend, her best friend, the only person she had ever told. 'It isn't all the time.'

'My God,' Tennessee Alice Moser had said, her gaze trailing after them like the tail of a kite, 'those are the most beautiful boys in human history. I have never seen anything like them in my life.' Even after they crossed the street at the end of the block and fell from sight, she kept her face turned towards the place they had been. She never said, *What were you thinking of?* She never said, *How could you have let them go?*

'Sometimes now I wonder,' Tennessee said.

'Wonder what?' Tennessee Alice Moser was there beside her in the bed and she pulled up the sheet and blanket as the room was cold.

'About what I did, giving up the boys.' Tennessee was confused now. They weren't at the park. She wasn't really regretting having let the boys go, not at this moment. She was regretting it all those years before. She thought she was saying it on that day they watched the children pass, Tip looking up, Teddy looking down. Tennessee Alice Moser says, *They are beautiful*, and she says in reply, *What have I done?*

'You'll never know how things might have turned out,' her friend said. 'Look at me. I wish I'd gone to the hospital sooner, though frankly I wonder if even then they would have put enough hustle into it to save me. I wish I hadn't died and I wish that I could have been the one to raise Kenya, but then I think, Look how nicely she turned out with you. Even though there were some things I would have done differently, I have to say she turned out golden. That's really all you can think. Your boys are good. They seem like happy boys. They may have turned out better with you and they may have turned out worse, but when you look at what you have to work with, you look at the way things are now, you'd have to feel it all went pretty much okay.'

Tennessee tried to pull herself into this present moment: her boys were grown, her friend was dead but here. She did not for the most part feel regret. She could look around the apartment she shared with Kenya, she could every now and then catch a glimpse of Tip walking into the Museum of Comparative Zoology, and she understood that the road from her living room to that museum would have been much, much harder than the road from Union Park. By offering them up, and by the blind good luck of where they landed, she knew she had given them something substantial, but that was not to say she didn't add up the losses every now and then. For some reason the losses were presently sticking in her throat. 'I know they're good, but I always wondered how much they suffered from not having a mother. I never thought about them winding up with no mother.' Tennessee went through a time of terrible doubt after Bernadette died. That was not what she had bargained for, that Teddy and Tip would be motherless boys. She kept waiting, thinking Mr. Doyle would marry again, but all those years she never saw a woman with them at the symphony, at the lectures. The only woman she ever saw walking the boys home from school was the housekeeper. Sometimes she wondered if it was a job she should apply for.

Tennessee Alice Moser poked her in the shoulder. 'It's not as if they don't have a mother, after all. They have a mother who's willing to get run over for them.'

'You know what I mean. It does boys good to be around a woman.'

'Good looking boys like that? I'm sure they've been around plenty. And anyway, you can't think about it like that. There's always going to be something missing. There is for everybody. If you gave them a mother then they would have suffered not having a father,' Tennessee Alice Moser said. 'Unless you think their father would have stayed around.'

For a moment Tennessee remembered that boy, how young he was, how his back had felt beneath her hands. It embarrassed her now to think of him.

'I think it would be nice if Kenya had a father,' Tennessee Alice Moser said.

'I'll try and find someone to marry.'

At this her friend let go a laugh too long and too rich for a hospital room.

'You don't think I could get married?'

She sputtered for a moment and then pulled the pillow over her face to calm herself. 'Really?' she said. 'No. No, I don't. You don't tell anybody anything. Who's going to marry someone who doesn't talk?'

'I talk. I'm talking to you.'

'You need to talk more. You should have made some other friends. Even if you didn't get married you could have done that.'

'How was I going to make friends? I couldn't tell them about my boys or about you or Kenya or even what my name was. I don't know how much there is after you take all that away.'

Tennessee Alice Moser ignored her and settled her head back into the cradle of her crossed arms. 'It would have been nicest if you could have married Mr. Doyle. I always thought that one day he was going to look up and see you. He was going to say, 'Excuse me, miss, but we must have an awful lot in common, seeing as how we are always going to the same places.''

'He's old,' Tennessee said. 'He's white. He used to be the mayor.'

'None of those things have hurt your boys.'

'And he's never seen me. I've spent the last twenty years making sure of that.'

'He saw you last night.'

Tennessee covered her face with her hands. She could feel the gentle tug of the IV needle in her vein. 'I don't know what I'm going to do about that.'

'Just be grateful. You're going to need help and he's the person who's going to help you.'

'I wouldn't take anything from him.'

'With Kenya,' she said, her voice at once so certain and so calm it seemed to take her by the hand and walk her forward. 'He's going to have to help you with Kenya.'

Tennessee would never say it, not even to her best friend in the world, but she did in fact have a fondness for Mr. Doyle that was a sort of affection. After all those years you get to know a person even if you've never spoken to him. She could tell that his moods were consistent for the most part and that he was fair. So many times she had seen him carry Teddy asleep to the car when he was young, or put a light hand on Tip's back when they were walking. He never pandered to the boys, he wasn't trying to make them into friends instead of sons, but he was proud of them, as proud as she was, and they had grown up in the light of his pride. She had seen him waiting for them, she had seen him frustrated, but she never heard him raise his voice or turn away when they were talking.

As a mayor there were things he could have done better, but as a father she had never faulted him. She did not fault him for trying to steer them towards politics. Tennessee understood that. What Mr. Doyle couldn't see was that the boys, while bright and dear and brave, knew nothing of sacrifice. They had never been asked to give anything up, not like Mr. Doyle had, not like she had. Even the place where Bernadette had been, Mr. Doyle filled that up by giving them twice as much of himself. And while she'd wished that he would find someone else, some nice woman who would replace what they'd lost, she often wondered if he felt that his wife was in fact irreplaceable. She imagined that he did not love her any less for being dead. She knew how possible that was. 'I guess Kenya could stay with them for awhile, until I was healed up.'

'At least you know he'll look after her.' Tennessee Alice Moser smoothed the covers out over them with the flat of her hand. It seemed like she was going to say something else, something important, but as long as Tennessee waited it never came.

'The boys would be good to her. She's always wanted to know them. She wants to have brothers.'

'And she'd have Sullivan, too.'

Sullivan, yes. He would be the easiest with her. He would be the one to buy her dresses. He would take her to Africa someday. 'I had a dream that he came to see me.'

253

'He did come to see you.'

'Really?' Now Tennessee had to think about it all over again. She was sure she had imagined everything.

'I think he has some problems,' Tennessee Alice Moser said.

'The truth is Tenny, we all have problems,' Tennessee said. 'I have a new hip.'

'And I'm dead,' Tennessee Alice Moser said, and laid an arm across Tennessee's chest and closed her eyes so that they could both get some sleep.

9

Kenya and Tip stood on the corner of Union Park and looked down the long, snowy expanse of Tremont for as far as they could see in one direction and then they turned to face the other. They found the world divided into three neat layers: blue sky, red brick buildings, white snow. The plows had come through in the very early morning and pushed everything from the middle of the street to either side, forming banks as high as Kenya's shoulder. She had to crane around them to see, but there really was nothing *to* see. The snow that was left on the street was packed into a hard white permafrost as impenetrable as the asphalt itself. When she scanned the few brave cars that skittered around with all the traction of ice cubes, none of them were taxicabs.

'What time is it now?' Kenya asked.

Tip didn't look at his watch. 'Eleven o'clock.' The cab was so late and they were so restless that they had decided to wait it out on the corner, but going to the corner did not produce the car. Tip was weighing it out: the wind, the cold, the crutches, the girl, the promise to his father that they would take a taxi, the likelihood of the taxi actually materializing in the next hour. Beneath her coat, Kenya was wearing a track suit brought from home. She was wearing Tip's backpack on her back and she had to lean slightly forward to counterbalance the weight of the books.

'I can take that bag,' he said, looking down at her, though he wasn't completely sure he could, given the compromised nature of his own balance. He needed the books in case he found the time to read for exams.

'I've got it,' she said, keeping her eyes fast on the road.

She appeared ready to spring at the first sign of available transportation, ready to sprint down the street and guide the cab back to Tip. Tip thought of her as a little peregrine falcon. Everything in her was designed to dart down, grab the rabbit. On the other side of the street the light turned green, instructing them to walk. That settled it. 'We're taking the T,' he said, and stepped into the street.

Kenya stayed on the curb. Tip was not following the plan. 'I told your father I'd make you take a cab,' she called in a loud voice. 'He gave me money.'

'Keep the money,' Tip said, working his crutches carefully against the hard pack in the street.

'At least call them again.'

'How many times can I call them?' Anyway, his cell phone was in his pocket and both of his hands were thoroughly occupied.

Kenya hesitated and then followed. If it would be wrong of her to take the T, it would be worse to let him go on alone. Besides, she didn't want to go back to the house. Teddy and Sullivan were both asleep and Doyle would be too bent on entertaining her if it was just the two of them sitting in the living room together. She had already listened to the Schubert quintet (ironically, he had played her *The Trout*, or at least Tip said it was ironic) and now she wanted to see the fish museum, the special part that was only for scientists, where she and her mother and regular paying customers were not allowed to go. She wanted to run on Harvard's track. She knew it was enormous and completely indoors because she had seen it once by peering in through the windows. More than anything, she wanted to get to the hospital so that she would be standing next to her mother's bed the minute she opened her eyes. She wanted to kiss her hands and put her head lightly to her chest and listen to her heart, the things she did on the nights she couldn't sleep. None of those things would happen on the curb. In two leaping steps she was right beside him again. She refused to dawdle. The light could change and strand her on the wrong side of Tremont. There was a chance that Tip might leave her there and even though she could catch him with no effort, she was not in the mood to cross against the light. She hooked her thumbs under the straps of the pack and hoisted it up. 'Let's at least go back and get the Silver Line.'

'We're taking the T.' He was nearly to the curb.

'But the T is four blocks at least. We can pick up the Silver Line on the corner and take it to Park Street.'

Tip didn't take the bus. He didn't like the bus. 'We're going to Back Bay.'

'That's insane.'

'Then I'm insane.'

She stayed quiet for awhile. She stayed beside him. 'You can walk with those things okay?'

Tip straightened his elbows, careful not to rest his weight beneath his arms. 'I'm getting the hang of it.' They were moving down Dartmouth Street at a good clip. He could have gone faster but every so often the rubber tips of the crutches would shoot out a quick inch or two on the ice and give him reason for sober consideration. The sidewalk was brick, charming, until you tried to shovel off the snow. It couldn't have been more than twenty degrees but he was dressed for it now. From Teddy he had borrowed a parka and scarf and the sheepskin hat with earflaps that he had often ridiculed his brother for. From his father he took a pair of soft leather gloves with cashmere knit lining that pressed up hard against his palms, expensive gloves that Tip himself had bought for Doyle as a present several Christmases ago. But even more than the layers, it was the work of moving forward that kept him warm.

'Isn't this the prettiest street?' Kenya said, her eyes forever turning up to the leaded windows and carved wooden doors that sat on top of straight stone staircases. 'Not as pretty as yours, but really nice.'

Tip stopped to shift his weight against the crutches. He tried to carry his left foot higher behind him and he felt the ache in his shin. The fiberglass casing of the boot that was designed to be so light was heavy. His foot was heavy. He took a moment to look around Dartmouth

258

Street while he caught his breath. Same old Dartmouth Street, a shrine to wealth and minutely polished taste, every narrow side street more precious and perfect than the one before it. He could feel his pulse pounding in the side of his neck and he wondered if it had to do with the Percocet or if he was just out of shape. Last night with Teddy he could have run from Cambridge to Newton and this morning he was struggling with the block. 'The street's gotten too gentrified,' he said, and so dismissed it. He was irritated with his ankle or with himself and in that irritation he took unfavorable notice of the brass mail slots in the doors, the shining knockers shaped like lions' heads. 'There's nothing interesting here anymore.'

'I don't know that word,' Kenya said. She was always in the market for a new word.

Tip turned his head up to see four stories of gentrification, left to right, front to back. The South End was a long way away from its squatter days, its fire-in-the-trash-barrel days. All of that had come and gone before Tip had even been born. 'The rich people came in and pushed the poor people out and fixed it all up so that every house looks the same.'

Kenya took inventory of the empty window boxes, the slender birch trees in the sidewalks, the stair rails fashioned in ornate iron-work. Even in the snow it all looked orderly and neat. She knew full well how lovely it would be once the purple vinca made a carpet around every tree and the geraniums filled the boxes. 'But it looks nice,' she said, coming to the street's defense. 'I can think of some places not too far from here that could stand to be gentrified.' To learn a word you had to know the definition, to own the word you had to use it in a sentence.

'You're missing the point,' Tip said, pushing off again. 'While they're fixing the windows and picking up the trash and planting the flowers, they get rid of the poor people too. I mean the black people, the brown people. They push them out into Cathedral and over into Roxbury. That's the gentry's idea of cleaning up.'

Kenya wasn't thrilled with the implication, that at some point in history she or someone very much like her had lived on Dartmouth Street and later had been swept away in the name of a tidy cleanup. 'You still live over here,' she said, imagining that one morning there was a note taped to every black door in the neighborhood: *Time for you to go.*

Tip didn't know anything about eleven-year-olds, how smart they were or weren't, how much they understood. It struck him that when he was eleven he would have made the same smart remark to his weak generalization and it frustrated him that he didn't know how to backpedal out of it. What he said was essentially correct, but her statement was indisputable: he had not been driven out of the neighborhood. He hadn't factored himself into the equation at all and now he was reduced to telling her the absolute truth as he knew it: 'You have to be poor and black to get taken out of this place,' he said. 'I was only black.'

When they had made it down all the stairs to

the T, Tip took out two tokens and fed them into the slot. The turnstile was a trick with the crutches and so he handed them over to Kenya and hobbled through as best he could. Everything in the city was dead today, including public transportation. People stayed home bundled up in front of their television sets, eating canned soup and watching the Weather Channel to see if there was going to be more of the same. For this Tip was grateful. If he was going to be slow it was better not to have a long line of impatient Bostonians jostling him from behind. They missed the first train because he couldn't run for it, but they were lucky and a second one came along before it should have. He would get the hang of this, he was sure, but for now the only thing he wanted was to be sitting down.

On the T, Kenya pulled off one mitten with her teeth and dug into her pocket. 'Here's the money for the taxi.' She handed the two twenties to Tip. She could not believe that Doyle had given her so much in the first place, but he had said there would have to be a taxi not only to the museum but to the track, and then to the hospital, and it was very likely they would need that much in the end.

'I told you to keep it,' he said, and put his hand over her hand and pushed it gently down towards her lap. There was no point in flashing money around.

'It's forty dollars!' she said, and held it up again. 'I'm not going to keep forty dollars.' What if Doyle thought she'd never told Tip about the money? What if somehow it got back to him that

261

it was her idea to take the train?

'So give it to him when we get home.'

But the more she thought about it the more nervous the money made her. Nothing good would come of her holding on to it. If something happened and she lost it (and she did lose things, no matter how hard she tried to be careful — she was thinking now about her favorite Red Sox sweatshirt left at a track meet last October), she would have to ask her mother to pay the money back. She straightened out the two soft bills against her thigh and laid them on the seat between them. 'Take it,' she said in a quiet voice. 'You give it back to him.'

Tip sighed and put the twenties in his wallet. He knew what Doyle had in mind giving her the money. He wanted her to feel grown up. He wanted her to feel that he had chosen her for a job. He had given her too much in hopes that she would pocket the change and have a little something for herself, something he didn't know how to give to her directly, but he had underestimated her. Maybe there was a way Tip and Kenya had had similar childhoods after all. She too had been attending lectures on social responsibility, sitting through the same crushing liturgies on the moral imperatives of honesty and humility. By growing up in the wake of his family she had inadvertently grown up with Doyle's curriculum as well. If Tip or Teddy found a quarter on the ground when they were boys they'd be half crazed with worry over who had dropped it and how they could possibly give it back. Doyle was always there trying to explain

262

that it was fine to keep the change that was out on the sidewalk and that it was in no way related to taking money from a cash register or a purse. Finding a quarter wasn't stealing, it was lucky, and even while they understood that rationally they were still left emotional wrecks by the thought that it could have been dropped by some very poor child straight out of Dickens. That was Doyle's fault. He had made them that way after all, high strung little do-gooders who had to live every moment of their lives as an enactment of the Nicene Creed. Maybe he'd done it to Kenya, too, without even knowing it. Doyle would just have to take the money back as a consequence of his parenting.

By the time they were halfway through Harvard Yard, Tip was seriously questioning the wisdom of his own decision to leave the house at all. His leg had progressed far beyond aching. The pain in his sciatic nerve was sharp and somewhat electrical in nature. It now extended from his foot up the back of his leg. He had, despite all better knowledge, dug the crutches into his brachial plexus and slowly crushed it, sending a radiation up his neck and into the back of his head that was like a persistent hammer slamming in a reluctant nail. He had to admit that from the standpoint of physiology it was interesting to feel his central nervous system unite. His wrists, for example, which he had been so careful to keep straight, had extended somewhere around the Science Center, and now the median, ulnar, and radial nerves were so sore from holding himself up that his entire arms trembled and burned in the warm sleeves of his brother's parka. His breath was labored and short. His sinuses were scorched from the freezing wind that pushed at him until he felt concerned for his own stability. Blind kittens were more robust in their nature. Once this was behind him he would not assume that pacing around the lab and lifting glass jars full of fish over his head sufficed for physical exercise. As for now he was thinking fondly of the living room sofa.

I can take her running, Teddy had offered.

Need I remind you that you were hit by a car last night? Doyle had said.

A fat yellow plow just as wide as the sidewalk snaked a lazy curve through the center of the yard while students who preferred not to walk through the snow filled the dry path behind it. Everywhere they looked the trees were black and wet and leafless.

'This is the most beautiful place in the world,' Kenya said in a tone best saved for walking up the nave of Chartres and not passing between two freshman dorms.

'It's nice.' Tip looked up and saw a handmade sign taped inside somebody's bedroom window, *Obama 2012.* The truth was Tip always felt better the minute he stepped into Harvard Square. He was a Cambridge resident by nature. Boston was a city that never understood him and therefore Boston was a city he never thought twice about leaving.

'Do you ever just look around and think, I can't believe I get to go to school here?'

Tip was concerned about the lack of feeling in his fingers. Cold? Nerve damage? It was impossible to tell. 'I guess I always thought I'd go to Harvard.' He was working to make his voice sound steady, conversational, to give no indication of what he was coming to see as his imminent collapse. 'I've been interested in the science department here since I was your age.'

Kenya pulled her mother's hat farther down on her head until the wind was cut from her eyes. It was hard for her to walk so slow but she did it. 'It's not like they let you in this place just because you're interested.'

The Museum of Comparative Zoology must have moved. It had never been this far before. By the time they got to the side door Tip didn't have the fine motor skills to put the key in the lock. After a few pathetic stabs of tapping the metal key against the metal door he dropped the ring.

'I've got it.' Kenya plucked the keys from the deep burrow of snow. She shook them off and made a pleasant jingling sound. 'Which one?'

Once they got into the lab, he fell into a chair and let his crutches slide with a great deal of clatter onto the floor. The place was empty. The snow had kept everyone away. Tip's chin dropped forward and he crossed his arms in front of his chest to try and stretch out the ache that was in his back. He had never been so grateful for a chair, for a room, for the warmth.

Kenya dragged another chair in front of him and lifted up his foot very gently. She did not mind that the sole of the boot was encrusted in watery gray ice. She did not put the well-being of

265

the chair before the well-being of the foot as Tip would have done. She picked a coat off the coat tree without any question of who it might belong to and covered his leg, then took down another and spread it across his chest. Tip didn't know who had left their coats behind, but they were always there, even in the middle of the summer. She pressed her small, neat fingers into the side of his wrist and stared at the clock over the door. When she did the math she pressed them in again to check herself. 'It's bad,' she said.

'It's all right,' he said, but his head was splitting.

Kenya walked away from him and a minute later she came back with a coffee cup full of water. 'Drink this,' she said. 'Do you have any medicine?'

Tip took a sip of the water and she held the cup. It was tepid. When he tried to reach in his pocket he couldn't get his arm to bend back far enough and she brushed his hand away and took the bottle out herself. 'Childproof caps,' she said, snapping the bottle open. 'I don't know who they think they're fooling.'

'They're fooling the people who can't read the instructions on the cap,' Tip said, but even he could hear the slur in his voice. He took the pill from her hand and swallowed it with the water she gave him.

'Oh,' she said.

He closed his eyes and took another breath. He would be fine. If he had to stay here another six to eight weeks until his ankle had healed completely he would manage. He knew how to

266

sleep with his head on his coat. He knew which restaurants delivered.

'Keep drinking,' she said. 'Little sips.' When the cup was empty she took it from him. She pulled off his gloves and rubbed each of his hands between the flats of her own small palms. He almost made a sound it hurt so much when she straightened out his fingers. Then she unwound her scarf and put his hands on either side of her neck.

It was like settling his hands on a radiator. He jerked them away and opened his eyes. 'What are you doing? You're going to freeze to death.'

But then, with admirable stoicism, she grasped his hands more firmly and clamped them around her throat, pressing them in with her hands so that for all appearances she seemed to be forcing him to strangle her. 'Just be quiet for a minute,' she said sternly. It was like holding a bird, a hot little bird cupped inside his frozen hands. She stood close beside him, her forehead practically against his chest. He felt every breath, every steady thump of her heart as it echoed through her carotid arteries. 'Who in the world taught you to do this?'

'Girl Scouts,' she said, not lifting her head.

'They give a badge for treating someone who's walking with crutches?'

'First aid. You have hypothermia.' She was speaking directly into his sweater.

'I don't have hypothermia.'

'You think.'

He looked at her, at the crown of her head bowed there beneath his chin, at the straight lines that ran between her braids. At some point she had taken off her hat. At some point her mother had put this child on the floor between her knees and parted her hair with such mathematical consideration that he could read her intentions in the child's scalp. This was a girl who was cared for, who would not be sent out of the house with her hair gathered into unequal sections. He could see all: hands, comb, soft hair, and for the first time he thought of the woman and the girl in this picture as people who had a tenuous connection to him. When as a child he had thought of the mother who gave him away at all it was as someone who was reckless and halfhearted, someone incapable of finishing anything she had begun. He pictured her apartment as a place that was full of half-read books, half-eaten sandwiches, a jigsaw puzzle of a clipper ship strewn across a table with only a dozen or so pieces fit together. By the time he was six he had named her lazy and selfish and closed the door on her there. He realized that this childish answer to the question of why he had been given away had somehow gotten stuck in the back of his mind without revision, and now it seemed the equivalent of being a scientist who still held with the theory that thunder was the result of God moving furniture around. After the death of his own mother he didn't have time to reconsider the mother who had given him away. He could only think of the one who had been taken from him forcefully, only think of the cancer that had started in her tonsils and then swept through her body in an irreversible tide. It occurred to him now for the first time with this girl in his hands how the two mothers were linked by their absence, and a wave of loneliness of the sort he did not allow himself came over him. He wanted both of them back, both the one who was living and the one who was dead. He gave Kenya's neck the smallest squeeze and then he let go. 'Let's stop this now before your neck freezes through and your head snaps off.'

She stood and looped her scarf back into position, then she stretched her arms up towards the fluorescent lights, making herself as straight and slender as a ruler. 'My neck will be warm again in just a minute,' she said, thinking that she was no longer holding up her end of the bargain as a heat source. 'You can put your hands on my stomach while we wait. That's the second warm place.'

Tip rubbed his hands together and pulled on his fingers until he felt the smallest indication that they were flexible and alive. 'No, thank you.'

'I won't mind.'

'You're a model scout.'

'You're feeling better, aren't you?'

He said that he was.

'Maybe you could write a note to my troop leader. We get extra points for practical application.' She bent back her shoulders and dropped the backpack to the floor, then she took off her coat. Her track suit was the pink of a dime store budgie with white stripes running up her legs and down her arms. 'It's warm in here.'

'It feels good.'

'That's because you have hypothermia.' Kenya

picked up a jar from the desk beside her and looked inside, agitating it gently left to right so that the long-dead fish rose up to swim.

Her touch was so light that he didn't feel the need to stop her. She didn't shake them the way a child would, she simply reanimated them. 'Do you want to help me finish up my work?'

'Sure.' She looked around at the long tables covered in papers and fishes. If they did everything that needed doing around here she'd never get a chance to run.

'I need to refile some of these and I can't carry them with my crutches, so I was thinking that you could carry the jars and I'll tell you where to put them back.'

'Just tell me where they go and I'll do it myself,' she said. 'I think you should keep sitting down.'

'Is that what the handbook says?'

'Don't joke,' she said. 'You could have died.'

'Well, I didn't, and now I need to get a little work done.'

Kenya made an assessment of the situation. She looked down the hallway in front of them and looked at the chairs. They were by no means shoddy in their construction. The fish department at Harvard clearly wasn't skimping on chairs. She had rolled around plenty of old people in the place where her mother worked and she knew a thing or two about how helpful a good set of wheels could be. 'Okay,' she said, giving her hands a single, authoritative clap, 'this is what we're going to do: you hold the jars and I'll push you. I think you can even keep your leg up if you work to steer the second one yourself.'

'I'm too heavy for that.'

His lack of imagination made her impatient. 'The chairs roll. I didn't say I was going to carry you.' Kenya got behind him and gave a demonstrative push. There was the practical application of the theory.

So Tip told her where the basket was and which jars should go in the basket and she brought them to him, stopping every time to hold the glass up to the overhead light and rock the occupants back into motion. '*Lepomis macrochirus*, immature bluegills,' Tip told her when she asked. '*Couesius plumbeus*, lake chub.' He didn't need to read the labels in order to know the occupants of all the jars on the desk. He didn't have to hold them or, for that matter, even get a very good look.

'Do you know every fish in this place?' she asked.

Tip shook his head, amused at the thought. 'There are over a million fish here.'

At that she held up her hand. 'Wait,' she said, and ran into the other room, into the endless rows of shelves and jars and fishes. She gave a small scream when she saw the full force of them there, the occupants of what appeared to be an entire ocean divided into jars and stacked into soldierly rows. It was a noise of pure delight. A scant half hour ago, Tip had considered telling Kenya she shouldn't be so impressed by things: the house, the street, the school, but his heart leapt that she did so love the sight of the museum's collection. She rushed back holding a larger jar in both of her hands, one enormous fish doubled over on itself, its pearly underside pressed tight against the glass so that every scale was clearly etched, its adipose fin pinned in snug to the body, its wide and rubbery lips kissing the bottom. 'What's *this*?' She was giddy, drunk on the abundance of marine life the way other children would have spun manically at the entrance of Toys R Us if they were told they could have any one thing they wanted.

'Don't go taking the specimen off the shelves,' Tip said. 'We're here to put them back.'

She raised the jar higher. 'Name that fish.' It was a threat, a dare, a sentence that said in no uncertain terms *You don't have a* clue.

'*Catostomus commersoni,*' he said. 'White sucker.' There were easily 1,295,000 jars she could have grabbed that would have left him with only an educated guess and very possibly not even that. Her random choice had been his luck.

'You're right!' she screamed in a voice worthy of a game show host and did one twirl with the sucker pinned to her chest. 'I thought that maybe you knew the ones that were out here because you were going to have a test on them or something.'

'I don't know most of them. You made a good pick.'

Kenya held the bottom of the jar up to her nose and did her best to shape her mouth to the mouth of the sucker. 'You've got to wonder what this guy looked like when he was still swimming.'

But Tip did know that. A sucker was not such

an uncommon sight. 'He would have had three irregular lateral blotches, right about here.' He touched the jar. It was then he realized how ridiculously glad he was to have been asked. No one ever asked him anything about fish. Doyle hated the MCZ. The only reason he ever came to the building anymore was because he had some cause to drag Tip out of it. Teddy liked to come. After he'd been upstairs to lose himself in the glass flowers or stare at the skeleton of the giraffe, he'd follow Tip around talking while Tip shelved the specimen, or he'd sit at Tip's desk to study, but he certainly never asked him what he was working on. He never picked up a jar and said, *Wow, look at this one*, or formulated a single question about what Tip knew or what Tip did. Teddy hadn't asked him a question about anything concerning school since approximately the fifth grade as he assumed, incorrectly, that any answer would be over his head. Tip would have been so glad to explain it: the function of gills, the placement of fins, the evolution of his beloved jaw structure. As for Sullivan, he just thought the whole thing was hysterical. He saw Tip's work not as a legitimate scientific pursuit but as some enormous, cosmic cruelty leveled against Doyle for his desire to steer his smartest son into politics. Most of Tip's friends were in the sciences and to them the fish were just disgusting. They regarded ichthyology as an elaborate smoke screen because for whatever reason Tip didn't want to admit that he was eventually going to apply to medical school like the rest of them. Yes, he had completed the prerequisites, but he wasn't going to medical school. He was going to stay in ichthyology for the rest of his life. Even the guys he worked with in the lab never pulled a jar off the shelf and said, *Name this*. He didn't expect them to. But in truth he was alone with a great deal of knowledge, knowledge that he would put into papers and eventually publish in scientific journals where his family and his friends and all the people he hoped would think well of him would never look at it.

'Do one more,' Kenya said.

Tip could neither sigh nor affect a world weariness of any kind. He would have played this game all day were it not for his fear of lessening her love for it. 'Put that one back first. It has to go exactly where you found it. Double check the numbers and turn the label face out.'

Kenya nodded, glad to exercise total obedience in Tip's domain, and then she was gone again, diving down into the crystal drink of alcohol solution. He listened to her tennis shoes lightly slapping away. She liked the fishes. She wasn't squeamish. She didn't make fun of the sucker or his name but instead showed an interest that was more than a simple mimicry in what Tip showed interest in, although that in itself would have been enough. Maybe she had a real mind for science and their shared predilection for evolutionary biology could be genetically linked, not that a gene for scientific interest had been identified but he imagined there was one. Tip had never given much thought to his own genetics before since the only person he had ever known to share DNA with had less in common with him than most strangers he passed in the Square.

She was back again, breathless, smiling hugely (those teeth!). She kept one hand flat on the top and the other on the bottom and held the jar out to him with straight arms, the label turned away. He knew it in a second. *Apeltes quadracus*. It was an excellent choice, not one made by any eleven-year-old girl who ran to grab the first thing she saw. These fish were from the third room. She would have passed several hundred thousand possible candidates in order to find them. It was also a kind choice since the pectoral fin still showed the slightest trace of red — the giveaway of the fourspine stickleback. In a living specimen it was the fish's bad luck, a bright red flag hanging beneath the gut like a bloody lure. When Tip told her what they were her face lit up with amazement. She looked at the label again and then stared at the fish as if she had no idea how they had appeared in her hands. 'You could do this on stage. You're like a magic trick.'

'It helps that you pick out the ones I know,' he said.

'I bet you're lying. I bet you know every fish in there.'

They added the stickleback to the basket and decided it was time to go to work. She got behind him and pushed. It wasn't a perfect system, they had to keep stopping and realigning themselves, but the floors were smooth cement and good for rolling. Tip used his good foot to help maneuver them forward. The doors between the rooms were as heavy as the doors on mausoleums and Kenya had to lean her shoulder into every one, but any way you considered it, it was a vast improvement over crutching. For every jar they put away, Tip gave a brief explanation of how their specimen related to the fish that sat on either side. It was so logical, after all, the redbreast sunfish beside the pumpkin-seed, the pumpkinseed beside the smallmouth bass.

'What's the oldest fish here?' she asked.

'Seventeen hundreds, all the way in the back room.'

Her eyes opened wide. 'And the newest fish?'

Tip shrugged. 'We'd have to go into the prep room and see what's there.'

'I mean when's the last time someone discovered a new fish.'

'Last week, the week before.' Tip picked up a slender jar of inland silversides and turned it around so that the label was face out. He wondered who would have left them there so carelessly. 'I don't know. People discover new species all the time.'

'I thought it was done,' Kenya said, her voice sounding slightly panicked.

'What was done?'

'*Finding* things. I thought it was all finished, everything was set.'

'Since when?'

'I don't know. Since they found all the countries. Since they found the oceans. How can there still be fish swimming around that nobody's even seen yet?' It unnerved her, the thought that things weren't settled, that life itself hadn't been completely pinned down to a cork-board and labeled. It made her feel cold, like anything could happen still. Why hadn't someone taken the time to name all the fish, and how many more fish were there room for? The shelves were already burdened. This place was like a submarine, dark and gray with dozens of different sized pipes running back and forth over the ceiling. Where were they going to put that many more fish? It would be one thing if he was talking about a dozen or two dozen, but if the number just kept expanding year after year, decade after decade, it was only a matter of time before the fish would have to go upstairs and take over part of the space that belonged to the birds. Then Kenya had a thought that seemed more terrible still: What if they hadn't found all the birds?

'The bottom of the ocean is a long way away,' Tip said. 'There are all sorts of things we don't know about living down there. And it isn't just the oceans. Most of the new species come from the Amazon. Scientists find new fish in the leaf litter all the time.'

'Leaf litter?'

'The dead leaves down at the bottoms of the rivers. You just need to take a stick and stir things around.'

'Are you going there?' The vision of him came very clearly, her brother standing in his waders on the banks of a wide, flat river, the jungle, sweet smelling and sticky, stretching out behind him, the shadows filled in with darkly twisting tropical vines. 'Don't you want to find your own fish?'

It had been a long time since Tip thought about fieldwork. There was so much to do on the species that other people were finding that he didn't consider looking for his own fish anymore. But when she asked the question he remembered himself as a boy, his father reading from Darwin, Tip falling asleep to dream of leaning forward over the prow of the *Beagle* as it sliced through the waves. 'Yes,' he said. 'Sooner or later I'll go.'

'Will you let me come?' If there were really still things in the world that needed discovering she wanted to see them for herself.

'You can come,' he said.

When Tip and Kenya had finished their work he took her to the single jar he loved above all others, a jar that he had found himself one night a year ago when he had finished putting things away and was simply wandering, as he was prone to do, and looking at what was there. He had not told his father about what he had found, nor Teddy, and when he mentioned it to Mr. Hartel who ran the lab he only said yes, of course he knew. Nine *Enneacanthus obesus* together in a black-capped glass no bigger than a can of shaving cream. He lifted it from the shelf and handed it to her so that she could read the label.

MCZ no. 40687
Banded Sunfish
Centrarchidae
Enneacanthus obesus
local: Concord, MA
Henry David Thoreau

She waited a long time, rocking the fish back and forth, knowing that it was something important and that Tip expected that she should be able to figure it out, but she couldn't. None of the words meant anything to her. She breathed and blinked. She tackled it again. It was a test, a kind of reading comprehension test, and if she paid attention to every last detail of what was in her hands she would understand it. She broke down the label word by word, she studied the fish again, and when it was clear that she was never going to come up with anything she closed her eyes and gave it her best guess. 'Are these the only nine sunfish left?'

Tip shook his head and tapped the bottom line. 'Thoreau.'

She looked hard at the name. *Thoreau!* she wanted to say. *I can't believe I missed that! There it is, right there in front of me.* 'He's the scientist?' she said weakly.

Tip took the jar from her and looked at it again. '*Walden,*' he said, trying to steer her to the answer. 'The Transcendentalist movement?'

Never lie about what you don't know, her mother told her. Somebody's always going to find out. 'I'm sorry,' she said.

Now Tip felt embarrassed. After all, she was only eleven. But at eleven he had been to the pond a hundred times. He went there with friends in the summer to swim and he went there on school trips. His father took them there on the weekends when he was pressed for time and couldn't drive all the way to the Cape. He and Teddy waded into the water, their pants rolled up to their knees, armed with mayonnaise jars made sterile by the dishwasher. They scooped up the sunfish and brought them back to the shore to identify them in *The Audubon Society Field Guide to North American Fishes, Whales & Dolphins*, even though, as Teddy liked to point out, they never found any whales or dolphins. They took out their pencils and printed the date at the top of the page in their field books. They wrote down the common name of the fish, their genus and species, number, and physical attributes. After they had noticed everything they could think of to see, they waded back into the water and gently, gently laid the jars on their sides to let the fish swim out undisturbed.

''The finest qualities of our nature, like the bloom on fruits, can be preserved only by the most delicate handling,'' Doyle said from memory. ''Yet we do not treat ourselves nor one another thus tenderly.''

Then Teddy, just a little boy who cared nothing about fish other than for their safety, repeated the line from *Walden* ten times until he had committed it to memory.

'He was a famous writer,' Tip said. 'He lived by himself at Walden Pond. Have you been to Walden Pond?'

Kenya shook her head.

The science teachers took classes there to make lists of plants and birds (marsh grass, nuthatch); their history teacher had taken them there to discuss the political majesty of Massachusetts, and their English teacher had taken them there to stand beside the pile of rocks that had once been Thoreau's cabin while she read aloud from *Walden*. How was it possible that any child could go to school in Boston and not get dragged out to Concord for something? 'It isn't far from here,' Tip said. 'When the weather gets warmer I'll take you. You can see where he lived.'

It was one thing to say to someone that one day you'd take them to the Amazon to poke around in the leaf litter, that was an abstract invitation. But it was something else to offer a trip to a place that was close by in a month that was not so very far away. Would he really want to drive her out to see a pond in the spring? She pictured the two of them in the car, the windows down, the landscape shooting past: apple trees heavy with white blossoms, the daffodils waving yellow flags beneath the boughs. They would hardly notice the scenery because they would be having serious discussions about matters of science. 'Thoreau studied fish out there?' she asked. She wanted so much to understand why this was important, why these fish were his favorites when there were over a million to choose from.

'He studied nature,' Tip said. 'All of nature. He had some pretty revolutionary ideas about how men should live. I used to study the fishes in that pond and I used to read Thoreau's books, so when I found these fish that he had caught — ' He stopped. His explanation captured nothing of what was important.

'That makes sense,' she said, lending him encouragement. 'You liked the same things.'

Tip nodded, but it was more than that. It was Doyle sitting on the shore, cutting up an apple with a pocketknife for the three of them to share, it was Doyle praising Tip for remembering the difference between the sunfish and the crappie. It was the beautiful water, clear and cold even in the summer. Tip watched his own feet stepping carefully between the rocks, and kept an eye on Teddy's feet because Teddy was dreamy and more likely to fall. All of that, and then the picture of Thoreau turning over his own cuffs and stepping into that selfsame water, living a life of studied isolation and yet still taking these fish, these very fish that he held, back into his cabin for study.

'I think,' Tip said, putting the jar back in its place, 'that we should call the hospital and check on your mother now.'

And so she rolled him back to the place they had started, unable to shake off the feeling that it had all been a test and that she had failed.

Kenya stood beside Tip at his desk while he called patient information and inquired about Tennessee Moser. When the woman on the other end asked if he was family he said yes, but he would have said yes if he was calling to check on a friend. It was an easy lie even if it might be the truth.

There was a pause on the line and then the woman was back again. 'She's still in surgery,' the nurse said. 'Everything ran late this morning because of the weather.'

Tip felt inclined to ask if it had snowed in the hospital but then thought better of it. 'Is there

282

any report on how she's doing?'

There Kenya stood, the watchful, big-eyed falcon.

'We won't have any information until she's out. She'll be in there another couple of hours and then it will be awhile after that before she's back in her room.'

Tip thanked her and hung up the phone. 'It's all going to be fine,' he said.

'How do you know that?'

'The nurse said she was going to be fine.'

Kenya reached up and pulled on her hair. 'I could *hear* what she said. I'm standing right here.'

Tip sighed and put his foot gingerly on the floor. Immediately, the blood rushed down into the boot and he knew there was going to be nothing good about standing up again. 'Let's go running,' he said. 'We've still got plenty of time.'

Campus security was good for a ride over to the track. They knew Tip well enough, finding him as often as they did asleep in the lab when they were locking up. His wrists didn't want to take the weight of his body on his crutches anymore. Every nerve and muscle protested his departure from the MCZ. He felt a sense of accomplishment just making it out to the curb.

'You must do a pretty mean mile in that boot,' the driver said when Tip told him where they wanted to go.

'Funny,' Tip said. Kenya folded into the backseat behind him, his crutches in the middle, his backpack keeping her angled forward. He had wanted all those books, thinking it was possible that he could get stuck in a hospital waiting room for hours, but now he saw them for what they were — dead weight that Kenya had to lug around on the off chance he might encounter boredom.

On the other side of the river the driver took them past the parking lot of Blodgett Pool and beside the football stadium where Harvard won its games like gentlemen year after year. 'Lots of kids calling to say they need rides this morning because it's so freaking cold,' the driver said, looking in the rearview mirror at Tip rather than at the icy road ahead of him. 'I'm sympathetic, mind you, but this isn't a taxi service. I tell them if they want a ride I'm going to have to see something broken.'

'Glad I could deliver,' Tip said.

Kenya kept her gaze fixed out the window, counting light posts, counting starlings. It was weeks ago, wasn't it? The police car and the snow and all of them squeezed in there together, her mother taken off in an ambulance and not knowing where to find her, not knowing anything. She had been out of her world for a long time now. She had been groping around in the dark for a month at least, not just since yesterday. She felt herself shiver unnaturally and she pressed herself against the door.

'This is as close as I can get you,' the driver said.

It was mercifully close. Kenya bit down hard on her back teeth and came around with the crutches, handing them to Tip like the dutiful scout she was. Inside, Tip took his ID out of his wallet and the girl behind the counter of Gordon Track, a girl who was simply fulfilling the contract of her financial aid package by working twenty hours a week, pointed at Kenya. 'They're getting younger, aren't they?'

'She's my sister,' Tip said.

'She needs to be a student.'

'She is a student. She goes to grammar school and it's closed today because of the snow.'

Kenya stood wide-eyed and silent, praying that this stranger, who had the most enormous assemblage of black curls she had ever seen on a white girl, would look the other way while she slipped beneath the turnstile. She was his sister, he had said so. She was a student. She was minutes away from touching her feet to the track.

'The rules are,' the girl said, and held her open hand up to a large, printed sign of rules instead of wasting her time repeating them.

'Look at this,' Tip said, and nodded down towards the boot that he was barely holding up behind him. The girl did him the courtesy of leaning over the counter. 'I'm not running today. We will only be taking up one spot on the track. I'm giving her my spot.'

'They're nontransferable. I'm the only one who'll get in trouble,' the girl said.

'Come in and watch her run. My sister's a track star. Nobody's going to ask her to leave.' He used the word 'sister' as a novelty. He kept expecting the girl to laugh at the joke.

But instead she sighed as if she had suddenly grown bored of the whole thing. Her calculus book was open and she rapped her pencil on the page. She had her own studying to do. 'Go.'

Tip continued to look at her, he took his hands off the bars of his crutches and spread them out flat on the desk. 'I'm serious,' he said, and for an instant he thought of Sullivan and so he smiled at her. Sullivan would have had the kid on the track five minutes ago. 'Come and see her run.'

She pointed with her pencil and nodded, not to say that she would be watching but to say that the show was over.

Kenya darted ahead, too aware that goodwill was a temporary condition. Once she was on the other side of the gate there would be no getting her back.

He never came here anymore. Sometimes he ran by the river if there was time, but he hadn't been to the track since freshman year. The light came down in a solid sheet from the high glass wall. It was lovely and quiet when there was nothing going on. Just the occasional squeak of some running shoes. He could come here to study sometime. It smelled warm, like sunlight on pavement. 'You better run fast,' Tip said to Kenya when he finally caught up with her. 'I've put myself on the line for you.'

Kenya was looking up to the banners hanging from the ceiling, Princeton and Columbia and Yale. She was looking down at the wide sweep of red track, so thick and soft she would spring halfway to the rafters with every strike. 'I do.'

There was a yellow-haired boy doing high-step and lunge in the straight sprint lanes that lay in the center of the track, two girls doing easy laps on the inside lanes, a third girl by herself running fast with a strong kick-back. The rest of the track was empty, and for a minute she wanted to go back to the girl at the desk and tell her, in case she didn't know, that only four people were actually using the facilities when there was enough space for every kid in her grade and the grade ahead of her plus all the teachers to run full on without bumping into one another. Who did the guardian of the gate think she was saving it for?

Tip sat down on the front bleacher and put his crutches on the floor.

'Put your foot up,' Kenya said, taking off her coat and hat and scarf.

'When did the Girl Scouts get so bossy?' he said and turned sideways to bring up his leg.

She wasn't listening to him anymore. She was hopping up and down now, a manic pink spring, ready to spend the ounce of herself that she had been holding on to tight, tight, tight. She put her hands on the ground and tried to make herself stretch but she didn't think she had the time. She felt certain if she waited another minute she was going to explode. It would all come raining down on her and the last thing she wanted to be was a girl crying on the Gordon Track. That would get her thrown out for sure. She stood and for an instant went up on her toes and then, at the crack of the gun that she kept in her head, she was gone.

She kept it light at first, swinging past the gently jogging girls who were locked in their own breathless conversation, *And so I told him . . .* , past the curve where the high-step lunging boy kept his legs so even and straight he resembled a mechanical doll. If there had been endless time she might have gone over and joined him but the need to run was so strong now she had to fight to hold herself back, keep herself from tearing out chunks of the soft red track with her heels. She needed to take it slow at first, to stretch down through her toes, to pump her elbows out behind her. The cold had settled in her bones, she felt it now. The cold from the high bedroom where she had slept the night before and the cold that had built up in her skin even before that, crouching down in the snow beside her mother, holding her mother's cold hand. She had absorbed her mother's cold into her and it had worked a frost along the inside of her veins. It had been cold at the hospital in the little room where they hooked her mother up to monitors while she slept. There hadn't been time to think about it then, how cold she was, how her hands ached, how her head was splitting from the ice that had built up in her ears. It was cold in the hospital waiting room with Teddy talking about the snow and cold at the piano though she had loved to play. It was cold in the kitchen and cold when she went back to her own apartment. It was every bit as cold there as it was outside. It was unbearably cold without her mother to wrap her in a blanket and fix her a cup of chocolate and talk about how the sun poured over everything in Kenya, the place for which she was the namesake, where they agreed they would go

288

together someday. In Kenya it was hot enough to make you forget that winter even existed.

And this morning? She had been freezing every minute of it. Her coat wasn't half as warm as Tip's and even though she'd brought a sweater from home she hadn't been able to wear it under her coat because then the coat was too tight to get her arms through the sleeves. Tip was on crutches, she didn't blame him, but he moved as slowly as the hands on a clock and she was having to practically nail her feet to the sidewalk to keep from running over him every step. She was picking up her pace now on the track, but not to where she would take it. She could have run this fast in the snow. She let herself float forward, every step a leap, her legs stretching out like scissors opened wide. She was a swimmer, a gymnastics star, she was a superhuman force that sat outside the fundamental law of nature. Gravity did not apply to her. 'Meditation in motion,' her coach would say. She heard his voice in her head as she lapped the talking girls, as she swept past the one who was there to run. From the corner of her vision she could see the step-lunge boy stand up straight and watch her pass. She dried off his forehead with the breeze she made. She wasn't even trying. She wasn't racing anything but the sight of her mother being hit by the car. That, and she raced the Doyles at their breakfast table saying she lived too close, and the girl at the front desk intimating that Kenya was not a person to be on this track any more than she should have a house on Dartmouth Street. She was racing Thoreau and his jar of fish because he continued to hound her. How was she supposed to know him? It was her plan to out-run all of that, and somewhere in that running she had started to fly. She no longer felt like touching all the dirt and the muck she had so patiently submitted herself to so that people would think she was a very nice girl. She was not such a very nice girl. Nobody who was very, very nice would ever work this hard to take something they wanted only for themselves. Nice girls did not demand that everyone stop what they were doing and look at them but that was exactly what she asked for and what she got. All the other runners on the track had stopped now, the way dancers will stop when the soloist steps forward to dominate the floor. The girl from the front desk was there, too. Kenya caught sight of her extraordinary hair as she blew past. Tip was there, his leg off the bench now and straight out in front as if he thought at any moment he might have to throw a rope around her and pull her back. Anger and sadness and a sense of injustice that was bigger than any one thing that had happened stoked an enormous fire in her chest and that fire kept her heart vibrant and hot and alive, a beautiful, infallible machine. They were no longer waiting to see how fast she could go, they knew how fast she could go. Now they wanted to see how long it would be before she crashed, and if that was what they were waiting for they might as well sit down and get comfortable.

Tip had never seen anything like it. Not just the speed but the utter effortlessness of it all, the way the toes of her shoes barely touched down before she set off again. She was a sprinter, clearly she was a sprinter, and yet she just kept going until he started to change his mind and wonder if she wasn't going to knock out a half marathon on the track while he sat there waiting.

'You weren't kidding about her,' said the girl from the front desk.

Tip didn't know how long she had been sitting on the bleachers beside him and even now he couldn't turn his face towards her. 'No,' he said.

'Are you a runner, too? Did you hurt your foot running?'

'I don't run,' he said.

'Something like that' — she shook her head — 'you'd think it would have to be genetic.'

'Maybe it is,' he said, watching her shoot past them again. Kenya's hands were open. Her face was easy and relaxed. She made none of those huffing sounds that would indicate the seriousness of her endeavor. 'Maybe I should give it another try.'

They were silent through the next lap and then the next. 'I'm going to call the coach so he can come over and see this,' the dark-haired girl said, because the runner had still not flagged. If anything she seemed to be getting stronger.

'Not today,' Tip said. He kept his eyes on Kenya every second. He felt like he was seeing greatness, like he was in the room watching Watson and Crick put the final touches on their model of DNA, or maybe he was seeing Rosalind Franklin with her magnificent X-rays. Wasn't it the girl, after all, who had actually found the key to life? Kenya was a flame, a thin pink wick. 'We've got someplace we have to be in a little while.'

'Well, somebody needs to see this,' she said.

'She's only eleven.'

'She won't stay eleven.'

There was a part of Tip that wanted to engage this girl, to flirt with her, but he couldn't turn his head. What would it be like to know at eleven the great thing you could do? This was what Doyle had always wanted from them, what Father Sullivan had wanted: a mission, a calling. Tip thought that he had found one in the fishes but it was nothing like this. Kenya running was pure ability: strength, grace, concentration, and the odd thing was that Tip believed her skill must be transferable. It wasn't just that he was watching her run: he was watching who she was. It seemed perfectly reasonable to think that she could take this energy and pour it into anything.

It was not too long after that the little bird started to land, her leaps coming back to a trot, her trot smoothing out into a jog. The black-haired girl began to whistle and clap, and the other runners who had been pressed to the side wall by Kenya's centrifugal force clapped as well. Tip clapped for her and she waved her hand while keeping her eyes straight ahead. The blond boy came up and started walking beside her and they talked back and forth, something Tip couldn't hear. This little girl from Cathedral and the Harvard boy were talking about — what, training techniques? She said something that made him laugh and he patted her on the shoulder and ran off at a modest pace while Kenya rounded her last turn. The three girls all came up and shook her hand, and then she headed back towards the bench.

'You're something, kid,' the front desk girl said to her.

'Thanks,' she said, and took a giant inhale, 'for letting me in.'

Tip shook his head. 'Secretariat.'

'Who?'

'It's a horse. A very fast horse.'

Kenya nodded, taking long, deep breaths. 'People say that to me. Not *that* horse. Some other one.'

'See you, Kenya,' the fast girl called as she left the track. Kenya waved.

'We should probably go pretty soon,' Kenya said.

'You can come back and run anytime,' the dark haired girl said. 'If I'm not here you tell them that Ariel said it was okay. I'll leave a note at the desk. What's your last name?'

'Moser.'

'You don't need to come in with your brother. Anytime you want to run, you come here.'

There was something about this easy dismissal of his necessity that bothered Tip but he didn't say anything.

Kenya spent a long time at the water fountain and then she walked another lap, stopping from time to time to stretch. 'I'm sorry I took so long,' she said to Tip when she finally got back in her coat. 'I had more running in me than I thought.' She hoisted up his backpack but he stopped her.

'Let me take that,' he said.

'Don't be crazy.'

'Really.' He took it from her hand and pulled the straps across his shoulders. 'I don't even know why I brought this. You shouldn't have to carry it.'

Kenya shook her head. 'I don't mind it, and anyway, you still don't feel good.'

'I'm better now.' Just watching her had made him stronger. He was perfectly capable of taking care of himself.

'Ariel can call the cab company.'

But Tip explained that the hospital was close. They could pick up the bus on the other side of the bridge. 'We'll be there in half the time on the bus.'

Kenya would have rather waited at the track. It was enough for her just to be in the building, standing on the right side of the glass, but she didn't want to argue with Tip about transportation anymore. In a way he reminded her a lot of their mother: once she made up her mind about how they were going to do something then that was the way it was going to be.

But when they were outside again she wished she had stood firm against him. She had sweated through her track suit and her coat offered no defense against the weather. The instant they turned into the wind she felt a paper-thin wash of ice form over her stomach and chest. They had forty dollars to spend! Tip was struggling, she could see that, and they weren't twenty steps from the door. 'Let's go back,' she said. 'We'll call security. They'll give us a ride.'

'It's right across the bridge.'

'I'm cold.'

'Anyone who can run like that has the fortitude to hang on for another block.'

Yes. That's what her mother would have said. *If you have the energy to run five miles, then I expect you have the energy to finish your homework. If you really are the fastest girl in the state, then let's see how fast you can pick up your dishes.* 'It's freezing,' she said. She did not whine but she wanted to tell him just in case the wind didn't get through the fancy down coat he was wearing. She could have been to the bus in ten seconds flat but instead they took steps that could be measured in inches. Tip was even slower now than he had been. She had to bite the inside of her cheek to keep from saying it. She could see the pain on his face, the sag in his shoulders as the crutches ground into his armpits. His foot was dragging behind him in the snow, but they kept pressing ahead, crutch, crutch. They weren't anywhere close to the bridge and the bus was on the other side of that. She said the word *Stop* very quietly but let the wind come inside her mouth and sweep the sound away. *Stop. Stop. Stop.*

And then, just like that, his left crutch turned against the ice and shot out as if it had been kicked away, and just as fast the right one went as well, but he pitched to the left, the whole balance of his body thrown into chaos by the backpack. His left arm splayed out to follow the trajectory of the crutch and Tip slammed into the ground without a moment to release his

295

hands, to curl his hands up around his head the way anyone would do if they were falling. Kenya heard the sound of his head hitting, distinct from the heavy sound his body made, the sickening thud of shoulder and hip and boot and books, the rush of air being forced from his lungs. He was a big man. It was easy to forget that about a person until you saw him fall.

'Shit,' Kenya said, and dropped to her knees.

They were still in the parking lot outside the track and when Kenya looked around she saw no one. Goddamn backpack. She pulled the crutches free from his hands and then tried to get him turned in such a way that she could pull the pack off of him and get him straight on his back, but he was heavy. His left arm was at a bad angle, both above his head and behind it. It also appeared to be longer. Her head darted up and she scanned every direction. At least he hadn't broken his neck, it wasn't that kind of fall. She moved his head and saw a smear of blood in the snow.

'Tip!'

'What?' he said, his eyes stayed closed, the left side of the face pressed into the snow as if it were a pillow and she was the one throwing open the curtains. *Wake up, wake up! It's time.*

'Can you move your arm and help me get this off you?'

Tip took a big inhale. 'One minute.'

She kept on tugging until finally she turned his shoulder the wrong way and he made a terrible face. His closed eyes pressed tightly down and he pulled back his upper lip to show his teeth the way a dog would show its teeth. 'Don't.'

She couldn't get anywhere without help. She struggled out of her coat, which seemed to be frozen to her torso, and lifted up his head. 'Lay on this.'

He panted a couple of times and then seemed able to compose himself. 'You'll get another badge.'

Kenya looked around again and then she filled her powerful lungs to their very edges with air cold enough to stop a life and she screamed, '*Help me!*'

'Shhh,' Tip said. 'I'm going to get up.'

She got up and tugged at his legs so they didn't look so twisted. It was wrong to leave him and impossible to stay. 'Two minutes. You stay here two minutes and don't move. I'm going to get help.'

'Smart,' he said, but did not open his eyes.

Two minutes, set your watch by it, because she was up and gone, a shot bullet hot from the fired gun. Back to Ariel who had dismissed her, to the arms of Ariel who now adored her, she flew, ripped the door open so that it banged the wall, letting the air fill the room with its arctic storm. 'He fell!' she screamed at the mass of curls bent over a calculus book, not a human head but a sheepdog poised over the desk, reading calculus.

Ariel could have been asleep. She shot up, startled. 'What?'

'In the parking lot. He fell. Get somebody!' And then she was gone. There was nothing left to say. One leap, out the door, one leap, down the stairs, and now she was crying, crying for her mother to come and save her from this, from having to be in charge of grown people. *Mother save me*, beat out her heart for one leap, one leap, over and over until she was beside him again. She skidded to the ground, taking his right glove into her mittened hands. 'I'm right here,' she said. 'Everything's fine.'

'Fine,' Tip repeated, 'except that I'm an idiot.' Then he squeezed her hand, and she cried even more because of it.

She had scarcely touched the surface of her own despair when she heard voices behind her calling her name, 'Kenya! Kenya!' It was the step-lunge boy, the nice boy who had asked her about her times and events. His arms were full of towels and he was running towards them in the snow, and Ariel was behind him and she was running, too.

'Help,' Kenya said again. She could not stop herself. It seemed to be the only word she knew.

Tip stirred in the snow just as they were coming up beside him. He wanted to take the weight off his arms but he couldn't figure how to do it. He thought about the myriad ways he had always been so lucky until now, and then he opened his eyes and saw her there. There was no one he could think of at that moment that he would rather have bending over him, no one more competent, no one who knew him better. 'Didn't this already happen?' he asked Kenya.

10

Teddy woke up in his own bed on the fourth floor but it took him a minute to figure that out. He had been running. He couldn't remember if he was running from something or to something but his heart was beating like a jackrabbit's and the covers from the bed were lying across the floor in sweaty twists. Teddy lay still in the bright light of his room, legs sprawled, and let the heat rise off of him. It was as if his body were working hard to warm the frozen air. He listened to his heart thumping inside his ears and that sound took every other thought away. He couldn't quite grab hold of where he had been and who else was there. While he had been running the dream had run faster, and before he could get his hands around it the whole thing slipped past him and was gone. He flipped over on his stomach and faced Tip's bed where Kenya had slept the night before. It was more expertly made than he had ever seen it, made the way he imagined a marine would leave his bunk, all the corners tucked in tight and the top spread smooth. Teddy closed his eyes against the sight of such order. He was sorry he had gone back to sleep. It never worked for him. The sleep he went back to was never the one he left. Now he was anxious, feeling like there was something important he had forgotten. If he had simply stayed awake, the only thing he would have to contend with would be exhaustion and that, comparatively speaking, was nothing at all. He got up, leaving his own bed unmade, and went to the dresser to tap the halo of his mother's statue three times, saying three fast Hail Marys to himself as he did every morning. Doyle had taken him to see a psychiatrist once when he was ten because he was certain that Teddy had an obsessive-compulsive disorder, but the psychiatrist had been unable to find any more taps than those three, and three, he said, was nothing to be worried about. 'Catholicism is an obsessive-compulsive faith,' the doctor said to Doyle without asking Teddy to step out into the waiting room. 'It's all ritual.' Teddy hadn't been able to touch the statue when he got up the first time this morning since he'd been sleeping on the couch, but now that he'd done it he felt more settled in his skin.

Teddy showered and went downstairs where he found his father and Sullivan sitting in the kitchen reading the paper, his father with the business section, his brother with a special supplement on travel. They turned their pale eyes towards him and blinked. There was such a similarity in their faces as they aged, the long straight noses, the way their eyes sat back in their sockets. It was as if they were two snapshots of one man spread thirty years apart. Teddy never thought about the ways his father and brother were alike because even when Sullivan was around they were so rarely sitting near each other. 'I didn't think you'd be up,' he said to Sullivan.

Sullivan was fading. The honey-colored tan

he'd brought home the night before seemed to be sliding into his socks, leaving behind a mass of darkened freckles on parchment backing. 'I tried to sleep,' he said, his voice exhausted. 'It didn't stick.'

'No,' Teddy said, opening up the refrigerator and peering inside as if the answer to whatever was haunting him were lodged behind a carton of orange juice. 'It didn't.'

'I called the hospital.' Doyle folded up his section neatly and placed it back in the stack of paper. 'She's still in surgery. She should be coming out soon.'

Teddy straightened up and closed the door without making any selection. Of course the dream had something to do with her, Tennessee and the hospital, all of them there, but what was confusing was that the part that felt like a dream now was the part he knew was real: he had left the house with Sullivan before it was light and they had gone to the hospital. He believed that the woman in the bed had been his mother, or was his mother, he didn't quite know how to phrase it in his mind.

'By the way, the nurse asked me for her insurance cards,' Sullivan said.

'She doesn't have any. They asked me last night, but they weren't in her wallet.'

'Kenya said she had them,' Teddy said.

Doyle took off his glasses and wiped them clean with a napkin. 'She probably did at one time, maybe with another job, but there's nothing there now.'

'Then we have to get her insurance,' Teddy said.

301

Sullivan shuffled through to find the cross-word puzzle. 'Too late.'

'It's not our problem, Teddy,' his father said.

'Then whose problem is it?'

Sullivan decided to get a piece of the action. 'The uninsured poor are such a compelling political issue until you actually meet one of them.'

'It's between Mrs. Moser and the driver of the car.'

'Perfectly done,' Sullivan said.

The bickering worked on Teddy's nerves, and they weren't in good condition to begin with. It was his intention to introduce something positive into the conversation. 'I'm going to bring Uncle Sullivan over to see her today.'

'John Sullivan?' Doyle said. 'You can't be serious. You're not going to drag that old man out in the snow. You'll kill him.'

'He wants to meet her,' Teddy said, because his uncle *did* want to meet her, even if the truth was more complicated than that.

'Did you stop to think about the fact that she might not want to meet him?' Doyle said. 'She will have just come out of surgery, and anyway, we don't even know who she is yet. I don't think we need to bring in the entire extended family.'

Of course he wasn't Teddy's extended family. Uncle Sullivan was the center of his family, the core, the magnet which kept the compass pointing north. 'He might be able to help her.' As soon as Teddy said it he wished he hadn't. Doyle had read about the goings-on at Regina Cleri in the paper and considered it to be nothing but an embarrassment. He didn't have a moment's patience with rumors of miraculous healing.

'It certainly takes care of the insurance question,' Sullivan said, and then stopped to yawn, giving his eyes a good rub once he had finished. 'He'll just go up to her bed and tell her to walk. She'll probably still have to pay for the room though.'

Doyle called forth his expression of deepest disappointment. 'Oh, Teddy,' he said. 'Tell me you don't believe he's actually doing that.'

Teddy picked up a rag and wiped the toast crumbs into the sink, keeping his back to his audience. 'It's nothing like that,' he said to the drainboard. 'A lot of people find him very comforting. Priests visiting sick people isn't exactly a new idea.'

'Can't you at least use a priest who's in better health than the patient?'

'He wants to see Sullivan and Tip,' Teddy said, trying another approach. 'He wants to see you. At least if he comes to the hospital — '

'I'm not going to the hospital,' Sullivan said impassively, swiveling the handle of his coffee cup back and forth with his thumb.

'What?'

'I've already been once today.'

'But we were all going to go together. Can't we do one single thing as a family?' It had never occurred to him that Sullivan wouldn't come. He had promised his uncle that. Sullivan was, in some shabby fashion, the payoff.

'She isn't *my* mother.'

He meant, of course, by simple mathematical extension, that his mother wasn't Teddy's mother either. Which meant that Bernadette, for whom he had lit a thousand candles, was the mother to whom his enormous love and devotion had no claim. A quaking rage rose up in Teddy's chest and he wanted to reach out and pull Sullivan's head off his shoulders. His anger was startling, murderous, like Death itself had glided into the room. It wouldn't take anything. Sullivan was smaller and weaker by half. His open arms draped across the back of the chair like an empty shirt. There was nothing to him. He could be eaten. But as soon as the thought had evolved in Teddy's brain he was sorry for it, and as soon as he was sorry the phone rang. Doyle stood to answer it, that ancient yellow phone that hung from the kitchen wall with its endlessly long cord curling into itself. All he said was hello, and after hello he was only listening. He didn't nod his head or cut his eyes back to look at his sons. He just stood there, all of the life pulled out of him, and listened to Teddy's punishment. Tennessee Moser was dead. That's what God had given him for his thoughts. That's how quickly retribution came.

'I want you to hold yourself together,' Doyle said finally. His voice was calm and ever so slightly stern. 'We'll be there as quick as we can. Can you do that? Can you stop crying? — All right, that's right. — Yes. You wait for us there.' When he hung up the phone he dropped his chin for a moment and looked at his shoes.

Sullivan and Teddy waited and watched him

but nothing came. 'She's dead.' Teddy said finally to save his father from having to say the words.

Doyle lifted up his face again, shocked by the breadth of his son's imagination. 'Oh, no, God, nothing like that. It's Tip. He fell on the ice outside the track. That was Kenya calling from the hospital. She said something happened to his shoulder.'

'An ankle and a shoulder,' Sullivan said. 'That's brilliant.'

Doyle ignored him. 'Get yourself together. We need to get over there.'

Sullivan had only made it through the first syllable of his explanation when Doyle raised his hand and stopped him cold. 'I wouldn't care if you were sixty,' he said. 'You've got two minutes.'

It was more than two minutes, of course. Doyle's car was still buried in Cambridge and so they were again reduced to looking out the window for the taxi that had been called. Teddy walked around the room with his hands stuffed in his pockets, staring at the floor like he was trying to find change, while Sullivan lay across one of the living room sofas in his coat, his feet hanging over the arm, one hand covering his eyes. He was thirty-three years old. He did not understand how such a short time in this house could have returned him to adolescence. He could package the place as hell's interpretation of the Fountain of Youth and make a fortune: just walk in the door and you're fifteen all over again. He tried to imagine how interesting this story would have been had he not been a part of it. He could have just as easily come home three months from now — three years! — and everyone would have gathered around to tell him the tale: Tip had been hit by a car, the missing birth mother had been found, there was a child and she was lovely but oh, the mother and the child had gone away again. He didn't think the entire story could possibly take more than ten minutes start to finish, and yet to live it, to actually be a part of its playing out, was an excruciating investment of time. Sullivan had used up his lifetime allotment for family drama by the time he reached twenty-four: other children had been adopted, his mother was dead, he'd killed poor Natalie and, in doing so, ended his father's career. The continent of Africa hardly knew such upheaval. By anyone's standards his previous involvement with the family story should have been enough. From now on he swore his visits home would be divided by decades and spent in hotels. This business of coming back to take your little part in the play you would never again be the star of was simply more than anyone should have to beat.

Doyle pulled back the curtain and, after carefully assessing the empty nature of the street, stared at his watch as if it might have something new to tell him since the last time he'd looked. 'I'm going to call the hospital back. Someone needs to tell Kenya why we're so late.'

'Ask her if they've found out what's wrong with Tip yet,' Teddy said.

'Leave her alone,' Sullivan said, but he hadn't taken his hand off his eyes. He didn't know that

Doyle had left the room.

After a minute Teddy stopped pacing and came and wedged himself onto the couch where Sullivan lay, working his hip against Sullivan's hip until Sullivan was forced to push himself back into the pillows and make some more room. 'I don't think Tip could really be hurt that badly, do you?'

'Do I think he's going to die of a shoulder injury? No.'

Teddy tapped his feet on the floor and stared towards the kitchen where Doyle had disappeared to use the phone. It appeared as if he might at any moment spring straight up from the couch and hang inverted from the light fixture in the living room. Sullivan could all but feel the nervousness pouring out of Teddy and into him at the point where their two bodies intersected at the hip. ''So first of all,'' Teddy said in a voice gone jittery and low, a voice that did not call Roosevelt's to mind at all, ''let me assert my firm belief that the only thing we have to fear is fear itself — nameless, unreasoning, unjustified terror which paralyzes needed efforts to convert retreat into advance.''

Sullivan uncovered his eyes and looked up at his youngest brother. 'Which means you want to do what, exactly?'

Teddy put his right index finger into his mouth, bit down. 'I was just thinking, if I slipped out right now I could go get Uncle Sullivan and meet you and Da back at the hospital. That way Tip is there and you're there. We could all be together. It would be a nice surprise.'

'Except that it's not a nice surprise since you already mentioned it to Da.'

'So not a surprise.'

'And by slipping out you mean leaving before he walks back into the room so that he couldn't stop you, and so I'd have to tell him where you'd gone.'

Teddy looked at his fingers. 'Something like that.'

'I have one for you,' Sullivan said. 'I know one you'll like.' He cleared his throat and then stretched back his neck as if to achieve a more sonorous tone. ' "There comes a time when people get tired. We are here this evening to say to those who have mistreated us for so long that we are tired — tired of being segregated and humiliated; tired of being kicked about by the brutal feet of oppression. There comes a time my friends when people get tired of being plunged across the abyss of humiliation, when they experience the bleakness of nagging despair. There comes a time when people get tired of being pushed out of the glimmering sunlight of last July and left standing amid the piercing chill of an Alpine November." '

'Sullivan, listen.'

But Sullivan only returned his hand to his eyes. He had no need to listen, only to speak. ' "We had no alternative but to protest. For many years, we have shown amazing patience. We have sometimes given our white brothers the feeling that we liked the way we were being treated. But we come here tonight to be saved from that patience that makes us patient with anything less than freedom and justice.'' Sullivan smiled, looking up at Teddy again. 'It's King, of course. Pretty good that I remembered that much. Except that the white brother part doesn't work exactly. It should be our black brothers. 'We have sometimes given our black brothers the feeling that we like the way we were being treated.''

Teddy reached down and took his brother's hand, kissed the knuckles gently, quickly. 'I owe you.'

'Yes, yes you do,' Sullivan said, but it didn't matter, since Teddy was already gone.

Teddy passed the taxi as he was running around the corner onto Tremont Street, and the sight of it only made him run faster. He had barely gotten away in time. The sound of the front door closing behind him and the blast of the cabbie's horn breaking up the crisp winter air came only a minute apart. Had Sullivan been able to remember the next paragraph his entire enterprise would have been sunk.

'It's like herding cats,' Doyle said when he and Sullivan were settled into the backseat of the car.

Sullivan nodded. 'It's true. You never had much luck in getting all of us together at one time.'

'Well, I never had much luck getting you anywhere.' Doyle looked for Teddy out the window but all he saw were sexless, shapeless bundles of humanity toddling down the street, trying not to fall on the ice. 'You could have made him wait.'

'You could have kept Tip from going out this morning. That would have saved us all a trip.'

There was nothing and no one who made Doyle think of Bernadette more than their oldest son. Sullivan was not like his mother. He did not possess a shred of her character, but he looked like her, and not just in the color of his hair. It was the way he held himself, the way he sat so easily in his own body, ankles, wrists, hands, all of that was hers. Bernadette would have been proud of the job Doyle had done with Teddy and Tip, but she never would have accepted his relationship with Sullivan. Whenever they were together he could hear her, pressing him to show more kindness, pressing for sympathy. Even the wreck Sullivan had made of his life would not have dissuaded his mother from her love. At thirty-three he was still the baby she had held in her arms. That was one of the many things Doyle had found so admirable about his wife: her ability to look at their children and see them at every age. She managed to hang on to every bit of love she had ever felt for them, while Doyle could only see the person they were at that exact moment in time. He didn't have to wonder if Bernadette might have changed if she had lived, if time would have worn her down to a lesser state of unconditional love. He knew it would never have happened. He tried to turn himself towards Sullivan now, to find the charity of spirit that Bernadette surely must have willed to him. 'We should have been allies,' he said finally, frustrated with himself for his inability to come up with anything better, and grateful not to have said anything worse. 'At least for the boys.'

Sullivan cracked the window and let a dose of

frigid wind brush his hair back from his forehead. 'But we're not.'

True, Doyle thought, but certainly some alliance is born of simply keeping up appearances. 'Is there anything we can agree on? I have to tell you, with this woman showing up and the accident, it would be a comfort to me.'

Sullivan sighed and rubbed at his eyes with his fingers. He was tired beyond measure, tired of not sleeping and tired of his family. 'I'm sure there are thousands of things. Global warming. You and I are both against global warming.'

'Jesus,' Doyle said. 'Roll up the fucking window.'

Sullivan raised his head, tried again. 'We both want the boys to do well, but the boys are going to do well, each in their own freakish way. It isn't what we'd wish for them but they'll find their happiness in the world.'

'Forget it.'

There was something in the flatness of his father's tone that seemed to jar Sullivan awake. For the first time since he'd left the hospital and Tennessee Moser in her bed waiting for surgery he decided to make a tentative engagement to the world. He considered the question and the deep canyon that sat between him and his father in the backseat of the cab. 'The girl,' he said finally.

Doyle was turned away from him now, his eyes tracing the shimmering surface of the frozen Charles. He said nothing.

'We are allies for the girl,' Sullivan said. 'Or we will be. We can agree on that.'

311

Doyle weighed out this offer, the pink-suited girl. 'What about the mother?'

Sullivan turned to him and, in doing so, inadvertently touched his knee to his father's knee. 'There you go. I offer the girl, you want the girl and her mother. Forget about the mother. Neither one of us knows anything about her. All I'm saying is that you and I can agree to get behind Kenya, to be helpful to her.'

Doyle could see her sitting in their living room, straight and still, listening to the music with her eyes closed. She made it through the first two movements of The Trout quintet and then he worried he was boring her. 'That's enough,' he said. 'I just wanted you to get an idea.' But she shook her head. She stopped him. And what she said then was that she could hear the stream in the music. 'She likes Schubert.'

Sullivan nodded. 'I believe that. She can play the piano a little, too. She played for Tip.'

This was better than anything he'd hoped for. She had wonderful hands. He had noticed them spread out flat on the kitchen table this morning, her fingers slender and long. It was with this image in his mind that he made his greatest admission to the son to whom he made a point of admitting nothing. 'I want to see if I can get her into Cathedral Grammar.'

Sullivan didn't like Cathedral Grammar, but that's because he didn't like the whole Cathedral system. He had been at Cathedral High School when his mother died. The nuns made every kid in the school send him a card, even the kids he had never heard of before. *Sorry about your*

312

mom, they said, one after the other. After awhile he stopped opening them. There was something luxurious about throwing away unopened mail. It seemed to him a very grown-up thing to do as he dropped entire stacks of cards into the trash. When he thought about his school what he saw were those envelopes sealed up tight, nestled in among the eggshells and coffee grounds. That probably wasn't reason enough to keep Kenya from going there. 'That's good. She'd do well there.'

A small peace washed over his father's face and Doyle smiled. Sullivan was genuinely horrified to see how little effort it took to make the old man happy. All he needed was the promise of a good deed, some task that he could concentrate on for the future. What would become of him once Teddy had left the house? What would become of him when there was no one left to meddle with? Sullivan wondered if Doyle would be waiting at the front steps of the school to pick Kenya up in the afternoon, if he would wait for her there all day.

'Here we are,' Doyle said, and he pulled out his wallet and paid the fare. He had one foot down in the snow when he turned back into the cab and pushed several folded bills towards his son who took them without a word and put them into the pocket of his coat.

There were several people in the waiting room but only one eleven-year-old girl in a bright pink track suit. She was sitting in the corner, away from the others, elbows on knees, her face in her hands. Doyle called her name.

She stood up quickly but when she turned to them she stopped, her eyes filling up with tears. They walked towards her and for one awful moment thought that they had misunderstood the gravity of the situation and were now about to receive the worst news possible from a child. 'He wouldn't take a cab,' she said.

Doyle took off his gray felt hat and held it by the brim. 'It doesn't matter,' he said, hoping that she would reassure him that the cab was the worst of it, but she said nothing. 'Is he all right?'

Kenya shook her head. 'He hurt his shoulder.' She crossed her right hand over to her own left shoulder, leaving it there for comfort. She was crying in earnest now. 'When they came and picked him up off the ground it was awful. He cried.'

Sullivan went to her and put his hands around her waist. He said one word, 'Up,' and then he lifted her so that her arms went around his neck, her long legs wrapped around his waist. In the moment that immediately preceded this very small leap and catch he was struck by the extent to which what he had said to Doyle in the cab had been the truth: they did agree on this girl, the one who now exhaled in long, damp sobs into the collar of his shirt. In many ways, Sullivan had been very good at his job in Africa. He had always known how to pick children up, how to comfort them without embarrassment, and in return the children found a solace in his skin, his hair. He made them hold their own weight by letting them cling to him. He didn't mind it. Kenya was too big to be carried, she was years past it, but Sullivan had always picked up the bigger children, boys or girls, anyone he could physically lift off the ground. In Africa, nobody weighed anything at all. It made him feel like a strongman, gathering up so many skinny arms and legs in his hands like bunches of sticks. He whispered into her ear, 'You didn't push him, did you? You didn't kick his crutch?'

She shook her head into the side of his neck.

'Then there's nothing to cry about.' He rubbed a circle on the small of her back.

Doyle came and stood beside them. 'I'll go in and see Tip and then I'll come back and tell you that everything's fine.'

Kenya nodded again but she couldn't raise her head. She had been put in charge, after all. She was the one with the money for cars.

Sullivan looked at his father, mouthed the word 'tired,' and Doyle nodded. 'We'll be right here,' Sullivan said. 'We'll wait for Teddy.'

'Will he be here soon?' Kenya asked, because now she was worried about everyone who wasn't in front of her.

'Oh no,' Sullivan said. 'He'll be late.'

Doyle did not need to ask anyone any questions this time. He knew the landscape. He knew that the door marked AUTHORIZED PERSONNEL ONLY was the one he was meant to walk through. What surprised him was that absolutely nothing had changed from the night before. The people even looked the same. The emergency room was like a casino in that way. It existed in a state of perpetual fluorescence that was meant to represent neither day nor night. It was a jar of alcohol solution in which time had been suspended.

'Ah, yes,' said Dr. Ball, bowing his head slightly to Doyle in a sympathetic acknowledgment of bad luck. 'Your son has come back to us.'

Doyle started, as if he had seen a ghost. 'Have you been here all night?'

Dr. Ball shook his head. 'No, no. I slept very well at home, thank you. It appears that I never leave, but then some would say the same of you. Your son, he asked for me. I have sewn up a cut above his ear. He said he did not care to see a plastic surgeon. It will be beneath his hair.'

Doyle thanked him and looked down the row of curtains, wondering where Tip was now.

The doctor sighed. 'I fear the shoulder is another story. It was dislocated in the fall. It's a very painful business, the shoulder coming out of the socket and then needing to be replaced. He's had a poor run of luck, your son, but this is not an uncommon circumstance. Crutches can be very deceitful at first.'

Doyle agreed, wishing to be out of his topcoat and scarf. There was a thin line of perspiration forming above his eyebrows. He found that he could hardly stand to be in this hallway again. The nurses, the lights, the empty gurneys lined against the wall, every bit of it struck him as unbearable. 'If I could see him now.'

'Certainly, yes.' Dr. Ball led him forward to the third bay. 'We have taken some X-rays. I want to see about the rotator cuff. It is probably fine but there is no point in his having to come back again. I've wrapped the shoulder to keep it stable. The bandages are not so much a medical necessity as they are a reminder for him not to use it.'

Doyle thanked the doctor for all of his attention and then he turned away. He did not want to see Dr. Ball again. He stepped inside the room and pulled the curtain behind him. Tip was stretched out, eyes closed, his shirt off. The white bandaging was extremely neat, binding the top of his left arm to his body as if it were a bad wing. The left side of his head was shaved in a four inch square above his ear that framed the six spiky black knots that were sewn into his skin, a perfect piece of modern art. His cheek was swollen and dark, and still, with all of that, the thing Doyle noticed first was how beautiful he was, how young and healthy and whole. His ribs expanded evenly with every breath and then made their gentle descent. Doyle put his hand on his son's forehead the way he had when Tip was a boy, a little wild boy who could not be comforted. 'How are you feeling?'

Tip opened his eyes and tried to focus. 'Like a fucking idiot,' he said.

'You fell.'

'She stood there and told me we had to take a cab.'

'Always listen to the girl.'

'I don't think of myself as a careless person, but twice in less than twenty-four hours makes you wonder.' He reached over and touched his shoulder very gently with the tips of his fingers.

'You were tired today. I never should have let you go out.'

Tip smiled slightly. 'I wasn't asking permission.'

'No one does. Not anymore.'

'Where's Kenya?'

'She's in the waiting room. She's pretty worried about you.'

'Is Teddy with her?'

'Sullivan.'

Tip raised his eyebrows.

'Teddy went to get your uncle. He thinks this would be the perfect moment for a family reunion. Anyway, Sullivan's doing fine. He likes the girl.'

'You have to see her run, Da,' Tip said. 'She's like a rocket. She's a hundred times better than either of us ever were. She looks like she could go to the Olympics tomorrow and wipe up the floor with everyone there. And she's a hell of a Girl Scout, too. She knew just what to do when I fell.' Tip didn't mention that she had in fact saved him twice, the first time being when he nearly collapsed on the way to the lab. In retrospect, it seemed a clear indication that the day should have been over when he could no longer get a key in the door. He also declined to mention her affinity for the fishes. It was a sign of maturity that he could recognize a peaceful moment and decide to let it stand.

'She seems to be an exceptional girl,' Doyle said.

Tip used his good arm to push himself up to sitting, then he slowly dropped his feet over the side of the table. 'Tell them I'm ready to go,' he said. 'We should all go upstairs with her, wait for her mom to get back to her room.'

Doyle started to form his objection, but then, in a similar moment of maturity, he thought better of it. Tip was right. They should go and be with Kenya. 'Let's get you dressed,' he said.

It had been a very long time since Doyle had threaded arms into sleeves or worked out another person's buttons. In this case it was all a pretty makeshift process that in the end left Tip looking like he was extremely broad chested and one arm short. Doyle went into the hall and found a wheelchair. 'Tell the doctor we'll be back,' he said to a nurse walking past. 'We're going up to check on someone.'

★   ★   ★

It wasn't until Teddy and his uncle were safely in the back of the taxi that he started to feel the weight of his mistake. There was Sister Claire standing in the snow without so much as a sweater, not waving goodbye but biting her lip, her arms wrapped around her waist. They had very nearly killed Father Sullivan just getting him dressed. Again and again he had buckled against them and asked to sit down, losing his breath the way another man his age might lose his train of thought — it was there, and then, just as quickly, it was gone. 'Maybe another day,' Sister Claire suggested, kneeling in front of the old priest and rubbing her thumbs across the tops of his hands. 'When it isn't so cold.'

'I'll be fine,' he said, losing his credibility when he had to stop and pant. 'Just ask Teddy.'

'I'll take perfect care of him,' Teddy promised. 'I'll bring him right back.'

'I don't think this is what's best.' She looked at Teddy very directly now.

But Father Sullivan waved her off. 'Don't scare the boy to death,' he said. 'I'm making the decision myself. No one's going to say I'm not old enough to make up my own mind. I can manage this fine. Everyone needs a little adventure now and then.' He had made his commitment, after all, and now he was settled on his decision. He had found that it was only uncertainty that made him anxious.

They couldn't get his shoes on because his feet were swollen. They weren't terrible, not as bad as they can get, but despite the wrestling and coaxing, nothing went on. In the end they put him in heavy socks and the sheepskin slippers that came up high on his ankles like Robin Hood boots and Teddy made promises to keep him out of the snow. Teddy had bought him those slippers for his birthday just two months before. Now Sister Claire wouldn't look at him at all as she got on her hands and her knees on the floor and tugged them up.

'Look how pretty the snow is!' Father Sullivan said in the back-seat of the taxi as they pulled away from Regina Cleri, Sister Claire growing smaller and smaller behind them. 'I get used to seeing everything from one vantage point and I start to forget, the world does not take place from a fourth floor window.'

'Could you turn the heater up?' Teddy asked the driver. Immediately they passed Mass.

General. If only last night's accident could have taken place near a hospital that was so close to them.

Father Sullivan exhaled heavily and leaned against Teddy's shoulder. 'I don't want to close my eyes. I want to see everything. There hasn't been a snow like this in years.'

'Get a minute's sleep if you can.'

The back wheels of the taxi lost traction and slid sharply to the left so that Teddy was half crushing his uncle with no warning at all. Then they found their grip again and they slid forward without comment. Giant, errant clumps of snow kept falling out of the branches of the trees overhead. They slammed into the windows in startling attacks and made the driver curse and swerve. That was one possibility Teddy had not considered: an accident. What would he do if he had to take his uncle out of the car in the middle of Storrow Drive? He could carry him, certainly. He could get him into a coffee shop, someplace warm, until he found another car.

'I didn't realize this would be so hard,' Teddy said, his heart cut in half by his own miscalculation.

Father Sullivan remained adamant in his good cheer. 'At least we're going to a hospital. If anything happens to me I'm covered.'

Teddy closed his eyes. He had propagated a disaster, possibly even a murder. He put his arm around his uncle and his uncle slipped down farther in his seat. Even the sitting, the riding, was a kind of cruelty. Hadn't Doyle looked at him directly and assured him that a visit would be a bad idea for everyone involved? Mother or not, Teddy didn't know Tennessee Moser, and while he was sorry she'd been hurt he could not understand what would have possessed him to risk the one person he could least afford to do without. Everything was going by them so fast. It set Teddy's heart racing. 'What if we went back now?' he said.

His uncle pushed himself up straighter to get a better look out the window. 'We're at the Citgo sign already,' he said. 'We're more than halfway there!'

Teddy used his sleeve to wipe the condensation from the glass, but still the river and streets and banks of snow looked all the same: damp and gray. 'The roads are still bad.'

'That's why there isn't any traffic. That's why this is the better day to go.'

By the time they finally arrived at Mount Auburn, Teddy had about decided they would never be able to leave. He wrestled the wheelchair out of the trunk of the cab and then wrestled his uncle out of the backseat while the driver stood by impassively, waiting for payment.

'Looks like you made it just in time,' the driver said, casting an eye to the pale uncle who was shivering inside the folds of his outsized overcoat. Teddy shelled the money out fast and ignored his change in favor of getting Father Sullivan inside. Once they had sprung through the electric doors and into the waiting rush of warm air his bad idea suddenly didn't seem so bad after all. There in the waiting room sat his entire immediate family: Doyle and Tip, Sullivan and Kenya, all together. The four of them turned their faces towards the gust of wind coming in through the open door and smiled. Neither Doyle nor Sullivan had ever been to visit him at Regina Cleri, and Tip had only come one time and then left after five minutes. To Father Sullivan it was as if this part of his family, these people whom he loved, had all packed up and gone to Africa. Now in the waiting room of the hospital they were returned to him. The joy swept across him like a wave of electricity. Teddy could feel it passing through him, the joy at seeing those very faces that Teddy had been unable to beg or cajole into a visit all these years. Whatever the price for bringing them all together to see the old man so close to the end of his life, it was worth it.

'Tip, Tip,' Father Sullivan said, trying to put some boom into his voice to cover over the tremor that was there. 'What a good man you are, getting yourself a chair so I wouldn't feel out of place.'

'I fell especially for you,' Tip said, and reached out to touch his uncle's hand.

'And my own namesake.' He put his hands on the armrests of his chair and made an attempt at bringing himself to standing but Sullivan leaned forward instead and kissed him on his cold cheek.

He loved them, each of them, for being themselves and for being part of his favorite niece and for being the family of Teddy, whom he loved above all others. 'Such a long time,' Father Sullivan said.

'A long time,' his great-nephew agreed. 'Now you're the famous one in the family.'

'Don't believe everything you read,' Father Sullivan said. 'Doyle, son, tell me who this is.' He pointed to Kenya, who was standing halfway behind Sullivan.

Doyle made the introductions, putting a hand on the shoulder of his wife's uncle. To see him like this, a small sack of bones in a chair, could only make him think what a long time ago it was that Bernadette had died. When she was alive John Sullivan was a tall man. He played softball with the boys in the street and smoked cigarettes on their front steps in the last hot days of summer.

Kenya stepped forward, hesitated for an instant, and then held out her hand. It was not because he was old, she didn't mind old, it was because he was familiar to her and her inability to remember him made her feel suddenly shy. Why should she remember? She must have seen everyone the Doyles ever knew at one point or another, in mass, at a rally, in the park. He put both of his cold hands around the warm one she offered him and held her there. It struck her how much his hands resembled certain pale, misshapen fish she had seen earlier in the day.

'It's your mother I've come to see, isn't it?' he asked.

Kenya nodded her head politely. She didn't know who he was coming to see but she would have thought it must be Tip. The one thing she was not feeling inclined to share at the moment was her mother. She assumed that once her mother was safely awake, all the Doyles would just go home and leave them there, and then this long and interesting foray into the other side of the glass would come to its natural conclusion.

'Teddy just wanted me to say hello,' Father Sullivan said.

'It's fine.' Kenya worried that her face had betrayed her. 'I just don't know how she'll be feeling.'

The group came to a unanimous agreement that since they were all together now it would be best to do whatever waiting that was left up on the surgical floor. That way Kenya would be sure to be there when her mother came back to her room. They went to the elevator in pairs, Teddy pushing Uncle Sullivan, Doyle pushing Tip, and Sullivan steering Kenya lightly by keeping his thumb on her shoulder. Kenya wanted to run up the stairs. There was no reason in the world to wait for an elevator when there were perfectly good stairs to be devoured. She was tired of so much holding back, pretending that she was as slow as everyone else. She would be slow when the time came to crawl into bed beside her mother. She would be careful and gentle then. She would stretch her thin frame down the length of her mother's side, bury her face beneath her mother's arm. She would not go away from her again. This time she would know better. In the hallway her legs jangled while they tried to stay still. Sullivan leaned forward, whispered in her ear. 'Wait.'

It took a bit of calculated arrangement but they all made it in. 'It's been a long time since we've been together like this,' Teddy said. Now that his fear had left him he remembered it only as over-zealous caution. He was proud of his accomplishment, bringing everyone together, making his uncle so happy. Even if nothing came of Father Sullivan's visiting Kenya's mother, and Teddy had let go of all of those expectations in gratitude that his uncle didn't die in the taxi, the trip would still be counted as a success. Kenya pushed the button for the third floor.

'I can't even remember the last time we were together,' Doyle said.

While everyone else was thinking about communions and confirmations, Father Sullivan came up with an answer. 'It was Natalie's funeral,' he said, and nodded his head as if agreeing with himself. 'That was a lovely service. A Jewish service, wasn't it?'

And with that question they ended the short trip up in silence.

'Who's Natalie?' Kenya whispered to Sullivan when they stepped into the hall. But Sullivan only put his finger to his lips and shook his head. The old man wrong, anyway. They weren't together that afternoon. Sullivan himself, the key player in the story, was missing. He had spent the day of her funeral in his own hospital bed, fast asleep.

What an entourage they made coming down the hall, Father Sullivan in his slippers, Tip in his boot and one empty sleeve, the long-legged black girl who walked with the redheaded man at her shoulder pulling out into the lead. It would have been impossible for anyone who saw them to know that they were all visiting one person. The two men in wheelchairs, one old and one young, both looked like they were patients being returned to their respective rooms. They glided past the nurses' station and, despite the size of their group, drew no attention. They knew where they were going.

But when they got to the room and found the door halfway open, they saw a woman sleeping in the bed and realized they were late rather than early. Everyone stopped but Kenya. She broke from them without word, as if they were people she had never seen before. While they each considered their own private hesitations, she went to her mother in her bed, asleep. As far as Kenya was concerned there was only one person in the entire world to see, and now that she was there right in front of her she was washed over in relief. Her mother didn't look too bad at all, a little swollen on the left side of her face, a bandage taped to her forehead, but she was completely whole and herself and the sight of her lying there brought Kenya to tears. She cried from happiness, a concept that had previously never made any sense to her at all. So strong was her love at the moment she felt her heart knocking wildly against her chest as if the heart itself was leaping forward to the woman in the bed. Two heavy white sheets and a thin green blanket with nearly all of the color washed out sat high up on her mother's chest. Kenya pulled back one side carefully, carefully to take her hand. 'Are you sleeping?' she said in a hopeful whisper, and thought of all the times she had said that before, only to have her mother open one eye and peer at her. 'Let me sleep,' she would say, and then open her arms for Kenya to crawl in beside her. Kenya wasn't expecting that now, not really, so when she got no reply she contented herself with her mother's hand. Ever so slightly her mother's hand squeezed back, a call as clear as if she had said her name. Kenya leaned forward to kiss that hand and then pressed it against her cheek.

Teddy stuck his head in the door. 'Is it okay if we come in?'

Kenya looked up at him, nodded, but she hadn't meant all of them at once. By the time they'd pushed in, the room was too small. They were lucky there was no one in the other bed.

'How's she doing?' Tip said.

'I think she looks good. Don't you think?'

Tip looked at her and he felt a chill pass over him. Teddy at the top half of her face, himself around the mouth and jaw. 'She does,' he said.

'She does what?' Tennessee said very quietly, and the members of the party all let out a collective *Hey!* Kenya's head pitched forward to the mattress and shook the bed. 'Careful, baby,' her mother said, her voice so light and low that only Kenya heard it.

'Awake!' Kenya said. She would not lift her head from her mother's side.

Dear God there was a pain in her stomach. Hadn't she said that to someone once? She would not be able to hold herself awake for long. It was like suspending a chin-up. She was too tired now. She wanted to see her baby but she wanted to swim back down into the darker water where she had been, where it was quiet.

'How are you feeling?' Teddy asked. He felt more comfortable there now than he had this morning.

Tennessee cracked open her eyes. All of them were there. Too many of them. It was more than she could imagine. 'Okay. Fine,' she whispered.

Tip knew he should say something, thank you or hello, but he only sat there holding on to the arms of his chair. His shoulder felt like someone was rooting around the joint with a paring knife and he moved it back and forth slightly to exaggerate the pain. The pain somehow forgave him for his silence.

'You're tired,' Kenya said to her mother, and when she didn't answer she said it to the room. 'She's tired.' She didn't want to be rude but she couldn't see the point in their staying now. They had seen her, she was sleeping, there couldn't be any more to it than that.

But Teddy had come too far to feel so easily discouraged. A prayer, on the chance that it could be beneficial, was certainly worth a try. He pushed Father Sullivan forward in his chair and since Kenya didn't make any effort to move he stayed down at the end of the bed near her mother's feet.

'I brought my uncle to see you,' Teddy said, his voice a fraction too loud.

Doyle shifted uncomfortably near the door. 'Maybe I should step into the hall. We're probably taking up all the oxygen in the room. Sullivan?' he said.

Sullivan looked to Kenya, who nodded her head at him. 'Okay,' she said.

'I'll go out, too,' Tip said. 'Just for a minute.'

Doyle was backing out of the room at the moment Father Sullivan leaned forward and for the first time got a closer look at the woman in the bed. 'Wait a minute,' he said. Doyle thought he was speaking to him and so he stopped, his hands on the back of Tip's chair. Kenya turned to face Father Sullivan and he looked at both of their faces together. 'I know you,' he said. 'I know you both. Teddy, don't you remember?' He looked at his nephew and then back to the woman in the bed. It wasn't his imagination. He was sure of it. 'This is Tennessee Moser. She worked at Regina Cleri years ago. We were close then, we were friends.'

'The priests' home,' Kenya said, nodding, because now she could place him as well. 'You lived there.'

'Tennessee,' the priest said.

Tennessee knew that voice and for that voice she opened her eyes. They had brought him out to her? In this weather? 'Father,' she said. 'My God, you shouldn't have come.'

'How do you know her?' Teddy said. 'I never saw her there.' He panicked at the thought. He couldn't have missed her at Regina Cleri! He felt that he could not endure such a failure, that he missed his own mother in the place he went to day after day.

But Father Sullivan wasn't looking at Teddy now. He was so pleased to have found his friends again, to have found everyone in so unlikely a

330

place. 'You came to see me a couple of times,' he said to Kenya. 'But you were so much smaller then! You've gotten so tall I didn't recognize you.'

'I didn't see her,' Teddy said.

Doyle and Tip pushed in closer now and Sullivan was close behind them, all of them watching. Father Sullivan did not think of what it meant for Tennessee to have worked in the place that he lived, nor did he think of what it meant for Teddy to have missed her. For the moment he was only glad to see this woman he had been so fond of. She came not long after he had moved to Regina Cleri, and she had always taken good care of him. He had thought he was so sick in those days, too sick to stay in the rectory anymore, but in retrospect he had still been in the bloom of health. Sometimes in the afternoons she would sit with him for awhile before she went home, talk about politics and things they had read in the paper. She liked to go to college lectures that were open to the public, and sometimes, she had admitted, ones that weren't open to the public, but it was easy to stay towards the back and no one ever asked her to leave. He remembered she brought him books from the library. How bright she was! Many times he had told her she should find a way to quit and go back to school, but when she left the job abruptly without coming back to tell him goodbye he felt unreasonably dismayed. With Tennessee there to visit, Regina Cleri had been bearable to him, and without her he felt like what he was: a useless old man who had been shelved away to die. 'I missed you so much after you left,' he said.

'You too,' she said honestly, though it took so much effort to say the words.

Father Sullivan did not speak of her to Teddy, come to think of it. His longing and disappointment once she had gone had made him feel too childish. Hadn't he even been worth a phone call, a note? It had bothered him for months, the unfinished quality of her departure, until finally he had disciplined himself not to think of her anymore. Now all this time later there was an answer, or at least a part of one. She was here. He pictured her coming into his room with his coffee in the morning. 'Are you still in that bed?' she'd always say to him.

'Tennessee,' he said, and rested his hand against the calf of her leg where it lay beneath two sheets and a pale green blanket.

His vision turned gray and then white, a fuzzy blurring of everything that was before him, as if the room had all been snapped away in a sudden wall of bitter wind. The awful cold of it rose up his arm and spread through his body, a cold that was worse than anything he had ever felt or imagined, colder than he had been the winter he was nine years old and broke through the ice on the Charles. He remembered now that black water pouring into his ears and down his throat, flooding his nose and eyes, the blind choking panic that came before his older brother pulled him out by reaching his hockey stick over the jagged edge of ice and into the water. Colder even than he was on that walk home, shaking beneath his brother's arm. He tried to open his ribs, to fill his lungs, but all the air inside him was frozen. His chest was frozen. There was nothing to breathe. It was as awful as any death is awful, like his own death would be awful, and then he wondered if that was what he was feeling, his own death now, surrounded by the people he loved. Tennessee had come back somehow to see him out of his life. He didn't understand why this would be the case but then what experience did he have with his own death?

'Uncle Sullivan,' Teddy said, and put his hands beneath his arms to pull him up. He could hear Doyle's voice from down the hall, the voice of never-ending authority, calling for a doctor. Teddy was there and Sullivan was there and Tip and this lovely child and they all seemed to be rushing towards him at once, everyone speaking to him, speaking over him, and then Teddy picked up both of his hands in his hands and raised them over his head and in that instant he let go of Tennessee's leg and the air seeped in. He took a shallow, broken breath. The hard block of ice that was pressed against his heart receded an inch and then two inches and then he felt the sudden release of a weight removed.

'Can you hear me?' Teddy said.

Father Sullivan nodded his head, though his own head seemed like too much weight to hold anymore. He wanted to let go of it. He was ready, truly, to give his life away. Everything was rushing. His eyes were closed but he was moving through the door. 'Help her,' he said, but he couldn't even hear the words himself. He was drowned out by the voice of a woman who was scattering the rest of them behind her, scolding as she drove them from the room. 'You never should have been in here in the first place,' she said. 'She's just come back from recovery.' And Father Sullivan heard this bit of news and he held on to it. The voice, or his memory of it, followed him all the way down the hall. *You never should have been in here in the first place.*

What came to his mind as he struggled to right the oxygen deficit in his lungs were those first two women who had come to see him in Regina Cleri, Nena and Helen, the ones he had supposedly healed, and he thought for the first time that he may indeed have helped them, because now he knew what it was to touch someone who was outside of help, to feel with what remained of your own life that which could not be saved. The doctor, in a horrible error of judgment, came to him and not to her, and the next thing he knew he was falling over the edge of the world, through the wondrous swirling sheets of snow and down deeper and deeper into sleep.

★   ★   ★

When Father Sullivan woke up again he was in a bed himself, a bed that was unfamiliar. There was a plastic tube lying flat across his body blowing oxygen into his nose, another tube dripping something into his arm, and Teddy was there sitting beside him. What he saw when he opened his eyes was Teddy's relief, Teddy smiling hugely. 'I thought I had killed you for sure,' he said.

Father Sullivan looked at him and knew from the simple expression of happiness on his face that whatever was coming had not yet arrived. 'Where's your mother?' he said.

Teddy hesitated for a minute but then he let it go. 'She's in her room.'

'Go back to her.' He tried to keep his voice calm.

Teddy shook his head. 'I'll see her later. I'm going to keep an eye on you for now. The doctor said you had an episode of ventricular tachycardia. He said that it could have happened anytime, but I know it was my fault, this has all just been too much. I was crazy to have brought you out like this.' Teddy hadn't called Sister Claire yet, even though he knew that too much time had gone by and she would be anxious now, imagining some terrible scenario that in fact would bear a remarkable resemblance to what had actually happened.

'Go find her doctor,' Father Sullivan said.

'You want the doctor?' Teddy was already on his feet.

'*Her* doctor.' Every word spoken was a flight of stairs to run. He gave himself a minute to concentrate on the air. The oxygen burned his nostrils, and still he wanted more than what he was getting. 'Go.'

Teddy eased back into his chair, picked up his uncle's hand. 'She broke her hip, do you remember that? She was hit by a car last night. But everything's okay now. She came through the surgery fine.'

'I know what happened.' He waited, pulled in breath. 'You brought me here to see her.'

Teddy shook his head. 'I didn't listen to you. You asked me not to do this and I just thought ... I don't know what I thought. I wasn't thinking. She's going to be fine. It's just going to take some time.'

Father Sullivan tried to imagine what Tennessee would want at the end of her life. He didn't know her well at all, and he didn't know anyone well enough to answer a question like that. He only knew that she had been good company, that the time passed more slowly on the days she didn't come in. He could picture her in his room as if she was walking towards him now, healthy and young. How she seemed to tower over him when he sat in his chair. 'How are you feeling today, Father?' she would say to him. 'Has your nephew been by to see you yet?'

'Get up now,' Father Sullivan said to Teddy.

Teddy did stand up and he pulled another blanket over his uncle's legs. 'Are you cold?'

'Why?' Father Sullivan felt a sob well up in his chest. He had wasted so much of his strength in life, run it out on nothing. If only he had the legs to carry him back to her. Maybe there was something that could be done. He couldn't save her but maybe he could find someone, a surgeon who could cut out whatever it was that was inside her. 'Go.' He closed his eyes and pulled in every bit of air he could manage.

'Look at you,' Teddy said. 'You've got to rest.'

'Then go.'

Teddy was stung but he refused to show it. His

336

uncle was old and ill and confused. His oxygen saturation was low. He was not responsible for anything he said. 'I'll stay with you. I'll keep everyone else out so that you can get some rest.'

Father Sullivan reached up for his nephew's hand. He wished he had the strength to squeeze it tight, to hurt him just enough to make himself heard. Teddy whom he loved above all others. Teddy who was his comfort and delight. It would be the last time he would ever see him as a child, the last time before all of the guilt and regret came to sit with him for the rest of his life. 'Listen to me, Teddy, I'm telling you.' His voice came out in nothing but a whisper. It was a strain to hear it at all over the hiss of the oxygen. 'Go as fast as you can now. Run.'

11

Doyle had insisted on arriving early. They each had a ticket but the seating was open and he wanted to be sure they could all find seats together. The ceremony was held in the symphony hall downtown, and while the entire auditorium offered good acoustics, acoustics were not what Doyle was there for. He wanted an unobstructed view of Tip crossing the stage and collecting his medical degree from Johns Hopkins.

'We should have packed a meal,' Sullivan said, crossing in front of the knees of parents who were even more neurotic than his own and so had arrived earlier.

'I've got some Life Savers in my purse,' Kenya said and patted the white leather bag at her hip.

'Always prepared,' Sullivan said.

Teddy dropped into the seat beside his father and opened his program. He rested his finger beneath his brother's name. 'Look at that, Thomas O'Neill Doyle — Warfield T. Longcope Prize in Clinical Medicine. Now that's something.'

'He should have gotten the convocation address,' Doyle said and looked at the two names above Tip's. 'He almost got it.'

'He didn't want it,' Kenya said. 'You know Tip doesn't make speeches.'

'They should have given it to Teddy,' Sullivan

said. 'The first non-medical school graduate to give the convocation address.'

Teddy rose to the call without hesitation. ''Duty — honor — country,'' he said in the voice of an old white man who'd been battered by war. ''Those three hallowed words reverently dictate what you ought to be, what you can be, what you will be. They are your rallying points; to build courage when courage seems to fail; to regain faith when there seems to be little cause for faith; to create hope when hope becomes forlorn.''

'Old patients never die,' Sullivan said, 'they just fade away.'

'You're going to need to start quoting yourself,' Kenya said to Teddy. 'Forget about all these dead people. Kids are going to want to hear Teddy Doyle speeches, wearing their Teddy Doyle T-shirts.'

Teddy smiled but shook his head. 'Nothing like that.'

'You should listen to your sister,' Doyle said. It was what he said about most things these days. It made no sense to him how Teddy could have turned himself towards politics and still be shy, and yet it seemed to be his very shyness that people found themselves attracted to. He won both his junior and senior class presidencies without regarding a word of Doyle's advice. He led the Student Coalition Against the War. He spent two summers working for the Massachusetts senator for whom he was named without letting Doyle put in so much as a phone call, and in fact it was that same senator and not Doyle who was so devoted to Teddy that he used all of his considerable sway to get him a spot in Georgetown law school in the fall. Contrary to all logic, the softer Teddy spoke, the more the room quieted down to listen.

'When Teddy's sworn in as president, will we have to get there early to stake out our seats or do you think he'll save them for us?'

Kenya shook her head. 'Saving seats isn't very presidential.'

'I don't want to be president,' Teddy said.

'You don't know what you want yet,' his father said.

'That's true. I don't know what I want. I only know what I don't want.' Teddy was working as an advocate for the homeless in Albany now, and while he had come to accept the fact that he needed the law degree, he was starting to think that political life was not necessarily a matter of elected office.

'I can see it now,' Sullivan said. 'Teddy will be the president, Tip will be the surgeon general, and Kenya will sweep the Olympics.'

Doyle was reading the program. He did not look up. 'Something like that.'

Teddy and Kenya both turned to look at Sullivan, but Sullivan only dropped his eyes and became interested in the program himself.

The addition of Kenya to the family had had the unexpected effect of giving Teddy much more sympathy for Sullivan than he had ever had before. He saw now how easily Doyle's attention had turned away from Tip and himself as it settled on her, just as it had turned away from

Sullivan twenty-five years before. The difference was that Kenya was magically exempt from everything the boys had had to endure. She didn't have to go to Kerry's fund-raising breakfasts. She was never once sent into the cold to hand out leaflets or canvass door to door. Politics, just at the moment that Teddy had finally picked it up, had ceased to be his father's driving interest. He had Kenya's spring meets now, her fall meets, her state championships, Junior Olympics, trophy halls. There was a never-ending stream of races for Doyle to follow now, and while they might not be for congressional seats, it could nearly be counted on that the gazelle of Union Park was going to win.

Not that it mattered. Teddy was as proud of Kenya as Doyle was, and despite what anyone might say when he wasn't in the room, he hadn't turned to politics to please his father. He had turned to politics in hopes of pleasing God. It was the pledge he had made in the hours before his mother's death, his second mother, or his first one, depending on how you counted them. While they waited for the outcome of her second surgery of the day, Teddy went into the stairwell of the hospital alone and swore to take on the heaviest mantle he could imagine. His hope was that God might forgive him, that God might even choose to spare the people Teddy loved. Teddy was responsible for what had happened, and his responsibility lay in the fact that he hadn't listened to anyone. The chance to do the right thing, say the right thing, spring into considerate action had presented itself again and again, and from the moment the car came bearing down on Tip in the snow Teddy had not moved fast enough. He did not think of reneging on his promise later that evening when Tennessee Moser died, nor did he think of giving it up the following summer when he lost his uncle. While Teddy had hoped for God's favor, it was not the contingency of the deal. His decision was his penance, in the same way medical school had been Tip's penance, though neither brother spoke of it as such. But both of them could see there would have been a benefit to being more like Sullivan, who had dealt with the mistakes of his life by setting himself adrift. Teddy and Tip had chosen the opposite course instead. Their punishment was to nail themselves down.

The lights in the symphony hall lowered and Sullivan whispered to Kenya, 'Here we go.' One by one the various deans and professors approached the podium and scattered their perfunctory pearls of wisdom over the graduates' heads. When they were finished the convocation speaker took the stage, a tiny Indian girl who had to bend the microphone as far down as she could in order to make herself heard.

'For four years we have worked alongside each other,' she began. 'And tonight we share a common dream.'

Tip, who sat in the first row of graduates by virtue of his placement in the alphabet, was fairly certain they did not, unless all of his classmates had in fact been privately dreaming of fishes. That was not to say they were all thinking noble

342

thoughts of medical science. Most of them, he knew them well enough to say, were probably thinking of dinner about now, about cleaning out their apartments and getting the hell out of Baltimore. But Tip alone was seeing the members of the faculty on the stage decked out in their doctoral hoods and bright academic finery as a pulsing reef of stoplight parrotfish, scrawled filefish, bright blueheads, and yellow-head wrasse. He was always seeing people as fish. He saw his patients as mackerel, as bass, that was how he remembered them. It was the device he used to endure their suffering and steel his interest in their complaints. And as he listened to little Soma Choudery, who had been his cadaver partner in pathology, and who but for that fact he might have dated, drone on about the nobility of their chosen profession, he realized medicine was not the profession he cared to choose at all. It was not helpful, normal, or beneficial to anyone for him to continue on with this particular mistake, no matter how far down the road he had taken it. It was at that moment, somewhere between Soma's charge that they never cease to learn from what their patients had to teach them and her hope that they would someday move towards a single-payer system, that Tip decided to return to ichthyology. He had always gotten his best thinking done during speeches. It came to him clearly and for the first time that he did not have to go through a residency and internship. He did not have to practice medicine in order to prove any more completely how sorry he was. At the end of the day what his father had always suspected about him was true: he did not find human beings as interesting as fishes. Their bodies lack the grace, the fluidity of motion. There were no new species of human to discover, and if there were Tip hoped that they would be left alone.

Not that he could completely regret what he had done. If medical school had not cured him of his grief, it had at least tempered it. His decision to shoulder this cross in the first place had come to him as quickly and certainly as his decision to lay it down: four and a half years ago in the waiting room of Mount Auburn Hospital when a nervous young girl in a lab coat that said 'Dr. Spruce' on the pocket explained that, unbeknown to anyone, there had been a slight laceration to the spleen at the time of the accident. Tennessee Moser, on her second brief appearance in Tip's life, was then rushed back into surgery and it was there that she died. She left behind a coat, a purse, a dark green hat, two yet-again-motherless sons, and one freshly minted motherless daughter. He could still see Kenya when she first came to live with them. For months she would only sit on the very edges of the furniture, looking like a girl who meant to leap up from the house on Union Park and run as fast as she could for home the minute they turned their backs.

After Soma had wrapped it all together on some pithy note about the implicit dignity of human life, the dean of the medical school began reading through the names of the class. When Thomas O'Neill Doyle was called, Tip crossed the stage and heard a small, unrestrained cheer go up from the middle of the hall. Tip's anatomy professor would be pleased to know that at that moment Tip was thinking about the spleen. That was specifically the thing that had driven Tip to medical school, an organ that ranked only slightly above the appendix in its unnecessary relationship to the human body. 'The spleen,' he had screamed at Dr. Spruce, because even as an ichthyologist he had taken human physiology his sophomore year. He gave himself four and a half years to wonder how any competent doctor could fail to inquire as to the state of the internal organs of a woman who had been hit by a Chevy Tahoe in a snowstorm, four and a half years to wonder if they would have failed had she not been black and uninsured. It wasn't until his third year during a surgical rotation that he understood that the laceration would have bled into the abdomen all night, the slowest drip a body would allow, and that they then gave her post-surgical blood thinners to prevent the possibility of blood clots to her lungs after her hip replacement, and that was the thing that opened up the flow so that by the time she was awake enough to grab at her own round, hard stomach and cry, she was already as good as dead.

Tip's penance was neither as cruel nor as abstract as his brother's. All he had to do was save someone else, if not someone stepping out in front of a car then at least that same person brought into an emergency room after the fact. He had thought the world was in need of a few decent doctors, ones who could see past the bones, and after his years at Johns Hopkins he was greatly assured that the world would have them. All the students he met were intelligent, many were compassionate, a few, like Tip himself, were true scientists. He did not regret the time he had spent there. The knowledge he gained could only improve him. After he got a doctorate in evolutionary biology he would be perhaps the first medical doctor of fishes.

Tip pulled up his mortarboard on the left side and discreetly scratched the scar over his ear which had never stopped itching. The ankle and the shoulder had turned out fine. He went running on the weekends and never gave it a thought, unless he ran with Kenya. He told her the ankle was the reason he couldn't keep up with the pace she set. It was Kenya who was always pressing him back towards the fishes, whose unwavering call he had on this night finally agreed to answer. **You are insane!** she e-mailed him day after day. **I am going to the Amazon without you.** Everyone knew that Tip had gone to medical school because he felt responsible for their mother's death, because he saw himself as too self-involved to even lift up his head and look through the snow for the lights of a car, and too scientifically limited to realize a leaking spleen when it presented itself. Only Kenya thought that this wasn't reason enough to give up the science he loved.

At the end of the program the graduates stood and repeated the Hippocratic Oath, the updated version that did not make the doctor forswear sexual relations with the male and female slaves in the patient's home, then there was a hearty round of applause, an orderly procession, and it was done. Tip turned his back on it all and set out to find his family. As he swam into the crowd, he was struck by the way everything looked different now. His heart was nearly bursting from the joy he had chosen to allow himself. There were no tonsils in front of him, no earaches, irritable bowels, cancer, cracked femurs. There was only an endless ocean of schooling fish, the quick and shimmering dart of life that he belonged to. He walked past all those happy parents snapping pictures of the young physicians they had produced, all those young physicians nervously thinking ahead to their residencies. It was not the day to break the news to Doyle, even if Tip believed the decision would not affect him as it would have in what they referred to as the pre-Kenya days. He milled through the people spreading out across the lobby and he saw them as anchovies, smelts, and grunions flashing silvery in the light. Ten feet away he saw Teddy wave his long arm above his head and Tip went to him gratefully.

'Dr. Doyle,' his brother said and kissed him unabashedly on the lips. 'I am so proud of you.'

'I can't believe you left the poor,' Tip said and put his arm around his brother's shoulder.

'The poor can soldier through for a weekend without me.'

Then the crowd shifted imperceptibly and opened up a narrow path for Doyle and Sullivan and Kenya to meet them. They were all together,

347

each one singing Tip's praises, giving their congratulations. 'Every family needs a doctor,' Sullivan said as Doyle arranged his children for a photograph.

Kenya, now impossibly tall and wearing a lemon yellow sun-dress, looped her lanky arms around Tip's neck and for a moment allowed herself to hang there. 'What a waste of a mind,' she said.

Doyle shook his hand and then clapped him hard on the shoulder. 'We have reservations,' he said. 'The Brass Elephant.' He looked at his watch. 'We don't want to lose them.'

Sullivan looked out over the milling crowd. 'Think of all those poor fools with no reservations.'

Together they trudged through the miserable neighborhoods of downtown Baltimore in the dark, feeling the car might as well have been parked in West Virginia. Tip, as the graduate, got the front seat, and Sullivan drove. Doyle and Teddy and Kenya crowded in the back.

'Well,' Doyle said and shook his head. 'It's a remarkable thing.'

'Not so remarkable. Didn't you see all those people graduating?'

'We saw the two people who graduated ahead of you,' Teddy said. 'We didn't care about the rest of them.'

'You only notice the ones who beat you in the race,' Kenya said.

Sullivan looked in his rearview mirror. 'Which would mean what, exactly? That you've never noticed anyone?'

348

Kenya leaned forward and slapped the back of Sullivan's head while Doyle slid a trim white box between the seats and tapped it against Tip's arm. 'This is from us,' he said.

The sight of the box made Tip strangely anxious. It was like getting a wedding present on the day of a broken engagement. 'You shouldn't have gotten me a gift,' he said. He meant it.

'A little something. Open it up. Kenya did the bow.'

'I'm a genius,' Kenya said.

Tip slid the ribbon over the top so as not to disturb his sister's work and rustled through the tissue paper. It was a stethoscope, a Littmann. He held the cool metal in his hands and wondered how many of his classmates were unwrapping their own Littmanns at this exact moment. 'It's lovely.'

'I know you have one,' Doyle said.

'This is much nicer.'

Sullivan smacked the steering wheel with the open palm of his hand. 'I think we should give him something else!' he said. 'What is a stethoscope on such a momentous occasion? We should give him something momentous!'

'I did my best,' Doyle said.

'This is plenty,' Tip said. What if he was wrong? All that money, all that time. Everyone they knew so full of pride and expectation. Already distant family members and friends of the family were waiting in the wings for free medical advice. Tip slid back the knot of his tie and flipped the collar button out of the hole.

'Give him the house,' Teddy said. 'He could

set up his office in the dining room.'

'Listen,' Tip said, because suddenly he was terrified of losing his nerve. It was starting to sound terribly childish even to him that something as cumbersome as medical school could be written off as lightly as a simple error in judgment.

'The house is too big,' Kenya said. 'He won't have any place to keep it.'

'I'd miss the house,' Doyle admitted. This was the day, the perfect day, all five of them together in the car, everyone laughing except for Tip and there was nothing new about that. That's why he had been the one to get through medical school. All that seriousness had paid off.

And then Tip hit on the one idea that could change everything. 'Give me the statue,' he said. It's what they all said now that they had moved away, all three of the brothers longed to have it with them. All three were ready to stake their claim to that one thing that could not be divided among them, and in the meantime it stayed where it was. But for the briefest flash Tip felt the depths to which this time he meant it. He was the least likely candidate for inheritance, neither the blood son that Sullivan was nor the soulful Catholic like Teddy, but he craved ownership every bit as much. Give him the statue and he'd go ahead with the plan, he would take that residency at Vanderbilt that he was already declining in his mind. Give him the statue and he would do everything he said he was going to do.

But his brothers only laughed, and Doyle

laughed with them. Finally Tip had made a really good joke. 'I'd sooner see you have the house,' Sullivan said.

Tip put the stethoscope back in its slender box and was free again. He would keep the gift to remember tonight. He would keep it in his desk as a cautionary tale when he was safely back with the fishes.

★　★　★

Doyle had rented a suite in a good hotel and the five of them slept there in Baltimore, he and Sullivan in one room, Tip and Teddy in the other, and Kenya on the foldout couch in the sitting room between them. They had laughed and talked all night. They had eaten too much and had too much to drink too late, and this time they all fell asleep fast and hard.

Except Kenya.

Kenya lay awake, her arms folded back behind her head. She stared out at the darkness and thought about her mother. It wasn't only nights like these she thought about her mother. She thought about her every night. But on a special night like this it was easy to imagine how it would have been, the two of them taking the bus down to Baltimore to stand outside the Meyerhoff Symphony Hall, the two of them watching as everyone went in and the Doyles went in, how her mother would have stepped aside and pretended they were waiting on someone and how she would have squeezed her shoulder hard when Tip went by, the cap in his hand, the black gown over his arm. She thought about things like this all the time but the problem with thinking about it tonight was that Tip never would have gone to medical school if Kenya's mother hadn't died, and so it was hard to figure out how her mother could have gone to the graduation. She would have the same problem again when Teddy graduated from law school. How could she think of her mother there? The present life was only a matter of how things had stacked together in the past, and all Kenya knew for sure was that if she had the chance to hand over everything she had now in order to regain what was lost there would be no words for how fast she would open up her hands. It had been fine out there with her mother, it had been paradise, when they were only watching.

In her chest she felt her heart beat faster and faster. She scratched at her head, her arms, until it was unbearable to try and be still. She got up quickly now and felt around for her clothes and shoes in the darkness: shorts, shirt, socks. She would lace up her shoes in the hall. It was easy to find the room key card because Doyle made everyone put theirs on the table by the door. She had meant to go and ask at the front desk how late the gym was open, but when she got to the lobby she could see the floodlights pouring over the parking lot, the parking lot that went all the way around the hotel, and so she stepped outside into the grass-scented air. It was a perfect night, clear and cool, with half a moon for company. She stretched up and down on her toes and then put her hands flat on the pavement. The night doorman looked at her, and, still bending forward, she waved. 'Running,' she said to him through the door, and he nodded back. Then she was gone.

She kept it slow on the first lap, making a clockwise sweep past the rental cars that fit together in neat rows. It was perfect really, bigger than she thought, bigger than any track she was going to find, and no one else was there. It was past midnight and she started to open up, but just a little. She wanted to save herself now, she wanted to run for a very long time. She didn't get bored by the loops she made. She didn't think about the cars. She was thinking about her mother. She liked to imagine that her mother had arranged everything as a way to get Kenya into that house, to have her live safely with her brothers. She pushed her shoulders open, stretched her neck up long. She filled up the great bellows of her lungs, then blew the air away. Her mother had it all fixed in advance. Fixed with the driver of the SUV, fixed with the men who drove the ambulance, fixed with the doctors, or maybe just one of them, maybe only the last one who took her away because it never made any sense, really, that she could have been fine and then so quickly dead. Or not dead. It was possible. Kenya listened to the tap of her own feet and spread out her steps to match her exhalations. She let her eyes trail from one lit up window to the next. What other way could she have done it if she knew that Kenya never would have gone willingly along with the plan, that she would have clung to her as tight as muscle to bone and cried and run straight back every time she was pushed away? And how else could her mother have gotten Doyle and the boys to love her unless she left her like a foundling on their stairs? Of course it wasn't likely. She was a smart girl, she knew what the chances were, but it was not entirely impossible either that even now her mother was watching her, that even tonight she was standing outside the symphony hall, or that she was in one of these cars that she ran past in circles, over and over again. Kenya kept herself out there just in case. She made sure to win her races so that her picture would be in the paper and she made sure that in every picture she was smiling, because if a person was willing to go through so much to give you what she thought would be a better life, it was the least you could do to look happy.

She would run all night, or at least until she was almost too tired to take the elevator back to her room, and in the morning her brothers would stand over the couch of the sun-soaked room and tease her about being so lazy. Her legs flexed out in front of her, pointed behind her. Without meaning to she was racing herself to the next Ford Taurus, to the stand of flowering cherry trees that framed the electric doors on either side. She decided that for a lap or two she would let herself run as fast as she wanted because she understood there was also a better than good chance that her mother wasn't watching her, and she was alone in that parking lot, in which case anyone who was around should know that there was never going to be a chance of catching her. When she was in her own room at night, the room on the fourth floor that once belonged to Teddy and Tip, she slept under the watchful eye of her mother and another woman in a photograph that Tip had found when they were packing up her old apartment at Cathedral. It was stuck in the *Field Guide to North American Fishes* that her mother had. It was one of the few pictures of her mother they found, and in this one she was definitely the happiest. Doyle took it to a photo shop and had it blown up to be as big as the picture of Bernadette. He framed it and put it on the dresser beside the statue. The three of them watched over her now, her mother and the woman she didn't know and Bernadette, who was both a photograph and a saint carved out of rosewood. Doyle had told her the story when he gave her the statue on her twelfth birthday, all about the grandfather in Ireland who stole it and his wife who wouldn't forgive him. He told her he had written it down that the statue would go to her, just in case anything ever happened, but that he figured they might as well put off telling her brothers for as long as they could because none of them was going to be happy about it.

'Then why give it to me?' she had said. She reached out and laid a finger on the gold of the halo. She had only owned it one minute and already she never wanted to let it go.

'Because you're the daughter is why,' he said. 'The statue always goes to the daughter.'

'But what would you have done if you didn't have one?'

Doyle put his hand on her head and pulled lightly on one of her braids to save her the trouble of having to do it herself. 'But we did,' he said. 'We did.'

Kenya looked down the long side of the hotel, a straight shot to the next right turn, and for a moment she closed her eyes. Maybe one of them was awake, Teddy or Tip or Sullivan or Doyle. Maybe one of them was standing at the window now looking at the parking lot, and he saw her flash by eight stories down, her long legs cutting through the night, her Johns Hopkins T-shirt flying out behind her. Maybe he never fully realized how fast she was until he had seen her at a distance, and so the one who was awake went to get the others up so that they could all stand at the window together and watch her run.

We do hope that you have enjoyed reading this large print book.

Did you know that all of our titles are available for purchase?

We publish a wide range of high quality large print books including:
Romances, Mysteries, Classics
General Fiction
Non Fiction and Westerns

Special interest titles available in large print are:
The Little Oxford Dictionary
Music Book
Song Book
Hymn Book
Service Book

Also available from us courtesy of Oxford University Press:
Young Readers' Dictionary
(large print edition)
Young Readers' Thesaurus
(large print edition)

For further information or a free brochure, please contact us at:
Ulverscroft Large Print Books Ltd.,
The Green, Bradgate Road, Anstey,
Leicester, LE7 7FU, England.
Tel: (00 44) 0116 236 4325
Fax: (00 44) 0116 234 0205

PAST CHANCES

Bernardine Kennedy

Abandoned by her mother, Eleanor spent her childhood in constant fear of her father's erratic behaviour. She's desperate to leave home and live independently like so many other girls in the seventies. When her best friend Marty, who works with her in a London hotel, invites her to share a house with him and the glamorous Megan and Venita, it's her chance to break free. But when Eleanor confronts her father with the news his reaction is catastrophic. And despite the support and guidance of her new friends, Eleanor cannot cope. Her rush into a love affair takes her down an ever more destructive path. Will Eleanor find the strength to take charge of her life or is it destined to spiral out of control?